KW-237-286

A DIAMOND FOR THE SINGLE MUM

SUSAN MEIER

A DEAL MADE IN TEXAS

MICHELLE MAJOR

MILLS & BOON

First Published in Great Britain 2019
by Mills & Boon, an imprint of HarperCollinsPublishers,
1 London Bridge Street, London, SE1 9GF

A Diamond for the Single Mum © 2018 Linda Susan Meier
A Deal Made in Texas © 2019 Harlequin Books S.A.

Special thanks and acknowledgement are given to Michelle Major for her contribution to The Fortunes of Texas: The Lost Fortunes series.

ISBN: 978-0-263-27203-1

0119

MIX
Paper from
responsible sources
FSC™ C007454

This book is produced from independently certified FSC™ paper to ensure responsible forest management.

For more information visit: www.harpercollins.co.uk/green

Printed and bound in Spain
by CPI, Barcelona

to mortgage everything they owned, she wouldn't be desperate right now.

Keeping his eyes on her, the doorman picked up his house phone.

"Mr. McCallan, you have a visitor. Harper Hargraves." A pause. "Yes. I'll be happy to send her up."

The doorman motioned to the elevator. She headed to the shiny steel door, and he followed her. When the door opened, he directed her to go inside and walked in with her.

He was keeping tabs on her. Making sure the scraggly woman with the baby didn't go anywhere else in the building.

Humiliation burned through her.

When the car stopped at the ninth floor, he didn't accompany her out, but stood waiting in the elevator as she rolled her stroller to Seth's door, then knocked.

The door opened, and Harper forgot all about the doorman watching her. Her husband's former best friend stood before her in a pair of gray sweatpants that hung low on his hips, as he wrestled a T-shirt over his head. He yanked the thing down his torso, but it was too late. She'd seen the rippling muscles of his chest and stomach.

Shell-shocked, she stared at him. He was taller, sleeker, more muscular than he had been five years ago. But with his perpetual smile and tousled black hair, he was the same heart-stopping handsome he'd been when they lived in side-by-side apartments. And those eyes of his. As black as the soul of a condemned man, they nonetheless had a strange light. Almost a knowing. As if the years had taught him to be careful…wise. Though he'd been a nervous nerd when he'd lived with Clark, he seemed to have found his confidence as a man.

It was easy to see why the tabloids gossiped about him being with a different woman every few weeks. Confident. Rich. Handsome. Built. He had everything—

Which she shouldn't be noticing. She'd had the love of her life. Their marriage had been fun, perfect. She missed Clark with every fiber of her being.

"Hey, Seth."

His gaze ran from her short cap of black hair down her simple T-shirt, along her worn jeans and back up again.

"Harper?"

She tried to smile. "It's me. I know I look a little different."

"A little different" didn't hit the tip of the iceberg. Since Clark's funeral, she'd had a baby, cut her long black hair and lost weight. She was suddenly grateful for the supercilious doorman. If he hadn't announced her, Seth might not have recognized her.

He gestured awkwardly. "I've never seen the baby."

"Her name is Crystal." Her words came out on a shaky breath, and she knew she had to get this over with before she lost her courage. "I need some help."

"I guessed that from the fact that you're here at eight o'clock on a Tuesday." He stepped back so she could enter. "Come in."

He held the door for the stroller. As Harper slipped by, her gaze flicked down his torso again. He looked so good in T-shirt and sweats. Fit. Agile.

Maybe a little intimidating.

That was probably why she kept noticing. Not interest. Fear. She'd never asked anyone for help. Never. She'd always made it on her own.

She pushed the stroller into the living room of the sophisticated open-floorplan condo. Motioning to the aqua sofa, Seth indicated she should sit, as he lowered himself to the matching trellis-print chair. She could see the white cabinets in the kitchen, along with a restored wood dining table surrounded by six tufted chairs the same color as the sofa, with a modern chandelier hanging overhead. Simple,

Sɯ

Susan M...Mills & Boon. *The Tycoon's Secret Daughter* was a Romance Writers of America RITA® Award finalist, and *Nanny for the Millionaire's Twins* won the Book Buyers' Best award and was a finalist in the National Readers' Choice awards. She is married and has three children. One of eleven children herself, she loves to write about the complexity of families and totally believes in the power of love.

Michelle Major grew up in Ohio but dreamed of living in the mountains. Soon after graduating with a degree in journalism, she pointed her car west and settled in Colorado. Her life and house are filled with one great husband, two beautiful kids, a few furry pets and several well-behaved reptiles. She's grateful to have found her passion writing stories with happy endings. Michelle loves to hear from her readers at michellemajor.com.

Also by Susan Meier

A Mistletoe Kiss with the Boss
The Boss's Fake Fiancée
The Spanish Millionaire's Runaway Bride

Manhattan Babies miniseries

Carrying the Billionaire's Baby
A Diamond for the Single Mum

And look out for the next book
Coming soon

Also by Michelle Major

Falling for the Wrong Brother
Second Chance in Stonecreek
A Stonecreek Christmas Reunion
Christmas on Crimson Mountain
Romancing the Wallflower
Sleigh Bells in Crimson
Coming Home to Crimson
Fortune's Special Delivery
A Fortune in Waiting
Her Soldier of Fortune

Discover more at millsandboon.co.uk

A DIAMOND
FOR THE
SINGLE MUM

SUSAN MEIER

For my son, Michael.

I'll probably miss you forever.

to mortgage everything they owned, she wouldn't be desperate right now.

Keeping his eyes on her, the doorman picked up his house phone.

"Mr. McCallan, you have a visitor. Harper Hargraves." A pause. "Yes. I'll be happy to send her up."

The doorman motioned to the elevator. She headed to the shiny steel door, and he followed her. When the door opened, he directed her to go inside and walked in with her.

He was keeping tabs on her. Making sure the scraggly woman with the baby didn't go anywhere else in the building.

Humiliation burned through her.

When the car stopped at the ninth floor, he didn't accompany her out, but stood waiting in the elevator as she rolled her stroller to Seth's door, then knocked.

The door opened, and Harper forgot all about the doorman watching her. Her husband's former best friend stood before her in a pair of gray sweatpants that hung low on his hips, as he wrestled a T-shirt over his head. He yanked the thing down his torso, but it was too late. She'd seen the rippling muscles of his chest and stomach.

Shell-shocked, she stared at him. He was taller, sleeker, more muscular than he had been five years ago. But with his perpetual smile and tousled black hair, he was the same heart-stopping handsome he'd been when they lived in side-by-side apartments. And those eyes of his. As black as the soul of a condemned man, they nonetheless had a strange light. Almost a knowing. As if the years had taught him to be careful…wise. Though he'd been a nervous nerd when he'd lived with Clark, he seemed to have found his confidence as a man.

It was easy to see why the tabloids gossiped about him being with a different woman every few weeks. Confident. Rich. Handsome. Built. He had everything—

Which she shouldn't be noticing. She'd had the love of her life. Their marriage had been fun, perfect. She missed Clark with every fiber of her being.

"Hey, Seth."

His gaze ran from her short cap of black hair down her simple T-shirt, along her worn jeans and back up again.

"Harper?"

She tried to smile. "It's me. I know I look a little different."

"A little different" didn't hit the tip of the iceberg. Since Clark's funeral, she'd had a baby, cut her long black hair and lost weight. She was suddenly grateful for the supercilious doorman. If he hadn't announced her, Seth might not have recognized her.

He gestured awkwardly. "I've never seen the baby."

"Her name is Crystal." Her words came out on a shaky breath, and she knew she had to get this over with before she lost her courage. "I need some help."

"I guessed that from the fact that you're here at eight o'clock on a Tuesday." He stepped back so she could enter. "Come in."

He held the door for the stroller. As Harper slipped by, her gaze flicked down his torso again. He looked so good in T-shirt and sweats. Fit. Agile.

Maybe a little intimidating.

That was probably why she kept noticing. Not interest. Fear. She'd never asked anyone for help. Never. She'd always made it on her own.

She pushed the stroller into the living room of the sophisticated open-floorplan condo. Motioning to the aqua sofa, Seth indicated she should sit, as he lowered himself to the matching trellis-print chair. She could see the white cabinets in the kitchen, along with a restored wood dining table surrounded by six tufted chairs the same color as the sofa, with a modern chandelier hanging overhead. Simple, but luxurious. Rich fabrics. Expensive wood. Even when a McCallan lived simply, he did it with understated elegance.

"I'm sorry to bother you, but I'm in a bit of a bind. I sold my condo yesterday, but the buyer wants it on Monday."

"That's great? Good? Awful?" He shook his head. "It's been too long. I'm not sure what to say."

She laughed, so nervous she couldn't even react normally around him. "It would be great, except I don't have another place to move into."

"Oh."

"The buyer paid cash and getting the place in a week was a condition of the sale and I really needed the sale... so I took the offer."

"You need money?" He frowned. "You own an investment firm."

And here was the tough part. Her wonderful, funny, smart husband had done what he'd had to do to buy Seth's share. Had he lived, that loan would have been a footnote in his life story. As it was, it had all but destroyed his legacy. The last thing in the world she wanted to do was tell Clark's best friend that he'd failed—

No, the last thing in the world she wanted to do was tell *her parents* Clark had failed. Seth, at least, would give Clark the benefit of the doubt. Her parents—her *mother*—would have a royal fit, then belittle Clark every time Harper mentioned his name.

"I had to sell the firm. Clark had leveraged it to get the money to buy your share and the market plummeted. It was like a perfect storm, Seth. I couldn't pay the loan and I couldn't sell the firm until I dropped the price to a few hundred thousand dollars over the amount we owed." She shifted the focus of Seth's disappointment from Clark to her. "And that money's almost gone because I needed it for living expenses while I had the baby and waited to sell the condo."

A hush fell over the room. Harper refused to say anything more. He might not belittle Clark the way her mom would when Harper finally told her parents she was broke, but Seth was an entitled rich kid. He'd dropped out of his family for a while, but when he and Clark had graduated university, Seth had used his connections to land them jobs in an investment firm. He'd gotten family friends to pony up the starting funds when he and Clark wanted to open their own company. When the business was more than on its feet, he'd found the money to buy out their investors. And when he needed to go to work for his family's company, after his dad's death, he'd easily handed over the firm's reins to Clark, not caring that he was giving up what could have been a gold mine if he and Clark had stayed around to run it.

Seth might have lived poor for a few years while he finished school, but he had no concept of genuine, lifelong struggle. And Harper wouldn't let him think less of Clark because he'd lost what he and Seth had built.

After a few seconds, Seth sighed. "And you sold your condo because that was mortgaged, too?"

"I didn't realize until after Clark died that we'd spent every penny he'd earned." She gave him time to digest that, then added, "He really liked you. He liked the life you brought him into. I know why he overextended us financially. And I'm not sorry he lived the way he wanted to while he had a chance. I'm not asking for anything except some help figuring my way out of this. Some advice."

"Even if you rent, you're going to need more than a week to find a place."

"I know."

Three-month-old Crystal stretched. Her head rose above the bundle of blankets she'd been snuggled into, revealing a tiny pixie face and a head full of short, shaggy black hair.

Realizing the baby was waking from the stroller-induced nap, Harper slid the diaper bag out of the bin behind the seat. "I'm going to have to warm a bottle."

Seth looked at Crystal. "Is she waking up?"

"Yes. She won't fuss if I have a bottle ready."

He rose, as if confused. "Okay."

"Just let me warm the bottle and I'll be all set."

She took the diaper bag into the kitchen and removed a bottle. As she opened the cupboard door to get something to hold enough water to warm it, she watched Seth peer into the stroller from about six feet away.

"You can actually get close enough to look at her."

Seth grimaced. "Not on your life. I have a niece a few months older than she is and I've never even held her."

Harper clicked her tongue. "Seth! Babies are wonderful."

"They look like they are. And my brother absolutely adores his. But they're small and fragile and they frequently leak bodily fluids. I'm keeping my distance."

She nodded, grateful for the small reprieve in talking about the mess she'd gotten herself into. She filled a mug with hot water and slid the bottle inside. Knowing it would take a few minutes to warm the formula that way, she walked back into the living room.

Seth said, "She's pretty. Looks a lot like my niece. Dark hair. Pale eyes."

"Sounds like your brother."

He laughed. "He has a talent for getting his own way about things." But Seth's laughter quickly died. His solemn dark eyes met hers. "You do realize how much trouble you're in."

"And you're about to tell me the only answer is to go back to my parents." She shook her head. "That has to be my last resort. My mother was abysmal to Clark until he started that business with you. Then she was constantly on his back to be more, to push for more, to have more. If I go home now and tell her that I not only sold the investment firm, I sold the condo to get out from under loans, she'll lose all respect for him."

Seth silently studied Harper. Still beautiful. Still tempting. And in so much trouble financially he wasn't even sure how to counsel her.

He spent his days haggling with contractors, hammering out contracts with some of the savviest businessmen in the world and fighting to make sure McCallan, Inc. stayed at the top of its industry. Yet he had absolutely no idea what to say to one little woman.

If she were anybody else, he'd easily tell her, "Suck it up, Buttercup. You've got no option but to move back in with your parents."

Except, she wasn't staying away from them for herself. She was holding back, probably waiting until she had herself on solid ground, before she had to tell her parents her husband had put her into debt. She was protecting Clark.

How could someone who'd fought his own condescending father most of his life not respect that?

The baby stirred again. Harper went to the kitchen and got the bottle.

Just as the little girl began to fuss, Harper was back, bottle in hand, lifting Crystal, settling her on her lap and feeding her.

It all seemed to simple, so easy. He'd seen his sister-in-law, Avery, do something similar. But Avery had tons of help. Not just Seth and Jake's mom, but Avery's mom, her dad and a nanny. He'd always thought Avery made being a mom look easy, but he'd apparently missed a lot about parenting in his years of avoiding babies.

"So, I'm kinda broke, but not really," Harper said, feeding the hungry baby. "With the sale of the condo I have a hundred thousand dollars to play with. Either to use for a down payment on a new condo or to live on until I find a job."

He sat back down, feeling oddly foolish for being so persnickety about kids as he watched Harper's baby happily suckle her milk. "Honestly, if you weren't out on the street in six days, I'd say your first order of business should be to get a job."

"But I am out on the street in six days. In that time, I have to pack and arrange for a mover, as I find somewhere else to live. You wouldn't happen to have an extra room?"

She'd said it as a joke, but he did have an extra room. She'd even have a private bathroom. There were only two problems with taking her in. First, he really wasn't comfortable around babies. Very few single men were. But he was super edgy around them. Preoccupied with a million little details for his job, he worried he'd step on Crystal, trip over her, knock her down.

But he knew that was just a cover for the real reason he didn't want Harper Sloan Hargraves to move in with him.

She was supposed to be his.

He'd adored her from the moment he'd laid eyes on her. But he wasn't the settling-down kind. His parents' farce of a marriage had ruined him on the fairy tale of happily-ever-after. The emotional abuse he'd suffered from his manipulative dad had made him far too cynical and too careful to want a relationship.

So, he'd let Clark ask her out.

And he'd become a playboy. He'd dated so many women he'd lost count. He traveled, was a regular in Las Vegas and couldn't remember the last Saturday night he'd spent alone.

"I was kidding about the room, Seth. You can talk again."

He shook his head. This wasn't about him. It really wasn't even about Harper. It was about Clark. He'd been Seth's best friend in every sense of the word. When he left his family home and his emotionally abusive father, Clark had found him in the library. Alone. Broke. And rich-kid stupid. Seth didn't even know he couldn't hide in the library stacks, wait for the lights to go out and spend the night. He didn't notice things like cameras and security guards.

Clark had asked a few pointed questions, gotten the real scoop and taken him to the run-down apartment he shared with Ziggy, next door to Harper. He'd told him he could stay until he got on his feet, but for three kids going to university, fighting for money for books and tuition, there was no getting on any feet. He'd found a job as a waiter, shared a room with twin beds with Ziggy and paid his part of the rent and food.

All his life, his dad had told him he didn't understand the real world and tried to teach him by withholding money, embarrassing him, belittling him, and Clark had taught him everything his dad couldn't in three years of paying for school and supporting himself.

Now here he was with an extra room, about to turn Clark's widow out on the street because he'd at one time had a crush on her?

That was ridiculous. He was a grown man now. A wealthy man in his own right who'd built exactly the life he wanted. He had his pick of woman and absolutely no desire to settle down.

She was safe…and so was he.

"You can have the room."

"What?"

He rose from the trellis-print chair. "You can have my spare room. Arrange to have your furniture put into storage. Have Crystal's crib delivered here." And just as Clark had said to him twelve years ago, he added, "You can stay as long as you need to."

Moving in together did not seem like a good idea.

Seth headed back down the hall, probably toward his bedroom. "As soon as you're settled, we'll go over your résumé, find you a job and start house hunting."

Because those were things Clark had helped him with.

He hadn't said it, but she realized this was nothing but payback for Clark's kindnesses and, honestly, she needed it. If her mother saw her, six days away from being homeless, she'd blame Clark and never forget.

Harper could not let that happen.

She said, "Okay," but he was already opening the door of his room.

Harper blew her breath out on a long sigh. This was not going to be easy, but it was better than living in the street.

After spending an hour contacting movers, Harper finally found one who had a cancellation in his schedule the following day. She booked the appointment and spent the rest of the afternoon, evening and the next morning packing. Right on time, the movers arrived and picked up her furniture and boxes of household goods, clothes and baby things. They drove first to the storage unit and dropped off everything but Crystal's crib and baby accessories, which were packed in the back of her SUV with a few suitcases of clothes.

She waved goodbye to the movers and headed for Seth's condo.

Though it was close to five, Seth had told her he worked until six and she knew he wouldn't be home. Which meant she could have everything set up in his condo before he returned.

But when she arrived at his building, the doorman wouldn't let her into Seth's apartment. Not that she blamed him. She'd thought Seth would have already made arrangements, but apparently he hadn't.

The doorman punched a few numbers into his phone

and within seconds was talking to Seth. Then he handed the phone across the desk.

"He wants to talk to you."

Oh, boy. He probably wasn't expecting her until Sunday. Plenty of time for him to get adjusted or change his mind. Instead here she was, a little over twenty-four hours later, her car loaded with baby things.

What did a playboy need with a baby and broke widow?

"Hello. Seth." Not giving him a chance to back out, she said, "I got lucky and found a mover who'd had a cancellation today. I packed last night and this morning, and now everything I own, except Crystal's things and a couple suitcases of clothes, is in a storage unit."

She hadn't meant to sound desperate, but oh, Lord, she had. She squeezed her eyes shut, but Seth easily said, "Okay."

Her heart started beating again.

"I have one more meeting before I can leave, but I'll call my next-door neighbor, Mrs. Petrillo. She has a key and will let you in. Just go ahead to the condo."

"Should I knock on her door?"

He laughed. "No. She's something of a snoop. It's why I want her to let you in instead of George. She looks out the keyhole every time the elevator arrives on our floor. This way she'll know I know you're there."

Harper laughed. Her first genuine laugh since she'd realized how much trouble she was in. She liked the idea of a nosy neighbor. It felt less like she and Seth were all alone.

Because they weren't. They had Crystal, the nosy neighbor and probably a hundred other people who lived in the building.

They would not be alone.

"I also have an extra parking space in the basement. I told George to get you a pass."

"Okay. Thanks." When she disconnected the call,

George handed her the card that would get her entry into the garage. "Is your car on the street?"

"Yes. I was lucky to get a spot right in front of the building."

"Good. I'll arrange to have your luggage and baby things brought upstairs. Then I'll park your car in Mr. McCallan's second space."

Balancing Crystal on her hip, she wondered how much Seth had promised this guy to be so accommodating. She handed him her car keys. "Thanks. It's the blue Explorer SUV."

He nodded once. "We'll have your things upstairs in a few minutes."

She rode the elevator to Seth's floor and just as Seth had predicted a short gray-haired woman stood by his door, waiting for her.

"Mrs. Petrillo?"

"Yes. And you must be Harper."

"Yes." She presented her baby. "This is Crystal."

The older woman lightly pinched Crystal's pink cheek. "She is adorable. Aren't you, sweetie?"

Crystal grinned.

Mrs. Petrillo inserted the key into the lock and opened the door. "Sorry about your husband."

"Thank you."

"Death is a terrible thing. I buried three husbands."

Harper gasped. Knowing the pain of losing Clark and the emptiness that followed, the loneliness that never seemed to go away, she said, "I'm so sorry."

"It never gets easier." She turned to Harper with a smile. "My soap is on right now. But I'm next door if you need anything."

"Okay. Thanks."

The petite woman waved goodbye and was gone within seconds, but her comment that it would never get easier haunted Harper as a new wave of missing Clark swept through her.

But she barely had time to catch her breath. The doorman arrived with her and Crystal's suitcases.

He led her to the extra room in Seth's condo. A queen-size bed and a dresser easily shared the space, leaving more than ample room for Crystal's crib. An adjoining bathroom with a shower made of black, gray and white glass tiles that matched a backsplash behind the white sink was small but not uncomfortably so.

The doorman left her suitcases on the bed and left. When he returned with the crib and high chair, he had two maintenance men with him. He introduced them, telling her they would set up the crib.

When they were done, Harper put Crystal in her bed to play with her favorite blanket and stuffed bear, and set about to unpack. She hadn't brought a lot, only enough clothes for her and Crystal for two weeks. Everything fit in the one dresser and the small closet. Another indicator of how much her life had changed since she lost Clark.

Not wanting to dwell on that, she carried Crystal to the living space. A quick glance at the clock told her it was only six. Her stomach rumbled. She hadn't eaten lunch. The mover was on too tight of a schedule.

Just when she would have gone into the tidy kitchen to see if there was something she could make for supper, something nice that could serve as a thank-you-for-keeping-us gesture, the condo door opened.

"Seth?"

The day before, she'd left as he'd walked back to his room to dress for work. She expected to see him in a suit, not a black crew-neck sweater with a white shirt under it and jeans.

Jeans to work? At his family's prestigious holding company, where he wasn't just on the board of directors, but was also a vice president?

"I canceled my meeting." He ambled into the room and tossed his keys and wallet on the counter, along with some envelopes she assumed were his mail. "How'd today go?"

She couldn't stop staring at him. Clark had gone to work in a suit and tie every day. He didn't cancel meetings. He never came home early. But Seth was a McCallan. From what she knew of the family, they did whatever they wanted. Especially Seth. Joining the family business obviously hadn't ended his rebellious streak.

"Busy. Exhausting."

He picked up the mail. Rifled through it. "Mine, too."

The conversation ended, and a weird silence stretched between them.

She sucked in a breath for courage. "I was just thinking about looking in your cupboards to see if there was anything to make for dinner."

He sniffed. "Don't bother. I'm pretty sure the cupboards are bare. There are takeout menus from a few local places. Order something for both of us. I have a credit card on file at all of them. Just tell them it's for me." He turned and headed back down the hall.

She frowned. "I thought you'd said you always have dates or dinner meetings or something?"

He stopped, faced her. "I did. Just like I canceled my last meeting, I canceled my date."

Harper blinked as he disappeared behind his bedroom door. *Canceled his date?*

An odd sensation rippled through her. Not happiness. Surely, she couldn't be happy that he'd canceled a date. She didn't "like" the guy. He was good-looking—well, gorgeous, really—but he wasn't Clark, a man she had loved. The feeling oozing through her was more of a recognition of how glad she was that she didn't have to be alone.

* * *

The door closed behind Seth and he leaned against it, blowing his breath out on a long sigh. When he'd invited Harper to live with him, he hadn't anticipated how uncomfortable it would be to have her in his house, but he was damn glad he'd canceled his date, so they could talk. About Clark. After a nice dinner, where he'd direct the conversation so she would remind him that she'd loved and married his best friend, he'd get his perspective back.

He took a quick shower. When he left his room and entered the living space, he found Harper at the table surrounded by boxes of Chinese food.

"I like Chinese."

"Good."

He walked over to the table, saw she'd found plates and utensils and took a seat.

"Your area of the city has just about every type of restaurant imaginable."

"It's part of the appeal."

He lifted a dish, filled it with General Tso's chicken, some vegetables and an egg roll.

"Oh, and I paid for it myself. I'm not destitute. And I'm not a charity case. I just need some help transitioning."

Point number one to be discussed. How she wanted to be treated. "I'm sorry if I made you feel that way."

"You didn't. I just wanted to fix some misinterpretations."

"Okay."

She turned her attention to dishing out some food for herself. Her short hair gave her an angelic look, enhanced by the curve of her full lips. Her casual, almost grungy clothes took him back to a decade ago, when he was a kid who listened to hip-hop and lived right next door to the girl he thought the most beautiful woman he'd ever met.

And that was point number two they had to discuss.

Eight years had passed since he'd had a crush on her and she'd started dating Clark. They weren't those people anymore. He didn't have a mad crush on *her*. He'd had a mad crush on the girl she'd used to be. Since then, she'd gotten married, lost a husband, had a baby alone. They weren't picking up where they'd left off.

He almost rolled his eyes at his own stupidity. He hadn't even asked how she was.

"So… How are you doing?"

She shook her head. "You mean aside from being almost homeless?"

"Don't make a joke. Clark was my best friend." There. He'd said it. Point number three that he needed to get into this conversation. Clark had been his best friend. "You lost him. You were pregnant. You went through that alone. And now you're facing raising a daughter alone. If we're going to do this—live together—we're going to do it right. Not pretend everything is fine. We used to be friends. We could be friends again."

She set down her chopsticks. "Okay. If you really want to know, I spent most of the year scared to death. It took me a couple of weeks to wrap my head around the fact that he was really gone. But the more I adjusted, the quieter the house got. And the quieter the house got, the more I realized how alone I was."

"And you couldn't even talk to your parents?"

"My mom never had anything good to say about Clark, so after a visit or two when I was lonely, I quit going over."

She stopped talking, but Seth waited, glad he'd decided to go this route. He needed to know what he was dealing with, and if she'd been alone for twelve long months she probably needed someone to talk to.

"I didn't shut them out completely. My mom came with me to a doctor's appointment or two and then we'd have lunch. But every time, the conversation would turn into a discussion of what I should do with my life now that Clark was gone."

"I'm sorry."

"Not your fault. My mother's a bulldozer. She sees the way a thing should go and she pushes. Whether it's the right thing or not."

"Have they seen the baby?"

"Yes. If I'd completely broken off ties, my mom would have mounted a campaign to get me back. So, I kept them at a distance. I let her stay and help the week after Crystal was born. But she couldn't stop talking about remodeling the condo to bring it up to standards, insinuating that with Clark gone I could do it right, and the whole time I knew I was broke and going to have to sell. Every time I'd try to tell her, she'd blast Clark." She lifted her eyes to catch his gaze. "That's how I knew I couldn't move in with them."

Seth leaned back in his chair. "I guess."

The room got quiet. Her mother wasn't the hellish dictator his father had been, but he wouldn't have wanted to live with her mom, either.

"So, what's up with you?"

He laughed, glad for her obvious change of subject to lighten the mood. "Not much. Jake's a much better businessman than my father was, so working with him is good."

"And your mom?"

He snorted. "My mom isn't quite as bad as your mom, but we have our issues."

She nodded sagely. "Sometimes the best you can do is avoid them for the sake of peace."

He'd never say that the feelings he had around his mother were peaceful. He had a million questions he'd like to ask. Like, why she'd said nothing when his father embarrassed or humiliated him and Jake. Or better yet, why she'd stayed married to a man who was awful as a husband and father?

She'd known he was cheating. She'd known he wasn't a good father. Yet she'd stayed. Forcing them all to live a lie.

Deciding he didn't want to burden Harper with any of that, he rose. "Do you like baseball?"

"Sort of."

"Sort of?" He sniffed a laugh. "There's a game on tonight that I'd love to see. If you want to watch, too, I can watch out here. If not, I can watch on the television in my bedroom."

"I don't want you to change your routines for me."

"I won't."

The sound of the baby crying burst from her phone. She held it up. "Baby monitor is attached to this. And it looks like I'm going to be busy for a while. Go ahead and put your game on."

Harper walked into her room sort of happy. It had been nice to talk about Clark, her mom and even being alone. She wasn't trying to make a new best friend, but she had been lonely. Having someone to talk to, to share a meal with, had been more of a treat than she'd expected it would be.

With Crystal on her arm she walked out to the common area and found Seth was nowhere around. Thinking he must have decided to watch the game in his room, she warmed a bottle, fed Crystal, played with her, let her sit in her little seat that rocked her sideways, then finally put her into bed.

After a quick shower, and still wired from their talk, she put on a pair of pajamas and returned to the living room to watch TV.

A few minutes later, Seth returned to the main living area. He held up his phone. "Work call. I also took a shower while I was back there." He set the phone on the center island and pulled a beer from the fridge. "Want one?"

She shook her head. "No. I might have to get up in the middle of the night."

That piece of information seemed to horrify him. "Really?"

"Crystal is a fairly good sleeper, but I never know."

He twisted the top off the bottle. "So, on the off chance that she'll wake up, you don't drink?"

"Yes."

He sat beside her. She liked his hair all rumpled from his shower. Whatever his soap was it made him smell like heaven.

Strange things happened to her pulse. Her breathing shifted. Probably so she could inhale the wonderful scent of his soap or shampoo.

She eased a few more inches away from him. It didn't help.

"What are you watching?"

She handed him the remote. "Nothing. Put the game on. I need to get to bed."

He frowned.

"You know…in case Chrystal wakes up."

"Right."

She walked into her room and closed the door behind her with a deep sigh. Her weird reactions around him shouldn't surprise her. Her husband had been gone a year and she'd all but locked herself in her house. Primarily to prepare for and then care for her baby. And she might be too needy to be around such a gorgeous guy. But she also couldn't risk slipping it to her parents that Clark had failed. Or, worse, having her mom or dad read her body language, realize something was wrong and grill her until she crumbled. That had kept her home, alone, more than she wanted to admit.

These feelings she was having around Seth were nothing but her reaction to being around a man again. A young, handsome, sexy-smelling guy who should not tempt her.

But he did.

Not because she was attracted to him. Though, she was. What woman wouldn't be? The real bottom line was a combination of things. Her having been sheltered for months combined with his good looks and their close proximity was making her supersensitive.

But it was Clark she loved. Clark she still missed.

She crawled into bed and closed her eyes, thinking about his silly laugh, how he'd loved to cook, how much he'd wanted their baby.

And all thoughts of Seth vanished.

In the middle of the night, Seth awakened to the sound of crying. Recognizing it was Crystal and he was repaying a debt, he rolled over to go back to sleep, but sleep didn't come. He put the pillow over his head. No help.

Finally, the little girl quieted, and he realized Harper must have given her a bottle or something. He fell back to sleep, woke when the alarm sounded and sneaked up the hall to the kitchen to make a cup of coffee. Their conversation the night before had been good, but they were still uncomfortable with each other. And he was still fighting that attraction. So better not to wake her.

"Good morning."

Damn. She was already up.

She wore the pale blue pajamas he'd seen the night before. They were much less revealing than things he'd seen in Vegas or Barcelona and his face should not have reddened. But it had.

She looked soft-and-cuddly sexy. Her sleepy blue eyes should have reminded him that she'd gotten up with a baby the night before. Instead they reminded him of warm, fuzzy feelings after sex.

"I just, uh, wanted a cup of coffee."

"Okay."

He neared the counter, where she sat holding the baby. The little girl looked at him.

"Hey."

Harper shot him a confused expression.

"Just, you know, saying, hey, to the kid…the baby… Crystal."

The little girl grinned.

"I think she likes you."

"Well, she terrifies me. In a good way," he quickly added. "I don't want to hurt her."

"You won't."

"Sure," he said, knowing he wouldn't ever hurt her because he wouldn't ever touch her.

He got his coffee and went back to his room, where he dressed in his typical work clothes of jeans and a halfway decent shirt. When he returned to the kitchen for his keys and wallet, Harper and the baby were gone.

Wincing, he walked back the hall and knocked on her door.

"Yes?"

"Just wanted to let you know I'm on my way to work."

"Okay."

He squeezed his eyes shut. The melodious sound of her voice drifted through him like a blast of sweet summer air. She sounded so happy and content that pride surged through him, tightening his chest. This time two days ago, she'd been facing homelessness and he'd fixed that for her.

He started up the hall and picked up his keys and wallet. What the hell was wrong with him? Helping her should feel good, but he wasn't doing this for her. He was doing it for Clark. To pay back Clark for taking him in when he needed help.

The very fact that he kept forgetting that meant it was time to get things moving along before his emotions got any more involved.

CHAPTER THREE

THAT EVENING, SETH RETURNED a little later than he had the night before, looking like a sex god in a T-shirt that showed off his chest and shoulders and a pair of sunglasses he'd probably bought in Europe.

Harper's breathing shivered. Her muscles froze. For the next ten seconds, she was sure her heart stopped beating.

"We're going to do your résumé tonight."

"That's great." She thought of Clark, realizing how happy he'd be once she was settled, and all the feelings she'd had about Seth lessened. "But I made dinner." A thought occurred. "You haven't eaten, have you?"

"No. But the résumé probably should come first."

"Or maybe we can talk about it while we eat?" That way they wouldn't have to discuss other things. Not that she hadn't appreciated the conversation the night before. She had. It was more that it had warmed her a little too much.

"Okay."

He set the table as she brought Crystal's baby seat over and strapped it to a chair. She'd already put the pot roast and potatoes and carrots into a huge serving dish and he carried it to the table.

"Smells good." His voice sounded funny, like he had caught the scent of the food and shivered around it.

"Thanks. I learned to cook after Clark and I got married. Mrs. Petrillo watched Crystal while I checked out the little grocery store a few blocks down."

They both sat. Each of them dished up a plateful of food.

Seth took a bite and squeezed his eyes shut in ecstasy. "This is fantastic."

It had been so long since anyone had complimented her that even a simple expression of pleasure went through her like warm honey. Luckily, they had work to do.

She bounced from her chair. "I'll go get my laptop."

She raced into her bedroom and found her computer. She turned it on, pulled up her résumé and headed to the dining area again.

When she got there, Seth was standing in front of Crystal's seat.

He glanced up at Harper. "I wasn't sure what to do. I knew you were probably okay with her sitting there. But I'm new to all this and when you were gone so long, I figured I'd better be safe rather than sorry."

Crystal grinned and he laughed. "She's really cute."

The sight of him by her little girl warmed her heart, but more than that, he was getting accustomed to her baby. Maybe growing to like her baby—

He wasn't supposed to like Crystal. Or her. She was here temporarily. They'd probably never see each other again after her short stay here. She needed to remember that.

"She's fine as long as the she's strapped in." She slid the laptop on the table. "Here's my résumé."

Seth returned to his seat. He angled the screen toward him and started reading.

After only a minute, he glanced over at her. "What kind of a job are you trying for?"

"I'd like to be somebody's assistant."

"Okay. Good. I think your qualifications should line up. But you do realize there'll be some other things like typing involved? Maybe writing reports."

"That would be fantastic. I like to work. I think I'd like a job that would challenge me."

He finished reading what she had in her résumé as he ate his roast and potatoes. After they'd cleaned the kitchen and dining area, she put the baby to bed.

When she returned to the living area, he pointed to the laptop, still on the dining room table. "Okay. We need to punch it up a bit, but we'll figure it out together. If I'm going to recommend you, I want to know what's in your résumé."

Her spirits brightened. "You're going to recommend me?"

"I saw how you worked when you lived beside me and Clark. I know you were dedicated to your clients. I know you put in long hours." He shrugged. "I'm the perfect person to recommend you."

She sat at the table in front of the laptop. He stood behind her.

Leaning in, he said, "Our first problem is that you haven't worked in five years. We have to downplay that."

The woodsy scent of his cologne floated to her. Her shoulder tingled because he had his hand on the back of her chair and every time she moved, she brushed it. Her mind tried to go blank, to enjoy the sensations, but she wouldn't let it. They had a job to do.

She turned to make a suggestion about how to get around the gap between her work experience and the current date, but when she turned, the way he leaned in put them face-to-face. So close, they could have rubbed noses.

Close enough to kiss.

Her chest froze. Where the hell had that thought come from? She did not want to kiss him. This feeling tumbling through her had to be wrong. Seth was her husband's best friend.

She started to turn away, but his eyes held hers. When she'd met him, she'd thought he had the eyes of a bad boy. Dark. Forbidding. But she once again saw the spark of wisdom or experience that she'd seen when he'd opened his condo door to her a few days before.

It was as if something had happened in the past five years. Something that had changed him. She knew what his dad had been like. She knew his mom had been oblivious—

She blinked to break eye contact. She wasn't supposed to be curious about him.

"I, um, thought maybe we could just admit that I got married five years ago and hadn't worked since."

He pulled back. "I think you have to. The worst thing a person can do is lie on a résumé."

Surprised, she laughed. "You think *that's* the worst thing a person can do?"

He turned away. "There are definitely worse things a person can do in general. But we're talking in terms of getting a job."

"Oh. Right." She faced her laptop again, moved the cursor to the spot she needed to change and started typing. But she couldn't stop thinking about his eyes. They were not the eyes of a serial seducer. They weren't the eyes of a poet, either. They were the eyes of a cautious man.

Probably because of what had happened in his family.

Sure, he was working for them…but he'd already mentioned not being close to his mom. Whatever had caused him to run from his family must not have been resolved. Or had they swept it under the rug like a good high-society family?

Curiosity rose and knocked and knocked and knocked on her brain, begging for attention.

She ignored it.

Her wanting to know about him could be nothing more than the curiosities of a lonely woman.

They fussed with her résumé for another hour before they got it right. Then she raced off to her room and Seth was left with the scent of her shampoo lingering in his nostrils, making him crazy.

But the fact that she'd run off proved to him that he wasn't the only one feeling things. He'd seen it when she'd sat staring into his eyes. She'd covered that by being strictly professional as they tidied her résumé, but her racing off brought back all his instincts that she was every bit as attracted to him as he was to her.

Clark's widow.

That made it doubly important that he help her with her job search, so she could leave.

The baby woke him again that night and instead of pulling the pillow over his head, curiosity had him sitting up in bed. He wondered what a mother and baby did in the middle of the night. Did Harper sing to Crystal? Read to her?

He plopped back down again and pulled the pillow over his head. This was nuts. He did not like babies. They scared him. He shouldn't care about Crystal and Harper. Or even just Harper. He knew better. It was why he'd stepped aside and let Clark ask her out. Clark had been the nice guy. The guy who loved kids and wanted a family. The guy who'd found one perfect woman and would have been faithful forever.

Seth was a womanizer.

But living with Harper seemed to be making him forget the wise move he'd made when he was twenty-two. Step back. Let her be with someone who would love her correctly.

He had to get her a job and an apartment, and move out of his house…his life. Before he did something stupid.

He went to work Friday morning and called Arthur Jenkins, whose assistant was at least seven months pregnant and should be going on maternity leave. His company was small. His needs were probably few.

He talked up Harper, honestly telling Art that she didn't

have office experience, but she was dedicated and a hard worker. When he mentioned that she was also funny and nice to have around, he clamped his mouth shut. Luckily, Art took everything he said in the context of an assistant and gave him a time to tell her to come for an interview Monday morning.

When Seth told her about the interview her eyes lit with joy, making him glad he hadn't canceled his date that evening. Or the one for Saturday night. Not wanting to take any chances being around her, he also left Sunday morning and didn't come back until late Sunday night.

Monday morning, he didn't knock on her door before he left for work. He texted her from his office to wish her luck on her interview and make himself seem appropriately distanced from the woman whose blue eyes could inspire poetry.

He didn't expect to hear back from her until after lunch, and relief got him through a morning of meetings. At noon, the sky was clear, the weather still warm. Feeling very good about helping Harper, he decided to accept his brother's invitation to join him for lunch at a nearby restaurant.

But as they strode toward the lobby door, Harper walked in.

He caught Jake's arm. "That's Harper."

"Harper?" His dark-haired, blue-eyed brother frowned. "Clark's wife?"

"Widow. She needed help finding a job." He craned his neck to see past the gaggle of people. "I got her an interview this morning."

Obviously surprised, Jake peered at him. "You did?"

He batted a hand. "It's nothing. But she could be here looking for me. Better go on without me."

Jake left. Seth caught up to Harper, who was standing in front of the directory. "Harper?"

She turned to him with tears in her eyes. "I didn't get it."

His heart sank, but he said, "It's your first interview. It's fine."

A tear rolled onto her cheek. "No. It's not fine. I need a job. I have a baby to support."

Her crying went through him like hot ice. He led her to the door and out onto the sidewalk, so she wouldn't stand in one place long enough for anyone to really see or hear her. Her words would blend into the noise of the city around them.

As they started up the street, she said, "Seth, it was like a whole different world. I was even dressed wrong."

She spoke stronger now. Her tears had scared him, but the fact that she gathered herself together humbled him. He thought he was helping her, but this was really her battle. She was a good woman, a good person, in a bad situation. And she was right. In her purple skirt and simple white blouse, she wasn't dressed to impress. It was like she was hiding her light under a basket.

He glanced around and saw a small boutique up ahead. He'd frequented the store to get gifts for his mom, his sister and girlfriends. The clerks were quiet, discrete. If he took Harper inside and told the saleswomen they needed to look around, they would smile and give them some space. And he could give her some pointers on dressing for an office. Somehow in those years of being self-employed, she'd gotten the idea that office workers needed to be dowdy.

He took her arm and led her into the store.

"What are we doing?"

"You said you felt you were dressed wrong."

She looked down at her white blouse and eggplant-colored skirt. "I *was* dressed wrong. I haven't bought clothes in two years, unless you count maternity jeans."

He pointed to the left at a long rack of tops beside a rack of skirts and trousers beside a rack of sweaters beside three rows of dresses.

"See the colors?"

"Pretty." Her head tilted. "And not a dark purple skirt or blouse among them."

"Go look."

She faced him. "I can't afford to spend a bunch of cash on clothes when I'm not sure if I'll need the money for a down payment on a house."

"Maybe. But because you've never worked in an office, I think you got the wrong idea about what to wear. Just look around."

She frowned, glanced back at the racks. He could see from the way her eyes shifted that she didn't just want to fit in. She almost seemed to long to run her fingers along the fabrics, try things on, get some clothes that would ease her into her next life phase.

"I can get you an account here."

She bit her lower lip. "If I have to use my profit from selling my condo as a down payment for another condo, God knows when I'll be able to pay it off."

"Why don't you let me worry about that?"

She closed her eyes. "I can't do that."

His heart melted. He could afford to buy the whole damn store and she wouldn't let him buy her a few dresses.

"What if we get the account, but you make the payments. Probably won't be too much if you spread it out over a few months. And new clothes will give you the confidence you need on your next interview."

She licked her lips. His libido sent blood straight to the wrong part of him, as his emotions zigzagged in four different directions. He'd always had a thing for Harper. But he'd also known her as his best friend's wife. He wanted to help her. Almost *needed* to help her. But he loved her strength, her pride, her longing to make her own way and be herself.

Hell, hadn't he fought to be allowed to be himself?

"Please."

She glanced at him. "I know you're doing all this to pay back a debt to Clark. But he never felt you owed him."

"I owe him everything I am today. Which is why I understand why you don't want to take the help."

She chuckled, then shook her head as if amazed by him. "You will let me pay the bill?"

"I'll consider forwarding that bill a sacred obligation."

"I do like that black dress back there."

He motioned for a salesgirl. "Then you should try it on."

They shopped long past Seth's lunch hour. She tried on dresses, pants, blouses, skirts, sweaters. Though Seth would have had her take it all, he let her sift through and find eight pieces she could mix and match, and three simple dresses.

The salesclerk happily tallied the price and boxed the first dress neatly. Expensively. From his days of living hand-to-mouth while at university and in his two years of working as a lowly broker for a big investment firm, he knew that little touches like a box with tissue paper made a person feel a bit better about themselves, about who they were.

He watched as the clerks tucked away the other two dresses, then the trousers, and started on the tops.

"Harper?"

The woman's voice came from behind Seth. He turned and saw a tall, black-haired woman with big blue eyes very much like Harper's.

"Mom?"

His gut almost exploded. Harper's mom wore an expensive suit, shoes that probably set her back thousands and a purse that had probably cost more. The diamond on her left hand could have blinded him. All of Harper's fears came into sharp focus for him. This was a woman who liked being rich, who thought more of money than people.

She reached out and caught Harper by the shoulders,

hugged her, then kissed her cheek. "It's so lovely to see you here."

He thought the comment odd until he realized this boutique existed purely for wealthy clientele. Harper's mom didn't know her daughter was broke. She believed her daughter belonged there.

"And buying things!"

Her mother sounded thrilled, but also proud. Knowing appearances meant everything to her, he understood why she was over-the-top happy.

Harper, however, looked like a deer trapped in the headlights of an oncoming car. She opened her mouth as if trying to speak but couldn't get any words out. Her eyes drifted to the stack of clothes, almost all packed into bags and boxes now.

Unconcerned about Harper's silence, Harper's mom faced Seth. "And who is this?"

He decided to pick up the dropped ball and held his hand out to shake Harper's mom's. "I'm Seth McCallan, Mrs. Sloan."

She took his hand with a gasp. "Seth McCallan. Of course. I've seen you at a few charity functions. I'm sorry I didn't recognize you. I'm Amelia Sloan. My husband is Peter. Please call me Amelia."

He smiled. "It's nice to meet you, Amelia."

Pleasure lit Amelia Sloan's face. "What are you d here with my Harper?"

"Just a little shopping."

The salesclerk finished boxing Harper's new clothes and casually handed the receipt to Seth.

Amelia's eyes narrowed, then widened slightly as she figured out Seth was paying for Harper's purchases.

"It's not what you think, Mom."

Amelia clucked. "And how would you know what I think?"

While the women seemed to be on the same page, Seth needed a minute to process why Harper was struggling. Drowning really. Here was the very person Harper wanted to keep her situation from, standing in front of them, seeing someone buying clothes for her daughter. She didn't know Harper was broke or that she intended to pay Seth for the purchases. And he realized explaining that might make things worse. Amelia would ask why Harper had to have someone else pay for her clothes, everything Harper was trying to hide would come tumbling out and the thing he'd spent a week of torture to avoid would happen.

Amelia Sloan would blame Clark.

There was only one way to fix this...

"We're dating."

The words came out of Seth's mouth in a rush, as if the quicker he said it, the quicker Amelia would stop going down a road that Harper didn't want her traveling.

But where Amelia's face glowed with happy surprise, Harper's mouth fell open.

Her reaction would have ruined everything if Seth hadn't thought to step closer and put his arm around her waist.

Amelia all but melted with joy. "You didn't want me to know you were dating one of the most eligible men in Manhattan? Harper! That's ridiculous."

"No, it's not. Because we're not—"

Seth squeezed her waist. "We're not serious. Just started seeing each other," he said, trying to mitigate the lie.

Amelia's eyes narrowed. "And you thought my Harper didn't dress well enough for your rarefied world?"

"No!" Seth assured her, scrambling for what to say. "She said she liked something in the window." Oh, crap. Another lie. "And I wanted to buy it for her." He *had* wanted to buy her clothes. "Because it pleases me to give her things." That, too, was the truth. Remembering the joyful expression on Harper's face when the clothes she loved had looked so good on her, he'd give away half his trust fund to see that look on her face again.

"Well, that's sweet." Amelia hugged her daughter. "I'd love to get coffee and chat, but I have something this afternoon. Why don't you and Seth bring the baby over some night."

"I'm sorry. We probably can't. We're kind of busy, too," Seth explained before Harper could answer. This might not be the perfect lie, but it would hold long enough to get Harper settled in a job and a house. Once they left the store and were away from her mom, he could tell her that. "But I'll have my assistant call yours tomorrow and they can set something up like dinner."

"That would be lovely," Amelia said, her eyes glowing.

Seth quickly grabbed the packages and herded Harper toward the door. "We'll see you then."

Amelia waved.

Harper reminded stonily quiet.

When they stepped out onto the street, he wasn't surprised that she pivoted on him. "You have no idea what you've done."

"I got you out of the store without having to admit anything to your mom."

"Yeah, but now she'll start snooping."

"Into what?" He laughed. "She can call the tabloids, if she wants, looking for times we went out, places we've gone. But she's not going to find anything."

"And she'll get suspicious."

"So what?"

"You are such a babe in the woods. I'm either going to have to come clean with her, and soon, or we're going to have to keep up this charade."

"Would it be such a big deal to keep it up?"

She cast him a long look. "You can't date anyone while you're pretending to be dating me."

"I feel uncomfortable leaving you alone at night, anyway." He sighed. He hated lying. His father had been the consummate liar. He'd used lies to control, manipulate, humiliate, belittle and bully everyone from his employees to his own children. If there was one thing Seth had vowed never to do, it was lie.

But this was a worthy cause, an unusual situation. Harper, a widow with a baby, needed time to get herself settled before she told her mom she was broke and it was Clark's fault.

Plus, her mom hadn't appeared on the radar of Seth's life before this. He didn't think she'd start now. Unlike his father's master manipulation lies, this little charade wouldn't hurt anyone.

"Needing to get out of this mess will step up your job search a bit and we might have to start looking for houses before you have a job...but I think I did what I had to do."

"You're willing to pretend to be my boyfriend for at least the next *four weeks*?"

The ramifications of that rained down on him. No breakfasts, lunches or dinners with any women except colleagues...and no sex.

She shook her head. "That's a long time."

Yeah, that was sinking in and not pleasantly.

"And my mother is relentless. You're a catch. She's going to want me to keep you."

That, thank God, made him laugh. "My reputation will save us. When we break up no one will be surprised."

"Oh, really?"

"Yes. You're taking this all too seriously. It's a few weeks. What can she possibly do in a few weeks?"

CHAPTER FOUR

WHAT CAN SHE do in a few weeks?

Harper groaned. "You'd be surprised. So, we do have to step up the job search and the apartment hunt."

"I already said that."

She glanced at the armful of boxes he carried and the bags she had in her hand. "I'm going to need a cab."

"No. Jake's car is just up the street." Juggling the boxes, he pulled out his phone, hit a few buttons and said, "Does Jake need you today?" He listened, then smiled. "Good. I have a friend who only has to go a few blocks, but she's been shopping and has bags." A pause. "Okay. We're not even a block up the street from the office. You'll see us on the sidewalk."

He disconnected the call. "He'll check in with Jake and be here in two minutes. I'll wait with you." He displayed the boxes. "Because I don't think you can handle all these."

They stood in silence until the limo pulled up. The trunk popped. The driver jumped out and took the packages from Harper, tucking them into the trunk. Seth handed him the boxes he held, and he stowed them away before returning to open the passenger door of the limo.

She turned to say thanks to Seth, but saw her mom coming out of the boutique—just in time to see her standing in front of a McCallan limo.

"Don't look now but my mom is behind you."

Seth's eyebrows drew together. "She is?"

"I told you, her curiosity knows no bounds."

"She's looking?"

"Of course, she's looking!"

"Then we'll just have to make this realistic." He leaned in and placed a soft kiss on her lips. The movement was smooth, a light brush across her mouth, but it rained tingles down to her toes. Her breath hitched, caught in her chest and froze.

She thought he'd pull away. He didn't. She told herself she should move back, but she couldn't. All those questions about him rose up in her, but so did the sweet sensations of being attracted to someone. Of feeling like a woman.

He took a step closer. She took a step toward him. His arms circled her waist. Her hands went to his shoulders. The kiss deepened. The press of his lips became a crush. Arousal blossomed in her belly, scrambled her pulse, shattered her concentration.

When he moved his mouth, she opened hers for him—

And common sense returned.

Not only was her mother watching, but Harper was also kissing Clark's best friend…and a womanizer. Even if he wasn't Clark's best friend, he was all wrong for her. And she missed Clark. She didn't want another man. Not yet. She didn't want to lose Clark's memory…to forget him.

She jerked back. Not risking another glance into those dark eyes of his, she took the few steps from the sidewalk to the limo. As casually as possible, she said, "I'll see you at home."

She slid into the limo. She didn't wait to see Seth's reaction, didn't peer at the boutique door to see if her mom was still watching. There was no need. The damage had been done. Not only did her mom think she was dating one of the wealthiest men in Manhattan, but that man had also kissed her. Greedily. Hungrily.

She could close her eyes and remember the kiss. Every movement of his mouth.

The limo sped off and she covered her face with her hands. She didn't know which was worse—her mom thinking she was dating a catch or liking the kiss of a man she shouldn't be kissing. Clark might be gone, but he wasn't forgotten. She'd adored him. She didn't want to replace him.

She wasn't even ready to *think about* replacing him.

She wasn't even ready to think about *liking* someone.

After flubbing her interview that morning, she'd thought her situation couldn't get any worse, and in the blink of an eye—or the brush of some lips—it had worsened exponentially.

Because worse than the longing that had sprung up inside her, worse than the kiss, worse than her mom thinking she and Seth were dating, was a deep sadness, a quiet reminder whispered from the depths of her soul that Clark was gone.

Seth stood watching the limo drive off. He'd kissed a lot of women in his lifetime but, somehow, he'd always known kissing Harper would be different. Every cell in his body had awakened. His blood had electrified. His mind shot back eight years, to when he should have asked her out—instead of stepping away so Clark could ask her out. Back to when he'd still believed in miracles, in magic, and he remembered his yearning to make her his.

He turned to walk to his building. Knowing her mom was watching, he kept his expression neutral. He didn't smile or frown or grimace until he was behind the closed door of his office, then he had to hold back a howl of misery. *He could not have that woman.* He was a serial dater. No. He wasn't even that nice. He was a one-night-stand guy.

Harper was a woman with a child. *A widow.* She needed security. He did not get involved with women like her because he didn't want to hurt anyone. His definition of making a woman "his" now was very different than what it had been eight years ago.

He could not kiss her again.

But he wanted to.

And that's what made him nuts. Until he'd kissed her he'd been curious. And, yeah, maybe a little needy for it. But he'd been smart enough to ignore the urge. Now that he knew how great kissing her was, he would think of that kiss every time he looked at her.

But he would also know he couldn't kiss her again.

And that would make him even more nuts.

He sat in his chair and threw himself into his projects as if his life depended on it. Around two, his stomach growled. He hadn't had lunch. He got a snack cake from the vending machine in the employee lounge and went back to work.

He should have left at six. He waited until seven. But he couldn't stay any longer. If he did, Harper would wonder why and probably realize a kiss that was supposed to be a show for her mom had been a little too real for him.

Of course, she had kissed him back.

Cursing himself for reminding himself of that, he rode the elevator up to his floor, then ambled down the hall. Using his key, he opened the door and stepped inside.

"I'm home."

He almost cursed again. He sounded like a husband.

"We're in the kitchen."

He walked into the main area and found Harper at the island, sitting on a stool, feeding Crystal a bottle.

The silence in the room was so thick, he scrambled for something to say. Anything to get them over the awkwardness. "So, she drinks milk?"

Harper glanced over at him. Probably confused by the

stupid question. Still, she answered it. "She drinks formula."

"Formula" sounded like something made in a laboratory. Sympathy for the kid filled him. Glad to forget his misery over kissing Harper, he sat on the stool beside them.

"She seems to like it."

"Do you think I'd feed her something she didn't like?"

After a few seconds, the bottle was empty. Harper rose and patted the little girl's back until she burped like a sailor.

She laughed. "Okay. That's enough for now."

She buckled Crystal into the baby carrier, which she fastened to one of the tufted chairs around the dining room table.

"I made dinner."

He wished with all his might that he could get out of eating with her, but his stomach growled. "What'd you make?"

"I was going to make spaghetti, but I think Mrs. P. plans to make that for you next week."

His mouth watered. Mrs. P. was a wonderful person to have for a neighbor. Which reminded him—

"How did she do babysitting while you were at your interview this morning?"

"She loved having someone to watch her morning soap operas with." Harper airily moved into the kitchen, over to the oven, and pulled out a casserole. "She told me that she'd be happy to keep Crystal anytime I have an interview or a condo to look at."

"That's good."

"She also loved the clothes we picked out." She lifted the casserole to the countertop, pausing for a second before she turned to Seth. "I'm sorry about my mom."

He reached for his mail to give himself something to look at other than her apologetic blue eyes. "It's fine."

"No. It's not fine. She's a snob and a gossip and just plain hard to get along with."

"I already told you my dad wasn't exactly a prince. In fact, he was so bad he makes your mom look good."

Her quick laugh told him he'd sufficiently gotten her past her embarrassment about her mom.

Now, if she'd just not say anything about—

"I'm also sorry you had to kiss me."

Just the mention of it turned him on again, while Harper still appeared apologetic. Only apologetic. Not breathless. Not curious. The kiss might as well have not happened.

A little annoyed, a little insulted, he tossed the mail on the counter. "It's not like I had to scoop up dog poop. Besides, I seem to remember the kiss was my idea."

And that she'd participated. She hadn't stayed still. It hadn't been like kissing a rock.

"Okay. Maybe instead of apologizing I should say thanks."

She should. She really should because he was suffering the torment of the damned and she'd gotten away from her mom without having to explain that she was broke.

He was a prince, a saint, to have helped her.

Especially since every time they discussed her mom, he thought of his dad. The humiliation. The fact that things weren't right with his own mom and would never really be right.

His phone rang. He glanced at caller ID and saw it was a female friend who visited New York only a few times a year. Glad for the interruption of his thoughts, he answered it. "Marlene! How are you?"

He drifted toward the sofa for privacy, knowing this was exactly what he needed. The reminder that he was a *happy* serial-one-night-stand guy. Not a knight who rescued nice women. Not a guy who thought too much about his past with an abusive father and a mom who turned a blind eye.

"I'm in town. Want to get a drink?"

"I'd love a drink." He needed a drink. "Where and what time?"

"I'm staying at the Waldorf. There's a lovely club just down the street."

"I'll meet you there in a few minutes."

He disconnected the call and headed for the door. "Sorry, but that was an old friend. I'm meeting her for drinks."

One of her eyebrows rose. He was absolutely positive she was going to remind him he wasn't allowed to date, so he added, "Seriously. She's just a friend. A business associate. If I pay, I can write this off as an expense."

"Oh. Okay."

He'd never heard two words said with such relief and that compounded the I'm-an-idiot feelings currently bubbling through him like stew in a big, black witch's pot.

All she was worried about was keeping the charade intact. While he was mad at himself for kissing Clark's wife, thinking thoughts about his parents that he'd believed he'd left behind when his dad died, and worried about his attraction to a nice woman when he was so unreliable, she was only worried about fooling her mom.

Not that he blamed her. He understood how hard it was to try to please an unpleasable parent.

"Have a nice time."

"I will." He headed out to meet Marlene.

He left for work the next morning after not much more than a few grunts in Harper's direction. Respectful of his mood, Harper didn't say anything, either. That kiss by the limo the day before had ruined the complicated but civil relationship they were developing. She knew that was why he'd eagerly accepted the chance to get out of the condo the night before. And why she'd been so glad he had.

The kiss had been amazing. Because of Clark, she'd talked herself out of making a big deal out of it. But it wasn't easy. Seth was an experienced kisser. She remembered every brush of his lips. Every sweep of his tongue. When she least expected it, she'd remember it, and had to admit, she'd liked it.

But maybe Seth hadn't. In fact, his edginess the night before and grumpiness that morning might be a sign he *regretted* kissing her. Not a sign that he'd liked it.

She smacked the side of her own head, hoping to knock some sense into herself. It was crazy, stupid, to think about it. The damn kiss had only been part of a charade. Plus, she had bigger problems that should be occupying her mind and her time. Like a job and a place to live.

While Crystal slept, she brought her laptop to the kitchen island and searched for jobs online, keeping her cell phone beside her with the baby-monitor app opened.

An hour into her fruitless search, her phone rang. The sound echoed through the quiet condo and almost made her jump out of her skin.

Seeing her mom's picture pop up on the screen, she grimaced. She'd want the juicy details about Seth. Harper was either going to have to continue the lie or tell the truth... which would open the can of worms Harper had kept tightly closed for the past year.

She took a breath. Blew it out slowly. Then answered. "Hey, Mom."

"Good morning, sweetie. How's Crystal today?"

"The same as always." She slid off the stool and paced into the area with the sofa and television, her feet drifting along the soft shag of the white area rug on the rustic brown hardwood floor.

"Has she said 'Nana' yet?"

"No. She hasn't even said 'Mom.' Right now, we're working on getting her to say 'goo.'"

"She'll say it. Then 'Mom' will follow and pretty soon

she'll be saying 'Nana,'" her mother said enthusiastically. "I'm calling because I haven't heard from Seth's people yet."

Harper squeezed her eyes shut, still undecided about what to say. Did she admit that she and Seth weren't dating? Did she say he was helping her find a job? Did she mention that he was letting her live with him—because she was nearly broke? And if she did, how would she handle her mom's anger?

She stalled. "It hasn't even been twenty-four hours."

"I know. But when a man like Seth is dating a classy woman like you, he's Johnny on the spot with things like dinner invitations."

She glanced down at her worn jeans and the shirt that had stretched out from too many washings. She was hardly classy.

But this was her opening to end the charade. She had to take it. She didn't like the lie—or Seth's regret. "Mom, this thing with me and Seth—"

"I know. You're not making a big deal out of it. In fact, you're probably brooding because of Clark, but it's time, Harper."

The easy way her mother dismissed Clark set her nerve endings on fire. "Time for what, Mom?"

"To let go. To date. To think about marrying again."

Oh, Lord. She already had them married? "Mom, Seth is thirty-one and he's never married—"

"Because he's particular. Many wealthy men wait until their thirties to marry, even their forties, because they have enough female attention that they don't need to marry the wrong woman. Though some do. Look at George Clooney. He waited until his fifties to settle down for good."

Harper frowned at her phone. Her mother certainly knew how to whitewash things she wanted cleaned and sanitized.

"That's one way of looking at it. The other is that they like dating, don't want a commitment, don't want kids."

Her heart pinged when she remembered Seth telling her he was afraid of kids. Even if that kiss had caused her to swoon, this was reality. Seth didn't like kids. She had a child. There would be nothing between them.

Her mind cleared. And while it was clear, she wanted it to stay clear. It was time to tell her mother the truth.

"Mom, what you saw yesterday—"

"Was adorable. Stop talking yourself out of liking Seth because you think he's is too good for you. Don't be angry, honey, but I know that's why you married Clark. Lack of self-confidence."

Anger burst in Harper's chest. "Mom, Clark was a gorgeous blond. He could have had his pick of women. I was lucky he chose me."

"You were young and thinking with your hormones. But we don't have to worry about that with Seth. He's gorgeous *and* has money. No. Not just money—a pedigree. He is someone."

"He's someone, all right. Probably a better person than you think he is." She opened her mouth to explain Seth was helping her out of her bad situation, but the words stuck in her throat. With the way this conversation was going, if Harper told her mother that she needed Seth's help because Clark had left her broke, her mom would explode. The only way *that* discussion went smoothly would be if Harper had a job and a place to stay when she told her parents that she'd had to sell the investment firm and her condo.

She needed time. Seth's lie bought her time.

"You know what, Mom? I think dinner with you and Dad is too soon."

After a short pause, her mom said, "Too soon?"

"We're barely dating." At least that wasn't a lie. "I think we just need to be on our own for a while."

Her mom sighed. "I get it."

Surprised that she'd given up so easily, Harper said, "You do?"

"Sure. Nobody starts out dating by introducing a guy to her parents. It was a fluke that we ran into each other, but that doesn't mean we can push the schedule along and ruin things." Her mom took a long breath. "But your father and I also can't ignore you, if we see you around town."

Relief and disbelief of her luck fluttered through her. "You won't see us."

Her mom laughed. "You're so sure of that? Your dad and I eat out five times a week. We go to parties. Now that you're with a man in our league, you're bound to run into us."

No, they wouldn't. Because she and Seth would never go anywhere.

Harper's chest loosened. Her blood began to flow again. She desperately needed the next few weeks to get her life in order. If it meant her mom had to think she was dating Manhattan's most eligible bachelor...so be it.

"Thanks, Mom."

"You're welcome." She paused. "You could still come by with the baby some afternoon when Seth is working."

"I have a few things I have to straighten out."

Her mom's voice soured. "Clark's estate still not settled?"

"Something like that." She winced, thinking of the whirlwind job search and house hunting in her near future and oh, so glad she hadn't ended the lie. "But as soon as I'm free, Crystal and I will be over."

"Good. I love you," her mom said in a singsong voice.

Harper said, "I love you, too."

She disconnected the call, wishing she could mean it. She knew her mom's intentions were good. But even as Amelia Sloan happily chatted about Seth, she'd subtly bad-mouthed Clark. When Harper finally told her mom that she'd lost Clark's investment firm because it was barely worth what he'd owed on it and sold the condo because Clark had mortgaged that, too, she had to have everything sorted or Amelia would have the kind of tirade about Clark that broke Harper's heart.

Seth had been correct. The lie really would hold for a few weeks. It had, too.

A little after six, Seth arrived home and Harper didn't waste a second. He'd run out of the apartment the night before and that morning because things were tense between them. She could fix that.

"My mom called this morning."

His expression shifted from neutral to cautious. "I forgot to have someone phone her about dinner."

"It's fine. I told her we had just started dating and needed a few weeks 'on our own' and she agreed."

His face contorted. "What does that mean?"

"It means she won't be calling or dropping by. We're fine."

He studied her for a few seconds. "I thought you said she was a meddler."

"She is. She's a smart one. She agreed to the pull-back to make sure she didn't ruin things before they start. But the bottom line is she's giving us a few weeks. Which means I can find a job, find a house, move out...and then tell her we broke up. Which will horrify her as much as Clark putting us in debt. I'll take most of the heat for her anger." She shrugged. "In a way, this charade is perfect."

Seth stared at Harper. The way she always deflected bad things away from Clark and to herself amazed him. But this time, it also made him a little angry with Clark that he'd put Harper in this position. Still, he'd never tell Harper that. And all things considered, he'd rather have their attention on her mom, than that kiss.

"So, you think she's going to let us alone?"

"Yes. We should be fine. As long as we don't go out."

The house phone rang. He walked to the island where it sat. Seeing the caller was Rick, another doorman, he answered. "What's up, Rick?"

"Your mother is here." There was a knock on his door. "I already sent her up."

Confusion made him frown, but he said, "Okay. That's fine."

He turned to Harper. "That knock at the door is *my* mother."

"Oh! Should I hide?"

The door opened before he could answer. He'd forgotten he'd given his mom a key in case of emergencies. Maureen McCallan looked past Seth and to Harper. She took in her torn jeans and bare feet.

"So, it's true. You *are* living with Harper Hargraves."

"It's not what you think."

"Really? Her mom bragged about it to everybody at the ladies who lunch meeting this afternoon."

He started to say they weren't living together in the conventional sense of the word, but then he'd have to explain the charade. If he told his mom the truth and his mom told someone, who told someone, who told Harper's mom, it would ruin everything.

He stuck to the lie. "It's more like we're dating."

"So, Harper's just here for dinner?" She sniffed the air. "You made French toast casserole?" She faced Seth. "You don't cook that well, Seth."

"I made it, Mrs. McCallan."

His mom gave Harper another quick once-over. "If you're dating my son, you can call me Maureen."

Harper swallowed hard and caught Seth's gaze. He hadn't believed her when she'd warned him the lie could cause trouble. Still, it was only for a few weeks and it wasn't like he was hurting a perfect mother/son relationship.

Maureen headed for the door. "Well, I have plans for tonight and don't want to interrupt your dinner. We'll catch up at the opening for the gallery on Saturday."

So much for not being seen in public. The gallery—Hot Art—was only reopening after his family had bankrolled renovations. He couldn't miss it. And now he couldn't go without Harper.

"Yes. We'll see you then."

CHAPTER FIVE

HARPER AND CLARK had gone to fund-raisers at various art galleries, and she knew most women wore cocktail dresses.

Shopping with Seth, she hadn't bought a cocktail dress, but she had bought a simple black sheath that she could dress up with pearls. The outfit was simple and elegant. She looked like the lady her mom wanted her to be.

Little black dress.

Dating Manhattan's most eligible bachelor.

Forgetting Clark.

Except she wasn't forgetting Clark. She and Seth weren't really dating. After her mom's promise to stay out of things, this ruse was supposed to be simple, easy, because they weren't really going out in public. Then his mom had showed up and now they were hip-deep in a lie.

She stepped out of her bedroom and Mrs. P. gasped. "Oh, you look so lovely. Old-style classy."

Harper laughed. "Did you just call me old?"

Wearing a tux, Seth came from behind Mrs. P.

He looked *amazing*. His long, limber body wore a tux with the elegant grace of a man accustomed to the fine things in life. But his face bore the oddest expression. His eyes had widened. His eyebrows had raised.

"She said you looked good. And you do."

"You don't need to be so surprised."

"I'm not. I'm just accustomed to seeing you in jeans."

Ragged jeans and worn T-shirts. Her chin lifted. She might not be allowed to be attracted to him, but that didn't mean she didn't have any pride. "You saw me in cocktail dresses plenty of times when Clark and I went to these functions."

"Yeah, but you were married then—and to my best friend. I never really looked at you."

Mrs. P. chortled. "You're digging yourself farther down, Seth. Quit while you're ahead."

"Baby's already in bed for the night," Harper told Mrs. P., handing her a short list of instructions.

Mrs. P. glanced at the paper. "If she'll probably sleep the whole time you're gone, why do I need these?"

"In case she wakes up."

"Ah."

Seth walked to the island and grabbed his keys. "Let's get this show on the road."

When his condo door closed behind them, she caught his arm to stop him. "I'm sorry."

"For?"

"This whole charade is turning into a big mess." She felt like a burden. A chore. A weird something attached to his life that he would soon grow to hate. And the thought that he'd end up hating her tightened her chest and made her wish she'd never asked him for help.

"It's not a big mess. It's a gallery opening. We'll show up, have a few drinks and be back in time for Mrs. P. to catch her eleven-thirty movie."

He said it so easily that Harper's chest loosened. "You're okay with this?"

"I started it, remember? It's a couple of weeks out of my life. We're fine."

They rode the elevator to the basement garage in silence, then stepped out into rows of luxury cars. She spotted her

Explorer quickly, if only because it was the one car valued at less than a hundred thousand dollars.

Which meant the Ferrari beside it was Seth's. "Wow."

He opened the door for her. "You like?"

"I love it." When Seth walked around to the driver's side and slid in beside her, she said, "Clark wanted one of these but thought the SUV was more practical."

"It probably was."

"Yeah, but it wasn't a convertible."

He laughed and started the car. "I'm guessing that means you want the top down."

"Oh, yeah." She couldn't deny it. She'd had a convertible when she was sixteen and had loved it. When she'd left home, left her parents' wealth and hypocrisy behind, it was the only thing she'd missed.

He pushed a button and the roof lowered, then he shifted gears and sent them roaring out of the parking garage.

The feeling of the wind in her hair made her laugh out loud. She'd been so concerned about involving Seth, getting a job and finding a condo that she hadn't had a second of peace. And this—the wind, the night air, forgetting her responsibilities for a few hours—was just what she needed.

"I forgot how this messes up hair," he said, shouting over the noise of the air circulating around them.

"I don't care," she said, and meant it. "Mine's so short, I can pull my fingers through it and get it in shape again."

"Good!" He hit the gas and sent the car speeding up the street.

The air felt fantastic. Freeing. Thanks to Mrs. P. and the need to shop for groceries, she'd had a few times away from the baby, but they hadn't felt like this. Like she was allowed to be herself. Not just a mom, not a cook, not someone scrambling for a job and maybe a place to live, but herself. Her old self.

She turned and yelled, "This is fabulous."

"I know. I sometimes drive to Jersey just for the hell of it."

She sucked in more air, let it wash over her like a spring rain renewing the world. But in the blink of an eye, they pulled up to the valet in front of the gallery. He opened Harper's door and helped her out of the low sports car as Seth got out on his side. Seth tossed him the keys, then took Harper's arm.

"Ready?"

She turned and smiled at him. "Yes."

Everything male in Seth awoke. She made the simple black dress and pearls stunning with her pale skin and big blue eyes. But her pleasure during their ride over with the top down had filled him with joy. He hated that this charade seemed to trouble her, and for one darn night he wished she could forget it all and have a good time. In fact, maybe that should be his mission. Not to romance her or steer clear of her for fear of feelings, but to show her a good time. Just because she was a friend.

The doorman didn't check the list for Seth's name. Everyone knew Seth was a McCallan. He opened the door, and Seth ushered Harper inside. As the door closed, the sounds of the city were immediately replaced by the noise of conversations rising to the high ceiling of the gallery and echoing back.

Harper said, "Wow. They've remodeled this place since the last time I was here. It's gorgeous."

She was gorgeous with her windblown spiky hair and her sheath outlining her trim figure. And for the first time in what felt like forever, he wanted to show off his date.

Who wasn't really a date.

But why not?

Most of the world thought they were dating anyway.

And he'd already decided he wanted her to have a good time. Maybe they could both enjoy this.

His brother, Jake, and wife, Avery, approached them. Avery's red hair and big green eyes paired with Jake's dark hair and blue eyes made them the perfect all-American couple.

Jake said, "Harper! It is nice to see you out and about again."

Harper sucked in a breath. "Thank you."

She was obviously nervous, and Seth prayed Jake wouldn't say something about Clark. The guy had been gone a year. Harper was showing signs of really getting beyond his death. If Jake said something now—

"This is my wife, Avery." Jake faced her. "Avery, this is Harper Hargraves. She's an old friend of Seth's."

Avery smiled and shook Harper's hand. She exchanged a quick look with Jake before she answered, "I remember."

But that was all she said. She didn't mention that she was with Jake when he got word Clark had been killed in an accident. She didn't say she'd been part of the search for Seth when he'd gone missing that night, or that they'd found him drunk and had to drive him home.

Seth hid a sigh of relief. Avery could have said any one of a million things. But his well-bred brother and his beautiful wife left out the sad details and welcomed Harper.

Jake said, "What do you think of the renovations?"

Harper glanced around. "The place is lovely."

"We wanted more space for displays, especially bigger pieces of art," Avery explained. "So, when the gallery came to us for help, we had it designed to fit almost anything."

"It's beautiful."

"Avery is the benevolent one," Jake said with a laugh. "I'd have given them the money and said have at it. She actually worked with the designers and architects."

Seth laughed at that. His brother was right about Avery

being benevolent, but Avery also had changed Jake, made him kinder and gentler. Though it would be a cold frosty day in hell before Seth told his older brother that.

"Hey, everybody." Seth and Jake's sister joined the group.

"Sabrina," Seth said. "You're probably too young to remember Harper, Clark Hargrave's wife."

Sabrina extended her hand to shake Harper's. "Of course, I remember. I'm only three years younger than you are, Seth."

Harper said, "How are you, Sabrina?"

She looked expensively elegant in her sparkly blue dress, which matched her blue eyes and brought out the best in her blond hair. "Overworked. Underappreciated."

Harper laughed, and Seth swallowed another sigh of relief. He shouldn't care if his brother and sister liked Harper, but he did. He blamed that on his fear that one of them would say something about Clark's death and ruin Harper's evening, but so far no one had. Which was odd. He'd have at least expected his brother to razz him about bringing a date.

He turned to his sister. "That's what you get for working for a charity."

Sabrina's chin lifted. "We're not a charity. Clients pay what they can for our services."

Seth addressed Harper. "Sabrina runs an organization that helps startup companies."

"That's interesting!"

"It's fabulous," Sabrina said. "People come to me with their ideas and I help them bring them to life."

Harper sighed with envy. "You wouldn't happen to need an assistant, would you?"

Seth quickly intervened. "Even if she does, she can't afford you. You need a job that pays you a fairly substantial amount of money."

Sabrina looked crushed. "Too bad."

Avery said, "I can keep my ear to the ground."

"I'd appreciate that." Harper shifted her purse from one hand to the other and Seth realized that her nails were painted. The little detail, another confirmation that she'd looked forward to this event, reinforced his vow that he would help her have a good time.

Which probably meant he should get her away from his family.

"Why don't we get a drink?" Seth said.

"Better yet," Jake said, "why don't you and I go and get drinks for the ladies?"

There was no way out of that without explaining he wanted to get Harper away from his family. He headed toward the bar.

Jake followed him. "I thought you were just helping her find a job? Now you and Harper are dating?"

He shrugged. "So?"

"So? Seth? She isn't just Clark's wife. You brought her somewhere she'd have to meet family. Are you serious about her?"

"It's not like that. We're together a lot because of updating her résumé, that kind of thing. Dating just evolved from that."

"Oh…that explains why you look so chummy."

He walked up to the bar, absently ordered a Scotch. "Chummy?" He laughed, suddenly seeing the humor in stringing this out and teasing his brother. "What the hell does chummy look like?"

Jake shrugged. "You know. Exchanging glances because you share information. That kind of thing."

"You sound like an old woman."

"No. I sound like a confused brother. During everything we went through with Dad, we've told each other everything. Now you show up with Clark Hargraves's widow and you don't think I'll be curious?"

For a split second, the ruse didn't seem so funny. He and Jake had been bound by a mutual need to get out of a bad situation. He could understand his brother would be curious as to why he'd kept something so big from him.

"Jake, I like Harper." He did. No lie there. "But she's Clark's widow. She needs help. I'm helping her."

"And dating."

"And dating. But neither one of us expects anything to come of it."

Jake laughed. "You are such a babe in the woods. That's exactly how love hits. When you least expect it."

"I'm fine."

"You think so but what seems like an innocent connection combines with sexual attraction, before you know it you're hooked."

The truth of that sank into his bones like a warning that had been right in front of him, but he'd kept missing. He'd always been attracted to Harper, and now they were sharing a condo. He was helping her. She was even cooking for him.

And tonight, he'd wanted to show her a good time...

"I think I'm smart enough to keep my wits about me."

"Too bad."

Just when he thought he had a handle on the conversation, his brother threw him another curveball. "Too bad?"

"Yes. She's nice." Jake's gaze drifted to Harper and Avery and Sabrina. "And Avery likes her. No better litmus test than that." Jake suddenly grinned. "Except Mom." Jake laughed. "Oh, it's going to be fun watching you explain this to Mom."

"She's already been to the house. She heard the rumor that we were dating, and she came by."

"Well, damn. I was kind of looking forward to the show."

"There is no show."

Or at least he hoped there wouldn't be. They hadn't yet

run into his mom. But now that Jake had mentioned it, he could be prepared for that, too.

Seth took a glass of champagne from a passing waiter then retrieved the Scotch he'd ordered at the bar. Jake did the same. When they returned to Avery, Harper and Sabrina, the three women were laughing.

Seth's breath stalled in his chest. He hadn't seen her laugh so deeply, so happily, since before Clark's death. But more than that, there was no one as beautiful as Harper when she laughed.

And suddenly he saw what Jake had seen. All those old feelings he had about Harper kept bubbling up when he least expected. And when they did, he froze or gazed at her, probably with adoring eyes.

Rather than panic, he decided that might be good. They were supposed to be dating. He could use these feelings, these instincts and impulses, while they were here, among the people they were trying to fool, and be warned of them when he and Harper were alone.

He rejoined the group as they subtly moved a little farther into the cluster of potential donors to the charity hosting the event. Before he took his final step in the move, Harper laid her hand on his upper arm and held him back.

"Your family put millions of dollars into the renovations for this gallery?"

"My mother enjoys being a patron of the arts." He grimaced. "We're actually silent partners."

The way her eyes brightened told him that pleased her. "Oh."

"We don't let a lot of the work we do, the things we own, get out to the general public." He paused, then caught her gaze. She trusted him with all her secrets. He could certainly trust her with one of his. "Sabrina paints. You'll find a lot of her work here under the name Sally McMillen."

"You guys didn't open this gallery for her, did you?"

He laughed. "No. The gallery discovered her but her first showing was a disaster. People bought her art seeking favors from my father or just wanting to have something done by a McCallan. She was embarrassed and upset. Wondered if people liked her work at all."

"I can understand that."

"Now her work is shown as Sally McMillen. She knows that the people who buy it like it for what it is. And she has a good job that acts as a cover for people."

Harper's gaze strayed to Sabrina. "She's so lucky to be talented."

"You're talented."

She turned back to him. "Not hardly."

"You cook. You care for a baby. Plus, I remember you having a booming business when we were at university. You made enough money for rent and tuition. While Clark, Ziggy and I had to live together, you could afford your own place."

She smiled sheepishly. "I was pretty good."

"You were amazing."

Their gazes caught and held. Everything Jake had said about Harper came tumbling back. He suddenly wondered what it would be like if they could have something. If *he* could do this. Fall in love. Create a life—

That was a lot to wish for from a guy who'd spent his thirty-one years knowing he'd never get married, never even get serious about a woman.

He directed Harper to catch up to Jake, Avery and Sabrina by putting his hand on her waist. One of Jake's eyebrows rose and Seth shook his head. Some days he swore his brother liked acting like a kid. Teasing him about a girl.

But not just any girl—the girl he would have let himself love if he hadn't been so scarred from his parents' marriage.

The conversation with his siblings and sister-in-law continued with everyone giving Harper tips on what skills she would need to be a good assistant. Harper matched them to things she had done as a dog-walker, gift-buyer and party-planner when she owned her own company.

Sabrina grew thoughtful. "You know, if you had a few months to get this business up and running, I might suggest that rather than find a job, you just pick up where you left off with your own business."

"I have a three-month-old. I can't leave at odd hours of the day or night to walk dogs."

"No," Sabrina said, still thoughtful. "But you could hire college kids to do that work."

"Oh! That sounds interesting."

Seth quickly intervened. "But you can't be newly self-employed and get a loan for a house or condo or even get yourself approved to rent something. You have to have a job."

All eyes turned to Seth. Everybody frowned.

"We're not just dating." He started seeing what Jake had been warning him about. He was dating a woman. Living with her. Being seen in public with her. Fooling his family for her. Because he liked her. He'd *always* liked her. "She came to me for help and advice and if that means I have to be the voice of reason, then so be it."

"Hello, darling."

Everyone turned at the sound of Amelia Sloan's voice. As Harper faced her mom, Amelia took her by the shoulders and pulled her in for a hug. "I told you we'd be running into each other."

She motioned to her right. "Seth, this is my husband, Harper's dad, Peter."

Peter shook Seth's hand. A tall brute of a man, he wore his tux with as much grace and elegance as Amelia wore her slim pink dress.

Seth said, "It's nice to meet you."

Pete's eyes glowed. "It's great to meet you, too." He

didn't say anything about Seth and Harper being an item. Amelia must have threatened him with death if he ruined this for Harper. But he didn't have to. His happiness over their dating was there in his eyes.

Everything sunk in a little more for Seth. This might be a charade to fool Harper's mom, but by the next morning most of the city of New York would believe he and Harper were an item. His family, his friends and the people he did business with would know he was dating his best friend's widow.

Because he was. That was the bottom line. What started out as fake was feeling very real. And maybe that wasn't bad. He'd always liked her. He'd always wanted to woo her. Tonight, he'd wanted to show her a good time, not for the charade but because he liked her.

He *liked* her.

Maybe this was his chance.

Older, wiser, maybe he could have something with her?

"Peter, Amelia, this is Jake and Avery, my brother and sister-in-law," he said, and Pete shook their hands. "And my sister, Sabrina."

"Nice to meet you," Pete said politely as he shook Sabrina's hand.

"Aren't the renovations divine?" Amelia said, taking in the tall windows that reached almost to the ceiling, which was two stories high.

"We're pleased with them," Avery said, her eyes brimming with happiness as she, too, admired the handiwork.

Amelia faced Avery. "You played a part in this?"

"I did a bit of work with the architects and designers who did the renovations."

Amelia inclined her head. "How generous of you."

"Not really," Sabrina said. "We enjoy the arts. We have several galleries in our neighborhood but this one holds a special place in our hearts. So, we're fairly healthy contributors."

"It does host some of the best events," Amelia agreed. But her eyes drifted to Harper and then Seth. They narrowed a fraction of an inch, then they lowered to gaze at their hands.

Even as Seth noticed that, he also saw that Jake had his free hand on the small of Avery's back. Possessive. But also, affectionate.

Seth smoothly raised his hand to the bottom of Harper's back. Harper shifted closer to him, as if she too had seen her mother's curious gaze.

"Who has the baby?"

"Seth's neighbor, Mrs. Petrillo."

Amelia's eyebrows rose. "*Seth's* neighbor?"

He let Amelia figure that one out for herself. If he and Harper really were dating, they'd be spending the night together. And if they were spending the night together, who better to keep Crystal than the woman next door?

Seth knew the minute Amelia pieced it all together. Her slim lips tipped up into a pleased smile.

Harper's mother liked him. If he and Harper were dating for real, Harper wouldn't ever again have to worry about her mom's feelings for Clark.

The man behind Jake tapped him on the shoulder and when Jake turned he said, "Jimmy! My gosh! How long has it been?"

Avery turned, too.

Sabrina mumbled something about needing to find her boyfriend, one of the artists whose work was being exhibited.

As Harper and Seth spoke with her parents, Jake and Avery drifted into the crowd. Then Amelia and Pete excused themselves to mingle. Seth followed Harper as she walked among the exhibits, thoroughly engrossed in the art and thoroughly enjoying herself.

The way she should. The way he *wanted* her to.

At eleven, Harper reminded Seth that they'd promised Mrs. P. they'd be back by eleven-thirty, so she could get into her pajamas to watch a movie that was playing that night.

They walked toward the door, Harper's mom's eyes following them, and nearly plowed into his mother.

"Seth, Harper." She smiled warmly as she took in their clasped hands. "I hope you enjoyed the evening."

"Most fun I've had in a long time, Mrs. McCallan."

"There's another event coming up in a few weeks, a ball. I think you'll enjoy that, too."

Harper reluctantly said, "We'll see," but Seth thought that was a fine idea. The more they got out, into dating situations, the more they'd be able to decide if they shouldn't make this real.

"We'll definitely be at the ball."

His mom smiled. "Good!"

They stepped out into the night air and Seth motioned to the valet.

"Are you sure going to a ball is a good idea?"

"We're dating. There's a ball." He almost laughed at his own cleverness. "You do the math. If we don't go, people will wonder."

The valet roared up in his Ferrari. The top was down but he didn't make a move to put it up.

When they were settled, he pressed the gas pedal to send the powerful car careening down the street. The moon was full, the air still warm as summer held on. Her laughter wove through him, pleasing him, relaxing him.

And he couldn't remember why he'd been fighting this.

Harper couldn't contain the joy that bubbled up and spilled out, as the glorious car roared up the nearly empty streets.

She loved the Ferrari, the smooth speed that took them effortlessly from stoplight to stoplight. But most of all she marveled at the ease of luxury. How simple life was when one had a good family and friends.

She wished the drive could go on forever, but she had a baby to care for, so when Seth pulled his beautiful car into the basement parking garage, she didn't sigh with disappointment.

She also didn't correct Seth when he put his hand on the small of her back, guiding her into the elevator. It wasn't easy to pretend they were together one minute and jump apart the next. She could understand his slipup. But she also had to admit it had felt pretty good to have his undivided attention that night. True, most of his actions were directed toward making sure her mother believed they were dating. But sometimes it felt as if they really were dating.

After a glass of champagne, she had to keep reminding herself they weren't.

He hit the button for the elevator to take them to his condo. She combed her fingers through her windblown hair.

He caught her hand. "Don't."

"Don't?"

"I like it sort of crazy like that."

She did, too.

Their gazes met.

He smiled.

Her insides trembled.

He stood near enough that she could touch him, and her fingers itched to. All she'd have to do is raise her hand to his face and run her fingers along the rough shadow of dark hair that had begun on his cheeks. She knew he was off-limits, Clark's friend whose money allowed him to date any woman he wanted. But she hadn't had this intense longing to touch someone in over a year. Fresh and surprising, it rippled along her nerve endings and tumbled to her fingertips.

"What's going on in that head of yours?"

She shook her head at the silliness of her thoughts. "Nothing."

"Didn't look like nothing."

That's when she realized he still held her hand. They weren't even two feet apart. And she wanted to touch him.

The elevator seemed to slow to a crawl.

He inched closer. "It looked a lot like something. And it made you smile." His lips curved upward. "Really smile. I know you enjoyed the ride in the Ferrari. I think you enjoyed the night. You wouldn't by any chance be considering giving me a good-night kiss to thank me?"

Her heart stumbled as her gaze fell to his full mouth. Funny how she'd never noticed how sensuous his mouth was. She should have. The memory of those lips on hers the day they'd run into her mom should have told her his mouth wasn't just plentiful; it was clever.

But so was she. Even if he was attracted to her, she'd already worked all this out in her head. Starting something with him wasn't right. No matter how lonely she'd been. She still missed Clark. That wasn't any way to start a relationship. Plus, he wasn't the kind of guy she'd date. Even as she told herself she needed to get them out of this, her heart pinched. Something about walking away from him just didn't seem right.

Still, when the elevator reached their floor, she slid her hand from his and stepped out into the hall, striding toward his condo door.

"You know as soon as Mrs. P. leaves you and I will be alone."

Oh, she knew that. And her pattering heart almost exploded with the possibilities. None of which she was ready for. None of which seemed any more right than walking away had seemed.

He walked up behind her and slid his arm across her body to put his key into the lock. His scent drifted to her and she could almost feel the heat of his body on her back.

Hard as it was, she wouldn't let herself shudder. Refused to let her mind go blank and her senses kick in. This man would kiss her tonight and call a girlfriend in the morning—

All the same…she couldn't remember ever feeling like this with a man. Part of her really wanted to see it through. Tease him. Kiss him again…

Mrs. P. opened the door. "Get in here, you goofs. My next movie is about to start." She edged past them into the hall as they walked inside the condo. "Baby was good. An angel. But she hasn't even stirred so my guess it you'll be getting a two- or three-a.m. wake-up call."

And that was reality. Harper wasn't the woman who dated playboys, indulged in their games, amused herself.

She was a mom.

A widow and a mom.

She also wasn't a coward.

Fortifying herself with a deep breath, she faced Seth. "I did have a good time." When she heard Mrs. Petrillo's condo door close, she added, "I did want a good-night kiss." And everything it might have led to. "Not because I'm crazy for you or even to thank you, but because I'm curious. I don't think you'd take advantage of that because I'd be a willing participant. But that doesn't make it right. You were Clark's best friend."

CHAPTER SIX

SHE TURNED AND walked to her bedroom, leaving Seth standing in the little space between his kitchen island and the living room. Challenge rolled through him, but it was tempered by something that stopped him cold. She was right. He wouldn't take advantage of her, but not because she would be a willing participant. Because he liked her. That's why he'd flirted with her. Teased her. Why he'd had the urge to toss caution to the wind.

He shook his head once, as annoyance with himself became red-hot anger.

Was he falling for her again?

No matter that he'd stepped back all those years ago and let Clark ask her out, he'd loved her. But even as a twenty-two-year-old, he'd known he was damaged goods. He hadn't become a playboy because he loved women—though he did. He'd become a playboy because he knew he couldn't settle down and he didn't want anyone to get hurt. Not even him.

Now, here he was, tempting himself with emotions he wasn't allowed to feel. With a woman he wasn't allowed to have. Which was crazy.

Still, lust had roared through him when she'd said she was curious. Since they'd already kissed that had to mean she was curious about other things. That had taken his brain straight to the gutter. Because he was curious about those other things, too. How different would it be to make love to a woman who wasn't just a friend, but was somebody he loved?

Had loved. Past tense. He might be getting new feelings for her, or resurrecting the old feelings, but now that he was aware he could stop them in their tracks. He did not want to hurt her. And he didn't want to find himself in a situation he couldn't get out of. A prison. To him that's what marriage was. He could see himself marrying Harper, simply so he wouldn't hurt her, and then living a life in a cage... or becoming his dad. A cheat. A man who justified being unfaithful because he was bored.

A cold chill sliced through him.

He would not be his dad.

Never.

Not ever.

He left the condo early Sunday morning, but the scent of her perfume from the night before lingered in the air and followed him to his car. Annoyed, he punched the accelerator and headed for the family beach house in Montauk for some time alone.

The huge, empty McCallan mansion gave him some perspective as his solitary footsteps echoed around him. He was a man meant to be alone. He loved solitude. He liked his own company. He didn't need to be around people. But when he wanted to, he could. He had tons of friends, and women loved him.

One of the family limos pulled up and his mom exited. Morris, the older driver his mother favored, followed her up the walk carrying bags as if she'd been shopping.

When they opened the door and saw him standing in the echoing foyer, they both jumped.

His mother said, "What are you doing here?"

He rolled his shoulders. "Looking for some peace and quiet. What are you doing here?"

She motioned for Morris to take the enormous bags to the kitchen down the hall. "I found the most adorable new cushions for the lounge around the fire-pit table on the back deck."

"And you had to bring them here today?"

Not happy with the challenge, his other's eyes narrowed. "Where's Harper?"

"With Crystal." *Clark's daughter.* Clark's baby girl. The child his friend had always wanted.

His resolve to not get involved with Harper strengthened. He might have to play his role, but he also didn't want his mom to get her hopes up. His time with Harper would definitely end. He didn't want questions or, worse, a scolding.

"Our relationship is casual." He shrugged. "I don't think it's going to lead to anything. Two weeks from now, we might not even be dating."

"You don't like her?" his mom asked, breezily heading toward the kitchen. "Or Crystal?"

The suggestion that he didn't like Crystal infuriated him. For a little squirmy thing she was no trouble. "If you're saying that I'd never settle down with Harper because she's a mom, you're wrong. There's nothing wrong with Harper or the baby. I'm just never getting married. And you of all people should know that."

"Seriously? You're still saying that?"

Fury rolled through him again. He knew it was time to back down, walk away before he said something they'd both regret. But he wouldn't let her brush his miserable childhood aside. "Yes. I'm still saying that. Because it's true." He rolled his shoulders again, trying to get rid of a tightness that wouldn't let go today. "You know what? You enjoy the day. I'm going back to the city."

She sighed. "Don't leave on my account. We could do

something together. Maybe play Scrabble or take a walk on the beach."

The things they'd done when his dad was MIA? "No thanks. I've gotta run."

He was at the front door before he realized he had nowhere to go and nothing to do. On a normal weekend, he'd have had dates lined up or fishing trips with friends. He might even be in Monte Carlo, just for the hell of it. To keep up this ruse for Harper, he'd bowed out of everything.

Antsy, he ambled to his car. Not only had he been edged out of his home, but the big house he'd hoped to be his sanctuary was also off-limits.

He managed to stay out all day by taking a long drive, getting dinner at a bistro close to his home and taking a walk to stretch his legs, only returning to the condo after he was sure Harper was already in her room for the night.

But seeing her sunny smile on Monday morning, he stopped dead in his tracks. Warming a bottle in his kitchen, she looked beautiful and sexy, slim and sensual in those soft blue pajamas that were probably still warm from sleep.

His feelings from Saturday night returned. That he liked her. That he wanted to make this real—along with her declaration that she wanted nothing to do with him.

Because of Clark. His friend.

"Okay. I have some early meetings," he said, forgoing coffee for a quick escape. "I'll see you after I get home tonight."

He raced to the front door, hearing her say, "Okay. 'Bye."

But the image of leaving her confused, standing by the kitchen island, burned in his brain. By the time he got to the office, he knew something had to be done about their situation. If proximity was causing him to get real feelings for her, then proximity was what he had to fix. He couldn't kick her out. But she would move once she had a job.

He'd already called the one friend who might have had an opening for an assistant. That had failed.

He decided on another route and marched to the Human Resources office.

Karen, Mary Martin's assistant, looked up. "Mr. McCallan!"

"I'd like to see Mary for a few minutes, if I can."

"Sure!" She tapped a few buttons on her phone, told Mary he was there and within seconds Mary's door opened. Fiftysomething with kind green eyes, she motioned him inside her office.

"What brings you here?"

He took the seat in front of her desk as she sat on her tall-backed chair behind it. "I have a friend who needs a job."

"We put a moratorium on hiring until February."

"I know. But I'm trying to help my friend and I don't know enough about the kind of job she wants to really understand how to assist her."

"What kind of work does she want?"

"Administrative or personal assistant."

"Lots of jobs like that out there."

He stifled a sigh of relief. Hope built. Maybe with Mary's help he could get Harper a job and put her out of range of temptation. "Good."

"What are her qualifications?"

"She ran a personal-assistant-type company before she married my friend. She walked dogs, planned parties, sent birthday gifts for guys too busy to buy them, that kind of thing."

Mary sat back. "Oh."

His hope crumbled itself into a ball and tossed itself into the trash can. "That was a bad 'oh.'"

"She doesn't have any *office* experience. She's probably going to have to start at the bottom somewhere."

"As what?"

"Clerk, typist, mail room."

His hope peered out of the trash can. "She's willing to do anything."

"She also needs to be willing to start at the bottom of the pay scale."

Knowing Harper wasn't picky, Seth and his hope perked up. "How low is bottom?"

She named a figure and he sucked in a breath. His hope collapsed and died. "She'll never support herself on that."

"No one can. Most people starting out get a roommate."

That's what he'd done. Two years *after* graduating university, he and Ziggy still needed to live together. He couldn't get his own place until the investment firm he and Clark started had become successful. Now that Mary had him thinking back to his very humble beginnings, he realized it didn't matter what Harper did. The only work she could do would not support her and a baby.

She was going to have to tell her mom…live with her mom.

The possibility upset him almost as much as he knew it would upset Harper.

He left Mary's office and ambled to his own, trying to think this through. The easy answer would be for her to let him buy her a condo, but if she wouldn't let him buy her a few sweaters, she'd never let him buy her a place to live.

He could afford a hundred houses and she wouldn't let him buy her one measly house—

He *could* afford a hundred houses. He could buy a condo, a beach house, a house in Connecticut… He could buy *anything* he wanted.

Maybe *that* was the answer.

He'd tell her *he* wanted a new place, something bigger or maybe an actual house, and his condo would be open. She'd never take it as a gift, but he could have an agreement drawn up where he sold her the condo interest-free and she paid him a minimal amount every month.

He'd make the deal sufficient that she would know he wasn't *giving* her his condo, but also so sweet she wouldn't be able to resist it.

He laughed. Once he found himself a place, their separation wouldn't depend on her finding a job. Though he would still help her find work. He just wouldn't be doing it while sleeping in the next room. He'd be in another condo or a house a state away.

He went home happy. Not because he wanted to be away from her, but because he didn't want to hurt her. He didn't like the idea that hormones or mixed-up feelings from the past or even proximity would lure him into something he couldn't get out of without hurting her. Or getting hurt himself. Finding himself a new place was the perfect answer.

He walked into his condo whistling. "Hey, I had a thought today."

Occupied with tucking the baby into her carrier, Harper peeked over. "You did?"

"You know how you need a house?"

"Yes."

"I also need a house."

At that she stopped tucking the blanket around Crystal and peered at him. "What?"

"Look around you. This is the condo of a guy who's got a little money but he's also frugal."

She gaped at him. "It's a beautiful place."

"I'm not saying it's not beautiful. I'm saying it doesn't suit me anymore."

"Oh. You want something a little more *McCallan*."

He winced. "No. I'd been tossing around the idea of getting a new home. I bought this about a year after Clark and I started the investment firm. I still didn't know if we'd make it or not. Then two years ago my dad died, and I'm not going to lie, Harper, I inherited some money."

"Seth, there's no crime in that. For people who have a ton of money, you and your family are very nice. Very normal."

Very normal? He almost laughed. He'd spent his childhood listening to his parents argue, his teen years being bullied by his dad and his adulthood avoiding all of it until Jake—the brother he loved and trusted—asked him for help running the family business and he'd agreed.

"Anyway, I realized I could sell this one to you."

She gasped. "Oh, Seth. I can't afford this."

"I know. Theoretically, you can't afford *anything* until you get a job." Or even after she got a job, but she'd realize that soon enough. "But here's the deal. I can sell you this and finance it for you."

"What?"

"I'll have my lawyer draw up papers that transfer ownership to you in return for you paying me a certain amount every month until the value of the condo is reached."

"You mean never."

He shook his head. "Most mortgages take forever to pay off because of interest. I was thinking of not charging you interest."

"You can't do that!"

"Why not?"

"It's too generous!"

"Hey, what Clark did for me saved me." Another thing he needed to remember when touching Harper tempted him. "Besides, there are other strings attached to this deal."

"What strings?"

"I have money but very little time. You have time on your hands. It would help me if you'd meet with a real estate agent and weed out the bad properties, so I'd only have to see the ones that really were contenders."

Her face brightened. "I'd do that for nothing…as your friend."

"You made my case for no interest. Just as you would help me find a house or a bigger condo because you're my friend. I should be allowed to sell you this place and finance it with no interest because I'm your friend."

"You're not going to bamboozle me."

"No. But you're not going to change my mind about no interest." He sighed. "This works for both of us, Harper. Take the deal."

The following morning, Mrs. Petrillo was happy to watch the baby while Harper and Seth met with Bill Reynolds, a real estate agent recommended to Seth by a friend. Rather than meet in his office, Bill suggested they get together at an empty condo not far from Seth's current home in Midtown. Harper might be the one doing the actual legwork of finding Seth a new place to live, but Bill wanted Seth to see a few condos, so he could get an idea of what Seth wanted.

When Seth and Harper arrived at the building, it was easy to see it had been renovated, but it had been done in such a way as to keep the "old Manhattan" charm of things like fleur-de-lis crown molding, pocket doors, elegant chandeliers and reclaimed hardwood floors.

Harper's face lit up when they rode the old-fashioned elevator to the top floor. But when she saw Bill Reynolds, her eyes widened. Dressed in a dark suit and white shirt with a slim tie, he wasn't buttoned down. His jacket swung open when he reached out to shake Seth's hand and his tie had been loosened.

Seth supposed the real estate agent's intent had been to look approachable but for some reason or another it got on Seth's nerves.

"It's a pleasure to meet you, Mr. McCallan."

"It's Seth."

"Seth," Bill said amiably. He turned to Harper. "And this is Harper?"

"Yes. She's the friend who will be helping me find a new home."

Seth swore the man didn't hear a word after Seth said, "She's the friend."

His eyebrows rose, and his smile grew as he shook Harper's hand. "I don't suppose you're looking for a place?"

"She's taking my current condo," Seth said, moving from the entryway into the living room. A white fireplace drew his eye first. Dark sofas sat parallel to each other atop a yellow area rug. End tables were thick, old wood. Lamps were dusty. Drapes hid the view.

"Look beyond the furniture, Seth," Harper said, walking to the window. "That crown molding is beautiful." She pulled open the drapes and gasped. "The view is fantastic. Everything else is cosmetic."

Bill inclined his head. "You're very smart about this stuff."

"No. I spent a year house hunting with my husband."

Bill deflated. "Your husband?"

"Deceased," Harper said quietly.

"I am so sorry," Bill said, but Seth didn't believe he meant a word of it. He gave Bill the side eye. Dark hair. Sharp green eyes, so colorful they had to be contacts. Clean shaven. Good suit.

Though New York claimed to be a city for all people, there were tiers of society. Seth and his family sat on the top tier with only a few other extraordinarily wealthy families. Below them was a tier of people almost as wealthy as the McCallans. Below that was a tier of people still wealthy enough not to have to work, but with less money than the two tiers above them. Below them were what Seth called the working rich.

That's where Bill fit. If Seth bought a condo through

Bill, his commission would be high six figures, maybe even seven. Sell eight or ten condos a year with that kind of commission and you earned yourself a place at good restaurants, charity fund-raisers, private parties attended by only the elite.

But though Bill wasn't truly wealthy, he was Harper's type. A man who worked hard to make something of himself.

Seth wanted to hate him but couldn't. *That's* what Seth had been, when he'd left home. That's what Harper had liked—maybe even what she'd loved about Clark. Harper had hated the life of luxury without substance. Clark had had substance. Hard-working real estate agent Bill had substance.

They breezed through a formal dining room, a den, an open kitchen desperately in need of a remodel and a maid's suite, then to a hidden set of stairs that led to three guestrooms and a generous master suite.

"I don't need all these rooms."

Bill laughed. "Of course, you don't. But space is money in the city. If you're paying twenty-five million dollars, you should get something to show for it." He pointed at French doors that led to a balcony. "Like that. Imagine that view at night."

He saw the skyline and knew that when it was dark, with hundreds of lights twinkling in the surrounding buildings, it was probably amazing. "I'm not the kind of guy who's going to stand out on the balcony in my pajamas—"

"None of which matters," Harper interrupted. "Because this place needs too much remodeling for you."

Seth faced her. "It does?"

"Yes." She smiled at him and he felt a little better. Not quite the snob Bill made him feel like. "If your condo furnishings are anything to go by, you like clean lines. You also like an open floorplan."

Bill brightened. "I have just the thing for you. Two build-ings down. Open concept. Kind of modified industrial."

They left the condo and walked up the street to the build-ing. Seth wasn't happy with that home, either. He also didn't like the third place Bill showed them.

Driving home, Harper said, "I think what you really didn't like was Bill."

Seth glanced out the window. "He was pretentious."

"He was trying to make a living."

"Actually, I think he was buttering me up, hoping to make an easy sale. He said we were only going out in order that he could get an idea of what I wanted but he thought I'd buy one of those three."

"Well, you didn't, and now that he's seen your taste, he'll try harder next time." She smiled again, and Seth felt better again.

"Besides, you won't have to go condo hunting until I narrow the choices down to two or three places I genuinely believe you will love."

He said, "That's good," then remembered she'd be alone with Bill Reynolds. Ambitious, centered, normal guy, Bill Reynolds.

Jealousy slithered through him like green slime. Sticky. Hot. Uncomfortable. He tried to shrug it off, but slime didn't shrug off easily.

"Maybe I should come with you?"

"You don't trust me?"

Damn. "Of course, I trust you."

She caught his gaze. "Then trust me to work with Bill."

He wondered if there was a double meaning behind what she said, then called himself an idiot. He couldn't have her. She'd been Clark's. He also wouldn't put himself into a po-sition where he could become like his dad. So, what did it matter if she found another man interesting?

He stopped the Ferrari in front of the condo building and

waited while she exited. She waved goodbye and walked inside, and he didn't stare after her like somebody so weak he didn't know good from bad. In a roundabout way, his dad had taught him good from bad. He'd married Seth's mom, but he hadn't been faithful. Seth had seen his mom cry, heard their fights. All because his dad had a roving eye and not one clue about loyalty or honesty. Especially not honesty with himself.

Seth shot off in the direction of McCallan, Inc. He was honest enough with himself not to pine after a woman he couldn't have, even if loneliness unexpectedly filled his soul.

CHAPTER SEVEN

THAT AFTERNOON, Harper called Bill Reynolds to discuss more homes for viewing. He pointed out six listings on the real estate company's website, she chose three and they arranged to see all three the next day.

She made Seth a special dinner. They'd almost made a huge mistake after the cocktail party. She'd wanted to touch him so much, she'd ached from it. But their being together was a bad idea.

Whatever he'd done on Sunday had helped him to accept that. He'd even happily decided *he* was the one who needed a new home. So, when he'd seemed horribly out of sorts while Bill showed them the condos, she worried it was because he was having second thoughts about moving. She appreciated his helping her get a place for herself and Crystal, and as long as he really did let her pay him for his condo, she wanted it. But if he had even one inkling of doubt about doing this, she wouldn't let him sell his home to her.

With the baby sitting in her carrier and dinner served, she casually said, "So, I made arrangements to see three more condos tomorrow."

He sucked in a breath. "Did you?"

Sucked in breath? Eyes down? That added up to avoidance. She was correct. He wasn't happy.

"Two are gorgeous. If they meet my standards, they might be contenders. The other one is actually two condos that could be combined into one."

He peeked at her. "That would mean renovations."

"I added it because I saw terrific potential. If you wouldn't mind a bit of renovating, you could really make that place yours."

"No. No renovations. I want move-in ready."

"Okay, I won't look at that one then."

His face registered relief. "So, you'd only be looking at two?"

That was confusing. Why would he possibly be happy there were only two condos instead of three? If he really didn't want a different home, he wouldn't want her looking at anything.

She had no choice but to push him to either stop knocking houses off the list or to admit he didn't want her looking at anything.

"Maybe I'll only look at one, if the first one is good."

His face brightened again. "If you like this first one a lot, maybe I should just come with you? That way if we both like it I can take it."

That didn't fit with either idea.

She set her fork down. "Seth, you don't want to buy the first thing you see. Options are good."

"Options mean more time."

"That's why I'm going out with Bill for the first look at every property. To weed out the ones that for sure wouldn't work."

"Yeah. I get it." He bounded out of his seat. "You know what? I'm kind of tired tonight. And there's a game on. I'm just going to go watch that."

He started down the hall, but she caught up with him. "Wait a minute. You have to tell me what's wrong."

"There is nothing wrong except I had a long day and I'm tired and there's a game on."

She studied his eyes. They didn't even flicker. But there was a shadow of something in them. Actually, it could be exhaustion.

Maybe he was right? Maybe he was fine. Tired, but fine.

Still, standing this close all her feelings from the night of the cocktail party crept up on her. Something about him drew her. Made her pulse jump and all her longings rise, reminding her that being with a man she loved was wonderful.

But they'd already talked about this. She'd told him anything between them was wrong and he'd listened.

Maybe that was what was going on now? He'd flirted with her on Saturday night and she'd rebuffed him. She'd told a sweet, sexy guy she didn't want him. She didn't think she'd hurt him, but she had said she didn't want anything to start between them.

Maybe he was keeping his distance because she'd asked him to?

Disappointment filled her. But she was the one who had nixed a relationship.

Because they weren't a good match.

She took a step back, away from him. They weren't right for each other. But they were still friends. He was kind enough to sell her his condo and she liked the idea of doing some work to help him find a new place to live. If she wanted their friendship to survive, maybe she had to stop pushing.

"Okay. Good night."

"Good night."

Wednesday morning, he was gone before she and Crystal came out of her bedroom. Knowing it was better for them to each have some personal space, she fed Crystal, ate breakfast, dressed to meet Bill at the first house and said good-bye to Mrs. Petrillo, who had agreed to stay with the baby.

She met Bill at the condo building, rode up in the elevator with him and strode down the hall like a business-woman doing a job.

Just the thought straightened her spine with confidence. She'd liked working. Not for money, but to have a place in society. To provide a service. The task Seth probably considered a throw-away job reminded her of the sense of purpose that she'd missed for the five years she and Clark had been married.

Bill unlocked the door and presented the space to her.

"Oh." She carefully eased into the beautiful home. "It's lovely."

Bill followed her. "I didn't think old-style charm suited Mr. McCallan. But this modern floorplan does."

She took in the gray hardwood floors, white wood trim, paler gray walls and modern furniture. "It's gorgeous."

They walked down a hall to the bedrooms. The entire condo was perfect. Very suited to Seth with clean lines and neutral tones that allowed for more colorful furniture and window treatments.

Riding down in the elevator, she told Bill that she definitely thought this one was a contender and he grinned.

"Good." He paused for a second then said, "So how do you know the McCallans?"

"My husband was Seth's best friend."

His smile warmed. "I see."

"I'm helping him find a new home and he's helping me with a few things."

Bill sniffed a laugh. "Don't be angry but I thought the two of you might be dating."

She pictured it. Having private dinners on the balcony of a gorgeous penthouse overlooking the city. Teaching him to love Crystal. More kisses like the first one they'd shared.

Her heart stuttered. Not just because the images gave her a warm, happy feeling, but because for a second, she'd forgotten about Clark.

She took a calming breath to steady her heart and ease the guilt. "No. Just friends."

"Well, that's good news for me then."

She frowned. "It is?"

"It means I can ask you out."

Ask her out?

He was attracted to her?

"Oh." The oddest sensation wound through her. Anytime Seth was close, her shivers were the good kind. This feeling wasn't like that. It wasn't revulsion. It was more like confusion mixed with lack of interest.

And once again, Clark wasn't anywhere in the picture.

This time when her heart squeezed, it wasn't from the thrill of being around Seth. It was her soul's gentle reminder that Clark kept falling out of the picture because he was gone. Had been for a year. The shock and sadness that had enveloped her immediately after his death had lessened to a dull ache that felt more like a memory than real pain.

She swallowed back the sorrow of that. It felt like the last step in losing him.

"That's very nice of you, but I'm not dating right now. My husband's only been dead a year. I'm just getting back in the world of work. I'm not ready yet."

He flipped a card from his jacket pocket and handed it to her in one smooth movement. "When you are, give me a call."

She smiled and took the card but the realization that Clark was gone—really gone—pressed down on her chest. It wasn't pain. She would have welcomed pain. But an empty, awful awareness that this stage was the end. And she really was alone.

Except for Seth. Kind. Generous. Seth.

Whom she'd given the brushoff after the cocktail party.

Her chest tightened, but she ignored it. She might be adjusting to Clark's death, easing him and their life together into a memory, but that didn't mean she was ready to date. Especially not someone like Seth. Social. Outgoing. Playboy.

She frowned. Those things were supposed to set her straight about him. Instead, she remembered being in his car, the wind in her hair—

No. Seth wasn't right for her.

Bill showed her two other homes, one of which was a maybe, but the third one that he'd added on the fly was a definite no.

By the time she was back at Seth's condo, soon to be *her* condo, it was nearly seven.

Seth and Mrs. Petrillo sat on the sofa, watching *Wheel of Fortune*, with baby Crystal tucked in her carrier, sitting between them.

"Hey."

All eyes turned to her.

"Sorry, it took longer than I expected. But the good news is, I think two of the condos he showed me today would be perfect for you."

She walked over to the sofa and lifted Crystal out of the carrier. Her little girl grinned at her. "I know why you're grinning. You should be getting ready for bed."

Mrs. Petrillo slapped her knees and hoisted herself from the sofa. "And this is my cue to leave." As she passed Harper, she whispered, "Seth told me it was okay to let her stay up."

Harper laughed. "She's fine. As long as I get her to bed by eight, I'm happy."

Mrs. Petrillo shuffled out the door and Harper turned to Seth. "I noticed that you didn't comment when I said I thought we might have found two condos suited to you."

"That's great."

"You don't sound like you think it's great."

"That's because I'm not sure I don't want a house rather than a condo. Someplace like Connecticut or Montauk."

The change surprised her enough that she forgot about herself, losing Clark and even being attracted to Seth. Though money wasn't changing hands, he'd hired her to help him. And she wanted to do this. Not just to get an interest-free home, but to pay him back for all the kindnesses he'd extended to her.

"Okay. I'll talk to Bill about it."

Seth rose from the sofa. "No. I'll talk to him. I'll call him tomorrow."

Confusion skittered through her. First, he was changing what he wanted, now he was edging her out? "Isn't that what I'm supposed to be doing for you?"

"No. You're taking the first look at what he comes up with." His voice was cool, serious.

All the fears she'd had the night before trembled back, sprinkled with the sense that he was trying to get away from her—or wanted nothing to do with her.

"What I'd like in a house is different than what I'd need in something in the city. Once I tell Bill, he'll find a few things. Then you're on the job again."

She nodded, but something odd filled the air.

"After you take care of Crystal then we can figure out what to do for dinner. I was thinking maybe a pizza."

"Pizza sounds great." She took Crystal back to her bedroom. As she changed the baby into pajamas, she tried to figure out what the odd thing was. She replayed all the conversations she and Seth had had since she'd moved in with him. He'd kissed her once—as part of a charade. The one time he had flirted with her, after the cocktail party, she'd told him she wanted nothing to do with him.

And now he wasn't mad. But he wasn't happy, either.

And why would he be? He was stuck in the same house with a woman who'd rebuffed him.

She had to find him somewhere to live—and quickly—before they grew to dislike each other.

In his office Thursday morning, Seth heard the sound of Jake and Sabrina laughing. His brow wrinkled. Sabrina never came to McCallan, Inc. She wanted no part of the family business and, given their history, Jake and Seth had understood.

Curiosity overwhelmed him, and he rose from his tall-back leather chair and strode out into the private reception area for the executive offices.

"Seth!" Sabrina raced over and kissed his cheek. "In all the mess after the showing over the weekend, I forgot to give you a new invitation to my exhibit on Saturday."

He pulled the embossed card from the white envelope. A McCallan didn't need an invitation to get into anything, except... He saw the name of the gallery—in Paris—and winced. "I'd forgotten all about this."

Sabrina's face fell. "You have to come! Pierre is flipping out. It's the first time we've done an exhibit alone together. It's the first time he's done an exhibit alone with *anyone*. Honestly, Seth, I worry he might just bail at the last minute and then it'll be Sally. All by herself."

Seth glanced up from his invitation. "Would that be so bad?"

Her face filled with horror. "He's the star. I'm the also-ran. If he bails, the exhibit is canceled. I'll need a shoulder to cry on."

"You'll have Jake."

Jake shook his head. "We're leaving early. Avery has a trial."

Sabina turned pleading blue eyes on him. "If Avery and

Jake can squeeze me in around a trial, whatever you have can be canceled."

"I…" He sucked in a breath, palming the invitation, which included Harper. He didn't know how this would go over with Harper, but the addition of her name to the invitation was more than a clue that Sabrina expected her there, too. And maybe being across an ocean, with Jake and Avery and Sabrina, would be better than running around the city all weekend, trying to figure out reasons to stay out of his apartment. "Sure."

Sabrina impulsively hugged him. "Thanks."

"You're welcome."

"And bring Harper's little girl."

Jake said, "That's a great idea. We've hired a nanny for Friday night and Saturday. She can keep Crystal, too. That'll give Abby someone to play with."

"Crystal's not much on playing. She basically sits in a carrier when she isn't sleeping."

"That's even better. That'll give Abby a chance to adjust to being around a baby for when Avery and I decide it's time to have another."

As Sabrina turned to the elevator, Jake headed back to his office and Seth stood alone in the quiet reception area.

Not only were he and Harper going to France, but it also appeared they were taking the baby.

How was he going to tell Harper they'd be spending the weekend in Paris? Leaving that night so they'd have Friday to adjust to the time change and be ready for the Saturday afternoon showing.

He called her. "I have something that might not be good news."

A light sigh drifted from his phone. "You decided you didn't want to move."

He shook his head, realizing that she thought of a lot of life in negative terms. Maybe because hers had been so difficult. First, a demanding mom, then losing her husband, then finding out their financial situation had been a lie.

"No. We're going to Paris this weekend."

"What?"

"My sister has a showing. Unless we want our secret to get out, we have to go. The whole family had promised we'd be there for her when Sabrina made these arrangements." He shook his head. "It kind of snuck up on me. Sorry."

She laughed. "You're sorry that you're taking me to Paris?" She gasped. "Oh. I can't go. I have Crystal!"

"Jake would like her to come along. He's got a nanny for Abby and he'd also like Abby to be around a baby. I think he and Avery are thinking of having another one."

"Crystal gets to come along?"

"I hope she's got a party dress."

Harper laughed. "I'm sorry, Seth, to be so excited about something that's probably a burden for you, but I've never been to France!"

"You haven't?"

"No. My parents didn't start traveling until after I left home."

"Okay, then. Pack appropriately."

"Do you think Avery would mind if I called to see what I need to bring?"

"I don't see why. She likes you." He winced. "Oh, and one more little thing. We're leaving tonight."

"Tonight! Good grief, Seth! I'll talk to you later! I have to call Avery and pack."

They flew to Paris with Avery, Jake and little Abby, and slept through most of the flight—without a problem or complicated explanation because Seth and Harper volunteered to take the bedroom with twin beds and give the jet's master suite to Avery and Jake. Though they'd left New York at eleven o'clock at night, given the flight time and the time difference, they arrived in Paris in the early afternoon.

They piled into the limo, which had two car seats already installed, and Harper secretly marveled at the ease of it.

The brothers joked about staying at the Four Seasons because their mother stayed at the Bristol and Avery sighed. "Your mother is lovely."

Jake said, "I know that. It's just that no man wants to stay in the same hotel as his mom when he's away from work." He gave Avery a significant look. "We want to have some fun."

Avery laughed.

Harper struggled not to gape at them. No matter how much time she spent with Avery and Jake, she still couldn't believe how normal they were. Or how equal they were. Jake managed behemoth McCallan, Inc., yet Avery's career as a small-town lawyer was every bit as important. They shared baby chores. Jake grilled burgers, hot dogs or steak once a week. And though they had a penthouse on the Upper East Side, they spent most of their time at a house in Pennsylvania.

The group checked in at the Four Seasons and separated when Seth and Harper got off on the floor of their suite and Jake and Avery rode to the penthouse.

Harper tried not to gape at the luxurious suite, but it was no use. The place was amazing. The door had opened onto a living room with pale furniture, bowls of white roses scattered everywhere and views of the city that took her breath away.

"There are two bedrooms. My assistant also ordered a crib."

At the mention of his assistant, Harper held back a wince. She might be staying the weekend in a suite like this, but next month she'd be the one ordering the crib for some other lucky family.

"We should get breakfast. It might be afternoon in Paris, but we're still on New York time."

Carrying sleeping Crystal, Harper opened the first bedroom door and saw a crib in the fabulous bedroom with a thick blue comforter and white furniture. With the pale blue curtains open, she had another view of the city.

She almost couldn't wrap her mind around the fact that she was in Paris. That Seth's family apparently flew here all the time. That their life didn't revolve around making money.

She faced Seth and said, "Sure. Breakfast is a great idea."

Seth eyed her shrewdly. "What's up?"

"I'm just a little blown away by it all."

He slipped out of his black leather jacket. "It is nice."

"It's amazing." His whole life was amazing. He worked, but it wasn't his life. He could have anything he wanted but he was down-to-earth. Maybe more than Clark had been.

He laughed. "Does that mean you want to go *out* to eat?"

"Avery said your mom has plans for dinner this evening. Crystal will be staying with the nanny for that. So maybe it would be best if we ate here." She paused then said, "If there's somewhere you want to go, you can. I just don't like to leave her for long stretches of time and she'll be getting up from her nap soon."

He plopped to the expensive sofa as if it were a beanbag chair. "Then I'll stay, too."

"You don't have to."

"Hey, we're supposed to be a couple. I can't go prowling Paris like a single guy."

She nodded. But her heart took a tumble. Just as she'd be somebody's assistant in another month, she'd also be away from Seth.

"For the weekend, let's be a couple. Let's do what we'd do if we really were dating so that there won't be any slip-ups with my mom."

"All right."

He angled his feet on the gorgeous cut-glass coffee table. "What would you and Crystal do on an afternoon in Paris?"

She thought about that for a second. "After I ate, I'd probably see if I could get a stroller and take Crystal around the city."

"See how simple that was?"

She laughed. "I suppose."

They ordered breakfast and just as they were finishing eating, Crystal woke. Harper brought her out and fed her a bottle, as Seth called the concierge for a stroller.

It arrived only a minute or so after Harper changed Crystal into a simple pink dress and sun hat.

As she tucked Crystal into the stroller, Seth said, "We can stroll around until five or so, then we need to get back to dress for dinner."

"It's formal?"

He shook his head. "No, but my mom is a stickler for time. She hates when anyone is late."

"Okay."

They rode the elevator to the lobby, which was filled with an abundance of flowers. The rich woods and marble gleamed in the afternoon sun.

Stepping out into the fresh air that smelled faintly of the rain that had fallen as they drove from the airport and onto gray brick streets, she inhaled deeply. The rich aromas of a nearby bakery teased her. "Makes me wish I hadn't eaten yet."

Seth slid on his sunglasses. Harper looked at him out of the corner of her eye. Not only did his life not revolve around money, but he also seemed so casual with her. As if walking the streets of one of the world's most wonderful cities with a widow and her baby was fun.

He turned to her, looking sexy and male in his leather jacket and shades. "Where to?"

"I don't know." She laughed lightly. "Let's just walk."

"If you only want to take a stroll, here's what we'll do." They started down the street and made a turn that took them to Champs-élysées.

She gasped. Leafy green trees and shops lined the gray brick-and-marble avenue, along with restaurants and vendors. The Arc de Triomphe stood like a sentinel at the end. Tourists bobbed and wove along the busy sidewalk.

"Because we're not going to be here long and most of our time will be spent at the gallery with Sabrina, I thought this might be the best way to see at least a little of Paris."

She inhaled again. "This is amazing."

"This is one of the best parts of Paris." He pointed at some shops. "You can buy anything from a cheap souvenir to a diamond tiara."

She gaped in awe. "I see that."

"Plus, it's the best place to get a real take on the people. On any day, you can walk into a designer store and see anybody from a rock star to a tourist who'd saved his whole life to get here."

She glanced around, still amazed. "I'd save to come back here." She shrugged. "Maybe see the whole city."

"Or sit at a sidewalk café and enjoy the show the tourists put on." He motioned to the right. "I haven't really had my morning quota of coffee. Do you mind if we stop? I'll buy you a croissant."

"I just ate!"

"Yeah, but sniff the air again."

She did and was rewarded by the scent of butter and vanilla, cocoa and coffee.

She groaned. "All right. I probably could eat a little something else."

They settled on seats at a round table in the corner of the café. Harper lifted Crystal from her stroller and set her on her lap as Seth ordered in French.

This time she didn't look at him as if he were special.

She was finally beginning to realize that his life allowed him to ease himself into other cultures, other worlds, places she'd probably never see.

She glanced at the baby on her lap and sort of understood her mother's fanaticism with becoming wealthy. Except her mom only wanted to lunch with the right people. She didn't understand the lush, broad life having money could provide. She just wanted to look good in Chanel. She was missing everything.

The waiter brought a pot of coffee and a tray of croissants and some things Harper didn't recognize. Her mouth watered.

Seth pointed to the tray. "These are madeleines, little cakes, and these are macaron." Glancing at her, he smiled. "My suggestion is take a bite of each."

That sounded like a good idea to her.

As he poured the coffee, she gingerly lifted one of the madeleines and bit into it. Her tongue rejoiced. "Oh, my God. There is no way I'm not eating this whole thing."

"Go ahead." He set a cup filled with coffee on the saucer beside her. "You're too thin, anyway."

And he'd noticed.

She shifted Crystal on her lap, took a sip of the rich, dark coffee, then finished the fluffy little cake that all but melted in her mouth.

Seth grabbed a croissant. He wasn't going to Paris and not eat a pastry. But he surreptitiously kept his eyes on Harper as she indulged in the treats. Not only did he mean what he'd said about her being too thin, but it also pleased him to watch her indulge.

Now that he knew she and Clark hadn't been on the solid financial ground that Seth had believed they were, he sincerely doubted anyone had ever spoiled her. Oh, her parents had given her things. Tons of things. All the things her image-conscious mother thought she should have. And Clark had given her things. All the things he needed for her to have to keep up the impression that he was financially stable.

But no one had ever spoiled her. His mission to show her a good time at the cocktail party had worked—until he'd flirted with her. So today he'd make it his mission to give her the best three days she ever had—without the flirting.

Crystal made a sound. Halfway between a "goo" and a "coo," the light noise floated over to him.

Seth tried to stay silent but couldn't. "Did she talk?"

Harper laughed. "No, she said 'goo.' I've been working with her."

"Working with her?"

"Getting a baby to say 'goo' is a way to get her acquainted with her vocal cords."

Seth never realized it was that complicated. His gaze stayed focused on Crystal. She looked at him and smiled before she pursed her little lips and said, "Goo."

He swore it was as if she knew he was curious. Mostly because she looked him right in the eye and seemed to say it to him.

His heart swelled. His throat tightened. It was so amazing to see a child learn that he was almost speechless from it.

Harper tickled her belly. "Are you chatty now?"

The baby giggled.

Seth sat mesmerized. Not because anything happening was so special but because it was so ordinary. He'd stayed away from babies all his life, thinking they were a nuisance or at least too fragile for him to be around. But Crystal wasn't. She was a little ball of cuteness.

He reached out and pulled her from Harper's lap. "Are you trying to flirt with me?"

When she giggled, he grinned. "Holy cow, she's cute."

CHAPTER EIGHT

HARPER STARED AT Seth as he held her baby at eye level and talked to her. Speechless didn't come close to what she was feeling. For a guy who'd only a few weeks before claimed he was afraid of babies, he held Crystal like a pro.

"You wouldn't be the first woman to try to steal me away."

Crystal patted his face. He didn't even blink.

Harper took a sip of coffee to ground herself in reality, but the delicious pastries were forgotten as he made stupid faces and talked with her little girl.

Warmth filled her, and she had to make a conscious effort not to let the amazing feelings she'd been having for weeks bubble up and form the word.

Love.

She could not love him.

She wasn't even supposed to like him, had struggled to keep her emotions in check. Yet here she was, with a feeling in the pit of her stomach that couldn't be denied. Love. Or at least the beginnings of it.

He was easy to be around, fun to be around, and he could no longer say he didn't like babies.

And she'd made her peace with Clark being gone.

She could love Seth. She simply couldn't do anything about it. He was a playboy, not the kind of guy to get serious. And even if he was…why would he pick her?

Clark's widow. She might be someone he'd play with, but that would be all.

Considering all these feelings were new, maybe they weren't fully formed? Maybe they were a possibility, not a total conclusion? Maybe she could guide them, so they wouldn't fully form?

She ended her debate with the knowledge that Seth was a great guy, worthy of her affection as a friend, and that settled her mind. It gave her great peace not to be fighting herself. She liked the idea of having feelings for him. She also liked the idea of controlling them. That was, after all, what adults did. Not let every little wisp in the wind drag them into things that were wrong for them.

That's how she could have a good time, not get hurt herself, not hurt or annoy Seth. Who probably wouldn't want to know she was feeling all this.

They spent the next hour with her pushing the stroller toward the Arc. But half the time Crystal wasn't in it. Seth picked her up and gave her her own personal tour of the city.

When Crystal tired, they went back to the hotel. Harper fed her and put her down for a nap, but she didn't go back to the sitting room with Seth. She took a long bath to pamper herself, then dressed for dinner early, knowing she had to take Crystal to the penthouse so the nanny Jake and Avery had hired could watch both babies.

She dressed Crystal in pajamas, then packed a diaper bag. When she came out of her room, Seth was nowhere in sight, so she left him a note that she was taking the baby upstairs to the nanny.

When she got to the penthouse, the luxury of it stole her breath. But Avery and Jake were so casual that she soon relaxed. She played a bit with Crystal, allowing little Abby to join a game of peekaboo, so both babies would be comfortable.

With the babies settled, they headed down in the elevator with Jake and Avery to get Seth because they were riding together to their mother's hotel for a predinner drink and then going to the restaurant.

Avery kept up a steady conversation with Maureen about projects the McCallans could support over the coming year, making dinner lively and even fun. Harper nearly volunteered to help with a campaign or two, but she kept her mouth shut. A month from now, she'd have a job. As a single mom, there was no guarantee she'd have time for projects.

The next morning, she and Seth ate breakfast in their suite and walked back to the café for lunch. Afterward, Seth played with Crystal while Harper dressed for the exhibit opening.

When she came out of her room, wearing a red sparkly dress that she'd picked up after her discussion with Avery about what to wear, Seth whistled. "See what a little croissant will do for you?"

She laughed. "I didn't gain weight overnight."

He handed her the baby. "You look amazing. Now, let me go get into my monkey suit and we'll be on our way."

"I'll take the baby up to the nanny."

Headed for his bedroom, he said, "Good idea."

Harper watched him go, feeling something she didn't want to describe. She'd settled this yesterday. Told herself it was okay to like him as a friend, a good friend, but it was wrong to fall in love. Though she couldn't deny the longing that rippled through her. She wouldn't let herself verbalize the wish that he'd fall in love with her. Knowing he didn't want a relationship with anyone was her one stronghold in reality. He might have gotten accustomed to her baby. He might even like Harper enough to flirt with her. But she'd never inspire in him the wish for anything beyond a one-night stand. She simply wasn't special enough. He was more the model, actress, rock goddess kind.

* * *

Two hours later they were hip-deep in a cocktail party. His sister, as always, dazzled in a blue dress that sparkled almost as much as her eyes did. In a city where her face wasn't instantly recognizable, she could easily be Sally McMillen for a couple of hours, mingle with fans and, in general, enjoy the fruits of her labors as an artist.

Still, she didn't hold a candle to Harper, who stood by Sabrina, in a circle of fans, listening to Sabrina talk.

Jake sidled up to him. "You know you don't have to eat dinner with us tonight."

He faced his brother. "What?"

"You and Harper could go somewhere alone. The nanny stays all night, so we could keep Crystal all night."

Not sure what his brother was hinting at, Seth stared at him. "What are you talking about?"

Jake nudged his shoulder. "You and Harper needing some time together. I see the way you're looking at her. Like somebody who doesn't get enough alone time." He leaned in closer. "Get a cab, take her to a restaurant with a view of the Seine. And be romantic."

Seth almost laughed. The last thing Harper wanted was for him to be romantic. She liked him as a friend. The nice guy who was helping her.

Although, he had decided that his mission this weekend would be to pamper her. A private dinner where she didn't have to listen to Sabrina's boyfriend Pierre whine, or worse, pout because Sabrina's work was getting more attention than his, would be a welcome treat. And not having to worry about getting up in the middle of the night would be even better.

His brother didn't have to know they weren't doing this for romance but to give her a weekend she'd remember.

"Thanks. I think we'll take you up on that."

He used his phone to find a good restaurant and his

name to get a table. A half hour before the reservation, he walked up to Harper with the slim wrap she'd brought for the evening chill.

"What's this?"

"I've decided you've had enough McCallan time and I made reservations for dinner."

She blinked. "You did?"

He glanced around to make sure there was no one close enough to overhear. "Don't worry. Nothing romantic."

She blushed. "I didn't really mean that as horrible as it sounded."

He helped her with her wrap. "I get it. Clark and I were friends. No widow wants to date her husband's friend. Worse, I'm not exactly the guy who's going to settle down." He smiled. "We're both safe. But we're also both hungry and a little sick of Pierre. Let's go."

"Okay."

They tracked down Sabrina, his mom and Jake and Avery to bow out of dinner with the family and were on the street at the same time their car arrived. On the drive to the restaurant, she talked about sending out a few résumés the following week and before they knew it they had arrived.

A tall, slim man in a black suit led them to a quiet table in the back with a view of the lights sparkling off the Seine. A waiter had glasses of wine in their hands within minutes.

She took a sip, sighed and sat back on her seat. "You cannot believe how good this feels."

"Sure, I can. I've had long days at work and I imagine that's what being with my family has felt like to you. Work."

She shook her head, then took another sip of wine. "No. I like your family. A weekend with my mom would feel like work, but I've been having fun with your sister and Avery." She grew thoughtful. "I'm not sure how I lost my girlfriends. You get married and your life starts to revolve around a man and before you know it, his friends' wives are your friends." She shrugged. "When Clark was gone, those friends drifted away."

Seth leaned a little closer on the table. "Then they weren't very good friends."

"I suppose not."

She pointed out the window. "Look at the lights. It's amazing how the world can be the same yet different."

"Sort of like the difference between the beach and the mountains?"

"It's more than that. Paris is…warm. The people seem to enjoy feeding tourists."

He laughed. "You've obviously never been to Italy or you'd know the way Parisians treat you is not all that warm. I once went to a restaurant where the chef actually came out and sat with me because he knew I'd enjoy his new dish."

"No kidding." She smiled. "Where else have you been?"

He thought for a second. "I haven't been as many places as I'd like. My work has taken me all over Europe and I've even been to the Middle East and some of Asia but what I'd really like to see are places like Dubai."

"I'd like to see Scotland and Ireland."

"Really?"

"They just seem so green and lush."

"And you have a thing for taverns?"

She laughed. "Maybe."

Their food arrived, and she again ate with gusto. Their conversations went from travel to Crystal to how grateful she was that he was selling her his condo. His mind clouded at the idea of her living in his condo without him. Luckily, by then their meal was long gone and their last glasses of wine had been finished.

Outside, he reached for his phone to call for a ride, but she stopped him. "Let's walk a bit."

The urge to take her hand rose in him, but he'd learned his lesson and kept his hands in his pockets. It was ironic that around his family, he could touch her as much as he wanted, but along the banks of the beautiful river, with the sensuous air of the romance of Paris surrounding them, he had to keep his distance.

Stars twinkled overhead. As the air began to chill, lovers huddled together, laughing, stealing kisses. But he and Harper walked along, quiet, not touching.

When she shivered, he said, "Okay. That's enough. It might be the most wonderful walk of your life, but I won't let you freeze to death."

He called for a car, then draped his suit jacket over her shoulders.

"You don't have to do that."

"I know." But he wanted to. Not because he wanted her evening to be special, perfect. Because everything in him warmed when he was around her. His life didn't seem work-driven. His family wasn't oppressive.

But she was the only woman who'd ever broken his heart. He wouldn't fall for her again. He wouldn't let himself.

The lights that winked off the Seine didn't have a thing on the glow inside of Harper. Standing without a suit coat, in his white shirt and bow tie, Seth looked like a picture from a magazine. She waited for him to say something, to step close and kiss her, but, of course, he didn't.

She'd told him not to.

They rode to the hotel in silence and stayed silent on the ride up in the elevator.

When he opened the door to their suite, she remembered that Crystal was staying the night with the nanny in Jake and Avery's suite and her breath stalled in her chest. His whole family believed they were sleeping together.

Maybe this was why Seth had let the romantic mood

pass as they walked by the Seine? He didn't want her to get any ideas about how the night should end?

Or maybe this was her chance? She was the one who'd told him no relationship. Because of Clark. Then she'd come to terms with Clark being gone, but she worried she wasn't the right woman for a man of the world.

The breath that had stalled in her chest burned in her lungs, as she stepped inside the suite. They were alone. But too many questions stood between them. Worse, the very fact that they were alone, in a suite, for the night meant she couldn't flirt or tease or even kiss him—even talk to him about her new thoughts about Clark—without looking like she wanted to seduce him.

There was no middle ground here. It was either friend or lover…temporary lover.

"Drink?"

She spun around too quickly and almost knocked herself off balance. "Um. No." She'd need her wits about her to get through this, and she already wasn't steady on her feet. Her whole body trembled with a combination of need and fear.

He took two crystal glasses from beneath the bar, anyway. "Are you sure? I know you had some wine with dinner, but you don't need to worry about waking up with Crystal. This might be your last chance for a long time."

She tried to smile. He was making a joke, but to her everything happening was deadly serious. Clark hadn't been her first, but there hadn't been many guys before him. Did she really want the first guy she slept with after her husband to be somebody guaranteed to break her heart?

"Maybe I will have something. More wine?"

He dipped down to reach below the bar again. "Coming right up."

She shrugged out of his jacket and laid it across the back of the sofa as he walked over with their drinks. He handed her the wine, then sat on the chair.

She frowned, feeling she'd gotten this situation all wrong. Oh, she still knew his whole family thought they were sleeping together. But he didn't seem to have any plans to seduce her.

"So, it was a good night?"

She nodded and sat on the sofa a few inches from his jacket, which still smelled like him and the air in Paris at night. Her heart lurched. Yearning spilled through her.

She whispered, "It was a really good night."

"I'm glad. I see how hard you work with Crystal. I know how hard your life is going to get."

She nodded. He wasn't making a move. He'd either gotten beyond whatever it was he'd felt at the cocktail party, or he was waiting for her. Waiting for her to say she'd gotten beyond Clark and was ready.

For one night.

Because she wasn't sure he would give her more.

Hell, she wasn't even sure he wanted her now.

Confusion overwhelmed her. She bounced from the sofa. "You know what? I'm more tired than I thought. I think I will take advantage of this night without the baby and sleep."

She caught his gaze, looking for what, she wasn't sure. A sign that he wanted her. A word that this wouldn't just be a one-night thing for him.

He looked down at his drink. "Okay. Good night."

She sucked in air to stop her shivering chest. "Good night."

CHAPTER NINE

SETH DIDN'T KNOW why he'd been foolish enough to think things between him and Harper might be changing. He wasn't even sure why he wanted it. He wasn't the guy who believed in happily-ever-after…so what had he thought might happen that night?

Caught between frustration and confusion, he kept his distance for the rest of their trip and even after they returned home. Days were easy because he worked. Nights, he scheduled a few house showings with Bill Reynolds.

The following Saturday morning, he slept in and in the afternoon, he took the Ferrari to Montauk to see if there were any houses with For Sale signs that he could tell Bill about. But Saturday night, he had no choice but to shower and dress for the ball.

He waited until the last second to come out of his room, only to find Harper was nowhere around. He looked left and right and suddenly her bedroom door opened and she stepped out.

Wearing a pale pink strapless dress that caressed her top, slid down her waist and belled out in layers of tulle from her hips to the floor, she knocked him for a loop.

She touched the diamond teardrop earrings that looked oddly familiar to Seth. "Your mother let me borrow these."

"Oh." *When had she seen his mother?*

"If you don't like them, I can give them back."

"No. They look great. Beautiful." She looked beautiful. Elegant yet somehow elfin. Like a fairy you'd see in the mists of Ireland. He almost said that. Almost told her that she probably wanted to visit Ireland because she'd belong there. But he held his tongue.

She walked over to him and smiled. "I really don't want to go to this any more than you do."

He held the gaze of her soft blue eyes for a few seconds, then blinked and looked away. "I actually enjoy this ball."

"Oh, then it really is me."

He busied himself finding his keys.

"I know we decided on no relationship. But I thought we were friends. We're supposed to be helping each other."

The slight tremble in her voice made him squeeze his eyes shut. All along his main goal had been not to hurt her, yet it seemed he had. Still, there was no way to avoid it. Just as he'd realized when he decided to sell her this condo, they had to untangle their lives, go their separate ways.

When he opened his eyes again, he grabbed his keys and slid them into his trouser pocket. "I've just been pre-occupied."

"Looking at houses?"

"That and with work."

"Was I not doing a good job finding you somewhere to live? Because that's part of our deal, Seth. I help you find a house and you sell me your condo interest-free."

He turned from the kitchen island. "The truth is I realized this was going to be a bigger job than I'd thought. I don't want to take you away from the baby."

"That's not the deal. I only agreed to no interest on my loan for this place because I'm helping you find somewhere else to live. If you change that, I can't take the deal."

Pride made Harper stand taller. She realized that a relationship wasn't in the cards, but she wasn't a loser. She was a grown woman with a child who was entering the workforce. She and Seth had made an agreement and if he dropped his end of it, then the deal was dead. No matter how much it disappointed her to lose this condo, which was perfect for her and Crystal, she would not take charity.

Seth shook his head. "I get it. I'm sorry. I won't see another house or condo without you. I really didn't know how much work this would be. Or that I wouldn't like being locked out of the process."

She breathed a silent sigh of relief, but she saw what was going on. "I won't lock you out of the process."

"It just seemed that you and Bill were so tight that I worried you'd knock out things that might have been right for me."

Because she didn't know him. He didn't have to say it. The first few weeks they'd lived together they were close. Then they'd gotten a little too close and the past week they had been like two strangers living together. It was as if those first two days in Paris hadn't happened.

"Then maybe we need to go back to you coming along on all the viewings. I can sort through the listings on Bill's website, choose three or four and have you go with us when we see them."

Seth turned away. "Okay."

She got her wrap from her bedroom, so they could ride in the Ferrari with the top down, but it wasn't as much fun as it had been the night of the cocktail party. That night, she'd felt so free. Tonight, disappointment rattled through her. Not that she wanted him to be falling for her. She'd sorted that out in Paris.

It was just that the woman in her was so lonely, so miserable. So empty.

The first weeks they'd lived together he'd put light back into her life. Now he barely spoke to her.

They'd made the right choice. She knew they had. But

the decision not to take things further had taken away their friendship and left a huge void, a hole in her heart.

A week ago, she would have included losing Clark as creating part of that hole. Now, she knew the truth. She was losing the first friend she'd made after losing Clark.

They entered the hotel hosting the ball the same way they'd entered the art museum for the first cocktail party they'd attended. The valet happily took Seth's car. A hotel employee cheerfully opened the doors for them. And Seth didn't even have to mention his name to get entry to the ball. Everybody knew him.

And maybe that was part of why she'd liked him so much. He was easy to be around, easy to laugh with. And she'd been alone for an entire year. She'd been vulnerable. Even if she hadn't realized it, she'd longed for somebody in her life.

With a fierceness that stole her breath, she suddenly missed being close to someone. She missed knowing somebody loved her. Missed having a place. Missed being somebody's love.

Seth's mom scurried over. "Our table is in front of the room."

Seth nodded. "We'll be up in a minute. There are a few people I want to introduce Harper to."

Maureen's eyebrows rose.

Seth laughed. "There are a lot of businesspeople here. Potential for Harper to find a job."

The jab burned through her. A reminder that she was nothing but a responsibility to him.

Because she was. Without a real relationship, she was nothing but a woman with a baby who desperately needed work. Not somebody he cared about. Not somebody he thought was beautiful. Or funny. Or nice to have around. A responsibility he was growing tired of.

They wove through the crowd with Seth saying hello

to at least fifty percent of the people they passed. Then he stopped and introduced her to John Gardner, a banker.

Harper remembered walking down the hall with Bill Reynolds the first time they'd looked at condos, feeling like a businesswoman doing a job, and she channeled that confidence.

Standing a little taller, she extended her hand to shake John's. "It's a pleasure to meet you."

"Harper's reentering the workforce."

John's gaze flicked to hers. "Really. What kind of work are you looking for?"

"Assistant," she answered before Seth could. She'd leaned on him far too long. She could do this now. She had to. She *wanted* to. "In college, I ran a small business where I did odd jobs for people with more money than time."

Tall, gray-haired John snorted. "I get that. I have some-one shop for the gifts I get my wife." He glanced around nervously as if realizing his wife could be close enough to hear him. When he saw she wasn't, he breathed a sigh of relief. "Can't let her know that, though."

Harper took the cue and assured him, "Confidentiality is the number one code of a good assistant."

"You better believe that." He glanced at his drink, then back at Harper. "And you think those skills will translate to an office?"

"Not in a traditional way," Harper admitted. "But wouldn't you rather have someone in your office who would find your last-minute gifts, as well as print the financials you have to review that afternoon?"

"I always had my assistant send my apology flowers."

Her confidence building, Harper said, "I'm also help-ing Seth find a new home right now. I'm looking at condos suggested by the real estate agent and weeding out the ones that are definite nos."

"That's a little above and beyond an assistant's job."

"True, but you never know what you're going to need from an assistant so it's good to have one who is versatile."

"So, what are you finding out there?"

"In the real estate market?"

John inclined his head.

"Are you considering moving?"

"My company is looking for an apartment for long-term visitors. It's okay to put someone up in a hotel when they are in town for a meeting or two. But when you have board members who are in town with their families or auditors or potential investors who'll be spending a week or ten days, it's better to have a condo they can use."

"I saw two a few weeks ago that Seth wasn't interested in. I can give you the name of our real estate agent and he can take you to see them."

"I'd rather have you stop by our office, talk with staff about what we're looking for and weed out all but three choices for us."

"Oh."

He pulled a card from his pocket. "My assistant's email is on there. Contact her Monday and we can arrange for you to come in for a meeting."

Happiness bubbled up from her chest and she knew it spread all over her face. "Okay. Thank you."

John ambled off and Seth said, "And *that's* how you network."

She slapped the little business card against his biceps. "Come on. It was a coincidence that he was looking for a condo."

"You think?"

She laughed but stopped suddenly, the expression on his face bringing her up short. With his dark hair and dark eyes, his black tux gave him a sexy, mysterious look that sent her pulse scrambling. Plus, he was smiling at her. Warmly.

The way he had the night she got the impression that he was attracted to her.

"Before you meet with him and his staff on Monday, we'll have to figure out a realistic amount you should charge for this service."

"What service? If they had someone who had time to meet with a real estate agent, they wouldn't need me to narrow their choices down for them."

"Exactly. The point is they don't have someone on staff who can take the time to look at condos. Thus, they hire you."

"So, I have a temp job?"

"No. You're a consultant. You have one of those rare opportunities where you can charge fifty or sixty thousand dollars for a few days' work."

She gaped at him. "Fifty or sixty thousand dollars!"

He grinned. "I know."

A tall red-haired man approached them.

Seth pivoted to face her. "This guy needs a full-time assistant. You'll get the extra cash from the real estate gig, but Max could actually hire you."

When the tall, red-haired man reached them, Seth took his hand and shook it. "Max Wilson. How have you been?"

"Great!" Max said, pumping Seth's hand.

Seth pointed to Harper. "This is my friend, Harper Hargraves."

"Hargraves? Related to Clark?"

Once again, she barely felt a twinge of sadness. She'd always miss Clark. Always have love for him in her heart. But she needed a job. This man needed an assistant. She couldn't blow this chance.

"Yes. He was my husband."

"I am so sorry for your loss. Hard to believe it's been a year."

"Yes. A year. That's why I'm out and about again. Even looking for a job."

Max asked, "What kind of work are you interested in?"

"I think I'm qualified to be an assistant."

His face brightened. "I'm losing my long-time assistant." He shook his head. "Feels funny to even think about hiring someone to replace her."

"I understand." She smiled at him. "I'm new at looking for a job. At university, I ran a virtual-assistant business. I bought flowers, walked dogs, bought gifts, sent reminders. I have a child now, so I want to shift those skills into a job that's more structured, so I can be home for dinner."

"That makes sense."

"But that doesn't mean I wouldn't enjoy the challenge of being someone's assistant. I had gotten to the point with some of my clients that I could anticipate what they needed. I kept logs of their friends' birthdays, anniversaries, that kind of thing, and kept them on track."

"Sounds a lot like what my assistant does." He took out his phone, scrolled to his schedule. "If you're interested, I have an opening at ten o'clock on Monday morning. Which means you'd need to come in at nine to talk with Human Resources first."

"I'm definitely interested."

"Give me your number. In case the timing doesn't work for HR."

She rattled off the number for her cell phone and he put it in his phone. "If you don't hear from her you're good for Monday at nine."

She nodded, and Max walked away to talk to a couple across the room.

Harper pivoted to face Seth. "That was great."

Seth beamed at her. "It was because you were great. Now you've conquered your I-need-a-job nervousness, you are amazing."

He said it casually, but after the words were out of his mouth, his face changed. He blanked all emotion from it, almost as if he regretted calling her amazing.

Sadness echoed through her again. Not about Clark. About Seth. Knowing there would never ever be anything between them. After he found a house and she found a job, they might not even remain friends.

The thought brought her up short, stalled her breath. If her interview worked out and Bill Reynolds came through with a house for Seth, this might be their last "date" together.

Cocktail hour ended with everyone taking seats for the dinner. They sat with Avery and Jake, Maureen and Sabrina and Pierre, who made dinner uncomfortable by complaining that nothing was up to his standards.

At the end of the meal, when he left to talk to a friend, Jake shook his head at Sabrina. "You need to dump that guy."

Seth said, "At the very least, send him back to France and forget his cell number."

Maureen said nothing, but her very silence confirmed she believed what everyone else did.

Luckily, dancing began. The band played a popular song and Jake rose to dance with Avery. Maureen gave Seth a significant look.

He glanced at Harper with a smile that was totally forced. "Would you like to dance?"

Harper almost refused. But Maureen sent her the kind of look that brooked no argument and Harper knew it would be near fatal to go against the McCallan matriarch.

"I'd love to."

By the time they got to the dance floor the song had ended. A slower song began. Seth hesitated but slid one hand around her waist as he joined their hands.

The terrible sensation of dancing with someone who

didn't want to be with her slithered through Harper at the same time she realized she was touching him. All those times her fingers had itched for it, she finally had her hand on his shoulder and her other hand held by his.

Her high heels brought them to eye level, but she didn't dare look at him while her hand was on the soft silk of his tux, making her blood shimmer through her. She tried not to notice his hand at her waist or that the distance between them seemed to shrink with every step, as if they were being drawn together by an unseen force.

She inched back and ruined their dance step.

"Relax."

"Easy for you to say. You've been to a trillion of these things."

"You came every year with Clark."

But she'd never felt these weird longings and curiosities with Clark. Of course, she'd always known Clark loved her. Maybe part of the yearning that coursed through her was simply an acknowledgment that Seth was unattainable?

Because she'd pushed him away.

"Clark and I did come to this ball every year."

"Do you miss him?"

For that she lifted her eyes until she caught Seth's gaze. "Not in the way that I did a few months ago."

She wasn't sure if it was her imagination, but she swore Seth's grip tightened on her waist.

"I'm sorry."

"Don't be. In the past few weeks, I've come to terms with the idea of moving on."

His head tilted. "Really?"

"Hey, I'm buying a condo, getting a job. I let go of the house that was our home. I've been alone for twelve long months. I was pregnant alone. Had a baby alone." She stopped, realizing she was about to tell him she was lonely.

She hadn't been. The first two weeks she and Seth had lived together had been fun. So much fun.

"That must have been hard."

"It's amazing what you can do when you have no choice."

"Weren't your parents around?"

She shrugged. "They called a few times. Came to visit a lot in the beginning to make sure I was okay."

"They love you."

"In their own way."

"And your mom's not so bad." He shook his head. "Look, I know firsthand how difficult family can be, but I think you should give your mom a second chance."

She ignored his suggestion, mostly because it made sense and it shouldn't.

"Do you regret going to work for your family?"

"No. This is my responsibility. I accept it."

She frowned. "Then what are you doing that you have no choice about?"

He caught her gaze, looked like he might say something, but stopped.

But he didn't have to say it. He wanted away from her enough to give her his condo and almost let her choose his next home. "You're unhappy that you took me and Crystal in, aren't you?"

"No."

The word was a wisp. As soft as a cloud but as strong as good whiskey. She thought for a moment that he was too kind to let her believe she was a burden. But his eyes held hers, serious, sincere.

He regretted that they couldn't have something together.

At the end of the song, Seth walked Harper back to their table, sorry that he'd brought up Clark. Not because it filled her with sadness, but because it hadn't. And that conjured all kinds of notions in his head.

She finally seemed happy to be moving on. Of course, he knew no one wanted to be stuck in grief for the rest of their lives. Getting out of that emotional quagmire might have been what she was happy about...

But whatever the reason, she was moving on.

They went back to the table and she got hoodwinked into working the crowd with Sabrina. His sister was always on the hunt for mentors for the budding entrepreneurs in her program. But she'd reminded Harper that she could use all the contacts she could to help with her job search.

He watched them move through the crowd. Sabrina in her simple white gown, charming the rich and generous. Harper was shy at first, then she gained her confidence and worked the room in a different way. She might be softer than Sabrina, but she was no less determined to get a job.

To move on.

She was more than ready.

When they returned to the table, Seth asked Harper to dance again and though it took three songs, the band finally played something slow and romantic. This time when he took her into his arms, he felt her tense then relax. Every few steps, he'd bring her an inch or so closer until she was almost pressed up against him.

That's when he stopped. She hadn't protested. But his conscience reminded him that she was a kind, wonderful woman with a child. A widow. And he was a womanizer. No matter what anyone said about the right person changing a man's life, Seth knew his reasons for staying single, staying unattached, were deeper and more important than those of the usual playboy.

It might soothe his ego to think Harper liked him but, in the end, he would hurt her.

He moved away from her when the song ended. "Shall we go back to the table?"

"Yes."

Her voice sounded a little shaky. Which didn't surprise him because being near her had him a bit trembly, too. To get them both past their discomfort, he said, "I saw you having fun with Sabrina."

She turned to him with a laugh. "Fun? The woman's a dynamo! I got the cards of three more executives who are considering adding another assistant to their staffs. I'm going to be employed before the month is out."

"That's good."

"It's fantastic." She took a long breath. "You know, the part about losing Clark was devastating. But I never realized how much I had missed when I decided not to work after we were married. Makes me wonder what else I missed."

She started walking toward their table again, but her comment had stopped Seth dead in his tracks. *What else she'd missed?*

He could guess a hundred things she'd probably missed, most of them involving his king-size bed. And, oh, Lord. What he wouldn't give to be the guy who showed her.

He headed back to the table chastising himself.

But watching her laugh with his sister, he remembered what she had said about losing her friends. She also didn't have a sister. He saw a different side of her as she laughed with Sabrina. A girlie side. The side she probably didn't have time for because of the baby and, soon, work.

When they got in his car to go home and the wind tousled her hair, sending her laughter to him on a wave of cool air, the conclusion he drew didn't surprise him.

This was a woman who was changing. She'd gone from devoted wife to single mom and would soon be an employee. And she wasn't sad about it. She'd finally found the fun in it.

What if she was done with the white-picket-fence dreams?

Or what if she'd put them on hold until she'd experimented a little?

What if this was his one small chance, his one tiny opening, to have the woman he'd always wanted. Not forever. Not for always. But for a season of time as she experienced life?

If he let her go, found a new house, moved out and never saw her again, would he be depriving them both of an opportunity fate seemed to have handed them on a silver platter?

Or was he crazy to be thinking like this? Thinking she wanted him? Thinking they could have something to remember forever before they both moved on?

He parked the car and they rode up in the elevator in silence. He unlocked the condo door and motioned for her to enter before him. Mrs. P. mumbled a quick report on the baby and an even quicker goodbye before she shuffled out the door.

And then they were alone. She headed toward her room, but he caught up to her at the kitchen island, grabbed her hand and turned her to face him.

Her pretty pink skirt ruffled as she pivoted. Her eyes jumped to his.

He saw the surprise, but he also saw the curiosity before she could hide it. He thought of the kiss all those weeks ago in front of the limo, thought of her eager response, and kissed her again, before he could talk himself out of it.

CHAPTER TEN

THE KISS STARTED off slow and smooth but quickly went deep. Not a sweet, thanks-for-the-nice-evening kiss, but a prelude to making love. The kiss of a man who wanted a woman.

Excitement, fear and wonder coursed through Harper. His hands slid along the bare skin of her back, along the curve of her waist, and raced back up again as his mouth worked its magic. She pressed her fingers to his chest, wanting to slide them to his shoulders, but they paused, savored. Everything was so much more intense than it had been with Clark. She wondered if that was because they had been so young when they married, or if Seth was simply a different kind of man.

Just when she might have made a move to slide her hands beneath the sleek material of his tux jacket, he pulled away.

Her gaze leaped to his.

"We've already said you and I aren't a good mix."

His strong, sure voice made the statement with a confidence that confused her after the way he'd just kissed her.

"We want different things. But I sense things have changed since Paris. You've adjusted to the fact that you're starting a new phase of your life, and I think you might want to try some things you could have missed because you were so young when you got involved with Clark. I'm not the guy you settle down with, but I am the guy you could find yourself with." His eyes searched hers. "Think about that. No rush on the answer."

With that he turned and walked down the hall. She didn't move a muscle. She wasn't even sure she breathed until he opened the door and walked into his bedroom.

Then her breath poured out in a long, almost painful rush that drained her of oxygen and left her even more light-headed than his offer had.

And it was an offer. No-strings-attached sex. A chance to find herself.

After a year of loneliness, she'd been thrust into the eye of a storm of getting on her feet financially, finding a job and a home for herself and her baby, and now he was giving her a chance to find herself as a woman.

She understood what he meant. She was different than she'd been when she'd arrived on his doorstep. But it was the scariest proposition anyone had ever made to her. Not because she wasn't sure what it entailed, but because it tempted her in ways she'd never been tempted.

For that reason alone, she knew he was right. She did long to find herself, figure out who she was. But with him?

That was the variable. She absolutely knew she'd be someone different with him.

Was that why Seth was so tempting?

She walked back to her room, her gown swishing around her, the diamond earrings his mother had lent her swaying back and forth. She tried not to think of him, what he wanted, what he thought she should want.

She stepped into her bedroom. A pale night-light illuminated the crib. Her baby. Her sleeping little girl.

She took off the earrings and laid them in the box Maureen had brought them in, then slid out of the fancy dress and tossed it across the room.

How could one little choice be so confusing?

* * *

Seth awoke feeling lazy and rested, then he remembered what he'd said to Harper the night before, remembered kissing her hungrily, remembered her greedy response…and that he'd propositioned her.

He pulled the covers over his head, then yanked them off again with a thump.

He'd never been ashamed of wanting a woman before. And she wanted him, too. She simply hadn't come to terms with it yet. But with time to think about it, maybe she'd changed her mind?

And if she hadn't, maybe he could help her with that?

He slid out of bed, found a pair of jeans and a T-shirt to slip into and headed out to the kitchen, his expectations teetering on the brink of believing she'd greet him with a smile, maybe a kiss—

When he got to the kitchen, she was feeding the baby.

Now what? He knew a kiss could get them over their morning-after awkwardness. And even with her sitting, he could walk up behind her, slide his arms around her and kiss the back of her neck, not giving her a chance to think about him or propositions or anything but the fact that they were attracted to each other.

Or he could just say "Good morning," and let her dictate what happened next?

She took the options out of his hands when she said, "Good morning," as he approached the kitchen island.

"Good morning."

Okay. That worked. But walking up behind her and kissing her neck was still a good follow-up.

She rose from the chair, set the empty baby bottle in the sink and wouldn't look at him as she turned toward the island again.

Suddenly, the neck kiss seemed highly inappropriate.

Still, he could walk up to her, slide his hands along her arms and kiss her...

She was holding the baby. Nestling her against her chest.

Confusion confounded him. How did couples with babies kiss?

In their beds probably.

And he had yet to get her in his.

She wouldn't meet his gaze again and he knew he'd missed his chance to kiss her. He couldn't believe he was losing his suaveness.

He would get this. He was the king of smooth. He'd just have to switch strategies a bit.

She slipped past him. "I was thinking of visiting my parents today."

"Visiting your parents?"

She wouldn't look at him. "They don't see Crystal often."

He knew that. He just didn't realize she'd rather visit her mother than hang out with him.

"Today's supposed to be nice."

She'd rather visit her mother than hang out with him?

"It is."

She motioned down the hall. "I'll just get us ready and be on our way."

"Okay."

"Okay."

He watched he walk to her bedroom, so desperate to get away from him that she was on her way to her parents' house.

At first, he wanted to kick himself for what he'd said to her the night before, then he realized a woman who didn't want anything to do with him would just tell him that. Quickly, like removing a bandage, she'd say "Forget it." But she couldn't tell him that because it would be a lie. So she was running.

His confidence returned. There might be a little thinking involved but he'd figure out how to woo her.

Having called for an Uber ride, Harper waited outside the building entry, talking with Hal, the Sunday doorman, who stood beside her holding Crystal's car seat. Close to seventy, he kept up a steady stream of light conversation, effectively keeping her mind off Seth until the car arrived.

He hurried over, opened the door and installed the car seat.

"Thanks, Hal." She was about to rummage in her purse for a tip, but he stopped her.

"It was just a car seat. And you're one of my favorite people." He smiled at Crystal. "Your baby is another."

His kindness released some of her tension. But not all of it. How did a woman say no to a man she really wanted? A man who'd looked like he wanted to kiss her that morning?

She had to stiffen to repress a shiver. She'd never experienced these emotions with Clark and though that made her feel a bit odd, it also revived her curiosity. Why were things always so intense with Seth?

No. "Things" weren't intense. They got along nicely until their attraction slithered into the room. Then her breathing changed. His eyes focused on her as if she were the only woman in the world. And the air disappeared from the room.

The driver began to chitchat and she had to reply. The light conversation eased Seth out of her brain and by the time she got into the elevator to her parents' enormous condo, she felt lighter.

No. Carrying her baby down the short hall to her mother's place, she felt like a single mom. Not a woman in a beautiful gown, wearing borrowed diamond earrings, being seduced by a man. Not a woman who wanted to throw caution to the wind, if only to satisfy her blazing curiosity. But herself. A woman with a baby who had to find a job, and who also needed a house. A woman with priorities that didn't include an affair.

A woman about to visit her parents with the baby they seldom saw because she was afraid they'd bring up all the wrong subjects.

She took a breath. Fortified herself.

She rang the bell and the maid answered, but her mom peeked out from behind the corner.

"The doorman said it was you." She smiled broadly and reached to take Crystal, as the maid took the car seat and tucked it in a convenient closet.

Glancing at her mom's taupe sheath, a nod to the fact that it was October, though fall temperatures hadn't yet arrived, Harper grimaced. "Be careful. I never know when she's going to throw up or pee."

Amelia laughed. "Diapers are stronger than they've ever been, and you threw up on me plenty." She headed for the elegant living room decorated in shades of sage, pale yellow and tan. "How are you today, sweet girl?" she asked Crystal as she tickled her tummy.

The baby giggled. Harper's dad rose from the sage sofa.

"What have we here? A rare Sunday visit?"

Harper kissed her dad's cheek, then gave the nonthreatening reply that would ease her out of having to give a real answer. "Bored today."

Her dad said, "Really? That's a good sign. For the past year, you've wanted nothing but to stay home."

Her mom sat on one of the tan chairs that complemented the sofa. "I agree. It's so nice to have you visit."

For the first time in about a decade, Harper relaxed with her parents. "Actually, it feels pretty good to get out of the house."

"And it's a lovely day," Amelia said, motioning to the huge wall of windows that displayed a panoramic view of

Manhattan. "Maybe if you stay long enough we can take Crystal for a walk in the park?"

"I didn't bring her stroller. It was hard enough carrying her, a diaper bag and the car seat."

Her mother smiled. "Maybe next time."

Harper's muscles and bones loosened a little more. She glanced around, realizing that maybe her mother wasn't the crazy wannabe rich woman that she had been. In fact, she'd actually seen a bit of that change when her mom agreed to back off from dinner with her and Seth. "That'd be great."

Her dad said, "Can you stay for lunch?"

Harper's stomach growled. "I haven't even had breakfast. If you wanted to feed me now, I'd be overjoyed."

Amelia rose and handed the baby to Harper's dad. "Let me talk to the maid. I'll bet she can have something ready in a half an hour."

"Wait." Harper rummaged through her diaper bag and pulled out the two just-in-case bottles she'd brought for the baby. "Can you put these in the refrigerator?"

"Absolutely."

When her mom was gone, Harper glanced at her dad. Crystal sat on his lap, patting his face. "She likes you."

"She should. I adore her."

Harper smiled, though her chest tightened. Her parents were a tad crazy, but a baby mitigated that. Or maybe Crystal brought out their softer side. Whatever the reason, this visit was going well, taking Harper's mind off Seth and into neutral territory.

"So, how's business?"

"Ridiculous," her dad said, with a sigh. "I can't keep up. I'll be hiring two new vice presidents in the next six months and the staff to go with them."

She almost asked if any one of those people he was hiring would need an assistant, but she stopped herself. Her parents' good, benevolent mood would die a needless death if she mentioned how desperately she needed a job.

Her mother sauntered into the room. "I'm back." She immediately took Crystal from her husband. "Brunch in thirty minutes."

"Thanks, Mom." It felt good to say that, good to mean it.

They chatted about Crystal until the maid came into the room and announced brunch was served. Harper was surprised to find her parents had a high chair with the proper padding and straps to balance a now four-month-old baby.

She ate eggs and toast, bacon and potatoes and topped it off with cheese blintzes and coffee.

"I'm stuffed."

"I'm glad to see you eat." Her dad reached across the table and patted her hand. "You're so damned skinny."

Amelia brushed away his concern. "She's fashionably thin."

"I liked her better with a little meat on her bones."

Her mother sighed. "Seriously, Pete. You're so behind the times." She turned to Harper. "What does Seth think?"

The reminder of Seth stole all the air from Harper's lungs.

What did he think? That he'd like to sleep with her. Without a commitment. No strings attached. No tomorrow.

She said the only thing that came to mind. "We haven't gotten that far in our relationship."

Her mom gasped. "You haven't slept together?"

"Amelia!"

She glanced at her husband. "What? It's a perfectly normal question in today's world. Especially since Harper doesn't want to let him get away."

"Away from what, Mom?" And they were back to their old relationship. The one that made Harper crazy. "Should I get a rope and lasso him? Or maybe drag him to the justice of the peace and force him to put a ring on my finger when he doesn't want to?"

"I'm just saying…"

"Things aren't like what they were when you were young. Marriage isn't the first thing people consider when they date someone." The lie stuck on her tongue. Not because it was a lie but because nothing about what she had with Seth, what she felt for Seth, was normal. They weren't dating. But they were living together. When they'd begun living together, they hadn't been interested in each other romantically. Now…

Now…

She thought he was fun and smart and extremely generous.

But he only wanted to sleep with her.

She pulled her cell phone from her pocket and arranged for a car to pick her up.

Her mother's eyes dimmed with concern. "Honey, don't leave because I said something you don't like. I agree our generations are different about how we see life and especially relationships. I didn't mean to upset you or criticize what you have with Seth. Sit down. Have some more coffee."

"I'm fine. I need to get Crystal to bed anyway." And maybe face Seth. Tell him she was not made for what he wanted.

"It's just that you seemed to have had a totally different relationship with Clark. I recognize you were younger. But he pulled you away from us. Seth seems to be making you comfortable being around us."

Anger burst through her. "First of all, Clark did not pull me away from you." But he also didn't encourage her to visit. In fact, most times she'd planned to see her parents, he'd made bigger, better plans.

She sucked in a breath. Shook her head to clear it because she didn't want to think about that. Not now. Not today. Maybe not ever.

"Second, it wasn't Seth's idea for me to visit you today." But he had told her to give her mom a break, not be so hard on her. And he'd created the charade that they were dating to help Harper get through the situation that Clark had left them in.

Her mother rose from the table and began unbuckling Crystal's high-chair restraints. "You know what? We had a lovely visit today. And I don't want to ruin that by an off-hand remark that rubbed you the wrong way. I love that you're dating Seth. I won't lie. But I love that you visited more."

"I liked the visit, too." She had. And she wasn't even angry with her mom. She was angry with herself because comparing Seth and Clark had her head spinning. Clark had been a great guy.

But he'd kept her from her parents and he'd left her broke.

All because he liked keeping up appearances, too.

Not wanting to sit around the house and mope, looking like a loser, Seth drove to Jake and Avery's house in Pennsylvania and dropped in on them unexpectedly. When he arrived at the huge house surrounded by trees, he could see the happy couple sitting on Adirondack chairs in the backyard near the pool. He drove his car up their long lane and walked across the lawn to greet them.

"Hey."

Jake set the paper he was reading on a convenient table and rose. "Hey! What brings you out here?"

Seth bent and kissed Avery's cheek. "I don't know."

"Where's Harper?"

"She left for the day. Visiting her parents."

And it was killing him. He'd never wanted a woman he couldn't have before. At least none that he remembered—

He frowned. Maybe he just had a really good PR system in his brain that made him believe he was irresistible?

Or maybe those other women hadn't had babies that kept him from being able to kiss them?

Because he couldn't explain any of that to his happily married brother without telling him he wasn't really dating Harper, he said the first valid excuse that came to mind. "But I wanted to talk to Avery. I'm getting a new condo and I thought I'd get some insights."

Avery perked up. "Where are you looking?"

"Everywhere. I can't decide between a really lavish condo or a house in Connecticut."

Jake laughed. "A house in Connecticut?"

"I'm thirty-one. I live in a condo that I bought when I was twenty-six, just becoming successful. I want something..." He gestured broadly. "Something that says..."

Unable to figure out what to say, he left the sentence hang.

Avery motioned for him to take a seat. Jake headed toward the big deck. "I'll get some lemonade."

As soon as the sliding glass doors closed behind Jake, Avery turned to Seth. "Okay, now that he's gone, tell me what's really going on with Harper. Did you have a fight?"

"No. Sort of. A little one." And that was all he was saying. Honesty was one thing, but he would not tell his sister-in-law he wanted to sleep with Harper, not get into something permanent. That would spoil the charade, too.

"I really do need help figuring out what I want in a new place to live."

Avery inclined her head. "Tell me why you want to move."

"I want a home that's more me. Something that not the home of a guy just beginning to make it."

"And you'll need more of a home for a family?"

"No." His brain almost scrambled trying to keep up with what was real and what was a charade. He decided he might as well do with Avery what he'd done with his mom. Disabuse her of any happily-ever-after notions.

"Look, don't get too invested in me and Harper. You know my relationships don't last. I just want a nice home. A good place to have parties."

Though Avery's eyes filled with curiosity, she took the cue and didn't question him. "And you said lavish?"

He laughed. "You know what I'd like? A den. My condo is open floorplan so the TV's right there in the sitting room, which bumps up against the dining area. Everybody can see everything. I'd like a den."

"So that you could have a formal living room?"

"Yes. And a bigger master bedroom."

"Okay. How about the kitchen?"

"The kitchen could be nonexistent if it was only me. But I'll need a kitchen for a caterer."

"Okay. Big kitchen."

They discussed a few more details of what Seth wanted. Jake arrived with the lemonade and took his seat.

"So how far did we get in the discussion of Seth and Harper?"

Seth groaned.

Avery gave her husband a significant look. "You know it's against family rules to be pushy about relationships. And speaking of that, you shouldn't have said anything about Pierre last night at dinner."

"He's a tool."

"And Sabrina loves him."

"I don't think she does," Jake said. "I think he pushed his way into her life and she just got accustomed to him."

Avery frowned. "Hmm. Now that you mention it, he was different in the beginning. *Pushy* might actually be the word for it."

"*Pushy* is exactly the word for it," Seth said.

The subject of Pierre died, and they drank their lemonade and talked about things Seth should look for in a new home. Twenty minutes later the baby monitor beside Avery squawked with the sounds of their one-year-old daughter, Abby, waking from her nap.

"I better go get her."

Avery raced into the house and Jake sat back on his seat. "So, what's really going on with Harper?"

Seth cut his brother a look. He had the same feeling he'd gotten the last time Jake had asked him about Harper, and it seemed wrong to be less than honest with him. He might not be able to discuss the ruse, but that wasn't his only problem with Harper. "I told her last night I wanted to sleep with her."

Jake winced. "You're not sleeping together?"

"In the beginning we were reluctant because Clark and I had been friends. But now, things are different. She's different. I think we should have an affair."

"And she wants to get married?"

"I'm not sure. But she knows I don't." He almost cursed. He hated talking about this kind of stuff. Even with Jake. "It's not like people don't have affairs. You had your share of them."

"True."

"And it's not like I didn't give fair warning, so she has time to think about it. We both have time to make sure it's the right thing. After all, she was Clark's wife." A wave of guilt hit him. The remorse about Clark that he'd felt before.

He groaned. "I'm paying back my debt to Clark by wanting to sleep with his wife."

"She's not his wife anymore," Jake said gently. "Seth, Clark is gone. And this might turn into something."

"It won't." He ran his hand down his face. He was tempting Clark's widow with an affair. Not marriage. Not even a relationship. Just an affair. Guilt rose in another warm wave. "You know how I am. I'm not the guy who's going to settle down like you did."

"How do you know?"

"A million things. Mostly Mom and Dad's sham of a marriage." He shook his head. "It all seems like a trap to me. A prison. I'll never shake that. I can tell the minute a woman begins thinking about something permanent with me, and I run. Eventually I'd run from Harper, too."

"Then I think you need to send your real estate agent the list of things you want in a house and tell him to get a move on. You liked Clark too much to hurt Harper."

"Exactly."

Avery walked out holding Abby and the little girl nestled her face into her mom's neck when she saw Seth.

As Jake pulled the baby from Avery's arms, he leaned in for a quick kiss with Avery.

Seth watched in amazement. The trick to kissing a woman with a child seemed to be taking control of the baby.

"What's this?" Jake tickled Abby's tummy. "Are you shy with Uncle Seth?"

She buried herself even deeper into Jake's shoulder.

Seth shook off his thoughts about kissing a woman with a baby because he didn't need them now that he had his thoughts about Harper straightened out. He looked at his niece with new affection since Crystal had taught him how to be around a child.

"I can't believe how big she is."

"One year," Avery said proudly. She sidled up beside Jake, slid her arm around his waist.

Seth saw that too. Even a one-year-old didn't get in the way of her and Jake being affectionate.

"We're thinking about having another baby."

"Or six," Jake said casually.

Seth almost choked. His stiff and stoic brother wasn't

merely casually affectionate with the woman he'd *married*. Now, he was thinking about having six kids? "You kind of hinted that in Paris."

Jake, a guy who had lived and breathed the McCallan legacy, finally had a life. A real life. And was happy. Though the temptation to tease him rose up in Seth, he couldn't tease about that. Not today.

Abby pulled away from her dad and looked at Seth. With her dark hair, round face and happy green eyes, she was the perfect combination of her parents.

"Hey, Abby."

She frowned.

"Come on. You can't be afraid of me. I'm Uncle Seth. I'm the one who will buy you the best birthday presents."

Abby's brow wrinkled.

Seth laughed. "I'm willing to wait until you're five for you to like me."

He reached out and kissed Avery's cheek, chucked Abby's chin and said, "Okay, I'm off. I'll see you tomorrow, bro."

Jake said, "Unless you're meeting with your real estate agent."

"Right."

The three-hour drive home gave Seth plenty of time to call Bill and talk in detail about what he wanted in his new condo. Always eager to please, Bill told him he would dig a little deeper and, satisfied, Seth disconnected the call.

He stopped at a nearby restaurant and picked up Chinese for supper.

Obviously glad for the food, Harper said, "Great," as he arrived with the bags.

But there was an elephant in the room between them. She hadn't answered his proposition. And despite his conversation with his brother, Seth still wanted her to say yes.

They sat at the table. Both dished out their food.

"Where's Crystal?"

"Sleeping."

"I went to see my niece today." Instead, he'd noticed at least two ways men and women could touch and kiss around a child.

Surprised, she glanced up at him. "You did?"

"Actually, I was talking with Avery about what I'd want in a condo and Abby woke from her nap."

Harper didn't say anything, and Seth realized his mistake. Harper was supposed to be helping him find a new home. "It isn't that I don't trust your judgment. It was more that I had no idea myself what I wanted. She helped drag some things out of me."

She ran her chopsticks through her food, playing with it more than eating it. Seth almost groaned.

Would he ever get anything right with this woman?

"What kind of things did she drag out of you?"

"A den, for one. A separate room for the TV and the sitting area. A bigger kitchen. A master that's more like a suite."

The hurt in her voice lessened. "That's all good."

"I called Bill. He's on the hunt for a few new places and he'll be calling you tomorrow."

She brightened a bit. "Good. I also have that interview tomorrow."

That's right. Max really had seemed interested. "And you have to call John Gardner about the condo for his company."

"I thought I'd call him first, maybe set a time for the afternoon with his people while I'm still dressed for the interview."

Seth laughed. "Good thinking."

And just like that, they were friends again. Seth would have breathed a sigh of relief except something about them easily being able to forgive and forget settled into his gut.

A feeling he'd never felt before. Not relief. Not exactly contentment. Something rich and right and totally foreign.

He'd had girlfriends. He had tons of friends. He had a brother and sister he was now close to. But this was different. This was special.

He told himself that was ridiculous, then watched a playoff game with her to prove to himself they could still be friends.

When it was time for bed, as they walked down the hall to their respective rooms, he remembered kissing her the night before, but tonight he didn't stop. He reminded himself that Clark had been his friend and if he really wanted to thank him for helping him get on his feet, he wouldn't hurt Harper.

No matter how flipping much he wanted to kiss her.

And now he knew how—take control of the baby.

He raced to his room. He would not hurt her, not kiss her and certainly not proposition her again.

CHAPTER ELEVEN

HARPER FELT FUNNY the next morning.

As Seth got coffee and she prepared a bottle for Crystal, the atmosphere of the kitchen was strange. If only being friends was the right thing to do, why did everything feel so off?

They didn't fight, weren't overly polite…but what had been ordinary and acceptable in the beginning of her living with him was now odd. Especially when he kept glancing at Crystal, looking like he wanted to say something or do something.

She supposed that might be because he'd seen his niece the day before. Maybe he'd gotten comfortable. Several times, it seemed like he wanted to pick her up, but changed his mind.

He'd held Crystal in Paris. Walked along the Champs-Élysées holding her, giving her a baby tour of the city.

Why did he hesitate now?

Seth left for work early—seven o'clock instead of eight or nine. Harper dressed for her interview and at eight o'clock called John Gardner's office and set up an appointment for one o'clock with his assistant to discuss Harper helping them find a company condo. Then she left Crystal with Mrs. Petrillo and went to her interview.

On the walk to Midtown, she realized she could have

left Crystal with her mom. Her mother would have loved that. The thought seemed to come out of nowhere, but it felt more right than the atmosphere in Seth's home that morning. She pushed those thoughts out of her brain and put her mind on possible interview questions as she finished the walk to Max Wilson's office.

The interview took two hours. She reported to his Human Resources department as Max had instructed and after twenty minutes of conversation she was given two tests. Then she was whisked to Max's office, where he made what seemed to be small talk, but actually delved into her life and the time she'd spent running her small business.

They shook hands and he promised he'd call before the week was out to let her know if she was a candidate for the job.

Though he hadn't hired her, he also hadn't said, "Thanks but no thanks." She left his office feeling great. So great, that when her phone rang, she answered with a perky "Hello!"

"Hey. It's Bill. I'm guessing Seth told you we'd talked, and he added a laundry list of things he wanted in his new house."

"Yes."

"He said to call and let you know when I had something, and I have two things. One we'll have to look at this afternoon, though. The owners are eager to sell. It's not going to last."

"I can meet you around three."

"Do you want to call Seth?"

She thought about how weird he'd been about her looking at houses alone and decided she should ask him to come along.

"Yes. I'll call him. I know it's short notice but if he can't make it, I'll see it alone. If he can make it, he might be able to decide today."

Bill laughed. "He might have to."

"Okay. I'll call him now and let you know."

She headed for a nearby coffee shop. Not only did she have time to kill, but she was also hungry. Her dad's comment about her being too thin echoed in her head, backing up something similar Seth had said in Paris, so she bought a premade sandwich and Danish pastry to go with her coffee. A far cry from the pastries she'd had in Paris. But this was her life now.

She found a seat and called Seth. "Bill has a condo he thinks is perfect for you but it's also going to go quickly. He said you'll have to see it today."

"This afternoon?"

"Yes. I'm to call him with a time. I won't be out of John Gardner's office before three, so what if we tell him three thirty?"

"Sounds good."

"Okay. I'll call him then text you the address."

She disconnected the call and ate her lunch. With food in her stomach and a great interview under her belt, she walked into John Gardner's office a confident woman. She explained to John and his staff that she'd been looking for condos with Seth, had a real estate agent she was working with and she would happily be the person who takes the first look at potential condos for them.

John asked for her fee. She gave him the number Seth suggested and within what felt like ten minutes, she was hired.

Shell-shocked, she walked out of the building and onto the sidewalk. With the money in her account from the sale of her and Clark's condo and the down payment on her services being wired in by John Gardner's company, she could afford a cab to get to the condo Bill wanted her to see.

She called for an Uber car. Now that she had more than a little bit of cash, she wouldn't be foolish…

Not that she'd thought Clark had been foolish.

She shook her head to clear those thoughts, got into the Uber car when it arrived and headed for the condo Bill wanted to show Seth.

As soon as she turned from paying the driver, she saw Seth standing just inside the double-door entrance, his hands in the pockets of his black leather jacket.

Her breath stalled at how gorgeous he was. His dark hair was just a little mussed, probably from a ride in his convertible. His dark eyes narrowed as he looked for her. When he saw her, his lips lifted into a warm smile.

Her heart flipped again.

She couldn't stop the tingles that coursed through her when she entered the lobby and he caught her hand. "You look fantastic."

She did a quick turn to show off her new outfit. A navy blue blazer over an orange flowered sheath and heels. It felt so good to be in heels again.

"It's amazing what new clothes will do for someone."

But she knew it was more than that. It had to be. She never felt more alive than when she was with Seth. Or more confused. How could she be happy around someone who seemed to be the exact opposite of the man she should love. Someone who didn't want what she wanted?

They told the doorman they were there to look at a condo with Bill Reynolds and he smiled. "Penthouse."

Harper and Seth exchanged a glance. "If that's the one Bill's showing today, then I guess we're going to the penthouse."

The doorman took them to a hidden, private elevator, and used a key card to set the car in motion. They rode in silence for what seemed like forever, then the doors opened on a huge great room with a wall of windows that displayed a view of Manhattan that looked close enough to touch.

She stepped out of the elevator. "Oh, my God."

Seth walked out behind her. "Wow."

The owner must have already moved because the place was empty. Shiny white marble floors winked at them.

Seth turned to the right and then the left. "I don't see a chandelier for the dining room or a kitchen."

"That's because they are separate rooms." Bill walked toward them, hand extended.

Seth shook it. "*This* is the living room?"

"Can you imagine having a party here?" Bill said, gesturing around the room. "Plenty of room for guests. But just think of that view at night. The lights of the city glowing from tall buildings. The moon hovering over them."

Harper could picture it. "It's so gorgeous," she said reverently.

Bill gestured to the left. "Let's take a look at the kitchen."

They followed him to a door that opened onto a butler's pantry with white cabinets and plenty of counter space to be a staging area for serving dinner, then into an all-white kitchen with stainless-steel, restaurant-grade appliances.

Harper walked from one appliance to the next, checking things out, and realized everything was new. "I'd get lost in here." She laughed. "It's huge. And everything's just been replaced. Why remodel and move?"

Bill shrugged. "Markets fall. Fortunes change. What this couple thought they could afford in January is now way out of their budget. If this thing sells today, they get a stake for a second chance."

Harper certainly understood that.

Bill showed them the dining room across from the butler's pantry, another room with spectacular views of the city. Two guest suites had the view on the other side of the building and the master suite—a sitting room, bedroom, dressing room, two closets and a bathroom the size of Seth's current kitchen—had yet another view of the city.

When they had gone through the entire place, Seth said simply, "I want it."

"There are two other bids."

"Do you know what they are?"

Bill frowned. "Sorry. No."

"Then let's come in at one-point-five million over asking."

Bill's mouth fell open.

Harper gasped. "Seth, that's a lot of money."

Seth didn't hesitate. He faced Harper. "When I see something I want, I go after it."

She gave him a curious look and he knew what she was thinking. He'd told her he wanted her, but after his talk with Jake, he'd backed off.

He might seem like a hypocrite to her, or a gentleman. He had no idea, and he also didn't care to find out. Things were better with them as friends, not even considering becoming lovers.

Even if he wasn't accustomed to walking away from things he wanted.

Oblivious, Bill said, "Let me call in your offer."

"Great. I'll call my bank."

Halfway through dialing, Bill stopped. "Are you telling me this is a cash offer?"

"Yes."

Bill grinned. "I think you just shot yourself to the head of the line. I'll need a cashier's check for a down payment to hold it."

The previous owners had left behind a desk, desk chair and two tufted chairs in the office. Seth excused himself to go into that room to call his banker. He made the arrangements, including having the check taken to Bill's office by courier, then he and Harper walked to his Ferrari.

"I hope you get it."

He opened the car door for Harper, realizing they were close again. Not just physically but emotionally. They were both thrilled that he'd found a home and if there was anybody he'd want to celebrate with, it would be her.

"I do, too."

"I've never seen views like that."

He scoffed, glad they'd found a safe topic of conversation. "Not even at your mother's?"

"No. And if she sees yours she's going to be house hunting again."

The second the words were out of her mouth, she shook her head, as if she regretted saying them.

Seth waited and finally she said, "I enjoyed my visit with my parents yesterday." She peeked across the car at him. "They loved seeing Crystal."

As much as she didn't want to admit it, she needed her parents, her family. Amelia Sloan might be a bit of an oddball, but Seth would bet with a few ground rules she'd be a good mother and a wonderful grandmother.

"That's great."

"It was."

Her voice had an unexpectedly wistful quality to it that made Seth want to ask questions, but he held back. Two years ago, when his father died, and Jake wanted him to work for McCallan, Inc., he'd agreed only to help his brother. But he'd worried about his relationship with his mom. Two years after his father's death, it felt odd still punishing his mother.

But it felt even odder thinking about getting warm and fuzzy with her.

When they arrived at his condo—soon to be Harper's if his offer went through—Mrs. Petrillo was watching a soap with Crystal happily sitting on her lap.

Harper needed to get out of her clothes, so she immediately walked back the hall to her room.

Seth debated a second, before he pulled Crystal from Mrs. Petrillo's lap. Not as a slick way to kiss Harper. She wasn't even around. Just as a way to hold her.

"I've missed you since Paris, kid."

Crystal giggled, then cooed. No prompting. No nothing.

"I think she likes me."

Mrs. Petrillo batted a hand. "She's been doing that all day. Laughing at nothing. Happiest baby I've ever seen."

She headed for the door.

"Don't you want to finish your soap?"

"No. Andrea annoys me. And she's on today. If there's one thing I know about soaps, it's that when a character starts off the episode, most of the scenes will have her in it. I'm going to make a sandwich, then get ready for bridge."

"Your friends coming to your house tonight?"

"We're meeting at a coffee shop." She grinned. "Something different. Old people usually don't like change, so my group deliberately shakes things up." She pointed a finger at Seth. "That's how you stay young."

Seth laughed as she walked out the door and when it closed behind her, he sat on the sofa, settling Crystal on his lap. "So, how are you today?"

He remembered Jake tickling Abby's tummy, so he tickled Crystal's belly.

When she laughed, he smiled.

That's how Harper found them. Crystal on Seth's lap, looking up at him with adoring eyes and Seth smiling.

"I'll take her."

Seth batted a hand. "No. No. She's fine. Besides, I thought I'd let you choose dinner tonight from the takeout menus. We have a lot to celebrate."

Harper only stared at him. She knew he'd made friends with Crystal in Paris, but it was more the look he was giving her baby girl that tripped something in Harper's heart. *He liked her.* Maybe he'd even grown attached to her.

She meandered to the drawer with the menus. "Is there anything a man who is celebrating likes to get for dinner?"

"I'll tell you what we should do. There's a steakhouse a few blocks from here that will deliver if I promise a two-hundred-dollar tip."

She laughed.

"I'm serious. And they have a wine list to die for."

"You want to get steak and wine?"

"And maybe some fries and a nice salad." He paused. "Actually, my mouth is now watering." He rose from the sofa, strolled over to her and handed Crystal to her. "Let me call."

The food arrived an hour later. The delivery man all but set the table for them and Seth generously tipped him, as promised. He pulled the cork from the wine and poured.

Harper had just put Crystal to bed. The room was quiet. There was no baby carrier on a chair or the table.

"This is nice." She hadn't meant to make the comment, but she couldn't take it back because it was true. It was nice.

She almost took a sip of wine, but instead held out her glass. "A toast. To you getting the most beautiful condo I've ever seen."

He clinked her glass. "I hope. I hadn't realized how ready I was to move or how much my life had changed. But it's time."

"And I benefit."

"Yes, you do." He met her gaze. "I never would have done this without you."

She snickered. "You needed someone to take your condo before you could get another?"

"No. I don't like to do things like look at houses. I have a hard time with salespeople."

She smiled at him. "It was my pleasure to help you. I would have done it for nothing."

"Don't sell yourself short."

"I don't."

"You do. You're a smart woman who is going to get an entry-level job and work her way up the corporate ladder."

She shook her head. "How do you know?"

"Because you have talent and ambition. I told you, I remember how hard you worked when you had the assistant company. Even then I thought the sky was the limit for you."

Warmth coursed through her, along with happiness. "I do have a baby to support."

"And you're a great mom." He held out his wineglass again. "Let's toast that. It's not easy being a working mom, but you'll do it."

"I will." Happiness glowed inside her. She couldn't remember ever feeling this good. She had a baby she loved, a condo soon to be hers, a consulting job that would pay her about a year's salary and she'd aced an interview.

She finished her wine and he filled her glass again as she picked up her knife and cut a piece of steak. When she tasted it, she groaned. "This is amazing."

"Aren't you glad I'm a nice enough guy that everyone's willing to deliver to me?"

"I am."

"So, tell me about the interview."

She told him about meeting with Human Resources first, then taking two tests, then talking to Max. He listened intently, didn't interrupt, didn't interject.

"He said he'd call either way. If got the job or didn't."

"He's a good man."

Harper turned thoughtful. "He really seems to be."

"He was one of the companies that refused to do business with my dad."

Because that was the last thing Harper expected to hear, she needed a minute for it to sink in.

"You like him because he wouldn't do business with your dad?"

"In a way, yeah." He set his fork down. "Max not even considering doing business with our company gave Jake the feeling he could have an ally when he eased our dad out of the chairman position for our board."

"Jake eased your dad out of his company's chairman position? I never heard any of this. Not even as gossip from Clark."

"Jake went behind the scenes to figure things out about McCallan, Inc. Our dad had been cheating subcontractors out of money, lying, fudging bids, that kind of thing, and Jake couldn't handle it. He got enough allies on the board to have someone else appointed chairman. Max became one of Jake's mentors. Which helped him when our dad died unexpectedly a few years ago. Our company now is nothing like what it was when Dad ran it. In a way, we have Max to thank for that."

"Wow." She almost couldn't believe what he had told her. But then again, she'd known there were reasons beyond rich-kid rebellion that Seth had left his family.

"I think you'd fit very well into Max's organization. You're honest and kind. You've won over our doormen and Mrs. Petrillo without blinking an eye."

She felt her face redden. "That was pretty easy. They're all nice people."

"See? Only a really kind person deflects praise."

She rolled her eyes. "Whatever." But she had to admit the fact that he thought her kind gave her another confidence boost. That and the way he felt she'd fit into Max Wilson's organization.

She almost told him about her mom, about the thoughts

she'd been having the past couple of days. That it was time to make up, but she wasn't sure how.

But the baby fussed, and when she went to her room to check on her, she couldn't get her back to sleep. Her eyes were red-rimmed from crying, her cheeks wet with tears.

She carried her out to the living room, where Seth sat watching a baseball game.

When he saw her, he said, "What happened?"

"I don't know. Could be any one of a number of things. I think I need to call the pediatrician."

"Give her to me so you can talk."

He took Crystal and settled her on his lap, but as soon as Harper started talking, she began to cry.

Seth got up from the sofa and walked with her, talking soothingly as he approached the windows at the back of the sitting area. He pulled open the drapes, showed Crystal the lights beyond the glass, and she stopped crying.

Harper stared at him at them, her heart aching. Whether he knew it or not, someday he'd make a great dad.

She watched them for a few minutes as she waited for the pediatrician to come to the phone. When he came on the line, he listened to Harper's explanation and suggested that Crystal was probably getting her first tooth. He told Harper to examine her gums, see if she could feel a bump or see any redness and to apply an over-the-counter gel.

As soon as she disconnected the call, Seth turned from the window. "What did he say?"

"That she's probably teething, I should look for signs of it and use an over-the-counter teething gel."

"Can we get it locally?"

"I already have it. Teething can start as early as three months, so I bought some for when her teeth began to come in."

"Smart."

She walked over to take Crystal from him. "I just know to be prepared."

They set the baby in her carrier and Harper looked at her gums. "They're red."

She swiped a finger along the space that seemed the deepest shade of red and felt the bump.

"Yep. This is it. She's getting a tooth."

"Did you hear that, Crystal? This time next week, you can be eating steak with me and your mom."

She laughed, then sniffled.

Harper rose. "Stand by the carrier while I get the gel."

She raced into her room, found the gel and was back in a few seconds. She smoothed it across Crystal's gums then rocked her until she fell asleep.

After taking the baby to her crib, she walked out to the sitting area and plopped down on the couch. "This might turn into a long night."

"Might?" He laughed. "I think you could be up every twenty minutes."

She turned her head along the back of the couch to look at him. "Unless the gel works."

He nodded. "Unless the gel works."

She couldn't get over how comfortable he was, not just with Crystal but with the teething. "The first night I stayed here, you woke up when she cried."

He shrugged. "I was a newbie."

"You were."

"Now I'm a pro."

"Not a pro but close."

He got up from the sofa and went to the kitchen, where he grabbed a beer. "I'd offer you one, but I take it you're on duty."

"I know. I'm glad I didn't drink that second glass of wine."

He ambled back to the sofa. "So, what are you going to do? Sit up all night and be available for when she cries?"

"Maybe."

"Seriously?"

"This my first baby. My first new tooth."

He laughed. "I won't drink this beer and I'll take a shift."

She gaped at him. "Don't be silly. You have work in the morning."

"I know. But I feel like I should help."

"We'll be fine."

But he put the beer back in the fridge. The TV still played softly in the background with the sounds of the baseball game turned down low enough that that didn't interfere, but when someone hit a home run and the crowd erupted with a shout, Seth looked at the screen.

"They're winning."

"They are."

"Clark loved the Yankees."

Harper nodded.

They were quiet for a few seconds, then Seth quietly said, "Ever feel bad that he's missing out on all these things with Crystal?"

She shook her head. "I should but I don't." She took a long breath, wondering what to say, what to hold back, and in the end she decided to be honest. "I don't think he'd have helped much with Crystal." She sneaked a quick peek at Seth. "Don't get me wrong. He wanted her. He wanted a family. But he'd have been more of an observer in her baby years. Happy to wait until she was old enough to throw a baseball or ride a bike before he got involved."

Seth looked shocked. "Really?"

"Yeah."

"But she's so funny."

"He'd have been able to resist her cuteness." She paused again. Bit her tongue once, but couldn't stop herself. She said, "He was more interested in business. I think he saw his place as being the one to provide the income and me the one to make the home."

"Sounds dangerously like my dad."

"Clark wouldn't cheat subcontractors."

"I know that. I'm sorry. It's just that my dad left all the home stuff to my mother, too."

The truth burned on her tongue. Not that Clark was bad, but that she was angry. Seriously angry that he hadn't involved her on decisions that had affected her future.

She felt herself losing the battle, knew she couldn't hold back anymore. "Do you know my name wasn't on our condo?"

He peered over at her. "Clark didn't put your name on the deed?"

"After I found the huge mortgage on the condo, I understood that he hadn't put my name on, so he could use it as an asset."

Seth's mouth opened then closed. After a long sigh, he said, "I'm not going to tell you that's normal because I think you know it isn't."

"He did a lot of weird things. More than juggling our money and assets. Things like scheduling things on the same day I had planned to visit my parents or the same day my parents were having a party." She sucked in a long breath, not quite disgusted with herself for talking about Clark, but not about to stop, either. "I don't think he kept me away from my parents for any reason other than he knew we didn't get along. In his own way, I think he was protecting me."

"Maybe he was."

"*You* don't do things like that, though. You don't tell me where to go or what to do. You've almost been a supporter of my parents."

He glanced at her, one eyebrow raised. "I'm the one who thought of the charade."

"Yeah, but you also say things like my mom's not so bad or she needs to see the baby." She pressed her lips together, then blew out a long breath. "I don't know where I'm going with this except that I had to talk to someone. Explain how I feel so I don't let my thinking go too far." She took another breath for courage before she said, "The month before I moved in here I stopped making excuses for Clark and started seeing him as a normal guy."

Seth didn't seem impressed. "We're all normal guys."

"I think all those months I stayed at home after Clark died, I was trying to hold onto the fairy tale. I didn't want to tell my mom Clark had failed because I didn't want to face it, either. I wanted to pretend everything was fine, even as my life was falling apart around me because of decisions he'd made."

"It's pretty difficult for a knight in shining armor to stay perched on a white horse his whole life."

She laughed. "I know. And I'm not angry with him. It just feels weird to settle into the knowledge that my husband wasn't perfect. That he had some pretty big faults. And he lied to me. Maybe not straight-out lied, but he didn't put my name on our condo, got a mortgage, leveraged the firm I thought was a cash cow."

"I understand. Try finding out your dad has a mistress… has had several mistresses. Kids think their dads walk on water. When I found out my dad was supporting a woman across town I was shell-shocked."

"That is bad."

"It gets worse. He never hit us, but he was a mean, spiteful person. He loved being in charge. He loved making people squirm. Even me and Jake." He shook his head. "Especially me and Jake. When we finally figured that out, we were at university, both broke, both jobless and soon-to-be out of our dorms because our dad hadn't paid for them, Jake learned to play the game. He got a job, earned money, said all the right things to our dad. I left my dorm and moved in with Clark. We both ended up the same… earning our own way. But it leaves a mark when someone you trust cheats you."

"It does." She caught his gaze. "Clark hadn't really cheated me, except for not putting my name on the condo. And I worry that when I tell this story to my parents, they're going to think I'm stupid."

"No. It might put another nail in their dislike of Clark, though."

She pulled in a breath. "So, how's your mom since your dad died?"

"Good." He frowned. "But we're not as close as I think she'd like us to be."

"Are you going to fix that?"

"A week ago, I would have said no." He shrugged. "Tonight, I don't know."

They both grew quiet. Harper looked at her watch and noticed the hour. "I better try to get some sleep. As soon as that gel wares off, Crystal will be up."

Seth flicked off the TV. "I'm going with you. I have to be up early tomorrow."

They headed down the hall, side by side. Quiet. Each lost in their own thoughts.

But when they reached her door, Seth stopped, too. "I know it hurt you that Clark kept so much a secret. But you've come out of this a very strong woman."

Pride shimmered through her. "Thanks."

She looked up as he looked down and the same temptation that always hit her when they were close eased through her. His eyes changed, went from happy to serious in a blink. Then he bent and kissed her.

The quick sweep of his mouth across hers raised goose-

flesh but there was more to it than that. There was no surprise as there had been in the first kiss, no demand as
there had been in the second kiss. Emotion warmed this
kiss. Genuine affection. They'd gone from two people unexpectedly attracted, to two people who cared about each
other and could talk to each other. She didn't have to be a
psychic to realize Seth probably didn't talk about the fact
that he and his mom weren't close.

Warmth filled her. Attraction blossomed in a new way,
a more potent way. If she touched him now, it would be
with affection, not curiosity. Which was stronger, more
powerful. She'd give every cent she had to take away his
pain over his dad, every cent she had to make him happy.

He pulled away, ran his thumb along her lower lip.
"Hope you get at least an hour tonight."

She laughed. "I was kind of hoping for two."

He smiled. "Good night."

"Good night."

She watched him walk down the hall to his room, new
feelings fluttering inside her.

He liked her.

He didn't feel sorry for her. Didn't feel he had to take
care of her, be around her out of obligation.

He liked her.

CHAPTER TWELVE

THE NEXT MORNING Seth woke up and tiptoed past Harper's room, careful not to awaken either baby or mother. He took the Ferrari to work, rode the elevator to the McCallan executive floor and walked to his office, feeling the strangest things.

Happiness, of course. He'd helped Harper get her life back on track, and last night he'd talked her through her resentment about Clark. To do that, he'd had to tell her about his dad, but he hadn't hesitated.

And she'd understood.

Which filled him with something he could neither define nor describe.

He tried to analyze it. She might have understood because Clark had done something similar to what his dad had done. Clark's sins weren't nearly as egregious as his father's. But there was a common thread there that had given them an understanding of each other's situation.

He was just about positive that was why he'd kissed her. And why the kiss had been so different, filled with emotion. What had started off as a light caress had formed a connection of some sort. Maybe a bond.

He'd forever remember Crystal's first tooth, remember Harper shopping for clothes, remember her struggling to right her life…and her listening about his dad.

It made him feel strange. Vulnerable in a way, but not really because he knew she'd never tell anyone. Not ever.

Which took him back to being happy.

Jake strolled into his office, a stack of contracts under his arm. "These are for you." He looked up from the contracts, saw Seth and frowned. "What's up with you?"

"Nothing's up with me."

"You have a silly look on your face."

"It's not a silly look. It's the expression of a guy who stayed up most of the night, listening for Crystal crying because she's getting a tooth."

"A tooth?" Jake laughed. "You are in for a lot of sleepless nights."

Worrying about Harper, he said, "How many?"

"I never counted Abby's, but it seemed like just when one tooth would come in, another would start." He winced. "It's not fun."

"We can handle it," he said, without really thinking it through.

Jake studied him. "But you don't like babies. And you're not sleeping with Harper. What were they doing there?"

"She and the baby have been living with me since Harper's apartment sold. That's how we slid into dating." He decided to shift the conversation back to Crystal. "When you're living with a baby, you either grow to like her or figure out someplace else to sleep."

"So, you like her."

"Have you seen Crystal? She's cute as a bug." Realizing he sounded smitten, he added, "But if all goes well, I could be out of my condo in another few days. Two weeks at the most."

Jake took a seat in front of Seth's desk. "You found a place?"

"I did. A couple remodeled a penthouse then couldn't afford it. Everything's new. I offered top dollar."

"So you can leave your apartment?"

"No. So Harper can have an apartment…and I can get a bigger place. Something more suited to my needs."

Jake frowned. "Are you breaking up with Harper?"

The question, though irrelevant because they weren't really dating, sent a shaft of confusion through him. What would they do when he moved out?

"We can still date."

Jake rose. "But you won't. Once you leave, I'm pretty sure you'll move on. Too bad." He nodded at the contracts on Seth's desk. "Legal team has those. They'll be briefing you in two weeks. It's your choice if you want to muddle through them now, then get their memorandums, or if you want to read the legal memos and then read the contracts."

Jake left Seth's office and he sat back in his chair, once again feeling strange.

It didn't seem right to leave Harper. Especially with Jake's prediction that once he moved out, he'd move on. Things weren't really settled for her. She might have had a good interview, but she didn't yet have a job.

He didn't have his new condo, either. As much as he liked it, maybe he should hope the deal would fall through?

His phone rang. Bill Reynolds's name and smiling face popped up on his screen.

Harper awakened after eight. In the crib by the bed, Crystal slept soundly, which was natural, given that she'd cried from three to five.

Grateful both she and the baby had been able to fall back to sleep until eight, Harper walked to the kitchen to warm a bottle and make herself a cup of coffee.

There were a million things to think about today. First, if Seth got his penthouse, she would be moving in here. They hadn't talked about furniture, but she had her own. Not that she didn't like his, but he could use it until he bought new or even donate it to a charity.

That meant she had to get herself onto the schedule of a moving company. The last time she'd been lucky that the mover had had a cancellation. She couldn't count on that again.

She also needed to think about her job. If she got the position with Max, she'd need a babysitter, maybe day care. But after talking with Seth, realizing that his dad had been the worst parent possible, she had begun wondering if she should offer her mom the chance to keep Crystal one day a week.

It was strange to consider her mom for such a big job. But talking to Seth the night before had settled so much of her thinking. She understood that she could love Clark and not like some of the things he'd done in their marriage. She saw that her mom could be a heck of a lot worse, and that it was time to mend their relationship. Giving her a day with Crystal might be a good first step, if only because by offering she'd be telling her mom she trusted her.

Because she did. And she wanted her family back.

Her good mood increased, and she knew she owed that to Seth.

Thinking about him reminded her of their kiss at her bedroom door and her heart contracted. The three best kisses of her life had all been given to her by Seth.

Seth.

With his kindness, commitment to his brother and the family company, commitment to helping her—the widow of a friend—and his obvious love for her daughter, he was amazing.

Crystal began to cry, and Harper took the bottle from the water warming it. She checked the temperature on her wrist, approved it and raced into the bedroom.

"Hey, angel."

Crystal blinked up at her mom.

"Are you feeling better?"

The baby smiled.

"That's a very welcome smile."

She lifted Crystal from the crib, changed her and took her to the kitchen for her bottle. But when she was done eating, the baby glanced around, as if looking for something...someone.

"Oh, you're wondering where Seth is."

She gave her mother a sleepy-eyed smile.

"He's at work. And pretty soon your mom will be going to work, too." Although staying home with Crystal had much more appeal. She thought about the idea Sabrina had so easily tossed around: resurrecting her virtual-assistant company and staffing it with college kids. She wondered if the hundred and fifty thousand dollars she had in the bank was enough for startup capital and money to live on until the business got off the ground and decided she'd call Sabrina and ask her. Seth's sister wasn't just a smart woman; she counseled start-ups.

She picked up her phone just as it rang. Glancing at caller ID, she saw Max's company name. Shifting Crystal to her hip, she clicked on the call.

"Hello?"

"Hello, Harper. This is Julie at Max Wilson's office. I'm calling to let you know that if you still want the job as Max's assistant, it's yours."

Her plans for resurrecting her small business weren't clear enough yet to refuse a sure thing. "I want it."

"Good. You start next Monday. Report to Human Resources at eight."

"Okay. Thank you."

Happiness bubbled up inside her, as she disconnected the call. She shifted Crystal to her other hip and dialed her mom.

"Harper?"

"Yeah, it's me. I'm calling to tell you I got a job."

"Oh. Well, that's great?"

"It is great, Mom. I didn't tell you that Clark had mortgaged our condo and I had to sell it, or that he'd also leveraged the investment firm and I'd had to sell that, too."

"Oh."

The surprise in her mom's voice was expected. What was unexpected was the ease with which she could pour out the truth of her life to her. She'd thought this conversation would be hell. Instead, the truth flowed out naturally.

"He'd used the firm to as collateral to get a loan to buy Seth's share. The market fell right after he died, and I barely got enough when I sold it to pay off the loan."

"That's awful."

Harper's breath caught. Her mom had sympathized, and her voice sounded sincere.

"It was awful. Seth and I aren't really dating. He was letting me live here until I straightened everything out."

"He's a good guy." Her mother huffed out a sigh of disappointment, but didn't say anything about the charade. She let it drop as if she understood. "You should have called. Your dad and I could have helped you."

"I wanted to handle it on my own." And now she was glad she had. Very glad. She'd gotten herself out of debt and learned to trust again. Seth helping her hadn't just staved off homelessness. It had given her back her faith in humanity.

She swallowed hard when that realization brought tears to her eyes.

He'd given her so much more than a place to stay.

"Anyway, I am totally on my feet now. But here's the interesting part. I thought maybe you'd like to take the baby one day a week. Not just because I'll be working, but because it would give you and Crystal a chance to get to know each other."

"Oh, Harper." The happy surprise in her mom's voice humbled her. "I'd love to."

"I'll have to find a daycare first. Then we'll talk specifics."

"That's fabulous. Your dad's going to be so thrilled."

"Thanks, Mom."

"You're welcome, sweetie."

"I have some more calls to make, so I'll talk to you once I know."

"Okay. I love you."

"I love you, too, Mom." Tears filled her eyes again as she hung up the phone. For the first time in eight years, she meant that.

When Seth arrived home for dinner, Harper had a feast waiting for him. "What happened?"

"What makes you think something happened?"

"You only go all out for dinner when you're nervous."

"I'm not nervous. I got the job."

His mouth fell open. Surprised and overwhelmingly pleased, he raced over, picked her up and swung her around. "That's great!"

"And I talked to your sister this afternoon about starting up my virtual-assistant business again. She says I can do it part-time for a year or two while I work for Max and see where it goes."

He looked up into her smiling face. "You've gone from no job to two jobs?"

"Yep."

He laughed and slid her down to the floor. He hadn't missed the easy way he'd caught her by the waist and lifted her up to swing her around. When she'd first come to his house, he'd never imagined they'd get this close. Yet here they were.

"I have a piece of news, too."

"Take off your jacket, wash your hands and sit down. You can tell me while we're eating."

"Okay."

He walked down the familiar hall to his bedroom, slipped out of the jacket and into the bathroom, where he washed his hands. Though Harper had never been in this room, everything about his condo seemed different tonight. Warm and cozy in the crispness of the October air. The scent of something Italian filling his nostrils. The sounds of cooing Crystal coming from the baby carrier sitting on the table.

"She sounds happy tonight."

"She is. The tooth isn't through by a long shot, but apparently babies get a break from the pain every once in a while. If you want to play with her after dinner, I would if I were you. We never know when the pain will be back."

Seth nodded, but sadness shot through him when he looked at Crystal and thought about how he'd soon be leaving.

Harper took her seat and handed him a spatula to dig out a helping of baked ziti. "Looks good."

"It's just one of those things I love to make." She smiled at him.

He watched her, his heart thrumming. He'd loved seeing her laugh with Sabrina at the cocktail party, thought there was no one more beautiful when she laughed…except she was more beautiful now. Contentment shone in her eyes. But also the light of expectation. She was securely on her new road in life now.

But so was he.

"I got the penthouse."

Her eyes widened. "Oh, Seth!" She bounced out of her seat and hugged him. "That's wonderful."

"Wonderful for both of us."

She returned to her seat, her head tilted. "More wonderful for you. I certainly want this condo and appreciate your generosity. But you wanted a new place to live, too."

He did. He loved that penthouse. "It's pretty awesome."

"Who doesn't love a kitchen fit for a caterer with a butler's pantry and a formal dining room?"

"I think more about a Christmas party in the huge living room with the lights of Manhattan as a backdrop."

Her eyes lit. "Can you imagine if it snows?"

"That would be cool."

"No, that would be ambiance."

He laughed and dug into his ziti, feeling a bit better about his move.

"What are you going to do about furniture?"

He took a bite of pasta, chewing as he thought about it. "This ziti is great."

"Thanks."

"I think I want to totally redecorate."

"Oh…that would be fun."

"Really?"

She playfully slapped his forearm. "Of course! I can almost see the beautiful rooms in my head and the possibilities."

He nearly asked her if she wanted to help him, then remembered that she had a full-time job, wanted to resurrect her assistant business and had a baby to care for.

He couldn't ask.

"I got the keys to the place today. It'll take a couple of weeks before it's officially mine, but because the owners are moved out and they happily cashed my check for the down payment, I got the key card to the elevator. The place is mine."

"That's great."

Harper had meant to say that with enthusiasm—instead her voice had faltered. Through all their weeks of planning for her to get a job and him to get a condo, they'd been hoping for this. Instead of being happy for them both, a thick, ugly sadness had planted itself in her chest.

"When does your job start?"

"Next Monday."

"Have you thought about daycare?"

"Already called. Four days a week she's in the daycare in the building of Max's company."

"Four?"

"One day a week she'll be with my mom. My dad's even thinking of taking the afternoon of that day off."

He sat back. "Wow."

"When I called her, my mom was confused at first about why I'd want a job, but I told her about Clark and the mortgage and leveraging the firm. Then I asked her if she wanted to babysit one day a week and she was happy." She bit her lip. "Actually, I told her I'd only been living with you. We weren't really dating."

"Oh." He didn't say anything for a few seconds, then he glanced across the table and caught her gaze. "How'd she take it?"

"It was barely a blip. I think she was so happy that I'd asked her to keep Crystal one day a week that she was stunned. I also think it's time for us to make up. To be a family again."

"So do I." He set his fork down. "It's like all your loose ends are tying up."

She nodded.

It felt right and yet wrong that she didn't need him anymore. Not that she wanted to depend on someone, more that it had been nice to share her burdens. Nice to have someone to talk to, someone to share her life with.

"When do you move into the penthouse?"

"I could go tonight."

She laughed, thinking he was kidding.

"I have a cot. Avery and Jake are meeting me at the house in the morning. Before work."

Her heart stumbled. "You're really leaving? Tonight?"

"It would be better to be sleeping there, so I'd be there when they arrive. Eventually, though, I'd have to come back for my things."

But by the time he got around to it, she'd already be working. He could come to the condo when she wasn't here, clear out his stuff, arrange for his furniture to be sent to a charity, and she'd never even see him.

Silence settled over the table. The ziti didn't seem so tasty anymore.

On the verge of tears, Harper noticed Crystal had fallen asleep in her carrier. "I better take her to the crib."

Seth's eyes took a slow trip over to Crystal. "Yeah. She looks beat."

"I wanted her to catch up on sleep today, but she wanted to play. Probably because she was feeling better."

"Maybe she'll sleep tonight."

"I hope."

She pulled the carrier off the table, but Seth suddenly rose. "Let me give her a kiss good-night."

He walked over and bent down to press a soft kiss on Crystal's forehead, something he'd never done before.

Harper's chest expanded with love, then flattened with regret. It had taken him weeks to get adjusted to the baby and now he was leaving.

Probably tonight.

By the time she got the baby into bed and returned to the kitchen, he was scraping his ziti plate to put it into the dishwasher.

"You're leaving now?"

She said it like a question, but she knew what was happening. All news was out on the table. She had everything she had needed from him. He had his new penthouse, a place he was clearly excited to get to.

They were done.

Ask him to stay.

The words popped into her head as a soft suggestion. She looked at him closing the dishwasher door, and tried to will her mouth to move, but she couldn't. She was the one who'd told him nothing romantic could happen between them.

But he was the one who'd told her he wasn't the guy to settle down with. He was the guy to experiment with.

She'd worked too hard and too long to get her life back in order. Wouldn't asking him to stay be like messing it up again?

Seth walked back to his bedroom, grabbed his jacket and a prepacked bag he had ready for spur-of-the-moment out-of-town trips and headed up the hall again.

Harper wore a strained smile. He knew what she was thinking—their change of fortune had happened too fast. He really didn't have to leave but even he saw the handwriting on the wall. A moment of weakness would be awful for them both. He'd told her his terms. He didn't do permanent, but he did do fun. If they got soft again with each other tonight, shared more secrets, another kiss, they'd end up in bed. He had to leave now—

Unless she understood that sleeping together didn't mean anything except a moment of happiness for both of them?

Ask me to stay.

He willed the wish across the room. Not so much because he wanted to sleep with her but because he wanted another night. Being vulnerable with her had been exquisite. He'd never shared so many of his secrets with anyone. Mostly because he knew other people wouldn't understand. She had understood. They'd talked things out. Both her troubles and his.

Now he just wanted one night of real closeness. If the sadness on her face was anything to go by, she wanted it, too.

"You know you don't have to go."

That wasn't what he wanted to hear from her. And she knew it. She had to ask him to stay, not tell him he didn't have to leave. He couldn't ask her. He'd already asked once. She had to say it.

Ask me to stay.

She pressed her lips together and stepped back. Shakily. "Okay, if you need anything…"

Disappointment tumbled through him. "I can call."

She nodded.

He looked into her pretty blue eyes, stalling to give her another ten seconds to change her mind. When she didn't, he headed for the door.

Regret tried to fill him, except part of the reason he liked her was her honesty. The sweet, sweet knowledge that she'd never lie to him, never manipulate him, only tell him the truth. She wanted more than he could give. He had to accept that.

He opened the door. Stepped out in the hall. Almost knocked on Mrs. P.'s door to say goodbye, but he thought better of it.

As much as this hurt, he needed the clean break, or he'd pine after her for weeks, maybe months, the way he'd done after Clark asked her out and she'd accepted.

CHAPTER THIRTEEN

SETH AWOKE THE next day to the sound of the house phone. Knowing only the doorman had the number, he raced to get it.

"Yes?"

"Your brother and sister-in-law are here."

"Send them up."

He slid into jeans and a big T-shirt and got to the great room just in time to see the elevator open and his brother and Avery step out.

Avery said, "Wow."

Jake agreed. "It's huge and gorgeous."

"Can you see the parties here?"

Jake laughed, but Avery walked around nodding. "Elegant parties."

"I'm not sure about elegant. I'm still young enough to be a little bad." But in his head, he saw what Avery saw: the room as neat as a pin, with sofas and tables, flowers and a fire in the fireplace, and the backdrop view. All because he had other rooms. A den. An office. A room that could be a playroom. A master suite big enough to have a nursery beside it.

He sucked in a breath. He knew why he'd had the thought, but he blocked it. He and Harper were not a good match.

The house phone rang again.

Jake winced. "I forgot to mention that I invited Mom. We had dinner together last night. I told her you'd bought a new place and somehow she wheedled it out of me that Avery and I were seeing it before work."

"It's okay." He picked up the phone. "If that's my mom, send her up."

Avery and Jake poked around in the butler's pantry, kitchen and dining room while his mother rode up in the elevator. When they heard the doors open, they returned to the great room.

"This is amazing," his mother said as she glanced around. "So much room." She faced Seth. "You have the entire top floor?"

"Gorgeous views from every room."

She nodded sagely. "Good for resale value."

He wished he could do what Harper had done. Come clean with his mom and get a fresh start. But Harper hadn't suffered humiliation, as he had. And his mom had turned a blind eye. How did they talk about that? Forgive that?

He turned toward the butler's pantry. "Wait until you see the rest of the place."

He took them through the kitchen area, dining room, guest bath, two guest bedrooms, the master suite and then another two guest suites.

"It's huge." His mother gaped at the view from the second guest suite. "Big enough for a family of six."

Jake laughed, but Seth shot him a withering look.

Jake only smiled, looked at his watch and caught Avery's elbow. "We have to go."

She glanced at her phone. "Yes, we do." She walked over and kissed Seth's cheek. "It's a lovely home. I'm sure you will enjoy it immensely."

When they were gone, Seth suddenly realized he was alone with his mother. Misery nagged at him. He had so many questions.

His mother put her hands on her hips. "What are you doing?"

Hoping she couldn't read his mind, he said, "Showing off the house I've always wanted."

"Where's Harper?"

Harper. He'd spent the night fighting thoughts of her. Thoughts of Paris. Thoughts of propositioning her and her not wanting what he wanted. Feelings had bubbled up, spilled over. But in the end, he'd done the best he could for her.

"Right now, I'm guessing she's enjoying the condo I'm giving her for cost."

Her eyes narrowed, and she made a sound of disgust. "Really?"

"You don't like that I'm not charging her interest?"

"I don't like that she's not here, helping you plan, talking about decorating this place, talking about a wedding."

Seth groaned inwardly. Now, he understood. And since Harper had come clean with her mom, he could come clean with his. "Mom, Harper and I were only dating because she had financial problems she didn't want her parents to know about. She'd sold her condo and didn't have time to get another. She would have been on the street, if I hadn't helped her."

She shook her head. "You like her. Maybe even love her."

He sniffed. "Where in the hell would you come up with an idea like that?"

She walked up to him and scrutinized his face. "From your eyes."

He turned away.

"You bought a house with a nursery attached to the master."

"Some people might look at that and see a reading room."

She tossed her hands in despair. "Seriously. You love that girl and she loves you. What is wrong with you?"

He spun around to face his mother. "How dare you ask me what's wrong with me when you know damned well why I think marriage is a sham! You and dad had the worst marriage in the world. He should have left you if he wanted every woman he looked at, or you should have kicked him out and saved your pride. Instead, you lived together like two miserable inmates in a prison..."

She gasped. "Seth!"

"It's true!"

"Okay. I'm going to let you get away with insulting me and your father since I've never talked about any of this with you. But this conversation is once and only this once. The truth is I tried to leave your father twice, but I had this crazy thought in my head that even a bad father was better than no father."

"I think we all know that's not true."

"Do you think he wouldn't have tormented you from a distance if I'd moved you out of his home? Of course, he would have. But first he would have told you lies about me. Your father was a miserable human being who would have used you, Jake and Sabrina as pawns. I knew it. No matter what I'd said or done, he would have ruined you three. As it was, he got a shot at you but not with the big ammunition he would have had if I'd left him and filed for divorce. He would have never accepted a divorce. A black mark. A failure. Everyone did his bidding or they suffered."

The air backed up in Seth's lungs. He'd never considered that his mean, manipulative father wouldn't have accepted a divorce. But why would he? Why should he? He was vindictive. Cruel. Sometimes, Seth even believed his dad had enjoyed being cruel.

Even if his mom would have left, his dad would have had visitation rights, maybe even filed for custody. He would have tormented them with lies about their mother. He would have tormented them period.

He rubbed his hands down his face.

"Do you understand?"

"Yes." Because his dad was a miserable human being. A master manipulator. A liar. "You stayed with him to save us from the third level of hell."

"Essentially, yes. But, Seth, not all marriages are like that. Look at Jake and Avery. They're happy. Not only that, very few people are like your father. Especially not Harper."

He sucked in a breath.

"She'd make you so happy." She shook her head. "No. She's already made you happy. You're calmer, content. When I heard you were looking for a new place, maybe even a house in Connecticut, I was sure you were nesting, making a home."

When Seth said nothing, she walked over to him. "I know you saw a lot of things a little boy shouldn't see. I'm sorry for that. But if you walk away from Harper because of your father, he wins again. He doesn't just strip you of your childhood or make your adolescence miserable, he steals your life. Your love. Your first real chance for happiness."

With that she turned and walked to the elevator, her footsteps echoing around him, reminding him of how empty his life had been until Harper moved in.

He glanced around at the huge room that Harper wanted to see decorated at Christmas, thought of the room in the master suite that could be a nursery and wondered if his subconscious didn't agree with his mom—

He'd bought this place for the family he so desperately wanted.

Harper's cell phone rang far too early. She looked at the time, saw it was close to ten and tossed off the bedcovers. A quick peek in the direction of Crystal's crib showed she was still sleeping. The baby had fallen asleep after her seven o'clock feeding and so had Harper. She'd tossed and turned the night before, miserable and alone without Seth.

She answered the phone with a groggy "Hello."

"Hey, it's me."

Seth.

Her heart broke all over again. He was probably calling to tell her about arrangements he'd made for his furniture or clothes.

"I'm still at the penthouse. I have a decorator coming around noon, and I wondered—"

"If I'd meet with her?" Her vision clouded with tears. She should say no. It was better not to see someone you wanted but couldn't have. But she couldn't take the quick separation. She needed to wean herself away from him. Needed to see him at least one more time. And even if he wasn't there while she met with the decorator, she'd have to tell him about their meeting. Maybe he'd even come here to talk?

"Sure. I'd be happy to meet with her. You go ahead to work."

"Actually, I'm going to be here, too."

Her heart jumped at the chance to see him. "Okay. I can be there at noon."

"How about eleven thirty?"

"I'll need to call Mrs. Petrillo…"

"You have plenty of time. I'll have one of the limos downstairs to meet you at eleven fifteen so you're here at eleven thirty."

That surprised her, but given that this was such short notice, it made sense. "Okay."

She drank her coffee, showered and dressed before Crystal woke.

When her little girl was fed, she walked her to Mrs.

Petrillo's door. The older woman took the baby with an expression of glee and Harper headed downstairs.

She found the limo just as Seth had said and took it to his new building. She walked inside and found the doorman.

"I'm Harper Hargraves."

He handed her the key card to the elevator. "Mr. McCallan said to give you this."

She almost winced. There was only one reason he'd give her the elevator key. As much as she liked him and wanted to remain friends, she couldn't take charge of decorating his entire penthouse. She knew what would happen. At some point, her willpower would disappear, and they'd sleep together…and he'd tire of her.

That was bitter reality.

She took the elevator to the top floor. The doors opened automatically. She stepped out into the echoing great room.

"Seth?"

"Over here."

He stood by the wall of windows, looking at Manhattan.

"I know you called me here because—"

He turned from the window, caught her gaze. "I love you."

Her heart stopped. Her breathing stopped. But she was positive that she hadn't heard correctly, so she said, "What?"

"I love you. I realized it last night. I wanted to stay, but you wouldn't ask me."

His words paralyzed her. Not because she didn't believe him. Because she did. He was too sensitive, too serious to lie about something so important.

Still, he might love her, but he couldn't make a commitment. And she needed a commitment—something. Even if it was just that they would live together.

"Seth, I get that you have feelings for me. But we discussed this." She shook her head. "You told me that you're not the guy who settles down. You're the guy to experiment with."

He had the audacity to laugh. "Things change."

Disbelief made her shake her head again. "Just like that?"

He got down on one knee. Pulled a ring box from his jeans pocket.

Her breath stuttered.

"I want to marry you."

She stared at the beautiful emerald cut diamond. "Oh, Seth." She wanted to believe him. But even as her heart leaped for joy, her common sense shuddered with vulnerability. "A person doesn't change overnight."

Still on one knee, he laughed again. "My mother tells me I've been changing since the day you moved in."

She could almost believe that because she'd been falling in love with him bit by bit since she first saw him standing in his doorway, yanking a T-shirt over his pecs and abs.

"But the truth is I loved you before Clark. I've loved you since I moved in next door to you. I let Clark ask you out because I knew I was damaged goods."

She kneeled in front of him, pressed her palms to his cheeks. "You're not damaged goods."

"I was. For the longest time I was. I thought I couldn't settle down, thought kids were scary, thought I'd hurt any woman who loved me." He caught her gaze. "You changed all that."

She whispered, "I did?"

"You accepted me for who I was, wasn't afraid to push me to do the duties a good friend should do and kiss like nobody I've ever kissed before."

She laughed. "It has been different."

"An adventure." He kissed her, light and brief, a promise of things to come. Then he presented the ring box to her. The gorgeous emerald cut diamond winked at her.

"Want to see where this adventure goes?"

Happy tears pooled in her eyes. She threw her arms around him. "Yes!"

The phone rang. "Good, because that call is probably the doorman telling me the decorator is here."

He stood up, reached down and helped her to rise. "I love you."

"I know." She searched his eyes, finding only truth and sincerity there. "I love you, too."

"Well, there you go. It certainly took you long enough to say it."

The house phone rang again. He strode over to answer it. "Hello." He winked at her during the pause. "Send her up."

"Ready to make this place a home?"

She stood on her tiptoes and kissed him. "Absolutely."

He caught her waist, hauled her to him and kissed her deeply. Her chest tightened. Her stomach tingled and everything inside of her suddenly wished they were back at the old condo with no decorator coming and a perfectly good bed, where they could try out this new love that they'd found.

The sound of the elevator door made them draw apart. Seth slid his hand around her waist and greeted the tall, slender woman.

"Mrs. Green?"

She walked over, hand extended. "Yes. It's nice to meet you. And this must be—"

"My fiancée."

A huge smile broke out on Harper's face, not just because he hadn't hesitated but because she loved him and he was hers.

Forever.

EPILOGUE

THEY MARRIED ALMOST two years later. Their August wedding was filled with lilac and pink, and a beige gown for the red-haired maid of honor, Avery. Crystal, two years old now, served as flower girl alongside Abby, who was nearly three years old—both wore pink.

Sabrina McCallan watched as Harper walked up the long aisle of the cathedral, her exquisite jeweled veil flowing behind her. Her mom's veil. Because it was so fancy, Harper had chosen a simple satin dress with cap sleeves and a skirt that eased out at the waist, into a long layer of satin that formed a train.

Sabrina's brother, Seth, watched his bride with love in his eyes. He looked good in his tux, and Sabrina had to admit she knew they were a perfect match. The beautiful waif and her handsome, strong, knight in shining armor.

Harper's father finished the walk up the aisle with his daughter and as he handed her off to Seth, Sabrina saw the tears in his eyes.

Then Harper and Seth stood before the pastor to say their vows and promise to love each other forever. Crystal fussed at the end of the ceremony and Harper stopped and scooped her into her arms before she and Seth walked down the aisle out of the church.

Jake and Avery, best man and maid of honor, also

stopped to get Abby. Avery looked amazing in the pretty pale dress, even with her six-month-pregnant belly.

Before Trent Sigmund, aka Ziggy, her brother's best friend and Sabrina's groomsman partner, could turn to walk her out of the church, Sabrina looked down at her own stomach. Six weeks along. That's what her doctor had said. She blew her breath out in a long, slow stream. In this family of people who loved kids, she was about to bring her own child into the fold.

Except she wasn't married.

And the baby's father didn't know.

And she had no idea where his globe-trotting behind was...

* * * * *

Chapter One

"I love weddings."

Gavin Fortunado glanced at his sister Schuyler, who stood next to him in the ballroom of the Driskill Hotel in downtown Austin, her long blond hair pulled into an elaborate braided updo. The understated opulence and elegant decor of the historic venue only made the starched collar of the tuxedo he wore feel even stuffier.

"I know you do." Gavin drained the glass of bubbly champagne he'd raised after his father's toast to another sister, Maddie, and her new husband, Zach McCarter. The fizzy liquid churned in his stomach, and he looked toward the crowded bar, mentally calculating how long it would take to get to the front of the line and order a whiskey neat. He had a feeling he'd need something more substantial than champagne to make it through this evening.

He placed his empty glass on a nearby table as Schuyler wrapped her elegant fingers around his arm. "Maddie is a beautiful bride," she said as she leaned against him, dabbing at the corner of one eye with her free hand.

"Yep." He patted his sister's hand. "You were, too." Schuyler had married Carlo Mendoza, vice president of Mendoza Winery, last spring in the sculpture garden at the winery in the Texas Hill Country outside the city. Just as he had this weekend, Gavin had flown in from Denver for Schuyler's big day. He loved his three sisters and appreciated that two of them, who were now married, had picked great guys. He liked and respected both of his brothers-in-law. Any guy who was man enough to take on Schuyler or Maddie was definitely ready to join the family.

Speaking of Schuyler's husband, where was Carlo now? Gavin could use a diversion before Schuyler started in on him.

Too late.

"I'm sure you'll find a beautiful bride, as well." Schuyler gave his arm a squeeze. The touch was gentle, but somehow Gavin felt like an animal caught in a steel trap. Sweat beaded between his shoulder blades and rolled down his back. He groaned inwardly as he noticed the line at the bar had gotten longer.

"You did a great job with all the wedding planning," he said, ignoring his sister's comment. "I know Maddie appreciated it since she's so wrapped up in the Fortunado Real Estate Austin office right now. I don't know how you convinced Mom to allow another wedding to take place here instead of in Houston. I thought she'd pressure Maddie and Zach to get married closer to home."

"It's only a couple hours' drive from Mom and Dad's house, but Maddie couldn't spare any extra time. She and Zach are burning the real estate candle at both ends these days."

Gavin loved all his sisters and brothers, but he and Maddie were only nine months apart in age, so they'd always been especially close. Her relationship with Zach had gotten off to a rocky start last year, as both of them had been vying to be named the new president of Fortunado Real Estate, the company Kenneth Fortunado had founded and devoted his life to for years.

Of the six Fortunado children, Maddie was the one most invested in the family business, although the baby of the family, Valene, was quickly coming into her own as a real estate agent. Their oldest brother, Everett, was a successful doctor. Connor worked as an executive at a corporate search firm in Denver so Gavin hung out with him on a regular basis. Ever since coming to Austin last year, Schuyler had joined the staff of the Mendoza Winery, heading up branding for the company. Gavin had spent his entire career with a corporate law firm headquartered in Denver. He knew his parents were proud of all of them, but Maddie had the same passion for real estate as Kenneth, and she'd gone toe-to-toe with Zach until they'd fallen in love.

It made Gavin smile to see his practical, pragmatic sister head over heels, especially since Zach was the perfect partner for her, as driven and dedicated to the business as Maddie.

"Maybe you'll be the one to tie the knot in Houston," Schuyler suggested cheerily. "I could see it at—"

"Stop." Gavin managed to extricate himself from his sister's grip without having to resort to chewing off his own arm. "I'm not getting married. What is it with everyone and this obsession with weddings? Mom and Dad have been dropping not-so-subtle hints since I stepped off the plane."

Schuyler sighed. "We want you to be happy."

"I *am* happy," Gavin insisted.

She arched one delicate brow in response. "You could be *really* happy."

Gavin rolled his eyes. He wasn't about to get into an argument about his level of contentment. Of course he was happy. Why wouldn't he be? He had a great job working with a prestigious law firm and was on track to be named partner within a year. He owned a fantastic loft in the bustling Lower Downtown neighborhood. The city was a perfect mix of urban and outdoorsy, with enough cowboy left to appeal to his Texas heart. Plus, Colorado offered almost limitless opportunities for the adrenaline-pumping adventures Gavin couldn't seem to get enough of during his downtime. He rock-climbed, mountain-biked and skied every weekend throughout the winter. Well, not this January weekend since he was at his sister's wedding, being subjected to the third degree by his well-intentioned family.

"Look at Everett," Schuyler continued, pointing across the room to where their brother stood talking to a friend of their parents'. His wife, Lila, was at his side, Everett's hand on her back. "He's happy."

As if on cue, Everett glanced down at Lila, and the

tenderness in his gaze made Gavin's chest ache the tiniest bit. Lila smiled up at him, practically glowing, and he drew her in closer. Gavin studied the couple, high school sweethearts who'd reunited last spring after years apart. There was something different about them tonight, a new kind of energy to their already strong connection.

Schuyler nudged him, drawing his attention back to her. "Don't you want a woman to look at you like that?"

"What I want is a drink," he told her. "And for you to drop the subject of my love life."

"When was the last time you had a serious girlfriend?"

Never, Gavin thought to himself. He only dated women who wanted the same things he did: fun, adventure and a good time. "Would you like a glass of wine?"

"You didn't answer my question." Schuyler placed her hands on her slim hips. As Maddie's matron of honor, she wore a burgundy-colored cocktail dress and matching heels that gave her a few extra inches of height. At six feet two inches tall, Gavin still towered over his petite sister. Her classic features and tiny frame made her look like any other beautiful young woman, but Gavin knew underneath the subtle makeup and coiffed hair beat the heart of a tenacious fighter. Once Schuyler latched on to a cause, she gave "dog with a bone" new meaning. It had been that determination that had led the Fortunados to the discovery that they were actually part of the famous Fortune family.

Schuyler loved a challenge and a quest, and Gavin didn't relish being her next one.

"Who says I don't have a serious girlfriend?" he

countered, willing to say just about anything to make her drop the subject. "Maybe I just didn't want to subject her to my crazy family."

"I don't believe you."

"Doesn't make it less true. If you all weren't such true-love tyrants, I would have told you about it before." Gavin smiled to himself. That should be enough to keep her occupied for a while.

He realized his mistake as her eyes lit with excitement. "Who is she? How long have you been dating? Why didn't you bring her to the wedding?"

"I'm heading to the bar," he said, invoking his big-brother selective hearing. "I'll get you a glass of Chardonnay. Oh, and it looks like Maddie is having trouble with her train. You have work to do, sis."

"Gavin, I want to hear about your lady."

"Maddie needs you. Gotta go." He moved around her, dodging like he was back on the high school football team when she reached for him.

"Valene can help. Wait… Gavin."

He waved over his shoulder and called, "Back in a sec," having no intention of returning to his sister. She'd regroup soon enough, anyway. Another glance over his shoulder showed Schuyler following him.

He tugged at his collar and glanced around, catching the eye of the slim redhead standing near the corner of the bar. Not exactly catching her eye, as he got the impression that she'd been watching him approach. Either way, she was a friendly face and he'd take it.

"Christine," he called, not daring to check on Schuyler's approach. He wrapped an arm around Christine Briscoe's shoulders. "Great to see you. How have you been? You look lovely. Shall we dance?"

"Um…" Christine, who'd worked for his father's real estate agency in Houston for close to a decade, seemed at a loss for words. That was fine. Gavin didn't need her to speak. As long as she came with him.

The man standing next to her, average height with dark hair and the start of a paunch that indicated he'd done too many keg stands back in college, frowned and made to step forward. Gavin took an immediate dislike to the guy but flashed a grin and held up one finger. "You don't mind if I steal Christine for a dance, right?"

He didn't wait for an answer. He grabbed Christine's hand—soft skin and fine-boned, he noticed—and tugged her toward the dance floor, breathing a sigh of relief as he saw that Schuyler had been waylaid by a distant cousin on their mother's side of the family.

The music changed from an up-tempo dance number to a slow ballad. Automatically, he wrapped his arms around Christine's waist, careful to be respectful of her personal space since he'd basically hijacked her for this dance.

She lifted her hands to his shoulders and glanced up at him.

"Hi, there," he said with his most charming smile.

"Hi," she breathed. "You, too. Well. Thanks. Yes."

He felt his mouth drop open and closed it again. "I think I missed part of the conversation."

She tugged her bottom lip between her teeth and his mouth went dry. He'd known Christine for years, but how had he never noticed the way her mouth was shaped like a perfect Cupid's bow, the lower lip slightly fuller and damned kissable, if he had the inclination?

Which he didn't. He couldn't. She was a cover to save him from his sister's meddling in his private life.

Clearly, Schuyler had messed with his head because he'd never thought of Christine as anything more than a casual friend before this moment—never gave her much thought at all if he had to admit the truth.

"I'm responding to your comments," she answered, somewhat primly. "It's great to see you, too. I'm well. Thanks for the compliment. Yes, I'd like to dance."

"Ah." He felt one side of his mouth curve. This time the smile was natural. Why did it feel so unfamiliar? "You're precise."

She frowned. "Oh, you weren't looking for a response? The questions were rhetorical." Color flooded her cheeks and it fascinated him to watch the freckles that dotted her skin almost disappear against the blush. "I should have figured."

"No... I..." He shook his head. "I'm a little bit off my game tonight."

"Your game," she murmured.

"Not that this is a game," he amended quickly. "It's a wedding."

"Your *sister's* wedding," Christine agreed, sounding amused.

"The Fortunados are dropping like flies," he said, glancing around for Schuyler, whom he thankfully didn't see in the vicinity. "Schuyler seems to think I'm next. Can you keep a secret?"

Christine nodded solemnly.

"I told her I have a girlfriend."

"But you don't?"

"No, and that's how I like it." He pulled her closer to avoid a couple trying some sort of complicated spin and tried not to notice the feel of her soft curves pressing against the front of his tux. This dance was about avoiding Schuyler. Nothing more. "For some reason, my sister can't seem to accept that. It was easier to lie, although I'm not sure she believed me."

"I'm sure you could find a girlfriend if you wanted one."

He grimaced. "But I don't want one. Not even a little bit."

"Oh."

He had the strange sensation that he'd disappointed her and didn't like the feeling.

"How's Denver?" Christine asked quietly after a moment of awkward silence between them.

"Good," he answered and struggled to come up with something better to say. Something interesting. Charming. Gavin was well-known for his charm. He had an easy way with women that made him popular, even with his ex-girlfriends. Where was that legendary charm now?

He couldn't figure out what the hell was wrong with him. Had he allowed Schuyler to rattle him that much? Hell, he came from a family of six kids. Good-natured teasing was nothing new.

"Did you cut your ski trip short to come to the wedding?"

He blinked. "I did, actually. How did you know?"

"Your sisters talk about you a lot," she said. She stiffened in his arms, making him regret questioning her. He liked dancing with Christine. She was just the right height and her body fit against his perfectly. She smelled clean and fresh, like strawberries or springtime or sunshine. Okay, that was stupid. Sunshine didn't have a scent.

He needed to get a hold of himself, but all he could

manage was hoping she'd relax into him again. The song ended and another ballad began. Gavin would have to tip the bandleader later for his sense of timing.

"Do you ski?" he asked, tightening his hold on her ever so slightly, splaying his hand across her lower back.

She laughed, low and husky, and his stomach flipped wildly. He hadn't expected that kind of laugh from strait-laced Christine Briscoe. "No skiing for me. I've never even been to Colorado."

"You'll have to visit," he told her. The way her eyes widened in shock was like he'd invited her to have wild monkey sex on the hood of his car. The image did crazy things to his breathing, and he pushed it out of his mind.

"Th-things are b-busy," she stammered, "at the office right now."

"That's right. You moved to Austin to manage the new branch. My dad mentioned that."

"I'm originally from Austin, and it was a great opportunity," she confirmed. "Of course, I loved working for your dad in Houston, too."

"Of course." He felt the sensation of someone staring at him and glanced toward the bar. The man Christine had been standing next to was still there, shooting daggers in Gavin's direction.

"Did I steal you from your boyfriend?" Even though it was no business of his, he didn't like the idea of this woman belonging to another man.

She shook her head, her full mouth pursing into a thin line. "Maddie and Zach invited everyone from the Austin office to the wedding. Bobby and I work together, but that's all, despite his best efforts. He's a good real estate agent but can't seem to understand that I'm not interested in dating him. In fact, you kind of rescued me."

"So then I'm your hero?"

Christine blushed again, and Gavin couldn't help but wonder what it would take to make her whole body flush that lovely shade of pink.

"I don't know about that," she murmured, her gaze focused on the knot of his bow tie.

He forced a chuckle, ignoring the pang of disappointment that lanced his chest at her words. What was going on with him tonight? He didn't want or need to be anyone's hero. "Already you know me too well," he said as the song ended.

Her eyes darted to his like she'd been caught with her hand in the cookie jar. "I should get back to…um… the bar." She squeezed shut her eyes then opened them again and offered him a lopsided smile. The first strains of a popular country line dance song started. "I'm not much for this kind of dancing."

"We have that in common," he told her then led her through the crowd. "Thanks for helping me out," he said as they stopped at the end of the bar. At least the guy from earlier was nowhere to be seen. He waited for her to say something, oddly reluctant to have this strange interlude come to an end.

She crossed her arms over her chest and nodded, barely making eye contact. "Enjoy the rest of your night."

"You, too," he said and took a step away, to be almost immediately stopped by an old family friend.

He glanced over his shoulder to see that Christine had already turned toward the bar. She was well and truly done with him.

Gavin didn't have much experience with being blown off by a woman, but he recognized the signs just the same. Christine Briscoe obviously wasn't having the same reaction to him as he was to her. He was more disappointed than he would have imagined.

Chapter Two

Christine picked up the glass of wine the bartender placed in front of her and drained half of it in one long gulp.

She'd just had her heart's desire handed to her on a silver platter and she'd made a mess of the whole thing. Gavin Fortunado might not be a hero, but he'd been her secret crush since the moment she'd set eyes on him almost ten years ago.

For ten years she'd harbored fantasies about her boss's adventurous, drop-dead-gorgeous youngest son. Then tonight, out of nowhere, he'd taken her into his arms, like a scene from every Hallmark movie she'd ever watched. And she loved a good romance.

Unfortunately, Christine hadn't even been able to put together a decent sentence. He'd actually flirted with her. Of course, Gavin flirted with everyone. Not that she knew him well, other than adoring him from afar, but he'd come into the Fortunado Real Estate Agency office in Houston often enough over the years.

She'd watched his easy banter with his sisters as well as the women who worked in the office. He was always charming but respectful and had a knack for remembering names and details. Half the women she knew in Houston had a crush on him, and she imagined it was much the same in Denver.

At first, when his gaze had met hers as he strode toward the bar, she'd thought he might call her out for staring. She'd been trying to ignore Bobby, who seemed to think he was God's gift to women. He was harmless but annoying, and Christine wasn't sure why he wouldn't give up on her. Maybe because she had very little social life to speak of so he assumed she should be grateful for his attention.

Irritated was more like it.

He'd been blathering on about some property he couldn't close, and Christine had been watching Gavin talk to Schuyler. Or rather argue. She was used to seeing Gavin smiling and jovial and hadn't understood the tension that made his broad shoulders appear stiff. Unlike her own, the Fortunado family was tight-knit so it bothered her to see the brother and sister at odds.

She'd been shocked when Gavin had approached the bar and taken her hand. It might have been a simple dance to him. For Christine, having Gavin pull her close, her body pressed against his, was the culmination of all her secret desires come to life. Of all the single women at the reception, he'd picked her. Did that mean something?

Probably not, but a girl could dream. Sadly, all she'd

be left with was her dreams since she'd been so discombobulated that she hadn't been able to truly enjoy the moment. Or relax. Or hold up her end of the conversation.

What was the point, anyway? Gavin lived life in the fast lane. She could barely get out of first gear. Normally, her boring routine didn't bother her. She was good at her job, had a cute apartment and a sweet rescue dog that adored her. She owned her own car and one designer purse she'd splurged on last year. The barista at her neighborhood coffee shop sometimes remembered her order, which never failed to make her feel special. She had a good life.

Only occasionally did she think about what it would be like to have more. To be fun and sporty like her sister, Aimee, or confident in the way of the Fortunado sisters. To be the kind of woman who could attract a man like Gavin.

She took another drink of wine and turned back toward the reception. The dance floor was filled with wedding guests, all of them laughing and swaying whether they had rhythm or not. Christine should join the crowd. Despite her two left feet, she loved to dance. But the thought of drawing attention to herself made her cheeks flame. Drat her pale Irish complexion. She had no ability to hide her feelings when her blush gave them away every time.

She had a travel-size powder compact in her purse. Maybe a little freshening of her makeup would help her feel more confident. Out of the corner of her eye, she saw Bobby heading in her direction. She grabbed the glass of wine and slipped into the hallway, turning the corner toward the bathroom, only to find her way blocked by Gavin and Schuyler. Immediately, she slipped behind a potted palm, curiosity about the Fortunados getting the best of her despite the fact that it was wrong to eavesdrop.

"Come on," Schuyler urged. "At least tell me her name. A name and then I'll leave you alone."

"You don't fool me for a second," Gavin said, amusement and irritation warring in his tone. "I'm not telling you anything."

Schuyler threw up her hands. "Because this mystery woman doesn't exist. Admit it, you aren't dating anyone."

Gavin opened his mouth, but Schuyler held up a finger. "At least not anyone serious."

"Oh, it's serious. It's also none of your business."

"Tell me something about her. One thing, Gavin."

"She has blue eyes," he answered without hesitation then added, "And fiery red hair."

"A ginger." Schuyler rubbed her hands together. "I need more details."

Gavin shook his head. "You said one thing. I gave you two."

"Where did you meet? Why didn't you bring her? How long have you been dating?"

"Schuyler, stop."

"I can't," she admitted with a laugh. "I need a new project now that Maddie's wedding is over. You're it."

"I'm not," Gavin insisted, running a hand through his thick hair.

He looked so uncomfortable and unaccustomedly vulnerable that Christine's heart stuttered. Tonight was the first time she'd seen this side of Gavin. He seemed almost human…not so picture-perfect, and it made her like him all the more. Which was dangerous, because she already liked him way more than was wise.

Without thinking, she took a step forward, away from her spot behind the fake plant. Gavin glanced up for one instant, and he looked so darn happy to see her. She wanted that look in his eyes to last. So instead of retreating, as her brain instructed, she moved toward them.

Schuyler glanced over her shoulder. "Hey, Christine. Are you having fun?"

Christine swallowed against the ball of nerves stuck in her throat. "It was a beautiful wedding, and Maddie and Zach look really happy. You did an amazing job with the planning."

"Thanks." Schuyler's smile was so genuine, Christine almost let the conversation end there. She was an honest person who valued her job and the relationships she'd forged with each of the Fortunados. But dancing with Gavin had been like eating a bite of cake after dieting for years. One taste wasn't nearly enough. She wanted the whole piece. "Please don't be upset with Gavin," she said, working hard to ensure her voice didn't waver.

Schuyler frowned. "Do you mean our argument out here?" She laughed softly. "Don't worry. It's a friendly brother and sister thing. I have to convince him to give up the name of the woman—"

"I asked him not to say anything." Christine wrapped an arm around Gavin's waist and leaned in close. "I wasn't sure if your dad would approve of us." She glanced up at Gavin and smiled. He was staring at her like she'd just sprouted a second head. Not exactly catching on to her plan, which made sense because she didn't actually have one.

"Wait." Schuyler gasped, her gaze ricocheting between the two of them. "What?"

Christine looked at Schuyler once more. "I hope you can understand…we wanted to keep things private. It was never my intention to deceive you, but—"

"Are you saying that you're Gavin's ghost girlfriend?"

"I know it probably comes as a surprise."

"Understatement of the century," Schuyler muttered. "You can't expect me to believe—"

"It doesn't matter what you believe." Gavin looped an arm around Christine, dropping a kiss on the top of her head that she felt all the way to her toes. "Christine isn't a ghost, but think about how you were giving me the third degree. I didn't want her to have to deal with that, not when I wasn't here to protect her."

Christine resisted the urge to whimper. Maybe it was the wine, but the thought of Gavin protecting her made funny things happen to her insides.

Schuyler's mouth dropped open. She stared at them for several long seconds. Christine tried to act normal and not like she might spontaneously combust at any moment. She rested her head against Gavin's chest, and as great as dancing with him had been, this took things to a new level. Without having to concentrate on the steps, she could enjoy his warmth and the feel of his rock-solid muscle. Not to mention the way he smelled, a mix of expensive cologne and soap. Would it be weird if she reached up on tiptoe, buried her face against his neck and just sniffed? Yeah, definitely weird.

She waited for Schuyler to call them out on the lie.

No way would anyone, let alone Gavin's perceptive sister, believe that they were a couple.

"Well…okay, then," Schuyler said slowly. "I'll admit I'm at a loss for words."

"Thank heavens for small favors," Gavin muttered.

"I still can't believe… I mean how long have you two been an item?"

"A while," Gavin said before Christine could answer. A good thing, too, because the reality of what she'd done was suddenly crashing over her.

"Don't tell your dad," she blurted, earning a frown from Schuyler and a gentle squeeze from Gavin.

"He loves you like you're part of the family," Schuyler told her. "You know that."

"He loves me *working* for the family," Christine clarified. "This is different."

"Gavin, tell her she has nothing to worry about from Dad or Mom."

"I have already, but you still need to honor Christine's feelings." He lifted a hand to Christine's chin, tipping it up until she was forced to meet his green eyes. This close she could see the gold flecks around the edges. She half expected to see anger or frustration for what she'd done, but he looked totally relaxed.

That made one of them.

"Christine makes the rules," he murmured and before she could react to that novel concept, he brushed his lips over hers.

The kiss started innocently enough. She had the mental wherewithal to register that his mouth was both soft and firm. He tasted of mint gum and whiskey, a combination that had her senses reeling.

She felt him begin to pull away and some small,

brave, underused part of her rebelled at the thought. She wound her arms around his neck and deepened the kiss, sensation skittering down her spine when their tongues mingled. A low moan erupted from her...or did the sound come from Gavin? The sound jolted her out of her lust-filled stupor and she jerked back. She'd had a couple glasses of wine, but not enough to excuse her basically mauling this man in front of his sister.

"I guess you guys are the real thing," Schuyler said with a laugh. "No one can fake that kind of chemistry."

"Right," Gavin murmured.

Christine kept her gaze on Schuyler. She had no idea what Gavin was thinking at the moment and was almost afraid to find out.

Schuyler wagged a finger at her brother. "Take care, big brother. Christine isn't like your usual girlfriends. She's special. Dad will kill you if you hurt her."

"I'm not going to hurt her," he said tightly, and Christine felt the arm still holding her go taut.

"He won't," she confirmed. She didn't need Schuyler reminding Gavin that she had nothing in common with the gorgeous, sexy women he usually dated. "He's amazing."

Schuyler laughed again. "If you say so. Shall we head back inside? I need a drink after this little bombshell."

"We'll meet you in there," Gavin said, and Christine wanted to argue. She wasn't quite ready to face his reaction to what she'd just done.

"Don't take too long," Schuyler told them, grinning at Christine. "Maddie should be throwing the bouquet soon. We need to position you front and center."

Christine tried to laugh, but it came out more like

a croak. "Sure," she managed and waved as Schuyler walked away.

When they were alone, she forced herself to turn to Gavin again. "I'm so—"

Her words were cut off as he fused his mouth to hers.

Gavin hadn't meant to kiss Christine again. He was still in shock from her announcement to Schuyler. He appreciated what she'd done. He'd been quickly running out of options when it came to distracting his sister from her obsession with his nonexistent girlfriend.

He owed her his thanks, but all he could think of was tasting her sweetness. His hands skimmed along the silky material of her dress, then over her hips, which held just the right amount of curve. And her reaction to him was a revelation. Straitlaced Christine Briscoe could kiss. She met him stroke for stroke, nipping at his bottom lip as if asking for more. Gavin lost himself in her, pulling her tight until her breasts pressed against his chest. As she had when they were dancing, she fit against him perfectly.

She was perfect.

How the hell had this happened?

Voices drifted from around the corner, and he took a step back, knowing the dazed look in her eyes probably mirrored the one in his.

"Hey, ladies," he called as a group of his mother's friends passed, several of them craning their necks to get a better look at Gavin and Christine.

He shifted so that he was shielding her from the curious gazes.

"We need to talk," he whispered when the women had passed.

Christine nodded, staring at the floor.

Gavin drew in a breath. Was she terrified of him now? She'd tried to save him from his sister, and he'd all but shoved his tongue down her throat. She'd seemed a willing participant at the time but now...

Another group of people turned the corner toward them, and Gavin automatically laced his fingers with Christine's and led her down the hall toward the hotel lobby. Her heels clicked against the pristine marble floors as they passed the stately columns that, along with the beautiful stained-glass dome, was the hallmark of the Driskill's famous lobby.

"Hey, Christine." The man she'd been standing with at the bar earlier, Bobby, waved from where he stood in front of the concierge desk. "A few of us are going to bail on the dancing and head to an Irish pub around the corner. Want to—"

"Oh, no," Christine whispered, her lips barely moving.

"She's busy," Gavin called and headed for the elevators along the far wall. She followed him in without protest but tugged her hand away as he hit the button for the fifth floor.

"Are you staying here, too?" he asked, not sure how to broach the subject of what had just happened between them. His wildly successful legal career had made Gavin believe he could talk his way out of any situation. Not so, apparently.

She shook her head, a lock of fiery hair falling forward to cover her cheek. Had he run his hands through her hair, loosening the elegant chignon? He couldn't remember but suddenly he wanted nothing more than to see the bright strands cascading over her shoulders.

He'd told his sister he was dating a woman with blue eyes and auburn hair. Maybe he'd been unconsciously thinking of Christine after their dance.

"Gavin, I—"

The door opened, cutting off whatever she was going to say to him. An older couple got in.

"Going down?" the man asked.

Gavin shook his head. "Up."

"We'll ride along," the woman offered. "You two look fancy."

"Wedding reception," Christine said quietly.

"I love weddings." The woman sighed. "Always so romantic."

Her husband snorted. "Except when your brother got sloshed and threw up on the dance floor at ours."

"He had food poisoning," the wife said, her tone clipped.

"Forty years." The man lifted his hands. "She still can't admit that her no-good brother's a drunk."

"At least he still shows up for holidays," the woman shot back. "Unlike your rude sister and her—"

"Our floor," Gavin interrupted when the elevator dinged. The door slid open, and he placed a hand on Christine's back. "I'm at the end of the hall," he told her when the door closed behind them with a snick.

His hand stilled as he realized her shoulders were shaking. Oh, God. Not tears. He could handle an angry jury or a recalcitrant witness. But tears killed him, especially the thought that he'd caused them.

"Don't cry," he whispered. "It will be—"

A sob broke from her throat. No, not a sob. Laughter.

She lifted her face, and he realized her tears weren't from anxiety, but amusement. "I know our relationship is five minutes long and a complete lie," she said, wiping her cheeks as she laughed, "but promise we'll never fight about your drunk brother."

He grinned and looped an arm around her shoulder as they started down the hall. "Fortunados can handle their liquor," he promised. "Do you have a sibling? I don't even know."

"A sister. Aimee is a year younger than me and perfect in every way."

"Perfection must run in the family."

As lines went, Gavin thought it was a pretty good one. Both subtle and charming. Christine only burst into another round of laughter. He was definitely losing his touch, although it was somewhat refreshing to be with a woman who didn't melt in a puddle at his feet. Gavin liked a challenge.

He wouldn't have pegged Christine as one, but this woman surprised him at every turn.

"I'm sorry," she whispered, clasping a hand over her mouth when a snort escaped.

He unlocked the hotel room door and gestured for her to enter.

"I hate to be indelicate," he said when they were both inside, "but are you drunk?"

She shook her head and drew in a shuddery breath. "It's just been a crazy night, you know?"

"I do. Would you like a drink now? I have a bottle of Mendoza red that was left in the welcome bag for wedding guests. Or water?"

"No, thanks." Now that her laughter had stopped, Gavin could almost see the wheels turning in Christine's brain as she became aware that she was alone with him in his hotel room.

"Would you feel more comfortable if I propped open the door?" He shrugged out of his jacket, tossing it onto the edge of the bed.

"I trust you," she whispered.

He blew out a breath, surprised at how happy the simple statement made him. He loosened his bow tie then undid the top button of his tailored shirt.

"Christine, I want to—"

"I'm sorry," she blurted. All the amusement from minutes ago had vanished from her features. "I shouldn't have butted into your conversation with Schuyler. You don't need my help to handle your sister and—"

"On the contrary. I want to thank you. You rescued me."

She wrapped her arms around her waist, and he could see her knuckles turning white from pressing her fingers against her rib cage. "I'm not sure what possessed me to get involved," she admitted. "I guess because you helped me with Bobby earlier."

"Bobby is a putz."

One side of her mouth curved, not a true smile but a step in the right direction. "That's true, which makes our situations different. Schuyler is your sister and she cares about you."

"She's also relentless." He took a step toward her, slowly, like he was approaching an animal that might spook at any moment. He didn't want to spook her. "Would you like to sit down?" He inclined his head toward the couch positioned in front of the room's large window. "We can talk about next steps."

Her cornflower-blue eyes widened. "Next steps. Okay."

He grabbed two bottles of water from the mini-fridge

and set them both on the coffee table before taking a seat next to her. "In case you get thirsty."

"You're really not mad?" She leaned forward and slipped off the heels she wore, revealing the most adorable painted pink toes Gavin had ever seen.

Hell, when was the last time he'd been with a woman? Granted, he'd been busy with work so his personal life had taken a back seat. But he was too far gone if a glimpse of toenail polish could mess with him like this.

"Christine, I'm grateful. I'd already made up a girlfriend. You made her a reality."

She tucked her legs underneath her. "And the kiss?"

"You'll never hear me complain about a beautiful woman kissing me."

She rolled her eyes. "I took it too far."

"You were convincing."

Color stained her cheeks. "Maybe I missed my calling. I should have been an actress."

"Hmm." Gavin didn't like the sound of that. It bothered him more than it should to think she'd been faking the kiss, even though that was what this whole thing was. A fake. He forced a smile, unwilling to let her see his reaction. Best to keep things light and casual, and he could do that better than almost anyone he knew. "I'm hoping you'll be interested in a repeat performance."

Christine made a sound that was somewhere between a yelp and whimper. "Of the kiss?"

Hell, yes.

"Actually, I was talking about you acting as my girlfriend." He ran a hand through his hair. "While I'm in Austin for the next few weeks."

"Weeks?" She uncurled her legs and dropped her feet to the thick carpet. For a moment he thought she was going to bolt. Then she placed her elbows on her legs and rested her head in her hands. "Weeks," she repeated on a slow exhalation.

"I'll make it worth your while."

Her head snapped up. "Like I'm a hooker?"

"Of course not." He shifted closer. "What I meant to say was it will be easy for you."

"You think I'm easy?"

"No. God, no." He leaned back, raised his gaze to the ceiling, hoping for some way to salvage this conversation. When he found no inspiration from above, he looked at Christine again, only to find her grinning at him. "That was a joke?"

She nodded. "You're different than I thought you'd be," she said quietly. "Not quite as perfect as you look at first glance."

"Is that a compliment or a criticism?"

She bit down on that full lower lip, and his insides clenched. "A compliment. It's good to know you're human."

"I don't usually like it when people tease me," he admitted.

"Oh."

"I like it with you."

"I'm glad." Another smile, this one almost shy. "I know you don't think I'm an easy hooker. You want me to pretend to be your girlfriend so your family leaves you alone. We'd have a fake relationship. That sounds simple."

Did it? Gavin wasn't sure what to make of his feelings for Christine, but they definitely weren't simple.

"Right," he agreed anyway. "One of the law firm's larger clients is based in Austin and we're finalizing a merger with another financial institution. Everything should be complete by the end of the month. It makes sense that we'd be together now, and then when I go back to Denver, you can break up with me."

"Like anyone is going to believe that," she said with a harsh laugh.

"Long distance relationships are tough. I don't think it will come as a huge surprise."

"The part where *I* break up with *you* is going to be the surprise." She sat back on the sofa, so close that he could feel the warmth of her body. "Your family knows you're a bit of a playboy."

"Am not."

She rolled her eyes. "How many women have you dated?"

He thought about that, grimaced. "Since when?"

"I rest my case," she told him.

"But this is different." He took her hand, laced their fingers together and looked directly into her eyes. "You've changed me."

Chapter Three

Christine felt her mouth go dry at his words. She'd changed him?

"At least that's what my family needs to believe," he clarified.

"Schuyler agreed not to tell anyone," Christine argued, although the thought of how she'd go about convincing people that she and Gavin were really a thing made goose bumps dance along her skin. Talk about the adventure of a lifetime.

"We *told* her not to tell anyone." He traced his thumb in circles against the sensitive skin on the inside of her wrist. "But there's no way she's going to be able to resist."

"So we'll need to convince your family this is real," she whispered. "Your parents will be upset they didn't know."

"They'll understand," he assured her. "I'll make sure they do."

"I hate lying to your father…to anyone in your family. They've been so good to me."

"This isn't going to change anything," he promised.

But Christine knew nothing would ever be the same. She should stop this charade right now, march downstairs and explain to Schuyler that it was all a big misunderstanding. Although she was sober, maybe she could pretend to be drunk. Blaming her crazy behavior on alcohol might give her a decent excuse.

Gavin's jacket began to ring. He stood and moved toward the bed, pulling his phone out of the pocket of the discarded tuxedo coat.

"Hey, sis," he said into the device. "No, I'm not coming back down." Pause. "Yes, she's with me." Pause. "I don't think she's going to care about the bouquet." Pause with an added eye roll. "Don't go there, Schuyler. I told you this is special. She's special. Let me enjoy it, okay?" Pause. "I understand and appreciate it. I love you, too." Pause. "Okay, I'll see you at the brunch in the morning."

He punched the screen to end the call then tossed the phone on the bed again.

"You missed the bouquet."

Christine stood. "I'm okay with that. You shouldn't be annoyed with Schuyler for calling. I don't want this to complicate things with you and your family."

He moved toward her. "My family is always complicated, especially now that the Fortunes are involved. My only concern is you. As much as I appreciate what you did earlier, if you aren't okay with this arrangement, we'll end it."

Here was her chance. A dance, a few kisses and she'd

go back to her normal life before the clock struck midnight, like some sort of Fortune-inspired Cinderella.

But she couldn't force her mouth to form the words. Despite this whole thing being fake, she wasn't going to miss her chance at getting to know Gavin. Under what other circumstances would a man like him choose to date someone like her?

Not that she was down on herself. Christine liked her life and felt comfortable with who she was. Usually. But she wasn't the type of woman who could catch Gavin Fortunado's attention. Until now.

"I don't want it to end," she said, embarrassed that she sounded breathless.

Gavin didn't seem to notice. He cupped her cheeks in his hands. "Me neither," he whispered and kissed her. Once again it felt like fireworks exploding through her body. The kiss was sweet and passionate at the same time. He seemed in no hurry to speed things along, content to take his time as he explored her lips.

Then his mouth trailed over her jaw and along her throat, her skin igniting from the touch. He tugged on the strap of her dress, and it fell down her shoulder. He kissed his way from the base of her neck to her collarbone. Her body was all heat and need. She wanted so much from this moment that she couldn't even put it all into words.

"You're so beautiful," he whispered.

The compliment was like a bucket of ice water dumped over her head. She wrenched away, yanking her dress strap back into place.

"Don't say that," she told him, shaking her head. "You don't have to say that."

Confusion clouded his vivid green eyes. "In my experience, women like to hear those words."

She swallowed. How was she supposed to respond without sounding like she was fishing for something more? That wasn't the case at all. In fact, she felt the opposite. She didn't want or need him to tell her she was beautiful because it simply wasn't true.

Christine prided herself on being pragmatic about her appearance. Growing up, she'd been a chubby girl with thick glasses and bright red hair that was more frizz than curls. Her mom had forced her to keep it in frizzy Annie-style curls that were anything but flattering. Christine had spent years enduring teasing, much of it led by her younger sister, until she'd become an expert at not being seen.

Aimee, with her larger-than-life personality and classic beauty, had been happy to step into the spotlight. She went to parties and on dates, while Christine spent most of her high school years in her room reading or listening to music. No one in her family seemed to notice or care as she slipped further into the periphery of their lives.

She'd decided to change things when she went away to college. She'd gotten contacts and started running, shedding the excess pounds that had plagued her for years. A bevy of expensive hair products helped her tame her wild mane, and the color had mellowed from the bright orange of her childhood. Her dad had called her "baby carrot" as a kid, and her sister had amended the nickname to "jumbo carrot" due to Christine's size. Even though she thankfully hadn't heard the nickname in years, it was how she still thought of herself.

She took pains with her appearance and she knew

she wasn't ugly. She was decent-looking, in fact. But beautiful? No, not to someone like Gavin.

"This is not real," she said, both for his sake and to remind herself.

Gavin's thick brows furrowed. "That doesn't mean—"

"What's your favorite color?"

"Um…blue."

"Mine's purple." She crossed her arms over her chest, aware he was still staring at her like he couldn't quite follow the direction of her thoughts. Join the club. Her mind and heart felt like they'd survived an emotional tornado, hurricane and maybe a tsunami thrown in for good measure, all in one night. "Favorite food?"

"Pizza."

"I like burgers and fries."

His mouth quirked. "That's kind of cute."

"Burgers aren't cute."

"You're admitting you like them as opposed to giving me some line about loving salmon and kale. That's cute."

"I take yoga classes and run before work. What do you do to work out?"

One brow arched. "So you're flexible?"

With a groan, she stepped around him toward the hotel room desk. "Do you want me to write all this down?" She picked up a pen and the small pad of paper with the hotel's logo.

"The ways you're flexible?"

"Gavin, be serious. You were the one who said your family would find out about us. We need to have our stories straight." Christine clutched the pen and paper to her chest and fought the urge to whimper as Gavin ran a hand through his hair. She could see the muscles of his arm flexing under his white shirt. "When did we meet?"

"We've known each other for years."

"Right. I mean when did we—"

"It was Thanksgiving break my senior year of college. I was getting ready to retake the LSAT after my not-so-stellar performance the first time around."

Christine inclined her head, surprised and charmed he'd remember the very first time they met. "You were studying in the conference room at the Fortunado Real Estate office. It was quiet because of the holiday."

"And I was bitter because my buddies had flown to Aspen for the weekend." He started undoing the buttons of his shirt, casually, as if it wasn't a big deal for him to be undressing in front of her. Of course, he wore a white T-shirt under the formal shirt, so it wasn't a true striptease.

Christine's heart stammered just the same.

"You were the only one in the office," he continued. "You kept bringing me coffee and takeout."

She shrugged. "It was my first week working for your father and I wanted to be helpful in any way I could."

"Do you remember what you told me after I'd complained to you for the millionth time about life being unfair?"

She shook her head. She hadn't remembered speaking to him at all. She'd graduated college a semester early and had felt lucky to be hired by Kenneth right away. It had taken almost a year on the job before she believed her boss wouldn't walk into the office and tell her he'd made a horrible mistake taking a chance on her. Having Gavin in the office during the quiet lull of the Thanksgiving holiday had made her so nervous. All she'd been able to do was refill his mug and send out for sandwiches.

"You told me to channel my inner Elle Woods."

Christine gave a soft chuckle. "I loved *Legally Blonde*."

"Clearly. You gushed about the movie. I didn't know what you were talking about," Gavin said with a grin. "I went back to my parents' house and rented it."

"You watched *Legally Blonde*?"

"Oh, yeah. I not only watched it, I was also inspired. I mean, if Elle Woods could get into law school, what excuse did I have?"

She snorted a laugh then pressed her hand to her mouth. "Tell me you didn't use scented pink paper for your admissions application."

"Not exactly." Gavin draped the crisp white shirt over the back of the desk chair then held up his hands, palms out. "If you tell anyone I said I was inspired by that movie, I'll deny it. But I might have Reese Witherspoon to thank for my law career." His smile softened. "And you."

Christine felt her mouth drop open. "I...had no idea."

"It seemed like a stupid thing to admit at the time. But I've never forgotten. You helped me then, and now you're saving my bacon once again. I owe you, Christine."

"It's not a big deal," she said automatically. But it was. It was that time he'd spent in the office poring over law books that had given her an initial glimpse of who Gavin truly was on the inside. Through the years she'd remained convinced he was more than the rakish attorney who was always scaling mountains or hurling himself down ski slopes in his off time. Back then he'd been nervous, vulnerable, and she hadn't been able to resist him. Just like she couldn't now.

She lifted the paper and pen. "We should still go over some more details if we're going to make this relationship believable." Not that it would be difficult on her part. One look at her face and it would be clear to everyone that she was already half in love with Gavin.

"How about we watch a movie while we talk?" He winked. "Elle Woods for old times' sake?"

"Sure," she whispered.

He picked up his jacket then patted the bed. "Make yourself comfortable. I'm going to order something from late-night room service. Can I tempt you with a hamburger?"

Christine started to shake her head but her stomach rumbled. "No cheese and medium-well, please."

He nodded. "Got it."

She placed the paper and pen on the nightstand and climbed onto the bed, butterflies racing across her stomach. She was in Gavin's bed. Or *on* it. Close enough.

He used the room's landline to place the order then clicked the remote to turn on the TV, searching until he found *Legally Blonde*. "I haven't watched this movie in years," he told her.

"It holds up," she said, choosing not to share that the movie was on her regular rotation of Saturday night rom-coms. It struck her that tonight was Saturday and here she sat watching a movie, as had become her weekly routine. Only tonight instead of curling up with her black lab, Diana, she was in one of the most beautiful hotels in Austin with Gavin.

She loved her dog, but this was way better.

Her nerves disappeared as soon as the movie started. She and Gavin talked and laughed, and then ate when the food arrived. He cleared the empty plates when the movie ended, placing the tray outside the hotel room door.

"I think you should stay a bit longer," he said, checking his watch. "The reception isn't scheduled to end until midnight, and knowing my family, they'll be closing down the place."

"I don't want to keep you from going to sleep," she said, stifling a yawn.

"Apparently, I'm not the one who's tired."

"It's been a kind of crazy night for me," she admitted.

"If you want to go I can—"

"We could watch another movie?" She smiled. "Something with lots of action to keep us awake."

"Good idea." He returned to the bed and flipped through channels until he found an old James Bond flick.

"Who's your favorite Bond?" she asked.

"Sean Connery." He moved to the center of the mattress. "In case you're interested, I make a pretty good pillow."

Her girl parts went wild. She scooted closer, and he lifted one arm, tucking her against his chest.

"I bet you're a Daniel Craig fan," he said, resting his chin on the top of her head.

"Every woman with a pulse is a fan of Daniel Craig."

She felt his chuckle against her ear, and the rhythmic up and down of his chest. As bizarre as the night had been, it was the stuff of her fantasies to be cuddling with Gavin. If only the night never had to end.

Chapter Four

Christine blinked awake, disoriented for a moment at the unfamiliar surroundings. The something—someone— moved next to her and the previous night came flooding back.

She turned to find Gavin asleep next to her, lying chest down with his hair rumpled and a shadow of stubble covering his jaw. Somehow they'd both ended up under the covers. He still wore his white T-shirt, and she was in her dress. The last thing she remembered was James Bond being served a shaken-not-stirred martini.

Now pale light spilled in from the room's picture window. She glanced at the clock on the nightstand. Seven in the morning.

Well, she'd successfully missed the end of the reception, but if she didn't leave quickly, she might run into the Fortunado family heading to breakfast.

With as little movement as possible, she slipped out of the bed. Gavin made a snuffling sound but didn't wake. Christine grabbed her shoes and purse. Without bothering to look in the mirror, she let herself out of the room.

She didn't need to see her reflection to know that she wasn't a pretty sight. She had no intention of allowing Gavin to see her this way, either.

The door closed with a soft snick, and she turned, only to come face-to-face with Valene, the baby of the Fortunado clan.

Her brown eyes widened. "Hey, Christine."

Christine smoothed a hand over her tumbling hair. "Hi, Val. Going to work out?"

Valene wore athletic shorts and a fitted tank top. Earbuds dangled from either side of her head. Her wavy blond hair was pulled back in a high ponytail. "Yeah. How about you?" One delicate brow rose. "That's Gavin's room, right?"

"Is it?" Christine's voice was a croak.

"And you're wearing the same dress from the wedding last night," Valene pointed out, none too helpfully as far as Christine was concerned. "Schuyler said Gavin left the reception early because he wasn't feeling well."

"I think he's okay now," Christine answered, purposely ignoring the question in the other woman's dark eyes. "Well, I should be going. Have a great day."

Without waiting for a response, she hurried down the hall, only taking a few steps before realizing that she'd be waiting for the elevator with Valene. Why did decisions made late at night rarely hold up to the light of day?

She breathed a sigh of relief when she noticed the

sign for the stairs, pushing open the door and racing down four flights. The stairwell led out to the parking garage. She shoved her feet back into the heels and made it to her Subaru hatchback and then away from the hotel without seeing anyone else she knew.

Thank heaven for small favors.

Quite small since she understood that although Valene had been shocked enough to allow Christine to escape this morning, there would be no avoiding the Fortunado sisters for long. Valene worked out of the real estate agency's Houston office but visited Austin regularly to help with establishing a new client base. Even if she didn't see Valene right away, the sisters would talk. Gavin seemed sure they didn't have anything to worry about, but Christine remained unconvinced.

Walking into her condo, she was greeted with an enthusiastic bark. Diana trotted toward her, tail wagging and ears pricked up. Christine smiled despite her tumbling emotions. Nothing like unconditional love to work as a distraction.

"Hey, girl." Christine crouched down to love on the dog. "Did Jackson take good care of you last night?" At ten years old, Diana was fairly mellow and low maintenance. As she did on nights when she worked late, Christine had asked her neighbor's preteen son to dog-sit Diana.

The dog pressed her head against Christine and gave a soft snort, making the tension in her shoulders lessen slightly. "Let me shower and change, and we'll go for a walk."

The dog turned in a happy circle at the mention of her favorite word.

"You would not believe the night I had," Christine

said as she placed her purse on the counter and headed for the bathroom, Diana following close on her heels. The dog had been her roommate and companion for so long, she thought nothing of carrying on a one-sided conversation.

She told Diana about Gavin and their arrangement. The dog inclined her head, as if truly listening. Christine was grateful for the sympathetic canine ear. Most of her girlfriends were in the real estate industry or knew the Fortunados, so she couldn't share the arrangement with any of them.

Her sister would have a field day giving Christine grief about only being able to find a fake boyfriend. Even as adults, their relationship was fraught with teasing, all one-sided. Christine had never allowed herself to think much of it, although it was strange that they couldn't seem to shake their childhood roles.

Aimee was beautiful, popular and funny. She worked as a hairdresser in a busy salon in one of Austin's tonier suburbs. She had tons of friends, a steady stream of rich boyfriends and remained the apple of their father's eye. Yet she never seemed to tire of pointing out Christine's shortcomings.

It had been easier when Christine lived in Houston. She'd come up with plenty of excuses over the years as to why she could only return to Austin once or twice a year for family functions.

But now that she'd moved back to her hometown, her mother made it clear she expected to see more of her.

After her shower, she dressed in a sweatshirt and loose jeans, laced up her sneakers and headed out the door with Diana. As always, the dog was thrilled to check out the scents along the walking trail situated about a block from the condo.

Christine waved to neighbors and tried to keep her thoughts from straying to Gavin. Why had she agreed to be his pretend girlfriend?

She had no answer, other than the fact that it was her best—and possibly only—chance of ever spending time with him.

Maybe that was a good enough reason.

Diana whined softly as they got to the open meadow that bordered the trail. Christine unclipped the dog's leash, and Diana sped off to investigate the nearby trees.

Christine's phone dinged, and she pulled it out of her pocket, drawing in a quick breath at the text message.

I missed you this morning. Talk soon?

She and Gavin had exchanged numbers in his hotel room, but it still shocked her to see his name on the screen.

How to respond?

Last night had been one of the best of her life, even though nothing had happened between them. Okay, she was disappointed nothing had happened. She'd spent the night in a man's bed and all he'd done was snuggle her. Did that say more about Gavin or her? She was afraid the answer was the latter.

Yes, she knew he respected her and she'd heard him tell his sister that Christine was special. Now, that felt like an excuse for keeping things basically platonic between them.

But he missed her.

That was a good sign, right?

She tapped in the start of several responses and almost immediately deleted each of them. Too sweet. Too trite. Trying too hard.

Finally, she sent a smiley-face emoji.

And immediately regretted it. Her mother sent smiley-face emojis about everything. All Christine needed was to add an "LOL" along with several exclamation points and she'd officially become the fuddy-duddy she was afraid might be her destiny.

Diana barked at a squirrel, and Christine pocketed the phone with a sigh. She wasn't sure what she'd gotten herself into with Gavin Fortunado, but there was no doubt she was in over her head.

"Where's Christine?"

Gavin made a show of checking his watch as Schuyler dropped into the chair next to him. For the morning-after brunch she'd traded her bridesmaid dress for a pair of slim trousers and a pale pink sweater, her blond hair in a low ponytail. He had the sudden urge to tug on it, as he had to annoy her when they were kids. "It's ten o'clock. Isn't that too early for an interrogation?"

"One question does not an interrogation make," she countered, forking up a piece of pineapple and popping it into her mouth.

"Hey, you two." His youngest sister, Valene, slipped into the chair on his other side. She wore a gray sheath dress and an understated pendant necklace around her neck. When had the baby of the family grown up so much? "What's the deal with you and Christine?" she asked Gavin.

He glared at Schuyler. "So much for keeping things on the down low."

"I didn't say anything," she told him, arching a brow at Valene.

"She didn't need to." Val sipped her glass of orange juice. "I caught Christine doing the walk of shame from your room this morning on my way to work out."

"Seriously?" Schuyler demanded, eyes narrowing. But to Gavin's utter shock, her stare was focused on Valene and not him. "You worked out already? Stop making me feel like a slacker, Val."

Val rolled her eyes and winked at Gavin. "So…"

"She wasn't doing the walk of shame," Gavin said through clenched teeth, wishing for something stronger than coffee in his china cup.

"Don't get me wrong," Valene told him, ignoring Schuyler's continued glare. "I approve. She's a definite improvement over that bimbo you were dating when I came to Denver last year."

"She's probably too good for you," Schuyler added absently. "How did you get her to take you on in the first place?"

"Feels like an interrogation," Gavin muttered under his breath.

Schuyler chuckled. "You know I'm joking. You're a catch, Gavin."

"It's just a surprise that you've let yourself be caught." Valene bit into a slice of bagel slathered with cream cheese.

"I don't want to talk about this with either of you." He inclined his head toward the rest of the family, who were gathered around Maddie and Zach on the other side of the room. "Especially not here."

"You need our expertise," Schuyler told him. "Christine is amazing. She's the kind of woman…"

"I'd want at my side for always," Gavin whispered, unaware that he'd spoken aloud until both of his sisters gasped.

Schuyler grabbed his arm. "Are you saying…"

"Did you ask her to marry you?" Valene leaned closer. "Are you and Christine engaged?"

Gavin felt his Adam's apple bob in his throat as he swallowed hard. "I didn't say that."

"It's true, though. I can tell by the look in your eyes." Valene let out a little squeal of delight then lifted her bagel and smiled blandly at the group sitting at the next table. "Try the blueberry cream cheese. It's amazing."

"Can you two be more obvious?" Gavin tugged his arm out of Schuyler's grasp.

"You're getting *married*," Schuyler told him, and he didn't dare contradict her. "You can't keep it a secret."

Fake dating to fake engaged in twenty-four hours. His stomach pitched as he thought about Christine's reaction to this new development.

"And there's no reason to." Valene dabbed at the corner of her mouth with a napkin. "Everyone loves Christine."

"She's a private person," he said, realizing the excuse sounded lame.

Schuyler nodded just the same. "I get that, but she's like one of the family to us. She's going to be one of the family soon. How soon? Have you set a date?"

He shook his head, trying to reel in his thoughts. What was he doing here? "Not yet. We didn't want to take any attention from Maddie and Zach."

Both of his sisters nodded in agreement.

"I'm sure that was Christine's idea," Valene said. "She's so thoughtful. We'll make sure she knows how welcome she is." She looked past him, her eyes widening. "Oh, they brought out a fresh tray of pastries. I need to get to them before Everett and Connor snag the best ones." She pushed back from the table. "I'll be right back. Who wants a donut?"

"Me." Schuyler raised her hand. "Bring one for Gavin, too. He's probably hangry and hungover."

"I'm neither," he said, although his head was starting to ache. Was it too early for a shot? "But I'll take a Bloody Mary, please."

Valene laughed as she walked away.

Schuyler wasted no time. She turned to Gavin and started in on him again. "Christine is going to get the wrong impression if you try to keep her a secret much longer, especially since you're in Austin for the rest of the month. She needs to start wedding planning, and I can help. Think about it, Gavin. She's going to be your wife. I get the business about being private, but if you make her feel like everything's okay, she'll believe it."

"Do you think I haven't?"

"I think you don't have much experience with a woman who you can be proud to bring home to Mom and Dad."

"That's not—" Gavin stopped, ran a hand through his hair. It was exactly the truth. Even though his relationship with Christine was a complete fake, he hadn't dated anyone with her amount of class and elegance in years. Christine was the kind of woman a man thought of spending his life with, and Gavin's stomach pitched at the realization.

"Bring her to the family reunion," Schuyler told him, breaking into his tumbling thoughts.

"What family reunion?"

"The one I'm planning to introduce everyone to the new Fortunes."

He shook his head. "I thought *we* were the new Fortunes."

She leaned forward, her eyes dancing with excitement. "There are more, Gavin. Dad has a half brother, Miles. He lives in New Orleans and has seven kids. Ben and Keaton put me in touch with the youngest son, Nolan. He's recently moved to Austin."

Ben Fortune Robinson had spearheaded the search for his illegitimate siblings after discovering that his tech mogul father was really Jerome Fortune, who'd faked his death years earlier. Jerome reinvented himself as Gerald Robinson and built his tech empire, but in recent years the family's focus had been on their new siblings. Keaton Whitfield, a British architect who was now living in Austin, had been the first of the secret illegitimate Fortunes Ben had tracked down. Together, the two of them had worked to uncover Gerald's other grown children and bring them into the fold.

Schuyler was the Fortune expert as far as Gavin was concerned, so he knew from her that Gerald's estranged wife, Charlotte, had actually known about his other children for the duration of their marriage and hidden the information from everyone. To learn there were even more previously unknown Fortunes out there… Gavin didn't know what to think.

"Schuyler, last year you were the one who wasn't sure if the Fortunes could be trusted. That was the whole basis for you infiltrating the family through the Mendozas."

She smiled wistfully. "Thank heavens for that brilliant idea. Otherwise, I never would have met Carlo."

"Can we keep on topic?" Gavin asked. Once again he wondered what it would have felt like to grow up an only child.

"We have to welcome the New Orleans Fortunes into the family, just like the Robinsons did for us. They're as innocent in all the family intrigue as we were, but we can't deny the connection. I'm going to make sure it goes well." She rubbed her hands together. "The reunion is going to be held at the Mendoza Winery. Nolan seems like a good guy. He promised he'd get his brothers and sisters to attend. I'm not sure about his parents yet, but I'm still hopeful."

"You never give up," Gavin murmured with a smile.

"It's one of my best traits," she answered. "I think the Fortune Robinson siblings are going to come, as well. I talked to Ben last week and he seemed amenable to the idea."

"What does Dad think of all this?"

Schuyler shrugged. "He's going back to enjoying his retirement after Maddie and Zach return from their mini-honeymoon, but I know he's curious about our new extended family. He and Mom have agreed to drive up and meet everyone. We'll all be here. Except maybe Connor. I'm not sure about his schedule and you know how dedicated he is to the search firm. He promised to try. Either way, the rest of the Fortunados will show a united front in welcome."

"It looks like you've worked out all the details."

"I'm doing my best. Now that Maddie's happily married, I can turn even more of my attention to the reunion." She wiggled her eyebrows. "And to making sure you don't mess things up with Christine before your big day."

I can't mess up something that doesn't really exist, Gavin thought to himself. Although he wasn't sure that rationale actually held water. It felt as if he'd already made a huge misstep by asking her to enter into a fake relationship.

He actually liked Christine quite a bit. More than he'd expected and definitely more than he had any other woman he'd recently dated. But it would complicate things if he tried to turn their pretend love into something real. Plus, despite what his sisters now believed, he still barely knew her. There was no explaining the connection he felt between them, yet he couldn't deny it.

"Don't tell me you've already done something stupid," Schuyler said, studying his face.

"No," he answered automatically then schooled his features. His sister was far too perceptive for his own good.

"You'll bring her to the reunion?" she asked again.

"You know she wants to keep our relationship private," Gavin argued weakly. "A Fortune reunion is the least private activity I can imagine."

Schuyler waved away his concern. "Valene saw her leaving your room, so someone else might have, as well. Besides, she'll want to start planning the wedding. Does she have a dress yet?"

"Um…I don't think so."

"Val and I will take her shopping. We have to plan the perfect bridal shower, too."

"Slow down, Schuyler." Gavin held up a hand like he was giving a command to an eager puppy. "All of this is going to overwhelm her. I don't want that. Even though we're engaged, Christine and I are going to take things at our own pace. If she wants—"

"You're in Austin until the end of the month, right?" his sister interrupted.

"Yes."

"Then it's no longer a long-distance romance where you can sweep her off to Colorado and have her all to yourself." She speared a piece of melon from her plate. "I assume that's what you've been doing. Unless you've been secretly coming to Austin for clandestine dates? Where did you get engaged, anyway?"

Gavin's heart started to leap in his chest. There were so many moving parts in this situation. He needed to talk to Christine to make sure they both kept them all straight. Hell, he wanted to talk to Christine again just to hear her voice.

"Colorado," he told his sister, deciding it was best to stay away from any pesky details. "Everything has been in Colorado."

"That makes sense," she agreed.

Good thing it did to someone.

"Austin is different than a lot of places. It's a big small town in some ways. You know that. It would be silly for you to try to keep things a secret, and I doubt it would work anyway. If you talk to Mom and Dad, they'll understand, but you can't keep trying to hide it. Mom will drive you crazy with attempts to nose into your love life, anyway."

Gavin pointed his fork at Schuyler. "I guess you get it honestly."

"Does that mean you'll bring Christine to the reunion?"

Out of the corner of his eye, Gavin saw Everett and Lila approaching the table. He might have to take his sister's advice and go public with his relationship with

Christine, but he didn't intend to reveal it this morning. "I'll invite her," he promised, "but the decision whether to attend will be hers."

"Oh, we can convince her," Schuyler assured him with a smile.

"No pressure," he said, pushing back from the table. "I mean it. I don't want you or Maddie or Valene to make her feel like she has to accept."

"Gavin, you have a protective side when it comes to your future bride." Schuyler grinned. "It's adorable."

He shook his head. "I'm going to talk to Mom and Dad. Let me tell them about Christine and the engagement, okay?"

"Sure," Schuyler agreed. "But I've already told you, the family loves her as much as you obviously do. There's nothing to worry about."

Gavin's stomach pitched at the mention of the *L* word. Those four letters were definitely cause for concern. Fearing that Schuyler would be able to read his emotions, he turned to greet Everett and Lila then made his way toward the rest of the family at the other side of the room.

He knew he needed to talk to his parents about Christine but didn't relish the thought of lying to them outright about his relationship. He told himself it would be better if he waited to speak to his dad in private. Although guilt sat heavy in his gut, he made it through the rest of the brunch then retreated back to his room, changed into a T-shirt and sweatpants and headed out for a run.

He expected to miss the bright sunshine and crisp air in Colorado but it felt good to be back in Texas. After a four-mile loop around downtown Austin, he showered, changed and then texted Christine to see if she could have dinner.

The challenge was knowing what to call the invitation. A fake date? A business meeting? In the end, he left it at "Want to grab dinner?"

His chest constricted when her return text lit up his screen. She had plans for the evening. Should he read more into the terse message? Was she angry that he'd texted instead of phoning? Could she be regretting their agreement enough to call off their arrangement?

Disappointment crashed through him, both because she wasn't available and due to the thought of her possibly backing out of the pretend relationship.

This discontent was new for him. Gavin didn't usually allow himself much time for reflection or self-analysis. Deep thoughts weren't really his deal. As a middle child in a big family, he'd learned early on that the best way to get noticed was action as opposed to introspection, which suited his restless nature just fine.

He'd climbed trees, raced his bike along dirt paths and generally careened through his childhood with an abandon that seemed to both amuse and terrify his parents. He knew they'd been happy when he finally settled on law school, and the constant challenges in his professional life kept his adrenaline moving just like the extreme sports he loved. But lately mastering even the most technical ski slopes hadn't been taxing enough to help him feel settled at the end of the day. Not like he had spending the night with Christine curled next to him.

He had friends in Austin who would be up for a night out, but the idea of going out with anyone but his fake girlfriend held no appeal. In the end, he pulled out his laptop and got to work preparing for the meeting he had scheduled with the firm's client next week.

His fingers itched to call Christine, but she hadn't given him any indication in her text that she wanted to talk to him. Not even a smiley-face emoji like the one she'd sent earlier. The simple plan for getting his family to stay out of his love life was already far more complicated than he'd expected.

Chapter Five

When the knock sounded on her office door Monday morning, Christine was already on pins and needles. She hadn't talked to Gavin other than a simple text about dinner the previous night. When she'd texted back that she had plans, he hadn't responded and she'd been too nervous to suggest an alternate time to get together.

She imagined him having second, third and fourth thoughts about their arrangement, especially after spending what to him must have been a boring night in his hotel room. Falling asleep after watching movies together—talk about a wasted moment. She figured she'd never get the chance for a do-over.

Maddie and Zach had flown to Cabo for a short mini-honeymoon. Neither of them was willing to leave the Austin branch for too long when business was picking up so much. Christine had no doubt they trusted her to run the internal side of things at the office, and Valene had postponed her return to Houston until they got back. Even Kenneth was pitching in despite his recent retirement. But she still appreciated their commitment and understood their mutual dedication to Fortunado Real Estate was part of what made them such a perfect couple.

Christine might have had a crush on Gavin for years, but what did they really have in common? She loved her work and knew he enjoyed his law career, but that was where the similarities ended. He was a high-powered corporate attorney who worked with big-name clients, and she was more comfortable behind the scenes, keeping everyone in the office organized and on track. She led a quiet life, and he was always off on some new adventure during his downtime.

It had pained her to say no to his dinner invitation last night, even if she was sure he was offering because they needed to confirm their stories before revealing their relationship to his family. But since she'd moved back to Austin, her mother had insisted she come to dinner every Sunday, sitting down to a meal with her parents and sister. And if she needed a physical reminder of why she and Gavin weren't a great match, her sister, Aimee, was more than happy to provide it.

Aimee was a talented hairstylist but had trouble holding down a job, bouncing from salon to salon so often that only her most loyal clients stayed with her. Still, she always made wherever she landed sound like the most exciting place on the planet to work. Her sister relished every opportunity to point out what a boring life Christine led and how old-fashioned it was to stick with the same company for a decade. Last night had been no exception. The owner of Aimee's most recent salon had invited her to go to the Bahamas for a weekend. Although the guy sounded like a total creep to Christine, her sister insisted Christine was just too much of a stick-in-the-mud to appreciate an opportunity for adventure.

Someone knocked again, more insistently this time, and Christine realized she'd been lost in her own thoughts.

"Come in," she called, pasting the polite smile on her face she knew any of her coworkers would expect to see.

Her jaw dropped when Gavin walked into her small office, and it felt like all the air in the room had been sucked out the moment he entered.

She shut her mouth and attempted to draw a breath but ended up choking and sputtering, reaching for the glass of water next to her computer. Her hand tipped it and water spilled across her desk.

With a yelp-cough, she jumped up, at least having enough sense to pluck the stack of contracts she'd been inputting before they were soaked through. She rushed to the utility closet in the corner of the office and grabbed a roll of paper towels, turning back to find Gavin lifting her wireless keyboard and phone out of the water.

"What a mess," she muttered then quickly cleaned up the spilled water, still coughing every few seconds.

She could feel her face flaming with embarrassment. Only when she'd dumped the last of the wet paper towels in the trash can next to her desk did she look up at Gavin.

"You're cute when you're flustered," he said, tossing the paper towels he'd used to dry the bottom of the keyboard and her cell phone case into the trash.

She gave a small laugh, which turned into a cough.

"Going to make it?" he asked, arching one thick brow.

"I'm fine," she whispered and took the phone and keyboard from him. "Mortified, but fine. Coordination isn't always my thing."

He winked, and her stomach felt like it had taken the first plunge on a roller-coaster ride. "Good to know."

"I didn't expect to see you here." She busied herself with rearranging the items on her desk, trying to ignore how close Gavin stood and how her body reacted to him.

"I'm meeting with my dad in—" he checked his watch "—five minutes."

"Oh." Disappointment washed through her at the knowledge that he hadn't stopped by to see her. Of course, why would he stop by for her when he could easily—

"Are you free for lunch after?"

Her mouth dropped open again and she pressed it shut. "Mmmhrmrh."

One side of his mouth quirked. "Is that a yes?"

"Yes," she breathed and was rewarded with a full grin.

It was like being struck with a two-by-four. She felt dazed, like she'd held her breath too long and was getting light-headed from the sensation.

Okay, maybe she was light-headed. *Breathe. Remember to breathe.*

"I'd like to speak to my dad about us," Gavin continued like she wasn't having an internal freak-out inches away from him. "If that's okay with you?"

"Us?" she squeaked.

"Our relationship."

"Our *fake* relationship," she clarified.

"Yes, well…" He massaged a hand along the back of his neck, and she wondered if she wasn't the only one trying to hide her nerves. "What would you think about a pretend engagement?"

Christine choked out shocked laugh. "Excuse me?"

"I…uh…my sisters… There was a little…uh…misunderstanding at breakfast the morning after the wedding."

"A misunderstanding that ended up with us engaged?" she asked, pressing her palms to her cheeks, which felt like they were on fire.

"It's not much different than dating."

The sound that came from her throat sounded like the creaking of the old screen door at her parents' house.

"I'm sorry, Christine." He started to reach for her then rubbed his neck again. "I should have said something, but they were so happy about it. I thought an engagement might be…uh…fun."

"Fun," she repeated. She started to shake her head, but Gavin was looking at her with so much hope that she couldn't stand to disappoint him. It was what she told herself but only part of the truth. She also didn't want her time with Gavin—pretend or not—to end. "Sure. It could be fun."

"Really?"

She smiled when Gavin's voice cracked on the word like a teenage boy.

"Yes," she confirmed and when he grinned, she had to believe she'd made the right decision. "So you're going to tell your dad we're engaged?"

He nodded. "Before I speak with him, I wanted to

make sure you hadn't changed your mind about the arrangement and now the engagement. When you blew me off last night, I wondered if—"

"I have Sunday dinner at my parents' every week," she interrupted. "The only thing that could get me out of it is a trip to the emergency room, and there's a good chance my mom would pack up the food and bring it to the hospital. She has this notion that eating a meal together will suddenly make the four of us into a happy family after almost three decades."

"That's great," Gavin murmured then shook his head at her frown. "I'm sorry. I don't mean it's great for you. It's not great that you have to deal with that, but I thought you were blowing me off."

She inclined her head as soft pink tinged his cheeks. Was Gavin Fortunado blushing?

"I wouldn't blow you off," she whispered, her voice sounding husky to her own ears. "Ever."

He drew in a breath like her words meant something to him. As if she meant something to him, which was impossible because before Saturday night they hadn't done much more than speak in passing throughout the past ten years.

Except he remembered the first time they'd met. He'd told her she'd helped convince him he could make it to law school.

Something tiny and tentative unfurled in Christine's heart. It felt a lot like hope. Possibility. Her chance for something more.

The same unfamiliar streak of boldness that had prompted her to act at the reception flashed through her again. She stepped forward, placed her hands on his broad shoulders, rose up on her tiptoes and then kissed him.

Their mouths melded together for a few seconds. She wouldn't allow it to go any further, not in her office. Even though the door was closed, several of her coworkers would feel no hesitation about knocking and walking right in.

When she started to pull away, Gavin gripped her hips with his big hands and squeezed. The touch reverberated through her body, sending shock waves of desire pulsing through her.

She moaned and then felt him smile against her lips. "I can't wait for lunch," he said, the rough timbre of his voice tickling her senses. "Suddenly, I'm starving."

Then he let her go, and she had to place a hand on the corner of her desk to steady herself.

Good gravy, the man could kiss.

"I'll meet you at the reception desk in twenty minutes?" he asked over his shoulder.

"Sure." She held up a hand to wave then pulled it to her side. What kind of a ninny would she be to wave to him like he was a knight heading to battle? He was going to talk to his father, and Kenneth Fortunado loved each of his six children and wanted their happiness above anything.

She only hoped Gavin's happiness wouldn't come at the expense of her heart.

"You look chipper today."

Gavin tried to wipe the grin off his face as he entered Maddie's office, which was currently occupied by their father. Kenneth sat behind the computer, a pair of wire-framed reading glasses perched on his nose. Although he'd officially retired last year, Kenneth was still in his prime and Gavin knew his dad was plenty capable of holding down the fort until Maddie and Zach returned.

One of the things Gavin missed most about living in Texas was spending time with his family. Despite occasionally wishing he were an only child, he truly loved being part of the Fortunado brood. His childhood had been idyllic, tons of love and laughter provided by the close bond his mother had fostered among all the siblings.

"It was nice to have everyone together for the wedding." He dropped into the chair across from the desk. "I also like seeing you in your natural habitat. Do you miss the daily grind of the agency?"

Kenneth smiled and shook his head. "I'm having a great time cheering on Maddie and Zach from the sidelines. It was one of my more genius moves to arrange for them to work together last year."

"Among a lifetime of genius moves," Gavin murmured with an exaggerated eye roll.

"Smart boy." His father steepled his fingers. "The smartest one remains marrying your mother. We're thrilled that Maddie's found so much happiness with Zach. It's what we want for each of our children." He raised a brow. "If you know what I mean?"

"As a matter of fact…" Gavin's stomach knotted even though his father had given him the perfect opening to discuss his relationship with Christine. He hadn't felt this nervous since he'd sat before his dad and explained that he was taking a position with a firm in Denver instead of the offer from one of his father's friends at a prominent Houston law firm. "I'm dating someone and thought—"

"That's wonderful, son." Kenneth's wide smile made guilt seep through Gavin's veins like poison. "Is it serious? Why didn't you bring her to the wedding?"

"Actually, it's serious and she was at the wedding." Gavin cleared his throat. "We've been keeping things private because she was worried about—"

"Worried?" Kenneth interrupted.

"About you," Gavin said softly. "What you'd think of our relationship."

"Why would I have a problem if she makes you happy?" He leaned forward, resting his elbows on the desk, the gold band on the third finger of his left hand shining. "Does she make you happy?"

Gavin thought about Christine's sweet smile and the way she looked at him like he was the only man in the world. "Yes," he murmured, almost more to himself than his father. "Christine makes me happy."

"Christine?" His father's expression went blank. "You're not talking about our Christine?"

"I am." Gavin drew in a deep breath as Kenneth frowned. "Although I wouldn't exactly say she belongs to the family."

"Would you say she belongs to you?"

Gavin thought about that then shook his head. "She's her own person. I like that about her." He held up a hand when his dad opened his mouth to speak. "But she's dedicated to you and to Fortunado Real Estate in general. Your approval of our relationship is important to her."

Kenneth inclined his head. "And you?"

"She's important to me," Gavin said immediately, surprised to find how much the statement resonated in his chest.

"Why haven't I heard about the two of you dating before now?"

"As I said, she wanted to keep things private at first to ensure it didn't impact her working relationship with anyone here."

"What's changed?"

Gavin fought the urge to grimace. It felt vaguely like facing a stiff cross-examination. "It's more than just dating, Dad. Christine and I are engaged."

"To be married?" his father asked, thick brows rising.

"That's the plan, and I'd like your support. You know I'm going to be spending the next few weeks in Austin. I don't want to have to hide anything or skulk around playing cloak and dagger if I want to see her. Plus, Schuyler is insisting Christine come to the reunion she's planning."

"I'm glad you talked to me," Kenneth said with a nod. "I don't like secrets."

Gavin chuckled. "Like discovering we're part of the famous Fortune family?"

"Some things even I can't control," his father admitted, almost reluctantly. "But you don't have to hide a relationship from us, son. I've told you we want your happiness above all."

Gavin didn't bother to explain how unhappy it made him that his family took such an interest in his love life. That feeling as though he were under the microscope had forced him into this arrangement with Christine in the first place.

But that wouldn't do any good at this point. Besides, he wasn't ready to end things before they even really got started. Pretending to be in love with and engaged to Christine might be a farce, but he liked her and knew they'd have a great time together over the next few weeks until he returned to Denver.

"Does that mean you approve?"

"You don't need my approval." His father smiled. "But of course I'm happy for you. Your mother will be, as well. You know how much we like Christine. Frankly, she's quite a step up in quality from the women you normally date."

Gavin rolled his eyes. "Schuyler said almost the same thing. I date decent women."

"Not in the same league as Christine."

"My girlfriends have been in Colorado," Gavin protested. "You haven't met most of them."

"Connor keeps us updated. He's ridiculously good with details."

"Connor should learn to keep his mouth shut. I'm not even sure he knows many of the women I've dated, so I'm not sure what makes him such an expert."

"He cares about you. We all do."

"I know."

"We care about Christine, too. Take care of her, Gavin. You aren't known for your staying power in relationships."

Ouch.

"Well, I'm committed to Christine now." Gavin smiled even as another wave of guilt crested inside him. His dad was right. Gavin didn't do long-term. It hadn't been a conscious decision, but he certainly had a habit of dating women who felt the same way about no-strings-attached as he did.

Christine was different. He knew that, even though their relationship was pretend. It was crucial he make sure they both remained on the same page so that she didn't get hurt.

"I'm glad to see it," his dad told him with a wide smile. "Your mom and I want you to be happy."

"Thanks, Dad. I *am* happy." He made a show of checking the Rolex that encircled his wrist. "I also need to get going. Christine and I are going to lunch."

"Enjoy," his dad answered, sounding pleased. "Let's plan a dinner with the two of you and your mom and me. I'm sure she'd be happy to come up from Houston to celebrate your engagement."

"Sure." Gavin walked toward the door. "I'll talk to Christine and we'll figure out a night that works."

"I'm really happy for you," Kenneth said, and Gavin left the office, trying to ignore the acid that felt like it was burning a hole in his stomach.

Chapter Six

Christine felt her smile falter as Gavin approached the reception area. He'd been sweet and flirty in her office earlier but now looked like a black cloud was following him. Had the conversation with his father gone badly? Was Kenneth angry that she and Gavin were supposedly dating?

"Lord, he's hot," came the appreciative whisper from behind Christine.

She looked over her shoulder toward Megan, the agency's young receptionist, who was staring at Gavin like he was the best thing on the menu at an all-you-can-eat buffet. "Um…yeah."

"Ready?"

She turned back to Gavin. "Sure. Is everything okay?"

"Fine," he snapped then closed his eyes for a moment. When he opened them again, the cloud had disappeared and a smile played at the corner of his mouth. He leaned in and kissed her cheek. "Don't mind me."

She heard Megan's gasp and felt color flood her cheeks. With a simple buss to the cheek, Gavin had effectively outed them to the entire agency. She knew that by the time they got back from lunch, everyone would know.

Maybe she'd order a drink with her meal. If only it was that easy.

"Be back in an hour," she said to the receptionist, purposely avoiding eye contact with the pretty brunette.

"I'll be waiting," came the reply. "We'll have a lot to talk about."

A drink couldn't hurt.

She and Gavin walked out into the hazy sun of the January afternoon, and she tightened the belt on her Burberry knockoff trench coat. She earned a decent salary with the agency but most of it went toward the monthly mortgage on her condo. She liked having a place to call her own more than she needed designer clothes.

"There's a new barbecue place a couple of blocks from here," she offered.

He stopped, inclined his head as if studying her. "I love barbecue."

Christine willed herself not to blush again. She wasn't about to admit she knew his taste in food from his sisters and from listening to stories of their family vacations over the years. That would make her seem like a total creeper.

"Me, too," she answered and started down the sidewalk in the direction of the popular restaurant.

Gavin fell into step beside her but didn't say anything more. When they stopped at a crosswalk, the silence became too much.

"Is your dad angry?" she asked, crossing her arms over her chest. "Does he hate the idea of the two of us? We don't have to do this. I mean, if it's—"

He reached out a finger and pressed it to her lips, effectively silencing her. She could barely remember to breathe when he touched her, let alone speak. "I'm sorry I've been quiet," he told her. "My dad is happy about our relationship."

The light changed and they began walking again. "Is there another problem?" she asked, glancing at him out of the corner of her eye.

"Everything's fine." He flashed a smile that didn't come anywhere near to his eyes.

Christine sighed. What now? Did she push him for the truth or let it slide? As much as she'd admired Gavin from afar for so many years, she didn't truly know him well. For all she knew, he had a toothache or had argued with his father about the Texans' chances in the playoffs this year.

They arrived at the restaurant, and he held the door open for her. She walked to the hostess stand and tried not to grimace as the woman looked between Christine and Gavin then did a double-take when he placed a hand on Christine's back, as though she couldn't imagine a man like him would be out with someone like her.

Sadly, Christine didn't blame the woman.

They followed the hostess to a table near the back of the crowded restaurant. Austin had plenty of barbecue joints but this was her favorite.

Christine made a show of studying the menu, almost disappointed when the waitress quickly took their orders.

She slipped the paper wrapper from her straw and tied it in a knot. As usual with this little ritual, the knot held when she made it but tore as she tightened it, and she sighed as the paper ripped.

When she glanced up, Gavin was smiling at her. "What's that about?"

She scrunched up her nose. "You never played the straw wrapper game?" She laughed when he frowned. "If the knot rips, someone is thinking about you. If not, you're out of luck."

"Yours tore off center," he pointed out.

"It always does."

"I'm thinking about you."

"You're sitting across from me," she said with a laugh.

"I thought about you all day yesterday," he continued. "About how much fun I had on Saturday night, especially the part where you curled against me in your sleep."

Her breath caught in her throat. "I don't remember that."

"You were asleep," he whispered and his voice took on a sexy edge.

"What exactly happened with your dad?" she blurted, somehow unable to let the subject go. "You haven't done a great job of convincing me he approves." Gavin's expression went from flirty to subdued in an instant. Way to ruin a moment, she chided herself.

At that moment the waitress brought their food. Gavin picked up his glass of iced tea, gripping it so hard his knuckles turned white. "He doesn't want me to hurt you."

"Oh," Christine breathed, knowing if she said anything more her voice would reveal that she shared the same fear.

"I don't want to hurt you," Gavin said, and somehow the words sounded like a promise. "I'm not going to hurt you," he added, almost like he was reassuring himself as much as her.

"Gavin." She reached across the table and placed a hand over his. He released his death grip on the glass and she saw his shoulders relax slightly. "We both know what this is," she said, even though it already meant so much more to her. "You aren't going to hurt me."

He nodded as if bolstered by her confidence. "I like you, Christine."

Warmth spread through her body at the simple pronouncement. "I like you, too."

"Do you think we could focus on that part?" He curled his big hand around her fingers. "We're friends who are getting to know each other better over these next few weeks. It doesn't have to be forced. I'm excited to hang out with you."

She swallowed. "You are?"

"Don't look so surprised," he said with a smile. "You're way more fun than you realize."

She laughed. "That might be the nicest thing anyone has ever said to me. I have a reputation for being organized, not fun."

"Then we'll work on your reputation."

She liked the sound of that.

"Is there anything else you need?"

Christine yanked away her hand and glanced up at

the hostess, who'd returned to the table in place of the waitress who had taken their order.

The raven-haired beauty was looking directly at Gavin as if he was the only one sitting at the table. "We're fine," he answered with a polite smile.

"Are you new to Austin?" the woman asked. "I haven't seen you in here before and I would have noticed."

Christine frowned as she picked up her chicken sandwich and took a bite. She couldn't believe the woman was flirting with Gavin right in front of her. Not that she could blame her. It was still almost difficult to look him in the eye some of the time. His gaze on her made her feel like her skin was on fire.

The hostess hooked two fingers in the waistband of her low-slung jeans, revealing the top edge of some kind of tattoo on her hip. She looked like she knew plenty about adventure and probably would have been friends with Christine's sister during high school. Certainly a woman who wouldn't have noticed Christine, unless she'd needed tutoring.

"I'm here for work," Gavin said, letting a bit of Texas drawl seep into his voice. "Originally from Houston."

"I could show you around," the woman offered with a sexy little half smile.

Christine figured if she tried that move she'd look like she was trying to hide something in her teeth.

Gavin returned the smile but gestured toward Christine. "I think we've got it covered."

The hostess's eyes widened. "You two are together?" She wagged one perfectly manicured nail between the two of them. "I thought she was your secretary."

"My fiancée," Gavin clarified without hesitation.

Christine drained her iced tea and held the glass out to the woman. "Could I get a refill?"

"Uh…sure." The woman took the glass and turned from the table.

"That was unexpected," Gavin murmured, digging into his own lunch.

Christine snorted. "You don't fool me. I bet women hit on you *all* the time."

"Not all the time."

She rolled her eyes. "Just on days that end in *y*?"

He grinned. "Something like that."

The hostess returned with the iced tea, placing the glass and a fresh straw on the table without a word and then walked away again.

Christine picked up the straw and pointed it at Gavin. "Why don't you have a girlfriend?"

"I was waiting for you," he said, making her laugh again.

"That's a bad line, even coming from your pretty lips."

He dabbed at one corner of his mouth with the napkin. "I've never been called pretty before. It suits me, I think."

"It's no wonder you became an attorney. You're such a smooth talker."

"I can't tell if that's a compliment or a criticism."

"An observation." She leaned in and repeated, "So why don't you have a girlfriend?"

He sighed. "You sound like one of my sisters."

"Which is not an answer to the question," she pointed out.

He studied her for a few long moments. "You do understand that I'm used to using my pretty mouth and fancy words to deflect questions I don't want to answer."

"I do."

"You're not going to let me get away with that?"

"I'm not," she said quietly. It might be the wrong thing to say. For all of Gavin's ease with people, she could tell he was a private man at heart. But she wanted to know that side of him, the part behind the handsome mask. Christine might not be the most adventurous or exciting person, but she knew how to be a good friend. She wanted to be Gavin's friend.

The waitress came to clear their plates, and Gavin gave her his credit card.

"Thank you for lunch," Christine said when the woman left again.

"My pleasure."

"Tell me about you and the lack of a girlfriend. Are you having trouble finding someone you connect with in Denver?"

He tapped a finger on his leather wallet. "I'm thirty years old," he said after a moment.

"Yes," she agreed. "Me, too. What does that have to do with dating?"

"At some point in the past couple of years, it changed. Expectations changed."

"Women got serious?"

"You could say that," he admitted. "Most of my friends got married. They settled down and bought real houses. Houses with yards in neighborhoods where you string up Christmas lights and build swing sets. Adult houses."

There was a thin note of panic in his voice, and she

wasn't sure whether to smile or roll her eyes again. "You're not exactly a 'failure to launch' type of guy."

"Being good at my job versus good as a husband and possibly a father are different things."

The waitress brought the bill, and after Gavin signed the receipt, they headed back toward the agency. A few clouds hung in the sky, and she was glad for her jacket to protect her against the brisk breeze blowing through downtown. Gavin didn't seem to notice the cool air, although that could be because he was used to winter in Colorado.

"You come from an amazing family," she told him.

He looked down and flashed a lopsided smile. "That's kind of the point. My dad is fantastic and my parents' marriage is as strong as ever. He always found time for each of his kids as well as my mom, despite how hard he worked. I know how to be an attorney, but that's nothing compared to being a husband or father. I don't know that I'm ready. I'm not sure I'll ever be ready. How could I compare to my father?" She noticed his hand clenched and unclenched at his side, a nervous gesture that was out of character for him.

This was it, Christine realized. This was Gavin behind the mask.

She reached out and took his hand in hers. "It's not a competition. Your parents want you to be happy, however that looks for you."

"I *am* happy," he insisted, squeezing her fingers. "I keep trying to tell them. I think maybe I wasn't cut out for more than what my life is now. I don't know how to admit that to anyone in my family. What if I don't have it in me to give more?"

At that moment a man burst from the crowd walking toward them, on his phone and clearly in a hurry, jostling people on either side. Before Christine could react, Gavin put an arm around her shoulder, tucked her to his side and shifted so that the man bumped into him instead of her.

Gavin didn't break stride or make an issue of it. He simply ensured that she wasn't bothered as he maneuvered them through the groups of working folks headed for lunch.

"You have plenty to give," she said, tipping up her head to look at the strong line of his jaw. She wanted to add that he just needed to meet the right woman. And maybe she could be that woman, but she didn't say those things because she couldn't bear to let herself believe they might be true. Despite his assurance, Christine understood that the only way to ensure Gavin wouldn't hurt her would be to not open her heart to him. A challenge, given how much she already felt.

They were almost to the agency office, so she started to pull away. Gavin didn't release his hold on her. He drew her into a quiet alcove between the buildings, turning to face her.

"When you say that, I almost believe it," he whispered. "I *want* to believe it."

"It's true."

She rose up on tiptoe to kiss his cheek, but he captured her mouth with his, his lips firm and smooth as they grazed over hers.

Her insides danced, electric sparks erupting along her spine. His tongue traced the seam of her lips and she opened for him, winding her hands around his neck and pressing closer.

Everything around her melted away as he deepened

the kiss. He made it too easy to forget that the only reason they were together was to appease his family. Christine hated that he had any question as to whether he could handle a real commitment. Even if their time together was temporary, at least she could spend the next few weeks proving that he was capable of opening himself to someone.

But right now all she wanted was to lose herself in this moment. And when he groaned softly, it was everything. She'd done that to him. A low whistle from the street had her pulling away.

"I can't… We shouldn't… This isn't the place."

He drew in an unsteady breath. "I'm sorry. You're right, of course. I just can't seem to control myself around you."

Now, *that* was definitely the nicest thing anyone had ever said to her. "I'm glad," she told him honestly, earning another smile. "But I do need to get back to work."

"Me, too." Then he leaned in and kissed her again. "When can I see you?"

"You're seeing me right now."

"A date," he clarified. "I want to spend time with you. We're friends. Remember?"

"Oh." She blinked. The way he was looking at her made her forget this was fake. "We could have dinner this week?"

"Perfect." He took her hand and led her back out into the street, stopping at the door of the agency. "Tomorrow night?"

"Okay." She swallowed. He wanted to see her again so soon, and not just because it was part of the charade.

She took a step away. "I'll see you tomorrow, then."

He kissed her one more time then walked toward the black SUV parked at the curb.

Christine straightened the collar of her jacket and then entered the office, shocked to find Megan along with two of the female agents staring at her from the waiting area.

"Gavin Fortunado?" Molly, one of the agents, practically hissed. "You've been holding out on us, girl. We want all the details of how you landed a fine man like that."

"He is so not your type," Megan said, shaking her head.

"How do you know my type?" Christine couldn't help but ask.

"I heard you were into Bobby."

Christine shook her head. "Only in his dreams."

"I told you so," Jenna, the other agent, said.

"Seriously." Molly took a step forward. "How long has this been going on with Gavin?"

Oh, no. Once again, she'd been so caught up in enjoying Gavin's company that she'd forgotten to clarify the details of their supposed relationship.

"A while. We're actually…" She cleared her throat. "Engaged."

"Are you joking?" Molly demanded. "How did you pull it off?"

Jenna swatted her on the arm. "You can't ask someone that."

"Come on, that man should be with a supermodel." She gestured toward Christine. "No offense. You're pretty but he's ah-may-zing."

"I know," Christine agreed immediately. She took a step forward. "I'll let you in on a little secret."

All three women leaned forward slightly.

"The way he looks isn't even the best part about him."

"Whatever," Megan said. "I'm not sure I'd be able to notice anything else."

Christine shrugged. "Then you'd be missing out."

There was a deep throat-clear, and all four of them turned to see Kenneth standing at the edge of the hallway. "Megan, could you pull our files on the Rosedale neighborhood? I want to compare comps for one of Maddie's clients looking at a house on Oakmont Blvd."

"Right away, Mr. Fortunado." The young woman scurried around to her computer.

"I'm meeting a client out in East Oak Hill," Jenna said quickly.

"I'm heading to an association meeting," Molly offered.

Christine noticed that none of them made eye contact with Kenneth. "Will you send me the listing information for the Hyde Park property when you get back?" she asked Jenna.

"Sure thing," the woman answered, her voice a nervous squeak.

Christine smiled as she approached Gavin's father and they walked toward her office together. "They're terrified of you," she said, patting his arm. "No one in Austin realizes you're just a big teddy bear on the inside."

He let out a low laugh. "Don't tell them."

"It's our secret," she agreed, turning into her office across the hall from the one Kenneth occupied this week.

"Speaking of secrets," he said in his deep baritone.

She schooled her features then turned. "Gavin spoke to you."

"You know you're already like one of my own daughters. Both Barbara and I feel that way. I'm thrilled that you'll be officially joining the family."

Emotion clogged Christine's throat as she nodded. Over the past decade working for Kenneth, she'd come to feel almost closer to him than she did her own dad. He never judged her for the things she wasn't but appreciated her for who she was.

"You never have to hide anything from me. I want you to be happy."

"Gavin makes me happy," she said, appreciating that she could give him a response that wasn't a lie. She suddenly had a clearer understanding of Gavin's mood earlier. It felt wrong to deceive Kenneth and the rest of the Fortunados.

At the wedding she'd acted impulsively, wanting to live out one of her secret fantasies and save Gavin from Schuyler's matchmaking in the process. But these weren't strangers whom she'd walk away from when Gavin returned to Denver and their relationship ended.

"I'm glad," Kenneth told her. "Barbara will be, too."

"I want you to know I'm still committed to the agency," she said quickly. "That won't change."

"I know." Kenneth frowned, his thick brows lowering over eyes that reminded her of Gavin. "I trust you implicitly, Christine. You just concentrate on staying happy, and I sure hope my son continues to be a part of that."

"He will," she whispered, somehow knowing Gavin would be the key to both her happiness and her heartbreak.

Chapter Seven

Gavin lifted his hand to knock on the door of Christine's condo the following evening, only to have it swing open.

"I can't go out with you," she whispered, her face pale and eyes wide.

He tightened his grip on the bouquet of roses he held. "Why? What's wrong?"

"It's Diana. She's sick." She took a step back, and he stepped into the condo. It was decorated in neutral colors but with colorful posters and pillows that gave it a homey look. Quite a bit different from the contemporary furnishings and unadorned walls of his loft in downtown Denver.

"Is Diana your daughter?" How had he missed the fact that Christine had a kid?

She gave him a funny look. "She's my dog."

He heard a low whine from the back of the condo, and Christine turned and started down the hall. She glanced over her shoulder at him. "I'm sorry. I'll call you tomorrow, okay? I've got to get her to the vet. They're staying open for me."

It was clearly a dismissal but Gavin wasn't about to walk away when she was so upset. He shut the front door and followed her into the kitchen, finding her kneeling next to a medium-size black lab that was on its side on the hardwood floor.

The dog looked up when he entered, gave a half-hearted bark then lowered her head to the floor again.

"What happened?"

"I'm not sure," Christine said, trying unsuccessfully to coax the dog to her feet. "Come on, Di. You can do it."

"I'll lift her," Gavin offered.

"She sheds," Christine told him, her voice hollow.

"It's fine. What kind of car do you have?"

"A Prius." She ran a trembling hand over the dog's head. "Normally, Di rides shotgun."

"We'll take mine. She'll be more comfortable in the cargo area. Do you have an extra blanket?" Gavin moved forward and knelt on the other side of the animal. "Hey, girl. Wanna go for a ride?" The dog's tail thumped as he pet her soft fur.

"You don't have to do this," Christine protested.

"I'm not leaving you."

He met her worried gaze, hating the panic in her eyes. "She's going to be okay," he said quietly, even though it was a promise he had no business making. But he would have told Christine anything at the moment to make her feel better.

She nodded and talked softly to the dog as Gavin scooped the lab into his arms. He straightened and started for the front door as Christine grabbed a blanket from the back of the sofa.

They got the dog into the back of his Audi SUV, and Christine told him which way to drive to get to the vet's office. Other than giving directions, she didn't speak, and he wasn't sure what else to say. He liked dogs well enough but couldn't begin to guess what had made hers sick. He reached across the console and took Christine's hand, wanting to offer whatever reassurance he could.

The vet's office was only a ten-minute drive from her place, and as she'd mentioned, the staff was waiting for the dog. The doctor, a gray-haired man in his midfifties, greeted both Christine and Diana by name as he instructed Gavin to follow him to the back of the clinic. Gavin placed Diana on one of the exam tables then returned to the waiting room and sat down next to Christine.

"I'm sorry," she whispered when they were alone. "This isn't your problem and—"

"I want to be here," he told her, lacing their fingers together. "I want to know you're okay. Tell me about Diana."

A hint of a smile curled her lips. "I adopted her from a shelter in Houston when she was only four months old. It was right after I started working for your dad. I'd graduated college and moved into my first apartment on my own so I wanted a dog for protection."

"How did she get the name Diana?"

"The shelter called her Princess. She'd been found as a stray. They don't know what happened to her mom or any other puppies from the litter. So I changed her name to Princess Diana."

He chuckled. "That's a funny name for a dog."

"Yeah," she agreed. "I might have entertained some girlish fantasies about my own Prince Charming back in the day. But despite the name, Di is so special. She was a holy terror when she was younger. Chewed everything she could get her teeth on. But it was love at first sight. We went for a walk tonight after work and she seemed fine. When I got out of the shower, she was on the floor." Her voice broke and she swiped at her cheeks. "I can't lose her. I don't understand what happened. I took her to the dog park after work, and she was acting a little out of it when we got home, almost like she was drunk. Then she settled down so I thought she was fine. Why didn't I realize something was wrong?"

"They'll figure it out," he assured her, wrapping an arm around her shoulder and pulling her close.

Normally, Gavin didn't do well with tears from women. Growing up in a house with three sisters, he'd seen plenty of crying in his day, but as an adult he steered clear of emotional scenes. Yet he couldn't imagine a place he'd rather be at the moment than at Christine's side.

She rested her head on his shoulder and they waited. Trying to distract her, he kept up a litany of questions about the dog, prompting her to share many of Princess Di's adventures over the years. Her love for the dog was evident as she spoke, and he hoped with everything inside him that the dog would recover.

The vet came out into the waiting room a few minutes later, studying a chart as he entered.

"How is she?" Christine leaned forward, clutching her hands tight in front of her.

"She's showing signs of poisoning, although I can't narrow down what could have caused it at this point. We've given her activated charcoal and IV fluids. You said on the phone she hadn't gotten into anything hazardous?"

Christine shook her head. "Unless it was something at the dog park that I didn't see. I've heard stories of dogs getting sick there recently but I didn't pay much attention."

The vet frowned. "It's possible, I suppose. Keep her on a leash for a while."

"So she'll be okay?"

The older man nodded. "We'd like to keep her here overnight. She should be ready to go home in the morning, assuming there are no complications."

"Can I see her?" Christine asked, her voice shaky.

"She's resting," the doctor answered gently. "It might be better if you wait until the morning. It's a good thing you got her here as quickly as you did."

Gavin frowned as Christine nodded. He could tell she was fighting back another round of tears.

They left the office, Christine's features a mask of pain. "I let this happen," she whispered as she climbed into the Audi.

"It's not your fault," Gavin assured her, squeezing her hands. "If some idiot put poisoned food at the dog park, there's nothing you could have done to prevent it."

"I was visiting with people while she ran around with the other dogs. I wasn't watching closely enough."

Gavin pulled the seat belt across her and fastened it. She was in no shape to take care of anything at the moment. It was painful to see Christine, who was always so quietly competent and capable, at a loss in this way.

"She's a dog at the park," he said, brushing the hair out of her face. "The whole point is to run around with other animals. The vet said she's going to be okay. It was smart that you brought her in for treatment right away."

She gave a small nod and leaned back against the seat, closing her eyes.

He got into the car and started back toward her house. They didn't speak during the short drive, but her breathing returned to normal and she seemed slightly calmer by the time he parked at the curb.

"Thank you," she said quietly, unbuckling her seat belt then turning to face him. "I'm sorry about the date." She shrugged. "Maybe we can take a rain check for later this week?"

"You aren't getting rid of me that easily." He turned off the SUV. "We can order pizza or whatever you want as takeout."

By the time he came around the front of the Audi, Christine was on the sidewalk. "I'm not great company tonight."

"Okay."

She threw up her hands. "Seriously, Gavin. You were such a huge help, but I'll be fine."

"*Seriously*, Christine." He reached out and brushed his thumb along the track of a tear that had dried on her cheek. "I wanted to hang out with you tonight. I still do. At least let me keep you company, since you're having a rough time. We don't even have to talk. Let's just eat and watch a movie."

"This isn't the night you planned."

"I planned to be with you," he answered simply and saw her draw in a sharp breath. "Let me stay."

She studied him for so long he felt himself wanting to fidget, but she finally nodded. "There's a pizza place around the corner. I have a menu inside."

"Pizza sounds great," he said, and taking her hand, they walked toward her condo.

By the time Christine finished her third piece of pizza, she felt almost human again. Maybe she should be embarrassed about her attachment to Princess Diana, but the dog had been a faithful companion and friend for ten years. She'd been a source of unconditional love and had seen Christine through several lousy boyfriends and always made her feel better about the strained relationship she had with her family. Everyone loved Di, even her unemotional father.

"She's going to be fine." Gavin repeated his words from earlier, as if reading her mind. She still couldn't believe how readily he'd pitched in to help with her dog and then comfort her. Sure, she could have managed, but it had been nice for once to feel like she wasn't alone.

"I know," she answered. "I just miss her. Other than when I'm away she's always with me at night." She thunked her palm against her forehead. "That sounds pathetically like my dog and I are codependent."

He flashed a grin. "Dogs are great. My roommate in college had a husky, and I loved hanging on the couch with that furry beast."

"You don't have any pets?" she asked, taking a sip from her second beer of the night.

"Nah. I like animals but I travel a decent amount. It doesn't seem fair."

"You could get a goldfish."

"I'll keep that in mind," he told her with a chuckle.

They cleaned up the dishes, empty beer bottles and the pizza box, and then moved to the sofa in her family room. "Are you sure you're okay with a boring night of television?"

"Being with you isn't boring," Gavin answered and the sincerity in his tone made her heart skip a beat. He sat close to her on the couch, and it felt natural to cuddle into him as they watched an action flick playing on one of the cable channels.

"Can I ask you a question?" His voice was a soft rumble against the top of her head.

"Sure."

"Why don't you have a boyfriend?"

She tried to stay relaxed but felt her body stiffen. Lifting her head from where it had been resting on his shoulder, she scooted away. "I haven't met the right guy," she answered, hoping that would be enough.

"I remember saying the exact same thing to you," he told her, raising a brow. "You didn't let me get away with it."

"But you're much kinder than me," she said hopefully.

He laughed. "Try again. When was the last time you were in a serious relationship?"

"I dated a guy in Houston for about two years, but we broke up before I moved back to Austin."

He whistled softly. "Two years is a long time."

She shrugged.

"What went wrong?"

"Well…" She took a deep breath and thought about

how to answer that question. "He wanted a schedule for…um…when we'd be together."

"When you'd go out?"

"When we'd *be* together." Color rushed to her cheeks. "In the biblical sense."

Gavin's eyes widened, and Christine wished for the ground to open up and swallow her whole. Why hadn't she just stuck to a vague version of the truth? They'd grown apart or wanted different things in life.

"He was a math teacher at a local community college, so logic and order were important to him. He created algorithms for our relationship and part of that was a schedule for the optimal timing of…you know."

"I know." Gavin nodded then quickly shook his head. "But I'm having trouble believing you."

"Maybe I shouldn't have made such a big deal about it," she said, echoing what her mother had said when Christine admitted to her the reason for the breakup. "I'm not exactly known to be adventurous. I've eaten the same type of cereal every day for breakfast for as long as I can remember. I'm not like you. My adventurous spirit is almost nonexistent. But that was too structured, even for me."

"Who says you aren't adventurous?" Gavin demanded softly.

She huffed out a harsh laugh. "No one needs to say it. Everyone knows it."

"I don't."

"You will," she countered. "You go heli-skiing and rock climbing and scuba diving." She held up a hand and ticked off their differences. "I'm scared of heights and speed and I can barely doggy paddle."

"There are other adventures you could have."

She wrapped her arms around her stomach and turned toward the television, hating the direction this conversation had taken. "At the end of the day, I'm a coward."

"I don't believe that."

"You're watching a boring movie with me and have dog fur stuck to your sweater." She rolled her eyes. "What's a typical date like for you in Denver?"

"Pretty similar," he said, deadpan. "Although sometimes I go for a crazy cat lady."

"I wish I knew how to let go and be wild."

Gavin leaned closer. "Do you have any memory of planting a mega kiss on me in front of my sister Saturday night?"

"Yes," she breathed.

He tipped up her chin and brushed his lips across hers. "That was not the work of a coward."

"It was different. I got swept away in the moment... in you."

"What's stopping you from doing that again? Every day, even?"

"Fear," she whispered, her eyes drifting closed.

She felt him smile against her mouth. "I love your honesty. There's no pretense with you."

"Too much talking," she told him, and deepened the kiss.

He let her take control, driving the intensity and pace. She pressed closer, and he lifted her into his arms. She ended up straddling him on the couch, loving the feel of his warmth beneath her. This was why it was a bad idea to schedule intimacy. The spontaneity of her connection with Gavin was one of the things that made it so special.

Well, that and the fact that it was Gavin under her. His big hands moved up her hips then under the hem of her sweatshirt, and she moaned when he skimmed his fingers along her spine.

"Lift your arms," he told her, and she automatically obeyed, too filled with need to bother being self-conscious. Her breasts were okay, she figured, and she'd at least had the forethought to wear a pretty bra tonight, preparing for all the possibilities before discovering Diana.

After tossing her shirt to the floor, he cupped her breasts in his hands then sighed with contentment. His thumbs grazed across her pebbled nipples, making heat pool low in her belly, but she wasn't going to be the only one half-undressed.

She pulled away from him and started undoing the buttons of his tailored shirt. He sat back against the couch cushions, seeming content to wait for her to finish.

When she did, he leaned forward so she could push the fabric off his shoulders. He shrugged out of the shirt then yanked the T-shirt he wore underneath over his head.

Christine thought for a moment that she'd died and gone to heaven. His body was absolute perfection. His shoulders were broad and his chest a wall of hard muscle. A smattering of golden hair covered his chest, and she splayed her hands over his bare skin, gratified when she felt his heart leap under her palm, and he groaned low in his throat.

He didn't try to hide that she affected him, even though she still had a hard time understanding why.

But now wasn't the time for second-guessing, not

with his touch driving her crazy with need. He leaned in and trailed kisses against the base of her throat, his hands snaking around her waist, pulling her up so that she was lifted to her knees. His hot mouth covered her breast and she moaned, threading her fingers through his hair as his tongue circled her nipple through the thin fabric of her bra.

It was too much and not enough at the same time. Christine wanted more, and as she had the other night, she forgot about being afraid or judged. All that filled her mind and heart was this man and how much he made her feel. How much she wanted to experience with him.

Then her phone rang, the sound like a bucket of icy water splashed over her head. She scrambled off his lap and reached for the device, which sat on the end table next to the sofa.

"Hello," she answered and then cleared her throat.

The overnight vet tech was on the other end of the line. As Christine listened, tears pricked the backs of her eyes.

"That's great news. Thanks for calling."

She disconnected the call and turned to Gavin. "Di just ate a bit of food and went out to do her business. She seems much better."

"She's definitely on the road to recovery."

"It sounds like it."

"I never doubted."

She nodded, then reached for her sweatshirt, suddenly self-conscious of sitting there in her bra.

"I should probably let you get some sleep tonight," Gavin told her, grabbing his T-shirt from the floor and shrugging into it.

Christine wanted to whimper in protest, both at him covering that amazing body and the thought of him leaving.

Of course, he was right. As much as she wanted to throw caution to the wind and rip all his clothes off, that would be the worst idea ever. The *best* worst idea ever.

"Thank you for tonight," she told him, standing and crossing her arms over her chest. "For dinner and your help and staying and…" Oh, Lord, she was babbling. She couldn't actually thank him for kissing her, could she?

"You aren't boring," he said as he buttoned his collared shirt. "Or a coward."

"Okay," she agreed, not wanting to talk about this. Hating that she'd admitted her fears to him. She had to remember to hold a piece of herself back; a lot of pieces, if she was smart. Because if she let Gavin all the way in, it would kill her when their time together ended.

"I had a great time being spontaneous with you," he said, his full lips curving at the corners.

That made her laugh. "Me, too."

"Will you text me tomorrow when you pick up Princess Di? I'd like to know how she's doing."

"I will," she said, and the fact that he cared about her sweet dog made her heart melt even more.

He took a step toward her, bent his head and kissed her. It felt like a promise of more, and Christine wanted all of it.

"Good night," he whispered. "Sweet dreams."

"Ya think?" she murmured without thinking, then blushed again as Gavin chuckled.

She locked the front door behind him, then straightened the condo and got ready for bed, missing Diana but comforted knowing the dog would be home tomorrow.

The happy glow Gavin had given her also gave a huge amount of comfort. And not just the crazy-good make-out session, although that had been…well…crazy-good. But his steady presence had made such a difference. Christine was used to doing things for herself. Even with past boyfriends, she'd remained steadfastly independent.

Her competence was her one inherent gift; at least that was how it felt growing up. She'd taken care of her family because that was the one way she knew to show love that they wouldn't refuse. It was unfamiliar to rely on someone else, and she would never have expected Gavin to be so easy to lean on for support. It made her goal of keeping her heart out of their arrangement even trickier.

But tonight she focused on how happy he made her. Wasn't she due for a little happiness?

Chapter Eight

By Friday Gavin's mood was as dark as the clouds that billowed across the sky above Austin, a harbinger of an impending thunderstorm. As much as he appreciated the predominantly sunny days in Colorado, sometimes he missed a good soaking rainfall.

Although not when the skies opened up as he parked two blocks from the restaurant where he was meeting Schuyler and Everett for lunch.

He dashed from his car toward the diner situated across from the Austin Commons complex, trying to stay under the awnings of the buildings he passed. Still, he was more than a little wet when he burst through the door. Schuyler waved to him from a table near the front, and both she and Everett grinned as he slipped into his seat.

"Where's your umbrella?" Schulyer asked, making a show of dabbing her napkin on the lapel of his suit coat.

"I don't own one," he admitted, making a mental note to find a store that sold umbrellas after lunch today.

"You've lived in Denver too long," Everett told him.

Gavin rolled his eyes. "I have an ice scraper."

His brother chuckled. "Not going to do you much good around here."

"I'll dry off eventually." Now that he was seated, he glanced around the diner's homey interior, appreciating the retro vibe of the decor. "What made you choose this place for lunch?"

"Best pie in town," Schuyler told him.

Everett nodded. "Lila wants me to bring her home a piece of lemon meringue. And cherry. And pecan."

"Wow." Schuyler glanced up from her menu. "I don't remember Lila having such a huge appetite."

"She's…uh…" Everett threw a look to Gavin then drew in a deep breath. "I'll share them with her."

"You could probably eat a whole pie on your own," Schuyler answered absently.

As he had at Maddie's wedding, Gavin wondered again if Lila and Everett might be expecting. But if his brother wanted to keep the news private for a while longer, he'd respect that.

"How's Christine?" Schuyler asked after the waitress had taken their orders.

"Fine." The truth was he hadn't spoken to Christine since he'd left her house earlier in the week. She'd texted him an update and photos of Princess Di, who seemed to be recovering nicely. While the dog was undeniably cute, Gavin had hoped for a little more. It was strange to find himself in this role reversal. Normally with women, he was the one trying to take things slow.

He'd learned early on in his dating life that if he didn't stay cognizant of managing expectations, he'd end up hurting women he cared about. So he'd established guidelines for himself around dating—how many times a week he could see a woman, the amount of phone calls or texts. Maybe it was cold, but he liked to think it had prevented heartache for his girlfriends and guilt for him.

Christine was different in so many ways. The romance might be pretend, despite their off-the-charts chemistry, but he liked spending time with her. An evening of a vet emergency, carryout pizza and an old movie had been the most fun he'd had in ages. He could be himself with her and wanted to make her see how much she underestimated herself. Gavin hoped their friendship would continue even after he returned to Denver, although the thought of moving into the "friend zone" and never kissing her again held no appeal whatsoever.

He'd expected her to call or reach out to him to let him know she wanted to see him again. That was how things usually went with women. He couldn't decide if Christine was playing it safe because of their arrangement or if she truly wasn't that interested in him outside of what was expected to maintain the ruse of being in love.

"Have you two thought any more about wedding plans now that you're in Austin?" Schuyler asked.

Gavin shrugged. "We're both busy."

"That's silly," she insisted. "Let me help."

"Schuyler could take care of everything," Everett added, none too helpfully in Gavin's opinion.

"Don't the two of you have enough of your own marital bliss to keep you occupied? How come everyone has so much time to worry about my love life?"

"We don't want you to mess it up," Schuyler said gently. "No one likes seeing you lonely."

Gavin felt the simple pronouncement like a sharp right to the jaw. "I'm not lonely. I have plenty of friends."

She shook her head then sipped at her water. "You have buddies to hang with and work colleagues. It's not the same."

Gavin darted a pleading glance at Everett. "Can you throw me a line here?"

"You have seemed at loose ends," Everett answered.

"Loose ends? How can you say that? I'm about to make partner."

Everett shrugged. "Having a good job isn't the same thing as having a good life."

"Coming from the man who was solely dedicated to his job until recently."

"Lila changed everything."

The waitress brought their food—a club sandwich for Schuyler and himself and a burger for Everett. As she placed the food in front of them, Gavin felt his frustration mount. This fake engagement with Christine was supposed to alleviate the pressure from his parents and siblings, not add to it. What would it take for them to get out of his business?

"I think it's great that the two of you are so happy," he said, forcing his tone to remain neutral. "Christine and I will start wedding plans when we're ready, but you have to trust that I can manage my own life. I'm not a kid who's going to make a stupid decision."

"Fair enough," Everett conceded, then took a big bite of his burger.

Schuyler looked less convinced. Despite the fact that she was one of the middle Fortunado siblings, she'd always been a caregiver for her brothers and sisters. Their mom found it amusing to watch Schuyler fuss like a mother hen, and Gavin knew she did it because she cared so much.

"You said you wanted to talk about the reunion," he told her.

She pointed a fry in his direction. "I'm going to let you change the subject because I love you. But know that we're all sticking our noses where they probably don't belong for the same reason. If you ever want to actually talk about your relationship with more than one-syllable answers to my questions, I'm here for you."

Gavin blew out a breath. Irritating as they could be, he loved his sisters and brothers with his whole heart. "I'll remember that. Thank you."

She smiled then popped the fry into her mouth. After she'd swallowed, she pulled out a pen and a small notebook from her purse. "I've confirmed with Nolan that his brothers and sisters will be there. They're flying in just for the party, so it will be a quick trip."

She flipped open the notebook. "The Paseo Fortunes aren't going to be able to make it because Grayson has some kind of rodeo award ceremony they're attending in Dallas. Nate promised they'd find another time to come to Austin to meet everyone."

"Lila heard that Gerald and the triplets' mom have rekindled their romance now that he's separated from Charlotte," Everett said between bites. "Obviously, it's a pretty big deal since Gerald and Charlotte were married for so many years. She can't be happy about losing him to his first love."

"Especially when she went to such great lengths to keep him from knowing about the triplets."

Gavin shook his head. When Schuyler first realized their connection to the famous Fortune clan, she'd traveled to the tiny town of Paseo, Texas, to talk to Nathan Fortune. Nate, along with his brothers Grayson and Jayden, were three of the illegitimate children of Gerald Fortune, who'd had a brief affair with their mother, Deborah, back when he'd been Jerome Fortune.

It was crazy to think that Jerome Fortune had been desperate enough to fake his own death and reemerge as Gerald Robinson as a way to escape his domineering father, Julius. And just as shocking to discover that their dad, Kenneth, was one of Julius's illegitimate sons, making them all Fortunes.

"Could you imagine Mom and Dad getting divorced at this point?" he asked his siblings, confident in his parents' love for each other.

"No," Schuyler answered immediately. "But I also couldn't imagine Mom trying to keep Dad from knowing he had three sons out in the world."

"Not just three sons," Gavin corrected. "Aren't there a bunch more illegitimate Fortune children out there?"

Everett nodded. "As far as the family knows, they've all been uncovered at this point. Apparently, Charlotte kept a secret dossier on each of them without Gerald's knowledge."

"It sounds like Gerald and Charlotte's marriage wasn't exactly perfect," Gavin said.

"Not at all," Schuyler agreed. "It still amazes me how open most of his legitimate kids have been about getting to know these half siblings. It's part of why I have such high hopes for the reunion. I really want all of us to feel like a family."

"Why is it important to you?" Gavin asked.

Schuyler was quiet for a moment before answering, "When I decided to infiltrate the Mendozas to get the goods on the Fortunes, I expected to be disappointed. Not only did I meet Carlo and fall in love, I also learned that the Fortune family is filled with a lot of decent people trying to make the best of difficult situations. I can't help but think that we have more in common with them than we might realize. Strength in numbers and all that."

Everett frowned. "As usual, it sounds like you've got everything figured out. Why do you need our help?"

"I'd like you to reach out to Gerald's sons. I know Ben and Keaton are willing to meet and I'm sure I can convince the sisters to attend, but I have a feeling the other brothers will respond better to a little 'mano a mano' talk."

"Don't you think Gerald's kids have enough to deal with right now?" Gavin took a long drink of iced tea. "First, all the illegitimate siblings showing up and then their parents separating? It's a lot to handle."

"But this is something positive," Schuyler insisted. "We're not a threat to them and neither are the New Orleans Fortunes. But we agree the Robinson siblings have handled all of the changes in their lives exceptionally well. I'm hoping they can help the rest of us."

"I'm willing to call Wes," Everett offered, mentioning Ben's twin.

Schuyler beamed at their eldest brother then turned her laser-focused gaze to Gavin. "What about you?"

"Big family parties make me itchy," he said, pretending to scratch at his arms and earning a fry in the face from his sister. "I'm more a lone-wolf type."

Everett let out a bark of laughter. "Not exactly spoken like a man who's ready for a trip down the aisle."

"I didn't mean it like that," Gavin amended, realizing he needed to watch what he said if he was going to make this fake engagement believable.

Schuyler seemed to take his comment in stride. "You can't spout that lone-wolf nonsense now that you're engaged to Christine. She's…" A wide smile split her lips as she glanced toward the door. "Speaking of your better half…" she said, wagging her brows at Gavin.

He turned to see Christine placing an umbrella in the stand next to the diner's entrance. She was with a woman he'd seen the other day at the agency office and the man who'd been hitting on her at Maddie's wedding.

His gaze narrowed as the guy leaned in to speak into Christine's ear. She laughed softly but shifted away, placing the other woman between her and her would-be suitor. Had the guy not heard she was dating Gavin? Was it possible he just didn't care?

As if sensing the weight of Gavin's gaze, Christine glanced toward him. His heart stuttered when she smiled as if the surprise of seeing him made her happy. Then her gaze flicked to Everett and Schuyler and he saw her draw in a sharp breath. She was nervous. He didn't want anything about their arrangement to make her nervous. She knew how much everyone in his family liked her. Although maybe that was part of it. She was afraid of what would happen when their time together ended.

He rose from the table at the same time she excused herself from her coworkers. The man—Bobby, if Gavin remembered correctly—gave Gavin a slow once-over then followed the other woman toward a table.

Christine walked toward Gavin and there was nothing fake or forced about taking her hand and brushing a lingering kiss across her mouth.

"Hi," he whispered against her lips.

"Hi," she breathed.

"Hey, Christine," Schuyler called from behind him. "Great to see you."

Gavin kept Christine's hand in his as he shifted so that she could speak to his sister and brother. It wasn't what he wanted. He wanted to pull her out of the restaurant and find a quiet place to reconnect with her, and if he was being totally honest, to kiss her senseless.

"Hey, Schuyler." Christine smiled. "Hi, Everett."

"How's the old man doing at the new office?" Everett asked with a wink. "Is he driving everyone crazy with his type-A personality?"

Gavin felt Christine stiffen next to him even though her smile remained fixed in place. "He's great, as usual."

Schuyler rolled her eyes. "Everyone probably feels like they're getting a break with him compared to Maddie and Zach. Those two are intense when it comes to real estate."

"We miss them, too," Christine said.

"Chris, we're ready to order. You coming over?"

Gavin felt his eyes narrow as Bobby called to Christine. "Who calls you Chris?" he muttered with a frown.

"Only my family and Bobby," she said. "I don't like the nickname."

"I don't like that guy," he said, dropping a quick kiss on the top of her head. "You can sit with us if you want."

"We're talking about the reunion I'm planning," Schuyler told her. "I'm so excited you'll be there, too. You're already like one of the family."

"Oh…uh…thanks." A blush rose to Christine's cheeks.

"Where's your ring?" Schuyler's gaze had zeroed

in on Christine's left hand. "I thought you'd be wearing it now that everyone knows about the two of you."

Gavin's stomach pitched. He hadn't thought about—

"It's at the jeweler being sized," Christine answered, squeezing his hand.

Schuyler nodded. "I can't wait to see it."

"It's beautiful," Christine said with a smile only he seemed to realize was fake. "I should go. Great to see you all."

Reluctantly, he let go of her hand. "I'll call you later?"

"Sure."

He leaned in to whisper in her ear, "And you'll answer?"

She nodded. "Of course."

"Great. I'm planning something for Sunday, so I hope you're free."

Her face went suddenly pale. "Sure. I guess."

Okay, that wasn't the response he'd expected, but he didn't want to push her for an explanation in front of his siblings.

He kissed her again, somewhat placated when she sighed and relaxed into him. That was more like it.

"Chris, come on."

"Can I punch that guy?" he asked in a tone low enough only she could hear.

"I don't think your dad would approve," she told him with a teasing smile before walking away.

"You've got it bad," Everett said when he sat down again.

"I'm ready for the wedding bells," Schuyler added in a singsong voice, then hummed a few bars of "Chapel of Love."

"You know Valene's still single?" Gavin grabbed a

fry from Schuyler's plate. "And Connor. I'm off the market so why don't you focus on one of them for a while?"

Everett chuckled. "You're such an easy target."

"Plus, you're only in Texas for a few weeks." Schuyler grinned at him. "Now that she's said yes, we've got to make sure you don't mess things up."

"I'm not going to mess up," Gavin said, pulling out his wallet when the waitress returned with the check. "Anything more we need to know about your reunion? I've got to get back to the office for a meeting."

As Schuyler went over details for the event, Gavin glanced behind him to the table where Christine sat with her coworkers. His gut clenched when she smiled at something the woman said. He didn't want to mess things up with her, but already their arrangement was more complicated than he'd ever imagined.

Mostly because of his feelings for her. She'd done him a favor as a friend by distracting Schuyler at the wedding and then agreeing to pose as his fiancée for his time in Austin.

It wasn't supposed to be more than that. He'd dated plenty of women and managed to keep his heart out of the mix with all of them. Why was Christine different?

She'd told him that she wasn't his type, and on the surface that might be true. But the connection he felt to her was undeniable. This crazy need to be near her made him both excited and anxious. He'd been joking when he made the crack about being a lone wolf, but it wasn't too far from the truth.

With her sweet smile and gentle spirit, it somehow felt like Christine was changing everything.

Chapter Nine

Either Gavin Fortunado had missed his calling as an actor or he was actually interested in her. Christine touched her fingertips to her lips when she was back in her office after lunch, imagining she could still feel the warmth of his mouth on hers.

Although she'd been a bundle of nerves running into him at the diner with Schuyler and Everett, he'd seemed relaxed and happy to see her. The way he'd taken her hand and then kissed her had made her feel like she was really his fiancée. But the rush of excitement brought on by that thought was followed almost immediately by a clenching in her heart.

If she let herself believe that, it could only end in heartache. When this started, she'd expected to put on a show when they were around his family. She would never have guessed she'd be going on actual dates with Gavin. And while she knew she should keep her walls up because of the risk to her heart, there was no way to deny how much she wanted to be with him.

She pulled her phone from her purse and dialed the familiar number.

"Christine?" Her mother picked up on the first ring. "What's wrong?"

"Nothing, Mom." Christine swallowed against the tension that accompanied every conversation with her mother. "I'm calling to say hi and see how you're doing."

"It's the middle of the day," Stephanie Briscoe pointed out as if she might not realize it. "Did you get fired?"

"No," Christine answered through clenched teeth.

"You said you were running the real estate agency those Fortunados own in Austin."

"I still am. It was a promotion."

"It sounds like a lot of work," her mother said drily. "I wasn't sure you'd be able to handle it."

"Mom." Christine sighed. How many times did she have to have some version of the "you can't handle your own life" conversation with her mother? "I've been working for Kenneth for ten years. I'm good at my job. They trust me. They rely on me."

"I worry," her mother whispered, indignation lacing her tone. "I'm your mother. That's *my* job."

"Okay," Christine agreed although her mother's concern had always felt more like judgment. "But I'm doing fine." She didn't mention the recent fall-off in business since the beginning of the year. In a meeting with Kenneth yesterday, they'd chalked it up to a normal post-holiday lull, but he hadn't seemed convinced and neither was she. Things had gotten off to a great start when Maddie and Zach had first taken over. She hated the fact that they'd be returning to trouble, even though it had nothing to do with Christine's role at the agency.

She wished she could mention the issues to her mother. It would be nice to have the kind of relationship where she went to her mom—or her dad, for that matter—for support and advice. But that wasn't the way of things and she didn't expect their family dynamic to change anytime soon.

"I'm glad," her mother answered. "I just want you to be okay."

"I know, Mom." She didn't bother to mention that it was the other Briscoe daughter who needed her mother's concern. Her sister, Aimee, had recently been fired from her job, and while she'd quickly been picked up by another salon, her spotty employment record was becoming a problem.

Christine had successfully graduated college and had a career she loved, but Aimee had floundered since high school, despite being a talented hairstylist. Their parents couldn't admit that the favorite daughter was the failure of the family, and Christine, whom no one had ever expected to amount to much, was thriving. She certainly wasn't going to point it out.

She decided instead to get to the real reason she'd phoned. "I'm calling about Sunday. I might not be able to make dinner."

"Christine, no. You promised when you moved back to Austin that you'd make an effort."

"I have," Christine insisted, hating being put on the defensive. "I've come for dinner every week."

"It's important to your father and me that the four of us spend more time together. Your sister is going through a rough time, and she needs our support."

Christine didn't want to hear about Aimee's rough time, which most likely stemmed from too many nights of partying with her friends and the monumental hangovers that seemed to prevent her from showing up to work on time.

"I understand, Mom. It's just one Sunday. I promise."

"Why can't you come?" her mother demanded. "Are you behind at work and need to catch up?"

"I have a date," Christine blurted.

Silence from the other end of the line.

"Since when?" Stephanie asked. "Who is this guy who wants to keep you from seeing your family? I don't like the sound of it."

Christine had to work not to growl into the phone. She loved her mother, but for some reason the love she received in return always manifested in criticism. It had been that way since she could remember. Her mother had constantly commented on Christine's weight or lack of friends, comparing her to Aimee with Christine always falling short.

"He's not trying to keep me from seeing you. I didn't mention it to him."

"Bring him to dinner," her mother answered simply.

"What?"

"You heard me. Unless it's some casual fling or you're worried we won't approve. I want to know more about your life, Christine. Let us meet your boyfriend. I want us to be closer. After the incident with my heart last year, you know I've been reevaluating things and focusing on what's important. You're important to me, sweetie."

Christine sighed. Just like that, all the fight went out of her. In addition to the position in Austin being a promotion, she'd taken the job to be closer to her family, and particularly her mother. Stephanie had a heart attack in March of last year, spending four days in the hospital then successfully completing months of cardiac rehab. Christine appreciated everything her mom was doing to make better choices in her life. She might not feel like she belonged in her adventurous, outgoing family, but she loved them.

In the hospital, her mother had told her she regretted that they hadn't been closer. She'd said she wanted another chance to repair her relationship with Christine. Wasn't that what every nonfavorite child wanted to hear from a parent, even as an adult?

"I'm not sure what time we're going out," she admitted. "But if it works, I'll bring Gavin to dinner."

"Gavin," her mother repeated, her tone gentler now. "I like that name. Does he make you happy?"

"Yes," Christine answered without hesitation. "So happy."

"Then I can't wait to meet him."

Christine said goodbye and disconnected the call. She'd purposely not mentioned Gavin's last name or that he was supposedly her fiancé. It was bad enough her mom would share with her dad and sister that Christine had a boyfriend. Christine still wasn't certain she'd have the nerve to take Gavin to Sunday dinner with her family, although the truth was he'd fit in better with them than she ever had.

She turned her attention back to her computer. Kenneth had tasked her with reviewing the agency's historical contract data to find a pattern to help determine why many of their deals were suddenly going south. It was worrisome but the task was something she could manage, unlike her feelings for Gavin.

Right now she needed to feel like she had control over something and it certainly wasn't going to be her wayward heart.

"We're doing what?" Christine felt her mouth go dry as she stared at Gavin.

"Ziplining," he repeated softly. "If you're up for it."

She concentrated on pulling air in and out of her lungs without hyperventilating. "Did you miss the part where I said I'm afraid of heights?"

He smiled.

"Deathly afraid," she added.

He took her hand and drew her closer. They stood in the area between her kitchen and family room on Sunday morning, light spilling in from the window above the sink. Gavin had arrived minutes earlier and looked even more handsome in a casual cotton button-down shirt and jeans than he did in his normal workweek uniform of a suit and tie. His hair was slightly rumpled and a thick shadow of stubble covered his jaw, like he hadn't bothered to shave for the entire weekend.

She was a big fan of this outdoorsy side of him.

Although not a fan of his plan for the day.

As if sensing her unease, Diana rose from her dog bed in the corner and trotted over for a gentle head butt.

"She can sense your fear," Gavin said, bending to scratch Di behind the ears just the way she liked. The animal promptly forgot about comforting Christine and melted into a puddle on the hardwood floor, exposing her belly for Gavin's attention.

"Traitor," Christine muttered.

"If you don't want to try it, we can do something else." Gavin glanced up as he rubbed the blissed-out dog's belly. "But you mentioned that you'd like to become more adventurous. The guy who runs the outfitter is a friend of mine from high school. I trust him implicitly so I figured this would be a safe way for you to face one of your fears."

"Safe," she repeated, testing the word on her tongue. How could she possibly be safe while harnessed to a cable and soaring through the air?

"I'll keep you safe," he said, straightening and looking into her eyes with so much sincerity that it took her breath away for an entirely different reason. A reason that made her knees go weak. "Do you trust me?"

She nodded, not convinced she could manage actual words at the moment.

One side of his mouth curved as if her answer made him happy.

"Are you ready for an adventure?" he asked.

She nodded again.

His smile widened. "I promise you'll be okay."

She said goodbye to Princess Di and followed Gavin out of the house, locking the door behind them.

When they'd gotten into his vehicle and turned onto the ramp for the interstate, he smiled at her. "How was your week?"

"Long," she admitted. "And busy."

"Maddie and Zach return later tonight, right?"

She nodded. "I'm glad they got away but it's too bad it was such a short honeymoon and they're coming back to—" She broke off, not sure how much to reveal about the drop in business at the agency.

"What's going on at the office? Is everything okay with Dad?"

"He's amazing as usual," she answered immediately. "Why do you ask?"

"You had a strange reaction when Everett asked about him in the diner the other day."

She shook her head. "It's not your dad. I'm not sure whether it's supposed to be a secret or not, but there have been some strange things happening with some of our deals lately."

"What kind of strange?"

"We're losing clients and having trouble with existing contracts. It doesn't make sense based on how strong business was right out of the gate. I'm not sure what's going on, but your dad's upset about it."

"Does Maddie know?"

"Not yet. It came to light this week, but there's definitely a pattern. Your dad didn't want to bother them while they were on their honeymoon. We're scheduled to meet to go over reports and trends tomorrow morning."

"She and Zach will figure it out," Gavin said, smoothing his thumb across the back of her hand. "There has to be an explanation."

"I hope so. We all had such high hopes for the Austin office." She stared out the window as the scenery changed from urban to more rural. It was one of the things she loved about Texas—the wide-open spaces. Even in the middle of the city, there was a sense of the cowboy spirit that made the state so special. Austin had a different vibe than Houston had, a more eclectic atmosphere with most folks taking the local slogan Keep Austin Weird quite seriously.

"Do you miss Denver?" she asked, glancing toward Gavin.

His fingers tightened slightly on the steering wheel. "I miss heading up to the mountains to ski on the weekends," he admitted. "Denver still has a bit of the cowboy feel to it, so it's not that different from Austin. A lot sunnier and less humid, I guess."

"My hair would love it." She tugged on the ends of her long locks. "Some days I'm a massive frizz ball no matter how much product I use."

"Your hair is amazing," he said. "The color is so bright."

She groaned softly. "They used to call me carrot top in school. I hated having red hair."

"It makes you special," he told her.

You make me special, she wanted to say but managed to keep her mouth shut. She'd told herself she would stay in the moment today and not worry about what might happen with Gavin or how much being with him made her heart happy.

Nope. She was keeping her heart out of the mix.

He exited the highway onto a two-lane road that led into the rolling hills north of the city.

"You doing okay?" Gavin squeezed her hand, and she hoped he didn't notice her sweaty palm.

"I can't believe I agreed to this." She leaned forward when the first zipline tower came into view, the seat belt stretching across her chest. "It's so high."

"You've got this," he assured her.

If only she had his confidence.

He parked in front of a cabin that seemed to be the outdoor company's office. Austin Zips read the sign above the covered porch.

Gavin got out of the Audi and walked around to her side. Her body felt weighted with lead, but she forced herself to climb out and pasted a smile on her face. "Looks like fun," she said, shading her eyes as she gazed up at the ropes course that had been built behind the office.

"Liar," Gavin whispered.

She laughed. "It's the stuff of my worst nightmares," she admitted. "But I'm going to face my fears."

Gavin leaned in to kiss her. "That's my girl."

"Fortunado!" A man's deep voice rang out from the door to the office.

"Hey, Marc," Gavin called. "Thanks for letting us come out on such short notice."

"It's our slow season," the man said as he walked forward. "But I'd always make time for you, buddy. I hear you're now one of the big-wig Fortunes."

Gavin's expression didn't change, but Christine felt a wave of tension roll through him. "You know how things go," he said casually. "It just means an even larger family."

"Sure," the man agreed affably. As he came down the steps, Christine couldn't help but smile. Gavin's friend could have been the Keep Austin Weird poster child. His sandy-blond hair was long enough to be held back in a man bun. Despite the temperatures hovering in the low fifties, he wore a pair of board shorts and a floral-print silk shirt like he should be hanging on a tropical beach instead of in the middle of nowhere outside Austin.

He shook Gavin's hand and did a couple of friendly back slaps then turned to Christine. "Gavin mentioned you have a bit of a fear of heights?"

She licked her lips and nodded.

"I want to reassure you," Marc said, leaning closer, "that you're in good hands with me. I've only had—" he tapped a tanned finger on his chin "—I guess that would be a half dozen equipment failures this year, but only one of them was fatal."

Christine took a step back. "Um…"

Marc threw back his head and laughed. "Joking with you, darlin'. We have a perfect safety record at Austin Zips."

"Right." Christine tried to laugh, but it sounded more like a croak. "Of course you do."

Gavin shook his head. "Not funny, Marc."

"Sorry." The man held up his hands, palms out. "We're going to make this easy and fun. By the time you're finished, you'll be shouting, 'More, Marc. Give me more.'"

Christine felt her eyes go wide.

"You seriously need to grow up," Gavin said, and his tone held a vague warning.

Marc seemed to get the message because he launched into an in-depth overview of the zip lines, the safety procedures and inspections that occurred each day and the standards his company followed to ensure a safe and fun experience for its customers.

Christine appreciated the information, and it gave her more confidence in Marc's level of professionalism.

"We're going to take the Mule out to the first platform. I have helmets and water already packed." He pointed to a four-seater utility terrain vehicle parked at the far side of the building. "You two load up while I grab my sunglasses and I'll be right out."

He jogged up the steps and into the building.

"You're going to be fine," Gavin said, wrapping an arm around her shoulder.

"Famous last words," she whispered, earning a chuckle from him.

"It's not too late to turn around. We can bag this whole idea and go see a movie or take Di for a walk. I'm just happy to have a day off and to spend it with you."

Christine appreciated the out, but she wasn't going to take it. "This is my chance to have an adventure." She flashed what she hoped was a confident smile as they got into the Mule with Gavin following. "Even if it's a miniadventure."

"The first of many," he told her.

The sun had warmed things enough to turn it into a perfect January day in Texas. She kept her focus on the blue sky and how nice it felt to be sitting so close to Gavin as Marc joined them and they headed across the rolling hills.

The zip line course was situated about a quarter mile from the building, traversing along the perimeter of the woods that bordered the property. As they got closer she realized the cables not only ran next to the woods but also through the trees, so that she'd actually have the sensation of soaring through the forest, if she could manage to keep her eyes open.

Marc parked then led them to the first platform. He gave another safety talk and explained how the two points of contact system with the safety lines worked. She and Gavin put on helmets and then the harnesses while Marc used his walkie-talkie to radio someone. A minute later an ATV sped toward them through the forest.

"This is Chip." Marc introduced an older man, who

was well over six feet tall and skinny as a rail. "He's going to be leading the two of you today and I'll follow."

Chip winked at Christine. "I'm going to go first down each run so you'll know it's safe."

She nodded then felt Gavin massage her shoulder. "You look a little pale," he said gently.

"Has anyone ever thrown up mid-zip line?" she asked Marc.

He laughed. "You'd be the first, darlin'. But don't worry about that. Do whatever's gonna make you feel better in the end."

"You've got this, Adventure Girl," Gavin told her as she clipped into the safety line then climbed onto the platform. Marc snapped Chip into the harness and with a playful wave, he took off across the huge open space between where they stood and the next platform.

"Wow," Christine whispered when Chip landed on the other side.

"Easy enough, right?" Marc asked.

Despite her racing heart and sweaty palms, she nodded.

He crooked a finger at her. "Do you want to go next?"

She shook her head. "Gavin will go."

"Are you sure?" Gavin asked.

"You need to be on the other end to catch me," she told him.

"I'll definitely catch you." He allowed Marc to connect his harness to the cable then took off, giving an enthusiastic whoop of delight as he sped from one platform to the next.

"I'd like to go home now," Christine whispered, earning a belly laugh from Marc. "Gavin made it look so easy. He's going to think I'm the biggest wuss in the world when I puke or pee myself on this harness. Could you imagine a worse way to end a date? I'm going to ruin everything."

"Darlin', I've known Gavin since we were stealing hootch from his daddy's liquor cabinet. I've seen lots of ladies on his arm over the years but never has he looked at one the way he looks at you. Don't worry about ruining anything. If you climbed down this platform and said all you want to do is go shopping at the nearest mall, that man would gladly hold your bags."

Christine smiled despite her fear. "I doubt that, but I appreciate you saying it."

"It's the truth."

"No shopping malls," she said, stepping forward. "I'm going to conquer my fear today."

"That's what we like to hear." Marc snapped her harness to the cable, explaining once again how to use the active brake if she felt she needed it.

Her knees trembled as she inched to the edge of the platform, and sweat beaded between her shoulder blades.

Gavin shouted words of encouragement, but she could barely make them out over the pounding in her head. She drew in a breath and took off, screaming first from terror and then with excitement as she sailed across the air toward the trees. She hit the brake lever the way Marc had shown her as she approached the next platform and a moment later Gavin's arms were around her. Good thing, too, because she wasn't sure she could stand on her own at the moment.

Chip unfastened her harness and she wrapped her shaking arms around Gavin's neck. "I did it," she whispered. "And I didn't pee myself."

Both men laughed and Chip patted her helmet. "Way to hold it together."

"You were amazing," Gavin said, kissing her cheek. "Are you ready to go again?"

She drew in a deep breath, most of her nervous butterflies replaced by exhilaration. "I am. Thank you for this day. It's the best ever."

He grinned and kissed her.

Marc joined them on the platform. "Okay, lovebirds. Let's hold off on the spit swapping until we're back to solid ground." He pointed at Christine. "Nice work. Next, we're going to show you how to curl into a ball to go faster."

The nerves returned, but Christine quickly tamped them down. She was going to try whatever Marc threw at her. The idea that she wasn't a total wimp made her feel braver than she ever could have imagined.

"I'm ready," she said, tightening the strap on her helmet. "For anything."

Gavin stood below the final platform, smiling as Christine rappelled down toward him, marveling at the change in her. As beautiful as she'd been at the start of their zip line adventure, there was something even more appealing about her now, a sense of abandonment that made her breathtaking. She was windblown with flushed cheeks and a smudge of dirt down the front of her shirt.

She hopped down the last few feet, grinning widely and doing a funny little dance with her upper body as Chip unstrapped the rock-climbing gear from her waist.

"She's a helluva sport," Marc said, handing Gavin a bottle of cold water. "I can't imagine bringing a woman who's deathly afraid of heights out here and having her handle it like a champ."

"She did great," Gavin agreed.

"You like her."

"She's extremely likable."

"Nah." Marc nudged his arm. "I mean, you really *like* her."

Gavin paused in the act of opening his water bottle. He hadn't mentioned the engagement to Marc. It was one thing with his family, but he figured it would be better to keep his story simple where he could. The pretend engagement definitely complicated things.

But he did really like Christine. Way more than he ever would have guessed at the beginning of their arrangement. Was that only a week ago?

How had his feelings changed so quickly?

"Where did the two of you meet?" Marc asked.

"She worked for my dad for years and now runs the Austin branch of the agency."

"So you thinking of moving back?"

Gavin felt himself frown. "My life's in Denver," he said quietly, suddenly understanding the point his siblings had been trying to make when they said a job was not the same thing as a life.

Marc slapped him gently on the back. "Not that I'm trying to skim your milk, but if the long-distance thing doesn't work out, I may have to swoop in to comfort her."

Gavin thought about the expiration date on their arrangement and his gut tightened. "No one's swooping in with Christine," he told his old friend.

Marc only laughed. "You've got it bad," he said, then walked forward to help Chip put away the equipment.

Christine grinned as she approached, pumping her fists in the air. "Did you see me?"

He smiled, pushing aside his discontent over the boundaries and timeline that defined their relationship.

"You were amazing." He wrapped his arms around her waist and lifted her off the ground. She smelled like a tantalizing mix of shampoo and the outdoors, fresh and clean. "Skydiving next?"

She laughed and kissed him. "Let's not get crazy."

When he lowered her to the ground, she cupped his cheeks in her palms. "Thank you, Gavin. I would never have done something like this on my own."

"I had no doubt you could."

Marc and Chip joined them and they rode back to the office. Christine laced her fingers with his like it was the most natural thing in the world, and damn, he wanted it to be.

"How about the ropes course?" Marc asked Christine with a wink. "It should be a piece of cake now that you're a master of heights."

Gavin expected her to decline, but she nodded and grinned at him. "Sounds great to me. What do you think?"

"Let's go," he told her and for the next hour they traversed the suspended ropes course, crossing bridges and climbing through obstacles. He could tell she was scared but never let that fear slow her down.

The sky was beginning to turn shades of pink and orange by the time they headed back toward Austin. Christine pulled out a pen and a small notebook from her purse and ticked off a list of other activities she wanted to try now that she knew she could overcome her fear of heights. Gavin's chest constricted as he listened to her plans.

He could see himself with her on every adventure, from bungee jumping to riding the roller coasters at the state fair. At the same time, he'd never imagined himself in a long-term relationship. Part of what allowed him to be so open with Christine was, ironically, knowing their time together had a built-in expiration date.

He could give himself fully because it was safe. But wanting more felt dangerous, both to him and to her. He didn't want to hurt her but his past had shown him that he wasn't the type of man who had more to give a woman like her.

"When did your fear of heights start?" he asked, needing to get out of his own head and the doubts swirling there. "You managed today like a pro."

Her grip tightened on the notebook. "My family went on a vacation when I was younger to a waterpark near Galveston. We were all supposed to go on this superhigh slide, but I didn't want to."

"Because of your fear?"

She tugged her bottom lip between her teeth. "Not exactly," she admitted after a moment. "I was overweight as a girl. It was a pretty big issue for my dad. He'd been a marine, and physical fitness was important to him. My younger sister was always into sports, and I never felt like I fit in. We're a year apart and as we got older, my dad started taking us on extreme vacations. I could never keep up so I think maybe I developed all my fears—heights, water and speed—as a way to have an excuse not to participate."

"So if you didn't participate, what happened?"

Her smile was sad. "The first couple of trips were

difficult because he'd try to force me to do things. Eventually, I just stayed behind with my grandma."

"While your family went on vacation without you?"

"It wasn't a big deal," she insisted. "In fact, I had a much better time with my grammy than I would have if I'd tried to keep up with the rest of them."

"Christine—"

"Anyway, that's how it started." She gave him a smile that was as bright and brittle as a piece of cut glass. "But today changed everything. Thank you."

"You don't have to thank me. I'm glad I could be there with you. Now, what are you thinking for dinner?"

She sucked in a breath and glanced at the clock on the Audi's dashboard. "Oh, no. Is it really after five?"

He nodded. "Time flies and all that."

"I'm supposed to be at my parents' for dinner by six. It felt like we zip-lined for thirty minutes."

"More like three hours plus time for the ropes course. Where do your parents live?"

"On the west side of Austin, near West Lake Hills."

"I could—"

"They want you to come, too," she blurted then covered her face with her hands. "I'm sorry. I should have said something earlier. I tried to get out of the dinner, but I told you my mom thinks that Sunday dinners with the four of us will somehow bring us closer."

"I don't—"

"I'm sure it sounds horrible," she continued, shifting her hands to glance at him from the corner of her eye. "I don't blame you for not wanting to go. But it's out of the way to go all the way back to my place. If you just drop me off at my parents' now, after dinner I can call an Ub—"

"I don't mind going," he interrupted, reaching out to tug her hands away from her face. "I'd like to meet your family."

She wrinkled her nose. "Why?"

"Because I want to know you better," he said with a laugh. "You know my family, and they all love you."

"My family is different from yours, and not in a good way."

"It doesn't matter."

"There's nothing to learn about me from meeting them."

"If your mom wants me there, I don't want to rebuff the invitation."

"Are you sure?" She sounded even more nervous than she'd been before the zip line tour. "I can make an excuse. This definitely wasn't part of our arrangement."

"I'd like to join you for dinner with your parents and sister," he said gently. "But only if you're okay with it. If not, I'll drop you off around the corner then come back and pick you up when you're ready to leave."

"Seriously?" she couldn't help but ask. "You'd do that for me?"

Gavin was quickly coming to realize he'd do just about anything for this woman, but he wasn't about to admit it out loud.

"That's what friends are for," he answered instead.

Chapter Ten

Christine tried not to look like she was about to throw up as she opened the door to her parents' house and led Gavin inside.

At this point she would have taken skydiving, maybe even without a parachute, over introducing him to her family. The prospect of it had seemed manageable during the drive, thanks to Gavin's quiet confidence, but the reality of it was a different story.

"Chris?" her mom called from the kitchen, and she grimaced. She hated the nickname her family still insisted on using. It brought back memories of being a chubby kid with an unfortunate bowl haircut that made her look like a boy. She'd tried her hardest to fit in but ended up feeling lousy about herself most of the time.

She wanted to believe she'd shed her self-doubts the way she had her extra weight, but it was easier when she was away from this house and her family.

"Hi, Mom," she said with a forced smile as she entered the kitchen.

Her mother looked up from where she was cutting tomatoes for a salad, her eyes widening at the sight of Gavin. Christine might not be the fat, awkward girl she once was, but she knew her mom wouldn't expect her to be dating someone who looked like Gavin.

Christine's dad walked into the kitchen from the family room. "Hey, kid," he said, taking in Christine's tousled hair and dusty clothes. "Looks like you need a shower."

"We went zip lining and didn't have time to change before coming here," she reported. "Mom and Dad, this is Gavin Fortunado. My...um...boyfriend." Cursing her fair complexion, she willed away the color she could feel flooding her cheeks. She hoped Gavin was okay that she didn't mention their pretend engagement to her family. She understood why it helped with the Fortunados, but the shock of her having an actual boyfriend would be plenty for her parents and sister.

"Fortunado? Like the family who owns the agency where Christine works?"

Gavin nodded. "Kenneth is my dad. Christine and I met at the office in Houston."

"I'm Stephanie and this is Dave," her mother told him, her tone almost dazed. "Are you a real estate agent?"

"Nice to meet you," Gavin said smoothly, walking forward and shaking first her father's hand and then her mother's. "I'm actually an attorney, and I'm sorry Christine and I are a bit of a mess. She just had to do the ropes course after we finished the zip line tour, and time got away from us."

Dave Briscoe gave a disbelieving laugh. "Chris on a ropes course? You've got to be kidding."

"I'm not." Gavin pulled out his phone. "She did fantastic. Would you like to see the photos?"

Her mother put down the knife. "I would."

"Did they have a harness big enough for her?"

The comment came from behind her and Christine turned, her chest tightening as her sister, Aimee, sauntered into the room. She wore a black tank top and tight jeans that hugged her trim hips. Aimee placed an empty beer bottle on the counter and gave a bubbly laugh, like this was all a big joke. "Oh, wait. She's not fat anymore. I always forget."

"I lost the weight years ago," Christine said through clenched teeth.

Gavin gave her sister the barest hint of a smile then took out his phone and pulled up the photos for her mother.

"Good for you, Christine," her mom said, taking the phone from Gavin and scrolling through the photos. "You don't look scared at all. Dave, look at these pictures."

"It was fun," Christine said quietly, darting a glance at her sister. Historically, Aimee did not respond well to Christine getting attention from their mother.

"Do you live in Austin, Gavin?" She moved around the counter, tugging on the hem of her tank top, revealing more of her world-class cleavage.

Christine glanced at Gavin, but he didn't seem to notice. How was that even possible?

"Denver," he answered. "I'm in Austin for a few weeks because of work."

"Do you ski?"

"Whenever I get the chance."

"I'm road-tripping up to Vail with some friends next month. I just ordered a new set of twin tips."

"Sounds great," he said, but shifted closer to Christine.

She tried to take comfort in his presence but couldn't seem to settle her nerves. "Aimee, Mom said you lost your job."

"I got another one," Aimee snapped. "A better one." She turned to Gavin. "We're looking to do the back bowls. Expert terrain only. You should meet us up there. It's an awesome group."

"Thanks for the invite," he said.

"Chris doesn't ski," Aimee announced as if Christine had tried to make Gavin believe that she did. "There's no way she'd be able to handle even the bunny hill." She laughed again. "Don't even get me started on a chairlift. With her fear of heights—"

"You should take a look at the photos," Gavin told Aimee as Christine's father handed back his phone. "She's got that fear of heights under control."

Christine glanced toward her father, who was studying her like he'd never seen her before. It had been so easy to believe she'd conquered the worst of her fears when they'd been in the middle of their date. Now she felt as awkward and bumbling as she always had with her family.

"It's nice to see you smiling," Dave said finally, inclining his head toward Gavin's phone.

Not exactly a ringing show of support but it felt like a huge endorsement from her normally recalcitrant father. Aimee must have noticed it, too, because her eyes turned hard.

"Let me show you my workshop while the women finish up dinner," Dave told Gavin. "Got a beer cooler out there stocked with cold ones."

Gavin nodded but looked at Christine's mom. "Do you need help with anything?"

Christine watched her mother's face soften. Her parents loved each other, but theirs was a traditional marriage with the bulk of the household duties falling to Stephanie. She could tell it meant a lot to her mom that Gavin offered to help. Once again Christine reminded herself that today was merely a detour on the trajectory of their relationship, which couldn't end in anything but heartache for her. How much of her heart she gave him was the only question.

"Thank you for the offer," her mom said, blushing slightly. "But I've got things under control. Dave is so proud of his workshop. You go with him."

"I'd love a beer, then," Gavin said to her dad and followed Dave toward the garage that housed his workshop.

"He's so handsome," her mom said when the door closed behind the two men. She fanned a hand in front of her face. "Makes me feel like I'm having a hot flash."

Christine knew exactly how her mother felt.

"It's difficult to believe you landed someone like him," Aimee said, opening the refrigerator to pull out another beer. The workshop was their father's man cave and a space where Christine's mother rarely ventured. Instead, she kept a few beers stocked in the kitchen fridge for when friends or her daughters stopped by. Of course, Aimee didn't bother to offer one to Christine now.

"He's great," Christine murmured, hoping to avoid

an in-depth conversation about Gavin. The Briscoe women might not be close, but she feared that her mom and sister would be able to read the lie of their relationship on her face nonetheless.

"What's he doing with you?" Aimee asked as she popped the top on the beer bottle.

"Be nice," their mother chided.

"We have a lot in common," Christine said, automatically going to the cabinet to begin setting the table. It was the second Sunday of the month, so that meant meat loaf. She could smell it baking, and the scent brought back both good and bad memories from childhood. Her mother had always been a great cook, although it still embarrassed Christine to remember herself as a girl, trying to take an extra portion at mealtimes or sneaking into the kitchen late at night to munch on leftovers.

Aimee took the napkins out of the drawer and followed Christine to the table. "Like what?"

How was she supposed to explain her connection to Gavin? On the surface, they were a mismatched pair, but he seemed to like her just the way she was. She saw beyond his polished playboy facade to the kindhearted man he didn't reveal to many people. That sort of connection would be lost on her abrasive sister, most likely chalked up to wishful thinking on Christine's part.

"Well, we both like zip lining." She grinned when Aimee snorted. "I'm also going to learn to water-ski this summer." Gavin gave her the confidence to conquer her fears. She'd never been a strong swimmer, mostly because as a kid she hadn't wanted to be seen in a bathing suit. But she could start doing laps in the pool at the gym where she belonged. By summer, certainly she'd be ready for waterskiing.

"Is Prince Fortunado going to teach you?" Aimee asked, her tone at once bitter and teasing.

"Maybe." Christine bit down on her lip. On second thought, Gavin probably wouldn't be around to see her water-ski, if she even managed it. Aimee didn't need to know that. She placed a plate at the head of the table and glanced up to meet her sister's gaze. "Or you could help me. I remember how great you were when we'd go out to Aunt Celia's place in the summer."

"That's a lovely idea," their mother said, clapping her hands together. "I'd love to see you girls doing something together."

Aimee looked torn between shooting down Christine and placating their mother. "If I have time," she agreed eventually. "We'll see."

Christine smiled even as her stomach pinched. She wished she understood where the animosity between the two of them had originated. Their parents loved them both, although Dave Briscoe had made it clear that he wished he'd had a son. Aimee had done her best to fill that void by being a rough-and-tumble tomboy growing up, interested in sports and cars and whatever else she thought would bring her closer to their father.

Christine had been the odd one out, so Aimee's constant resentment didn't make sense, but it had persisted just the same.

Maybe it was silly that she still wanted a relationship with her sister, but she couldn't help it.

"It's obvious Gavin really likes you," Stephanie said, ignoring her younger daughter. "I like seeing you this happy."

"Thanks, Mom."

Aimee grumbled a bit more but they managed to get

dinner on the table without an outright argument. Christine's father was more animated than she'd seen him in years during the meal. It was clear he liked Gavin, and Christine felt the all-too-familiar guilt that she was exposing her family to their fake relationship. Obviously, her parents would be sorely disappointed when she and Gavin parted ways. But she consoled herself with the knowledge that at least now they saw her as more than just their boring, awkward daughter.

Thanks to Gavin, she felt like so much more.

She made an excuse about needing to prepare for a Monday meeting, and they said their goodbyes soon after dinner. The sun had fully set while they were at her parents' and she was grateful for the cover of darkness so she had a bit of time to regain control of her emotions.

The ride back to her house was quiet, and she wasn't sure what to make of Gavin's silence. Her family and her role in it were the polar opposite of the tight-knit Fortunado clan. Even discovering the connection to the famous Fortunes had only seemed to bring them closer. She couldn't imagine anything that would truly bridge the distance in her family.

When he pulled up in front of her condo, she pasted on a smile and turned to say good-night, only to have him lean across the front seat and fuse his mouth to hers.

Her breath caught in her lungs, and she immediately relaxed into the kiss even though the intensity of it shocked her.

"That was fun," he whispered against her lips.

She pulled back with a soft laugh. "You must be talking about the kiss because dinner with my family was about as much fun as a root canal."

"They don't give you enough credit," he said, his tone serious.

She shrugged. "It's hard to break old patterns. You wouldn't understand because your family is perfect."

"Hardly," he answered with a snort. "I don't think any family is perfect."

They both looked out the front window as headlights turned down the street, illuminating the front of the Audi. "I need to take Princess Di for a walk," she said, her heart suddenly beginning to pound in her chest. "Any chance you want to join me?" It was such a simple question, yet it felt funny requesting something from Gavin. He had initiated most of the time they'd spent together, and it felt strange to be so nervous—like somehow she was imposing on his evening.

He flashed a small, almost grateful smile. "I'd love to."

They walked to her condo hand in hand, and she unlocked the door, immediately greeted by the dog. While Gavin got busy loving up Diana, Christine pulled on a heavier jacket and took the dog's leash from its hook in the laundry room. She grabbed a flashlight, as well, and they headed out to the street.

"My family sometimes feels larger than life," Gavin said as they walked, Princess Di happily sniffing the edge of the sidewalk as she trotted along. "We all have big personalities."

"It's one of the things I liked best when I first started with Fortunado Real Estate," Christine admitted. "Your dad is great and it was fun when any of the kids or your mom stopped by the office."

"Yeah. We're a ton of fun." Gavin scrubbed a hand across his jaw, the scratchy sound reverberating in the quiet of the evening and doing funny things to Christine's insides. "But growing up it was hard to get noticed—there were so many of us doing different activities. Honestly, my mom is a saint for handling all of it. But that's part of how I became an adrenaline junkie. All of my antics were a way to get attention."

"Really?" Christine was shocked by the admission. "The adventurous side of you seems so natural."

He shrugged. "I guess it is by this point, but sometimes it feels like a compulsion rather than something I do because I love it. Don't get me wrong, I like to have fun, but I wonder if there's more to me than working and taking off on the weekend for more thrill-seeking."

"I think there is," she said softly.

"I don't even own a houseplant," he told her out of nowhere.

She frowned. "Um…okay."

"I know that sounds random." He shook his head. "But I'm not exactly known for my skills at adulting. I have a great job, but even at the firm I'm the guy who woos the prospective clients. I move too fast to be able to stay with one for the long haul, so much that it's a shock I'm in Austin for so long. I admire your dedication and how steady you are."

"Thank you," she whispered.

"And your sweetness and loyalty," he continued. As the dog blissfully investigated a nearby shrub, Gavin turned and cupped her cheeks between his palms. "Your family doesn't have any idea how lucky they are to have you."

She swallowed the emotion that threatened to clog

her throat. She wanted to believe that. It didn't matter that she was a grown woman and had made a wonderful life for herself. The fact that she'd never fit in with her parents and sister was like an itch that she couldn't seem to scratch, always distracting her from allowing herself to be truly happy.

"I'm lucky to have you," he continued, and her heart soared. "Even if it's only for a few weeks, I'm grateful for our time together."

Right. Like a balloon that had been stuck with a pin, her happiness deflated, thanks to the reminder that their arrangement was temporary. Gavin might enjoy being with her, but he wasn't looking to make this into something real. He had no problem remembering the parameters of their relationship. Why did she?

"We should head back," she said, pulling away and tugging on Di's leash. "I actually do have a meeting first thing tomorrow with Maddie and Zach."

He frowned but dropped his hands. The cool night air swirled around her, making her body miss the warmth of his touch.

She purposely kept a greater distance between them as they returned to her condo. What was the point of letting him close when he was just going to walk away? She might not be the most confident woman in the world, but she had enough self-respect to not allow herself to turn into a blathering idiot begging him to want more. At least not to his face.

"Can I see you this week?" he asked, placing a hand on her back as she unlocked her door.

Whenever you want, her heart shouted. It felt like her emotions were rattling her insides like bars on a prison window. What would happen if she threw her self-respect to the wind and invited him in? Would he take her up on the invitation?

Instead, she smiled and shook her head. Physical distance was the only way she could think of to keep her feelings for him from spiraling out of control. "It's going to be crazy around the agency with your sister and Zach returning. I think it would be better if we waited until the reunion next weekend."

"Oh." Gavin's thick brows drew together over his gorgeous green eyes. "Is everything okay?"

I'm falling for you, she wanted to tell him. *I don't know how to stop it or protect my heart.*

But she did know and, unfortunately, it involved keeping her distance unless they had to be together for the ruse. She hated pushing him away, but what choice did she have?

"Everything's fine, but I'm busy and I'm sure you are, too. I mean, the sooner you close the new client, the sooner you'll be able to head home. Right?"

"I guess," he said slowly. "I'm in no hurry."

"Me neither," she admitted before she could stop herself. Princess Di gave a soft whine, ready to be in bed for the night. "Let's talk in a few days," she told Gavin with fake cheer. "Thanks again for the adventure, and for joining my family for Sunday dinner—an adventure unto itself."

He stepped back, studying her face as if trying to figure out why she was acting so remote. She couldn't explain it to him, couldn't bear for him to deny that he would hurt her.

Already her heart ached more than she could have imagined.

"Good night," she said and slipped into her quiet house.

Chapter Eleven

Gavin tugged on the collar of his crisp white shirt as he approached Christine's front door Saturday night. He hadn't been this nervous about a date since…well, he'd never been this nervous.

Other than a couple of awkward phone conversations and a few random texts, he hadn't spoken to her since the previous Sunday evening. He wasn't sure what went wrong. They'd had a perfect day, even if the visit to her parents' had been a tad uncomfortable.

Actually, the new understanding of the role Christine played in her family made him furious. Beyond her dedication to his father and the family business, Christine was an amazing person in her own right. Maybe he hadn't noticed her understated beauty and charm at first—or in the ten years he'd known her. But now that he'd spent time with her he couldn't envision his life without her sweetness and light in it.

Except that was exactly what was going to happen at the end of the month. He'd mentioned the predetermined finish to their arrangement, hoping to coax some sort of reaction from her, but she hadn't batted an eye. Not that he blamed her. He'd all but told her he was a bad bet for a relationship. Why wouldn't he expect her to take him at his word?

In fact, her mood seemed to change after he revealed his feelings about his own childhood, the ones that left him riddled with guilt for being an ungrateful schmuck. His family was fantastic and what did it matter if he had to work to be noticed in the midst of so much love? But he'd gotten so used to pushing himself for the rush of adrenaline that he didn't know any other way to live.

Yet with Christine it was easy to slow down and enjoy the moment, whether walking her dog or watching her conquer her fears. She made everything a little brighter, helped him breathe easier than he could ever remember.

He'd gotten himself onto a crazy treadmill of working hard and playing hard, a cliché overachiever in every area except the one that counted the most—his personal life. He'd always doubted he had the capacity for the kind of love his parents had, the kind Everett, Schuyler and Maddie had found. As crazy as it was and despite the unexpected way their connection had come about, he saw that potential with Christine. And now he doubted she'd give him a chance to prove it.

He knocked, smiling as Princess Di gave a loud *woof* on the other side of the door.

"I'm ready," Christine said as she opened it.

Gavin started to smile then felt his jaw go slack.

"Wow," he murmured as he took her in.

"Is this dress okay?" She smoothed a hand over the front of the soft fabric. The dress was black and strapless with a thin sash around the waist and fell to just above her knees. She'd paired it with a delicate gold necklace, dangling earrings and a pair of the sexiest heels he'd ever seen. This was a Christine he hadn't seen before. Her hair was swept to one side and fell in soft waves over her bare shoulder. His fingers itched to touch it, to touch her. He wanted to pull her close and hold on all night. "Schuyler said cocktail attire, but I don't want to seem overdressed."

"You're perfect." He shook his head, his brain jumbled as if he were the ball in an arcade pinball machine. "So damn beautiful."

She laughed and a blush stained her cheeks. He'd missed seeing that rosy glow. He'd missed her so much it made him feel like a fool. It had been six days. Barely any time at all and yet...

He leaned closer, breathing in the delicate scent of her.

"What are you doing?" she asked with a laugh, taking a step back into her condo.

"Making sure you hadn't changed shampoos since I saw you last."

"You're crazy," she told him.

"For you," he confirmed.

Di nudged Christine's legs, trying to reach Gavin. "Hey, girl," he said, bending to scratch behind the dog's furry ears. "I missed you, too."

"Gavin." Christine's tone was serious. He frowned as he straightened, wondering what he'd done wrong now. "Yes?"

"You look nice, too," she said, almost shyly.

He swayed closer, ready to meld his mouth to hers,

but she turned away, grabbing her purse from the entry table. "We don't want to be late. Schuyler wants the family there before the New Orleans Fortunes are scheduled to arrive at four."

"There's plenty of Fortunados to handle the welcome." He moved closer, crowding her a little. Her breath hitched and it gave him so much satisfaction to know she wasn't as unaffected by him as she acted.

"It's important," she insisted.

He sighed. "You're right, of course."

"Of course."

"First, I have something for you." He pulled a small velvet pouch from the inside pocket of his suit jacket.

Her mouth formed a small O as she watched him take a six-prong diamond solitaire engagement ring from the pouch. "I think you need to be wearing a ring when we get to the reunion."

"Yes," she breathed then pressed two fingers to her lips. "I mean, you're right. You didn't actually ask me anything." She stared at the ring. "But, yes, just the same."

It made him ridiculously happy to hear her say yes. He slipped the ring onto her finger. "It's on loan from one of the firm's clients who owns a chain of jewelry stores throughout Texas."

"A loan," she whispered, seemingly unable to pull her gaze from the sparkling diamond. "You have some darn good connections."

"Thank you again for doing this, Christine."

"Of course." Her gaze lifted to his as she closed her left hand into a tight fist. "We should really get going."

He stepped back so she had room to close the door and resisted the urge to take her hand as they walked toward the Audi. Clearly, he'd spooked her last week with something he'd said or done. Now he'd given her an engagement ring. Not exactly taking things slow, even when it was all pretend. He appreciated that she was still willing to uphold their arrangement, but he worried that one wrong move on his part would send her running.

Which was the last thing he wanted.

He opened the passenger-side door then walked around the front of the Audi, wishing he'd thought to bring her flowers or something—anything—that would have given him an excuse to linger at her place and have her all to himself.

The drive to the winery was only thirty minutes from Christine's place, and she spent most of it asking him about his week.

His shoulders relaxed as he shared progress on negotiating the merger of one of his firm's larger manufacturing clients with another company. He'd been focusing on cultivating the client relationship and on making sure they were abiding by all the local, state and federal laws that governed the industry. In turn, he asked her for her take on the continuing saga of Fortunado Real Estate's Austin branch. He'd talked to Maddie after she'd been back a few days, and his sister had seemed both frustrated and confused by the falloff in business.

Christine didn't have any more answers than his sister had but was clearly just as upset by the issues.

They arrived at the Mendoza Winery, situated in the picturesque landscape of the Texas hill country, and Gavin took Christine's hand as they approached the entrance.

"It's Schuyler's big show," she whispered, and her

words made him stop in his tracks. "What's wrong?" she asked as she turned to face him.

"I'm glad you're here with me tonight." He reached out and trailed a fingertip along her jaw. "Not because of our arrangement. It's more than that. You make me happy, Christine."

She hitched in a breath, and he could almost see the struggle as she tried to remain distant. He inwardly cheered when she went up on tiptoe to give him a quick kiss. "You make me happy, too," she said with an almost reluctant smile.

At this point he'd take reluctant. He'd take anything she was willing to give.

He glanced up as Schuyler called his name.

"Here we go," he whispered, and they continued toward the rustic yet modern lodge surrounded by acres of weathered grapevines. He hadn't been there since Schuyler's wedding and, once again, appreciated the beauty of what the Mendoza family had created.

Schuyler greeted Christine with a warm hug and a friendly chuck on the shoulder for Gavin. "You're late."

"I'm here now."

She rolled her eyes. "I bet the only reason is Christine."

"Maybe," he admitted.

"You would have skipped my reunion?" She glared at him, but he could see the sisterly amusement in her eyes.

"I would have made it eventually."

"Go on in." She waved them past her. "Our family's already here, along with Olivia and Alejandro." She glanced at Christine. "I wish I had a cheat sheet to give you for keeping all of the Fortunes straight. Olivia is one of Gerald Robinson's daughters. She and Alejandro Mendoza first met when he came to Austin from Miami for a wedding. They're pretty cute together." She checked her phone. "Nolan just texted. He and his brothers and sisters are on their way."

"Are his parents coming?" Gavin asked, thinking of his father.

Schuyler's mouth pinched into a thin line. "Their names are Miles and Sarah," she said quietly. "They didn't make the trip from New Orleans. Some kind of prior commitment, according to Nolan." She shook her head. "I don't think that's the truth."

"How did Dad respond?"

"He's taking it in stride. I think he's disappointed, but hopefully the Robinson siblings will show. That would help take his mind off Miles as well as the trouble with the agency. Apparently, Fortunado Real Estate isn't the only company having problems. Olivia told me her dad is stressed out because of some glitch with a processor manufactured by Robinson Tech. There's talk about a giant recall. It's as out of the blue as the trouble at the agency. I'm hoping this night will help everyone focus on more positive things."

"It's so nice that you put all of this together," Christine said. "Family is important, no matter how different the members of it might be."

"I couldn't agree more." Schuyler beamed. "I'm so glad you're here. We all are."

Gavin saw Christine's shoulders stiffen slightly, although not so much that Schuyler would notice. He knew what it meant and quickly ushered her into the winery.

"We're going to be okay," he told her in a hushed tone. "No one is going to get hurt in all of this."

She smiled but her eyes remained strained. "I know." Glancing around the interior of the winery, her features softened again. "It's gorgeous."

"Weren't you here for Schuyler's wedding last year?" It embarrassed him that he didn't remember, but surely she would have been invited? Christine was important to his family. She'd been a constant in their lives for a decade. The thought made guilt wash over him once again. Why hadn't he noticed her before now?

She shook her head. "I was invited but couldn't attend. My mom had a heart attack last spring so I spent a lot of time with her."

He stopped and stared down at her. "I didn't realize. She seems healthy now."

"She is," Christine said with a nod. "It's part of why she's so intent on the family dinners and all of us getting close. She's gotten a new lease on life."

"You have some explaining to do, son of mine."

At the sound of his mother's voice, he turned to see her approach, her arms held wide. "Hi, Mom." He bent to hug her, breathing in the familiar scent of the perfume she'd worn since he was a kid. "You look lovely."

"You look like you've been keeping secrets." She pulled away and wagged a finger at him. "I'll deal with that in a minute," she said, then turned to Christine. "First, let me say hello and congratulations to this beautiful girl."

"Hi, Barbara." Christine leaned in to hug his mother. "It's nice to see you."

"You, too, dear." Barbara took her hand. "Kenneth

tells me you're doing great things in Austin. He had such fun working with you last week."

"It seemed like old times," Christine admitted. "I'm surprised he was willing to hand the reins back over to Maddie and Zach without a fight."

Barbara laughed. "Don't let him fool you. He's loving every minute of retirement."

"Probably because he gets to spend more time with you," Christine said, and his mother looked pleased at the compliment.

Seriously, how was it that Christine hadn't been snatched up before now? Beautiful, sweet, smart and possessing one of the kindest hearts he'd ever met. Some man was going to be lucky to have her as his wife.

The thought that it wouldn't be him made Gavin's stomach turn like he'd just eaten food that had gone bad. But he knew she deserved someone better. Someone who could give her the kind of devotion she deserved.

"Speaking of spending time with people..." His mother turned her knowing gaze back to him. "Why was this relationship kept a secret?"

Gavin opened his mouth to answer, but Christine placed a hand on his. "It was my decision," she told his mother. "I wanted a chance for us to get to know each other—just the two of us—before we shared it with the family."

His mom smiled. "We can be a bit much."

"In the best way possible," Christine said, and Barbara gave her another hug.

"We're thrilled for both of you," his mom said. She held up Christine's hand. "It's a beautiful ring, lovely and classic just like the woman wearing it. I hope this means—"

"Mom." Gavin grimaced. "Please don't give us pressure about planning a quick wedding like Schuyler and Maddie have been. We're taking our time."

She took Gavin's hand and squeezed. "I was about to say I hope this means you'll be spending more time in Texas. And not that we're going to lose Christine to Colorado."

"I'm in Austin until the end of the month," he said, choosing not to directly answer the question. Of course, his mother already knew his plans for the next couple of weeks. But he wasn't about to address his future with Christine, not when his hold on her at the moment felt tenuous at best.

His mom inclined her head to study him before her attention was drawn to the front of the room. "Our New Orleans guests have arrived. I'm going to collect your father and go say hello."

Christine moved to his side as his mother crossed the room. "What is it about the Fortunes, legitimate or not, being so darn attractive? You have some mighty gorgeous genes in your family."

He chuckled despite the tension running through him. Each new leaf uncovered in the mess of a family tree Julius Fortune had planted added additional complications to all their lives. Of course, last year the Fortunado branch had been the ones complicating everything.

As Gavin watched his parents greet the new arrivals to this odd family reunion, he had to agree with Christine. Seven of the eight newcomers to the party were clearly related, he assumed, based on how they resembled each other, much the way he and his siblings looked alike.

He'd done a bit of research on Miles Fortune and his

New Orleans family. Nolan, who was the youngest son and a recent transplant to Austin, looked the most comfortable. Gavin guessed that had something to do with the woman on his arm, a brunette with long hair and a sweet smile. The rest of the group seemed hesitant to join the party, and Gavin didn't blame them. They were all making the best of a difficult situation.

"None of us got to meet Julius Fortune," he said tightly, "but by all accounts he was a sorry excuse for a man."

"Yes," Christine agreed, shifting closer so that the length of her body was pressed against him. Was it an unconscious move on her part or could she possibly know how much comfort he took in her nearness? "Despite that, his sons have good lives and from the looks of it, amazing families. I think that says something about all of you. If nothing else, remember you have that in common with your new relatives."

"Thank you," he whispered, placing an arm around her shoulder. "You make everything better."

She tipped up her chin to stare at him as if his words surprised her. He couldn't resist kissing her soft lips and didn't care that they might have an audience of his family, both new and old.

"Ah, young love," his brother Connor drawled as he gave Gavin a hearty slap on the back. "You two are damn adorable."

Gavin threw an elbow, but Connor dodged it with no problem. "And you're a pain in the—"

"Hi, Connor," Christine said, breaking apart from him.

His brother leaned in for a quick hug. "Hey, lovely lady. It's great to see you." He hitched a thumb in

Gavin's direction. "How did you get mixed up with this clown?"

"Just lucky, I guess," Christine answered, taking Connor's teasing in stride.

He winked. "Well, let me know if he gets out of line. I'd be honored to step in as your overprotective brother."

Gavin snorted. "You realize the two of us are actually related? What happened to you being too busy to come down for this?"

"Blood relations can't be helped," Connor answered. "And I wouldn't have missed this reunion. What do you think of the new crew?"

"I think we can all appreciate what they're going through, dealing with the knowledge of our shared family history." He shrugged. "I also think it's interesting that Dad's half brother isn't making an appearance tonight."

"I don't see any of the Robinsons here tonight, other than Olivia," Connor added. "I'm a little surprised at that. They've all seemed fairly open to this bizarre turn of events."

"I'm sure it's been tough with Gerald and Charlotte separating. Maybe that changes things for some of them? I couldn't imagine Mom and Dad ever breaking up."

"Thank heavens for that," Connor agreed. "I've heard that Charlotte hasn't taken the separation well."

"Can you blame her?" Christine asked, and Gavin realized there were things she didn't understand about the situation.

He shrugged. "Apparently, she knew about her husband's infidelities and kept some kind of a dossier on the illegitimate kids he'd sired."

Christine's big eyes widened. "That's awful."

"No doubt. I'm going to grab a drink then head over to introduce myself to the newcomers," Connor told them. "Can I get either of you something?"

"I'm fine for now," Christine responded.

Gavin shook his head. "Me, too."

When Connor walked away, she took Gavin's hand. "It means a lot to Schuyler that all of you are here." She glanced to where his sister and Carlo were talking to Nolan Fortune, tall and lean with dark brown hair. He held tightly to the hand of the woman at his side. "I think we should join them."

He nodded, unsure of why he felt so out of sorts or how to explain the way having Christine at his side soothed him. They approached the foursome, and Schuyler smiled gratefully.

"Let me introduce you both to my brother," she said. "This is Gavin and his fiancée, Christine Briscoe." She inclined her head toward the other couple. "Gavin, meet Nolan Fortune and *his* fiancée, Lizzie Sullivan."

"Thanks for coming tonight. I heard you've moved from New Orleans to Austin recently."

The man nodded, his brown eyes warm. "I'll always love NOLA, but my heart's in Texas so this is where I belong." He leaned in and dropped a gentle kiss on the top of Lizzie's head. "It's good that we all get together."

"I couldn't agree more," Gavin answered.

"Carlo and I are going to check on the food," Schuyler said. "If you or any of your siblings need anything, Nolan, just let me know."

"Will do." The man glanced around as Schuyler and Carlo walked away. "I think I could use a glass of the Mendoza wine I've heard so much about."

Gavin motioned to one of the servers holding a tray of wineglasses. "I can help with that."

Each of them took a glass of wine, and after thanking the server, Gavin lifted his glass. "A toast to new family and friendships. Sometimes the best endings come from the strangest starts."

Nolan and Lizzie shared a long look.

"I feel like we should ask how you two met," Christine said. "There's a story there."

Lizzie smiled. "It is a strange start," she admitted. "I saw Nolan playing in a jazz band in Austin the holiday season before last and we struck up a conversation from there."

Nolan draped an arm over his fiancée's shoulder. "But we didn't reconnect until this past December. I tried my best to mess things up, but she gave me another chance. Best moment of my life."

Gavin watched Christine's eyes light as she listened to the other couple. For all of her practicality, he realized she was a romantic at heart. And how had he honored that? With deals and arrangements, boundaries and timelines. What a fool he'd been.

"How about the two of you?" Lizzie took a slow sip of wine. "How did you meet?"

Gavin's stomach dipped as Christine's face fell for an instant before she flashed a too-bright smile. "We've known each other for years," she said airily. "It's the classic friends-first scenario."

"Friendship is key," Lizzie said, obviously sensing Christine's discomfort at being put on the spot.

"Actually…" Gavin leaned in, as if he was sharing a deep secret. "I'd had a crush on her for years."

"Who could blame you?" Nolan asked gamely.

"Exactly," Gavin agreed. "But I didn't think she'd ever go for a guy like me."

"He has a bit of a reputation," Christine offered, then added in a stage whisper, "As a *player*."

"No." Lizzie patted a hand on her chest, feigning shock.

"But I knew I'd have to be a better man to earn my place at Christine's side." Gavin twirled the stem of the wineglass between two fingers, the truth of that statement hitting him like a Louisville Slugger to the chest. "So I…"

"You became one," Lizzie finished.

"Working on it," Gavin clarified.

"Most of us are a work in progress." Nolan lifted his glass to study the burgundy liquid inside. "This wine is fantastic."

Gavin was grateful his new relative was giving him an out on a subject that cut a little too close to home. "It's a private vintage. They only bring it out for special occasions."

"I'm sorry my dad wouldn't—" Nolan cleared his throat "—couldn't be here for this."

"I know my parents would love to meet him."

"What about the other brothers?"

Gavin felt his mouth drop open. "What other brothers?"

"You don't know about Gary and David?"

He shook his head.

Nolan ran a hand over his jaw. "Our fathers weren't Julius Fortune's only illegitimate sons. He had two more."

"I wondered about that," Schuyler said, rejoining the group. "I heard Ariana Lamonte—or I guess Fortune now—the reporter who married Jayden of the Paseo triplets, made a reference to there being 'others.'"

"Why didn't you say anything?" Gavin asked, his gut tightening once again.

"From what I could tell, the Paseo Fortunes were ambivalent about all of this. It was before Gerald and Deborah had reconciled so Jayden seemed to care more about protecting his mom from being hurt again than uncovering any more Fortunes. I think Ariana dropped it out of respect for Jayden's wishes."

"Our dad has known about his birth father for a while," Nolan revealed, leaning in closer to his fiancée. "He's done some research on his own over the years."

"Julius Fortune was a real piece of work," Gavin muttered.

"Quite true," Nolan agreed.

Schuyler shook her head. "We've got to stick together in all this. There's too much stressful stuff going on already and we can't let Julius's mistakes continue to haunt us. I only wish the rest of the Robinsons had been able to make it. They—"

As if on cue, Olivia hurried over to them. She held her cell phone in front of her like it was a poisonous snake. Glancing around wildly, her gaze settled on Schuyler.

"What's wrong?" Schuyler asked as Olivia took a shuddery breath.

Conversation in the lodge fell silent as everyone's attention focused on Olivia.

She swiped her hands across her cheeks. "A fire," she whispered. "Someone set fire to our family home. The Robinson estate has been destroyed."

Chapter Twelve

Christine registered the collective gasp that went up in the room at Olivia's words.

Schuyler wrapped her arms around the other woman's slim shoulders as the Fortunados and New Orleans Fortunes moved to surround them.

"What happened?" Kenneth asked, making his way through to the two women.

Olivia blinked several times as Schuyler released her. Alejandro Mendoza took his wife's hand, and Olivia leaned into him, clearly needing the support. Christine knew Olivia's courtship with Alejandro had been a whirlwind, and she'd even heard whispers that the engagement had been a sham at the beginning. Clearly, the two were soul mates and she couldn't help but wonder if she and Gavin might also have a happy ending to their strange beginning.

Olivia shook her head as Alejandro pulled her closer.

"We don't know exactly how it got started, but my brother Wes overheard the fire chief talking about suspected arson. Dad's the only one living at the estate at the moment, although Deborah is there quite a bit and each of us stops by when we can." She glanced at Schuyler. "We were all getting ready to come here. I think if someone did this purposefully, they must have known the estate would be empty tonight. In fact, things would have been worse except..." Her voice broke off as a sob escaped her lips.

"What is it?" Schuyler demanded. "Is everyone okay?"

Olivia shook her head. "I asked Ben to stop by the house and pick up a couple of photo albums. Apparently, he got there when the fire was really raging. He called 911 but tried to fight it on his own before the firefighters arrived. He—" She paused again, placing a hand over her mouth as she shook her head.

Christine automatically reached for Gavin's hand.

Kenneth placed a gentle hand on Olivia's arm. "Tell us," he whispered. "Is your brother okay?"

She gave a small shrug. "We don't know. He's on his way to the hospital. The EMTs tell us it's severe smoke inhalation." She dragged in a shuddering breath. "Alejandro and I need to leave. I have to get to the hospital— everyone's planning to stay there until we hear more about Ben. But I wanted you to understand..." She placed a hand to her cheek and shook her head. "I don't know what since none of this makes sense. The Fortune Robinsons would have been here, Schuyler. I promise."

"Of course. What do you need us to do?" Gavin's sister asked. "Please, Olivia. Let us help. We're your family, no matter how crazy the circumstances."

Olivia flashed a watery smile. "Would you go out

to the estate? It kills me that there's no one from the family there, but our priority is Ben. It's the house we all grew up in, and no matter what kind of problems Mom and Dad have been having recently, there are so many memories."

Although her parents' house didn't exactly fill Christine with sentimental thoughts, she thought about the Fortunados' stately home in Houston. She'd been to Kenneth and Barbara's home a number of times through the years and it had always struck her as such a happy place, as if the walls held on to the memories of children growing up there and of the bond among the Fortunado children. If the Robinson estate was anything like that, the loss of it would be far greater than simply physical property.

"Of course," Schuyler said and the entire room seemed to nod in unison.

"I've got to go," Olivia whispered.

"Do you need someone to drive the two of you?" Gavin asked, stepping forward. "With the shock and upset—"

"Thank you," Alejandro interrupted. "But we'll be fine."

Olivia nodded. "My family and I appreciate your willingness to help. We're grateful for each of you."

With that, she and Alejandro turned and walked out of the winery. There was a moment of heavy silence before the room exploded in shocked murmurs and muted conversations.

Gavin quickly grabbed a chair from a nearby table and climbed up. He shot Christine a grateful smile when she lifted two fingers to her mouth for a sharp whistle that drew everyone's attention to him.

"The fire at the Robinson estate is a tragic turn of

events," he began, "especially if the cause of the blaze turns out to be arson." He drew in a breath as if he felt the shocking possibility like a blow. "But the Fortune Robinsons need us now. All of us. We may not know each other well yet, but this is the time when we become one family."

Pride bloomed in Christine's chest as she glanced around to see all eyes riveted on Gavin as he spoke about the importance of solidarity and support. Even though most of his work was done in boardrooms with company leadership, she could imagine him in a courtroom, commanding the attention of judge and jury.

He tasked Valene and two of the New Orleans Fortunes—the oldest brother, Austin, and the baby of the family, Belle—with rounding up blankets, snack baskets, clean clothes and toiletry kits to take to the hospital for the Robinsons during the time they were keeping vigil for Ben. He asked Everett, his doctor brother, to head directly to the hospital to use his connections to facilitate whatever he could for the family. Schuyler volunteered to coordinate meals, and Maddie offered to secure a furnished rental house for Gerald Robinson and stock it with groceries and other household items before he got there.

Christine smiled and nodded as Gavin met her gaze across the sea of Fortunes. How was she supposed to do anything but fall in love with this man?

Oh. She placed a hand on her chest as panic washed through her. She was in love with Gavin. It was more than a crush or infatuation. So much for guarding her heart so she wouldn't be hurt at the end of this.

The knowledge that the end was inevitable did nothing to stem the tide of emotions she felt for him. The week of keeping her distance was forgotten like yesterday's news. After easing herself away from the group as Gavin mobilized everyone who was left to head to the estate, she hurried to the bathroom and splashed cold water on her face.

Nothing had changed about her outward appearance. She saw the same blue eyes and red hair holding its style thanks to a truckload of product, pale skin that looked a bit pastier than normal thanks to her panic-inducing revelation.

But inside her was a tumbling avalanche of doubt and fear. It was difficult to believe that her heart, which was so sure and full at the moment, could be in grave danger of shattering at the end of the month.

She took a few steadying breaths then headed back out.

Gavin waited in the dimly lit hallway.

"You don't have to do this," he said quietly, his face a stark mask.

Had he somehow read her mind? As if she had a choice on what her heart wanted—*who* her heart wanted. It had always been him.

She swallowed and tried to figure out how to explain her emotions to him without sending him running in the other direction. "I—"

He moved forward, taking her hands in his. "You've been great tonight. The best. But I know that it's overwhelming, all these Fortunes, and now the fire. It goes way beyond what you signed up for with us."

Did it ever, she thought.

"I can drop you at home before heading to the estate. I totally understand that you might not want to be a part of this mess. We're not your problem so—"

"Stop." She shook her head. He'd completely misread her reaction, but she couldn't blame him. She'd *tried* to pull away this week. Look where that had gotten her. "I'm going with you to the estate if you want me there."

"Of course," he answered without hesitation. The intensity of his gaze made her breath catch. "You've been the most amazing sport about all of this."

She choked out a laugh. So much for his devotion. A good sport? It was as if she could feel her heart splintering into a thousand pieces. She swallowed and tried not to let her emotions show. This was her chance. He'd given her an out. She should be smart and take it.

"It's all part of our deal," she answered with forced cheer.

His brows drew together, and he opened his mouth as if he wanted to argue with her assessment then snapped it shut again. "Are you ready?"

She nodded and followed him out of the winery. The only people left were servers, cleaning up the deserted party.

"You did an amazing job of rallying everyone," she told Gavin as they pulled away from the curb.

"We attorneys like to hear ourselves talk," he said with a wink.

"You do that too much."

He chuckled. "Talk?"

"Downplay the good things you do," she clarified and saw his knuckles tighten on the steering wheel. "Maddie told me you do pro-bono work with low-income families in the court system in Colorado."

"I've had a lot of success in my career. It's easy to give back in some small way."

"According to her, you devote a ton of hours to the cause."

"I have time on my hands when ski season ends."

"Gavin." She adjusted the seat belt strap so she could turn toward him. "This is what I'm talking about. I'm not sure why you want everyone to see you as this cavalier party guy, but it's a mask."

"Hiding my insightful thoughts and hidden depths."

"Yes," she answered simply. "You're a good man. I wish you could see yourself the way I do."

A muscle worked in his jaw as he accelerated onto the interstate. "I wish I could be the man you see," he said after several long minutes.

They drove the rest of the way to the Robinson estate in silence, although it was more comfortable than awkward. At some point Gavin reached across the front seat and laced her fingers with his. She was coming to expect the way he seemed to need to touch her as if she grounded him in the midst of the chaos swirling around them.

They exited the highway and drove through an upscale neighborhood of mansions. Christine gasped when the estate came into view. She hadn't seen the house in person before today, but given Gerald's success in the tech industry, she'd imagined it as spectacular.

It probably had been prior to today. But now she could only describe the scene in front of her as horrific. Fire trucks still lined the driveway, although the fire had been out long enough that the remains of the building were no longer smoking. The west section of the mansion, which clearly housed the garage, was still intact for the most part. As for the rest of the building, the walls that were left were no more than a blackened shell. Most of the structure was rubble and ash.

"Do you really think it was arson?" Christine asked as they parked behind Kenneth's Mercedes.

Gavin seemed as stunned by the scene as she felt. "I can't imagine who would do something like this. I've never heard rumblings that Gerald has any sworn enemies. If a person set a fire intent on doing this much damage, they must really hate him."

"It's unbelievable."

They got out of the SUV and joined the rest of the family who had assembled on the driveway in front of what should have been the front door.

"Has someone talked to the fire chief?" Gavin asked his dad.

"Not yet." Kenneth shook his head. "I think we're all paralyzed in the face of this much destruction. They're lucky Ben was the only one injured in the blaze. The level of damage blows my mind."

"I'll find him," Gavin said and jogged off in the direction of the row of fire trucks.

Barbara rested her head on her husband's shoulder. "It's awful but we both know home is where the heart is. Gerald and his family will survive this. He can rebuild and make new memories while holding on to the old."

Christine agreed, but that fact didn't make the devastation more palatable.

"I wonder if Charlotte knows," Connor murmured.

"I'm sure someone called her," Kenneth said. "Although I imagine she has everything of either sentimental or monetary value that belongs to her out of the house. I know Gerald wanted to make a clean break, especially after reconnecting with Deborah."

Gavin returned at that moment. "Normally they wouldn't allow access to the house so soon after firefighters got things under control. Apparently, Olivia told her dad we were coming out here. Gerald made some calls to ensure we'd be good. He has friends in high places. The chief says we can go in the areas they've deemed safe but to be careful of debris."

They each nodded.

"Let's split into groups," Gavin told them. "Connor and Savannah, you take some of us and start at the far end of the house nearest what's left of the garage. Mom and Dad, you take a group and start in the center and spread out. Christine and I will lead a crew to the far end of the rubble. I'm guessing that's where we'll find the master suite."

He gazed at what used to be the estate's main structure. "Look for clues as to what the room might have been used as and base your search for salvageable items there. As an example, you might find an appliance or two that tells you that room is the kitchen."

"What are we looking for?" Savannah asked, glancing over her shoulder toward the house.

"Anything of value, either financial or sentimental. Don't worry too much about pedigree or authenticity on any of the pieces we collect. This day is going to haunt the Robinson family, and I'd like them to know we were able to save something."

As his family and the Fortunes from New Orleans split up to tackle the first step in helping to heal their Robinson relatives, Gavin returned to Christine's side. She could see the tension around his mouth and eyes, feel the tension radiating from him.

"What if someone did this to my parents' house?" he asked softly. "It's unimaginable."

Once again she tamped down her doubts and wrapped her arms around his waist. "We're going to get them through this," she promised. "You're one family now. That matters."

He blew out a breath and kissed the top of her head. "You have no idea how glad I am that you're here with me."

"There's no place I'd rather be," she assured him, and together they followed his family into the wreckage.

Chapter Thirteen

It was almost midnight before Gavin walked Christine to the door of her condo.

"This was not the night I'd planned," he told her, rubbing a hand over his eyes.

They'd stayed at the Robinson estate until darkness made it dangerous to pick through the destruction. Although the house had been effectively torched, they'd managed to find a number of personal mementos that remained undamaged. They'd put the items into boxes and driven them to the rental house Maddie had secured.

It had seemed a sorry collection pushed into one corner of the empty garage, but Gavin hoped they'd bring some comfort to Gerald and the rest of the family.

They'd gone to grab dinner with Maddie, Zach, Schuyler, Carlo and Connor. Somehow Gavin needed the tangible reminder of his connection with his siblings. With everything going on from new Fortune revelations to the trouble with the family business to the fire, being able to laugh with his family was a balm to his soul. Had he been wishing for life as an only child just a couple of weeks ago? What a fool he'd been.

His family was a gift, just like this time with Christine. He'd taken both for granted. That was his problem and why he knew he had to let Christine go at the end of all this. He didn't have enough inside him to give her what she deserved.

"No one can plan for tragedy," she said, pulling a key ring out of her purse. "It's how a person handles it that shows what they're made of." She turned to him. "You were strong, articulate and compassionate tonight. It says so much about you as a person."

Damn. He wished he were a better man because walking away from Christine was going to hurt like hell.

"Right back at you," he said, then did a mental eye roll. He must have used up all his decent words earlier because he couldn't seem to form a coherent thought at the moment.

She unlocked the door and opened it to allow Princess Di onto the small porch. The dog's tail wagged enthusiastically as she greeted first Christine then Gavin with a head butt to the legs before trotting down the steps to do her business in the bushes.

"Do you need to walk her?" he asked, smiling at the dog. He really needed a pet. Maybe having something to come home to would help his outwardly exciting life feel not so lonely on the inside. "I could—"

"One of my neighbors took her out earlier." Christine

leaned inside and flipped on a light. "She'll be ready to hunker down for the night after her potty break."

"Right." Gavin rubbed a hand along the back of his neck. "I guess I should—"

"Would you like to come in for a bit?" she asked, almost hesitantly.

"Yes," he breathed, thanking the heavens for her invitation. It was ridiculous, this constant need to be with her. Reckless to allow himself to depend on her in any way. But he couldn't help himself. She was like a cool drink, and he'd been in the emotional desert of his own making for far too long.

She whistled for the dog, and Diana came loping back up the steps and into the house.

"Let's talk about your mad whistling skills," Gavin said as he closed the door behind them.

She grinned. "What can I say?" His insides tightened as a blush stained her cheeks when she added, "I'm good with my mouth."

If she'd smacked him over the head with a sledgehammer, he couldn't have been more shocked. He felt his mouth drop open, and desire pounded through him, flooding his veins with a sharp yearning.

Before he could get his muddled brain to form a response, she turned away. "Would you like a drink?" she asked over her shoulder. "A glass of water?"

"Sure." She toed out of her strappy heels and just that innocuous movement made another wave of need crash through him. Once again her pink-painted toes were the sexiest thing he'd ever seen.

She continued to the kitchen, hanging her purse over a chair. She took a dog biscuit from the cookie jar on the counter and then tossed it to Princess Di, who expertly caught it. The dog padded over to her bed while Christine pulled two glasses from an upper cabinet and filled them.

All the while he stood rooted in place, every cell in his body tingling with awareness and—Lord help them both—unbridled lust.

"Gavin?" She stared at him with wide eyes from the kitchen as if he were a hungry lion and she was the proverbial lamb invited to his feast. "I was joking about the mouth comment," she said with a hesitant laugh. "I went too far. I'm sorry."

Her apology jarred him from his lust-filled stupor. He ate up the distance between them in three long strides. "You never need to apologize," he said, cupping her face in his hands. "Yours is the most tantalizing mouth in the universe." He kissed her, nipping at the corner of her lips. "I thank my lucky stars each time you kiss me."

She moaned in the back of her throat as he ran his tongue along the seam of her lips. "Open for me," he whispered, and she did, her tongue mingling with his until his mind was swimming once more.

He ran his fingers through her hair, the way he'd been longing to all night, plucking out the thin pins that held the style in place.

At this moment he didn't give a damn that she was too good for him. He couldn't find it in himself to care about anything except the feel of her pressing into his chest. Her curves, her scent, the sweetness of her very essence.

Then she pulled away, and Gavin wanted to growl his protest. Was she going to send him away? Close herself off the way she had in the past week? He wasn't sure he could take that distance again.

"Why haven't we had sex?" she blurted, her eyes a little hazy but otherwise focused intently on his.

Just when he thought she couldn't surprise him anymore, another inadvertent blow sent him reeling.

"Um… I'm trying to respect you," he said, the words ringing false even to his own ears.

Her delicate brows drew together until she wasn't so much frowning as glaring at him. "You only sleep with women you don't respect?"

"No," he answered quickly. "I didn't mean that. What I'm trying to say is…" Oh, hell. What was he trying to say?

"You don't want me like that," she supplied and it took a moment for her words to register in his muddled mind. Right now the majority of his brain cells had gone on hiatus, allowing the lower half of him to take over the controls. That half wasn't exactly known for its good judgment.

"I want you in every way possible." He moved forward, and she stepped back as if putting distance between them was an unconscious response. No. He couldn't let her put up a wall between them. Not tonight.

He softened his tone and let his need for her flood his gaze. His career and the choices he'd made to keep himself closed off in his personal life had made him a master of the poker face.

He wondered if he'd ever been like Christine, whose beautiful emotions were written on her face.

"You agreed to help me because of the pressure from my family," he said slowly, needing the words to come out right. Knowing this moment mattered. "I don't want to take advantage of that…of you."

One side of her mouth kicked up. "What if I want to be taken advantage of?"

"Christine."

She studied him for a moment, and he could almost see the emotional war going on inside her. Which side would win out?

"I want you, Gavin."

He could have dropped to his knees in thanks. At the same time he didn't want her to have any doubts or regrets so he asked, "Are you sure?"

She took a step closer and wrapped her arms around his neck. "Never more sure," she promised and kissed him.

He let her set the pace and gave himself over to her slow, seductive torture. He couldn't remember the last time he'd been this happy, and it was all because of the beautiful woman in his arms.

More.

That was the refrain echoing in Christine's mind as she kissed Gavin. His hands reached up to stroke her bare shoulders, thumbs grazing over her collarbones. The featherlight touch made goose bumps break out along her skin, and all she could think was *more*.

She broke off the kiss, gratified when it took a few seconds for Gavin's gaze to focus on her. He'd given her the choice tonight, and she loved him for it. For so many reasons. Despite her doubts and the understanding that heartbreak was inevitable, she wanted this moment. This man.

Hitching in a breath, she pushed the suit coat off his shoulders and tossed it onto the counter. Gavin's nostrils flared as she moved closer and tugged on his tie, loosening the silk and sliding it from the collar.

"You can probably do this with more efficiency," she said, her voice husky as she started at the buttons of his shirt with shaky fingers.

"I like you undressing me," he whispered.

With every button, another inch of his muscled body was revealed. The shirtless Gavin she'd seen in photos from Fortunado beach vacations over the years didn't do justice to Gavin in the flesh. Heat radiated from him, and his skin felt soft yet firm under her touch.

When he'd shrugged out of the shirt, she took a moment to admire his body in a way she hadn't been able to the night of Diana's trip to the vet. Her girlie parts screamed to get on with things but she hushed them. This was every one of her fantasies come to life, and she had every intention of savoring the experience.

He gave her a sexy half smile. "I had no idea I could be so turned on just by how you look at me."

She reached out a hand and smoothed it up the hard planes of his chest. "How about when I do this?" she asked, wondering where in the world this confident seductress had been hiding.

Or perhaps not hiding. Maybe she'd simply been waiting for the right man to unlock her passion.

No doubt that Gavin held the key to everything.

"I love it."

She took her other hand and skimmed it across the front of his trousers, and she knew without a doubt he wanted her. He let out a soft groan as she cupped him then he encircled her wrist with one hand. "You're making me crazy, and I love it."

"It's an adventure," she told him, earning a low laugh.

"The best kind," he agreed, lifting her hand to his

shoulder. Then he reached around and unzipped the back of her dress. The silky fabric slid down her body and over her hips with ease, pooling at her feet.

Although inwardly cringing at standing in front of this perfect man in nothing but a black strapless bra and pair of lacy panties, Christine forced herself not to squirm. As she had minutes earlier with him, Gavin took his sweet time studying her, his chest rising and falling sharply as his gaze wandered along her body.

The need and desire she saw there gave her confidence, and for the first time she tried to see herself through Gavin's eyes. Clearly, he liked what he saw. Although she hadn't been overweight for over a decade, Christine still viewed herself through the lens of the chubby girl she'd once been. The misfit. The loser.

But she was a different woman now, and it was past time she start embracing who she'd become. She refused to allow herself to be stuck in her old insecurities.

Biting down on her lower lip, she reached around her back and unclasped the bra strap, tossing the thin piece of fabric to one side. Then she hooked her thumbs into the waistband of her panties and slid them down her hips.

All the while, Gavin's gaze remained on hers as his breathing grew more ragged.

"You have too many clothes on," she whispered.

"Damn straight," he agreed, his voice shaky.

He made quick work of his shoes and socks then unfastened his belt buckle and took off his pants, pushing them down his hips along with his boxers.

Suddenly, Christine had the realization that they were standing at the edge of her kitchen. Now what? She'd only been intimate with her previous boyfriend, and that had strictly been a lights out in the bedroom type of affair. Spontaneity was new for her, and while her body was a big fan, her brain wasn't quite sure how to deal with the reality of her new adventure. "Oh, my gosh."

Gavin chuckled. "I've gotten a lot of reactions in my day, but that's a new one."

"We're in the kitchen," she told him.

His grin widened, and he stepped forward. "You've never christened your kitchen?" he asked with a wink.

She shook her head.

He moved closer, reaching for her. "I like watching you try new things, and I have lots of them planned for tonight."

"You have a plan?" Her voice came out in a squeak.

"Do you trust me?" he whispered against her mouth, licking across the seam of her lips.

"Yes," she breathed.

"Good," he said and lifted her into his arms.

She gasped. The feel of his body was even more amazing than she could have imagined. Then she gasped again when her backside hit the smooth wood of the kitchen table.

Gavin trailed kisses along her jaw then down her neck and lower. He cupped her breasts in his big hands. When he took the tip of one, and then the other, into his mouth, she moaned from the pleasure of his mouth on her body. One hand moved lower, grazing her hips before gently pushing apart her legs and inching closer to her center.

She thought the attention to her breasts was enough to drive her mad with desire, but this was something else entirely. His fingers found a rhythm that had her craving more, the pressure in her body building with excruciating sweetness until she finally cried out. It felt as though a thousand stars were crashing over her, bathing her in a bright light that was like nothing she could have imagined.

Gavin kissed her, deep and slow, as the pulsing release subsided.

"I'll never look at this table the same way again," she whispered when he pulled away.

"I'm going to take that as a compliment," he answered with a husky chuckle.

"But you didn't…" Christine cleared her throat. "We aren't finished?"

"Not by a long shot." He gave her a sexy half smile that made her toes curl. Then he bent and took a wallet from his pants' pocket, pulling out a condom wrapper. "The next part of my master plan is moving to the bedroom."

"I like that plan."

She went to stand but before she could get to her feet, Gavin picked her up, one arm under her knees and the other cradling her back.

"Down the hall?"

She nodded. "You're pretty good with your hands," she told him, placing a hand on his bare chest. "But you haven't turned me into so much contented jelly that I can't walk."

"Pretty good?" He made a sound low in his throat. "That sounds like a challenge. And I could carry you for miles."

She bit down on the inside of her cheek when a denial popped to her lips. She might not feel confident about her body, thanks to years of being overweight, but she knew enough not to point out her flaws to Gavin.

He seemed as enthralled with her as she was with him, and that thought only served to open her heart to him even more.

"I can hear you thinking," he told her as he entered her bedroom.

She laughed softly as he tugged down the comforter and sheet and placed her on the mattress. "Then you'd better distract me."

"Exactly what I had in mind."

He opened the condom wrapper and, a moment later, skimmed his hands up her body until he was leveraging himself over her. She could feel him between her legs, but he held still as he smoothed his thumbs along the sides of her face, gazing into her eyes with an intensity that stole her breath.

"You're amazing," he whispered.

She automatically shook her head. Christine knew she was many things. Smart. Loyal. Dependable. Okay, that sounded more like she was describing her dog, but it was difficult to argue with the truth.

Gavin gripped her head and said again, "You. Are. Amazing."

Oh, no. She blinked several times. There was no way she was going to cry in front of him because he'd said something nice and she wanted desperately to believe him. She lifted her head and kissed him. Then he was inside her, moving in a rhythm that she knew was unique to the two of them. It was everything, and she still wanted more. Pressure built again, consuming her, but this time she wasn't alone in giving in to the pleasure. Gavin stayed with her, in her, until they lost themselves in the moment and all the things she felt but couldn't put into words.

And Christine knew the emotion…this night…this man…would change her life forever.

Chapter Fourteen

The next morning Gavin blinked awake, disoriented for a moment by his surroundings. The bedrooms at both his loft in Denver and the Driskill, where he was staying in downtown Austin, were decorated in a neutral color palette and dark wood furniture, so the pale blue walls and creamy white furniture he woke up to weren't what he expected.

The woman curled against him, still fast asleep, was another unexpected occurrence. Well, not exactly unexpected. He'd spent most of the night making love to Christine, which had been better than he ever could have imagined.

But Gavin didn't typically spend the night with the women he dated. More than typically. He didn't ever stay over an entire night. He also hadn't had a woman stay overnight with him since... Well, Christine's sleepover in his hotel room after Maddie's wedding had been the first.

It was part of his unwritten list of relationship rules not to complicate things. Simple was easier when it came to women, but Christine and their unorthodox arrangement were changing everything, especially his self-control.

He thought about sneaking out quietly but couldn't quite force himself to move. Her bright auburn hair was messy—thanks to him, most likely—and he loved how relaxed and unguarded she appeared in sleep.

Scratch that last bit. He liked it very much. Not loved. He wasn't a man who threw around the word *love* in any capacity with the women he dated. Dangerous territory that led to expectations he couldn't possibly meet.

Maybe that was why it was so easy to let down his guard with Christine. Their built-in end date was a safety net for his heart. So why did it feel like he was walking on an emotional tightrope with nothing but cold, hard ground beneath him as a landing?

He shifted away as a reality he wasn't willing to accept pummeled at his defenses, a tornado of doubts and long-held beliefs tearing at his walls.

Christine sighed then opened her eyes, her gaze soft and sleepy. Damn if he didn't want to pull her close, bury himself inside her and try to give her everything he'd never thought himself capable of offering a woman.

The mental reminder of his own shortcomings was enough to have him jerking away and climbing out of bed as if she'd just tried to bite him.

He was a damn coward.

She sat up, lifting the sheet to cover her beautiful breasts. Now that he knew firsthand the sweet taste of her skin and the way she fit with him, he had to force himself not to crawl under the covers again.

"Good morning," she said, and he hated himself for the doubt that clouded her eyes.

"Hi. I've got to go."

"Oh." The smile she gave him was shaky at best. "I understand."

She couldn't possibly because he was fumbling around with no playbook for this moment. Clearly, since he was making a complete mess of it. "I had fun last night," he said, even as he pulled on his trousers.

At some point during the night, he'd brought his clothes into the bedroom and put on boxers to sleep. Now he fastened his pants and reached for his shirt even as he shoved his feet into his loafers.

"Me, too," she said, tucking a loose strand of hair behind one ear. "Have you heard anything more about Ben or confirmation on the cause of the fire?"

Gavin glanced at his phone sitting on the nightstand. He hadn't even thought to touch the thing since she'd invited him in, so caught up in Christine as he was. He shook his head. "That's why I need to leave. I want to check on Ben."

She nodded, although the doubt remained in her gaze. "Let me know how he's doing. Maybe later we could—"

"I have a meeting tomorrow morning with a client and a presentation I need to finish. It's going to be a late Sunday in the office for me."

This time she didn't nod in agreement, and when her eyes narrowed as she studied him, a bead of sweat rolled down between his shoulder blades.

"Is there anything we need to talk about?" she asked,

and he could tell how hard she was working to keep her composure. He couldn't admire her or hate himself any more than he did at this moment.

"Nope," he lied.

"Right." She shifted to the edge of the bed, still holding the sheet up to cover her body. "I need to get dressed and take Di for a walk." When he didn't move, one delicate eyebrow arched. "Which means you should leave now."

Bam.

He thought he couldn't admire her more, until she went and gave attitude right back to him. Good for her. His Christine was stronger than she believed herself to be.

No. Not his. He was in the process of messing it up, because that was how he handled real intimacy.

He wasn't sure if it helped or made things worse to know he was an idiot.

With a sigh, he bent to kiss her goodbye. She turned her face at the last moment so his lips landed on her cheek.

"Have a nice rest of your day," she told him, refusing to make eye contact.

"I'll call you later," he promised.

"You can text me," she advised. "It's simpler that way."

Simple. Right. His new least favorite word in the English language.

"Have a good day," he said quietly. "And thank you again for last night…for everything. I—"

"It's fine, Gavin. We have an agreement. I get that. I hope you get positive news about Ben." With those polite words, she showed him that he was—without a doubt—the biggest jerk on the planet.

He didn't want to be. He didn't want this arrangement or the way she made him feel more than anyone ever had. But he couldn't find the words to make it better. Not when the hollowness inside his chest was a gaping pit that he couldn't seem to escape.

So he gave her a charming smile, even knowing she saw through that tired mask, and walked away.

"You look like hell."

As Gavin climbed in the passenger side of his brother's car, Everett studied him over the lenses of his mirrored sunglasses.

"Just drive," Gavin muttered, buckling the seat belt.

Everett chuckled and pulled away from the hotel's entrance. They were heading to the hospital to check in with the Robinson branch of the family. Gavin had spoken to Wes Fortune Robinson earlier. Ben's twin had reported that his brother was in stable condition but they were still monitoring him to ensure there was no additional injury to his lungs.

Gavin's sisters had taken care of the rental house for Gerald, as well as baskets of snacks at the hospital and a meal service for each of the Robinson siblings for the next week while they were still in the early days of processing the tragedy of their family home being burned to the ground.

Gavin couldn't imagine what they were going through, losing so many precious memories and family heirlooms. And all that on top of the troubles at Robinson Tech.

He still had trouble processing that the fire had been

ruled arson, as Wes had confirmed earlier. The tech industry might be cutthroat but who would have it in for
Gerald so much that he or she would be willing to burn
down the man's house? Couple that with the recall of
one of their processors, and Gavin couldn't imagine
things getting much worse for the tech company tycoon.

There was no doubt that Gerald had a crack legal
team in-house or on retainer, but Gavin wanted to offer
his help in whatever capacity was needed. Everett had
offered to pick him up so they could drive over together.
His brother had a friend on staff so he was monitoring
Ben's recovery.

"Don't tell me you've already messed up things with
Christine?" His brother gave a low chuckle even though
Gavin didn't find any humor in the question.

"She's fine," he said through clenched teeth.

Everett shook his head and turned onto the boulevard
that led to the hospital. "You messed it up. Did she dump
you and give back that pretty rock she was wearing?"

"It's not like that."

"What's it like?"

How was he supposed to answer without lying? He'd
been lying from the start, but his feelings for Christine
didn't feel fake. Spending the night with her hadn't been
part of their arrangement. The relationship was real and
not real. And yes, he'd messed it up.

"I still don't get why everyone cares so much about
my love life," he muttered.

"We want you to be happy." Everett gave him an
annoyingly perceptive big-brother glance. "We love
you, man."

Gavin pressed two fingers to his suddenly pounding

head. Christine made him happy. Could all his doubts and fears be wiped away by something so simple?

"I *am* happy." He felt like a broken record. "I've got a great life. My life is the envy of everyone around me."

"Are you trying to convince me or yourself?"

Gavin sucked in a breath but didn't respond.

"No one would have guessed you and Christine would be such a perfect match. On paper, you're two very different people."

"I don't care what other people think." Which wasn't true since the whole reason this had started was to appease his family.

"She's good for you," Everett said, ignoring Gavin's opinion.

"Yeah," he murmured. "She's amazing, which means she should be with someone who can appreciate and take care of her the way she deserves. I'm not a great bet when it comes to long-term."

"That doesn't have to be true."

"But it is," Gavin countered. "We both know it. Since I've been in Austin, I think every single member of this family has warned me about hurting her. There's a reason for that."

"We're not used to seeing you like this, but we believe you can make it work."

"Right."

"You can make it work, Gavin. Just stop being an idiot."

Gavin laughed softly. "Easier said than done."

"Maybe," Everett agreed. "The right woman makes it worth it. I can't imagine my life without Lila."

"Speaking of you and Lila..." Gavin arched a brow.

"Are you ready to talk about the new adventure you two are embarking on?"

Everett slanted him a look that answered the question without words. "You're more perceptive than you look. She wants to wait a few more weeks before announcing the pregnancy."

"I won't say a word." Gavin reached out a hand and squeezed his brother's shoulder. "But congratulations."

"Thanks." The smile Everett flashed was so full of love and happiness, it made Gavin's chest pinch. Would he ever feel that way? It was suddenly so easy to imagine a daughter with Christine's bright hair and sunny smile. But not if their relationship stayed in the pretend realm.

Everett pulled into the hospital parking lot a few minutes later. They weren't able to see Ben but they talked to Wes and Gerald. The police still had no suspects but the fire investigator had determined that the blaze originated in the master bedroom. It was strange, especially since Gerald hadn't been home at the time.

Although he didn't know the Robinsons well, Gavin still felt an overwhelming anger on their behalf toward whoever did this. It felt vindictive and personal. They needed to discover who was behind it. If an enemy was targeting Gerald Robinson, would they try something else or was destroying the family's home an isolated incident?

Gavin also had some things to work out in his own life. Namely his not-at-all-simple feelings for Christine. Was it as easy as Everett made it seem? Surely not. But he could manage it. All he had to do was talk to Christine and explain...

Explain what?

That he was terrified of hurting her. That he didn't believe he could make her happy. Neither would give her a reason to make their fake relationship real.

Scratch that. It was already real. Last night proved it. He could manage the rest. After all, it wasn't like he needed to drop to one knee.

He'd be going back to Denver at the end of next week. Why couldn't they have a long-distance relationship? He wasn't necessarily looking to have his cake and eat it, too, but why not?

Weekends and holidays together but enough separation that she wouldn't get the wrong idea about what he was able to give. They didn't have to be engaged. He might feel more for her than he had for a woman since…well, since ever. But that didn't change who he was at the core.

Why should it? He liked her. He had fun with her. Yet he didn't have to commit more than he could. At some point his family would give up with their insistence on seeing him settled. They'd understand he didn't have it in him. Surely, Christine would understand, as well.

He was an attorney, after all. He just needed to make his case to her.

Chapter Fifteen

Christine transferred a call to Maddie's office then continued entering data into the spreadsheet pulled up on the computer in front of her. Megan had called in sick, which was a bad habit the receptionist had on Monday mornings. They'd have to discuss expectations of the job, but for now Christine was filling in at the agency's front desk.

Two new clients, both looking for large family homes, had everyone feeling a bit more positive about the future. Maddie and Zach were both talented, dedicated Realtors, and Christine knew they'd find a way to overcome the recent setbacks.

She'd do everything she could to support them, even if it meant long hours and little rest. Staying busy was a good distraction from the tightness that had gripped her chest ever since Gavin's abrupt departure yesterday morning. As promised, he'd texted her last night, but she'd been too emotionally drained to respond with more than a few quick keystrokes.

They'd spent an amazing night together, but now she felt as unsure about his feelings as she had weeks ago. Did he still see her as a friend doing him a favor? The phrase "friends with benefits" came to mind, causing pain to slice across her stomach. That wasn't what she wanted from Gavin…from any man. Christine wasn't built for a casual fling and mentally kicked herself for believing it was more.

Needing a short break to clear her head, she popped over to Facebook. A sidebar advertisement for a popular Hill Country wedding venue on the screen, and she couldn't help but click on the link.

A moment later she sighed as she looked through the slideshow of charming, rustic wedding snapshots. The couples looked so happy, and she could clearly imagine futures of babies, family holidays and years filled with both laughter and tears. Not that her biological clock was exactly ticking at the moment, but she wanted to marry and have a family one day. It wasn't difficult to picture children with blond hair running through a backyard or cuddling up with a mini version of Gavin to read a bedtime story.

"Oh. My. God."

She started as Molly hovered over her shoulder.

Christine clicked the mouse, wanting to navigate away from the jeweler's website, but the young Realtor swatted at her hand.

"You're making plans," she said, excitement clear in her tone. "You and Gavin are really getting married. April is the perfect month for a wedding. It's not hot as an oven yet, and the bluebonnets will be blooming."

Christine shook her head. "I told you we want a long engagement not—"

"Did you say an April wedding?" Jenna joined them, leaning over the reception desk with wide eyes. "I bet Gavin will have a whole bunch of hot groomsmen."

"If Gavin's friends are half as hot as him, it's going to be the best weekend ever," Molly said with a laugh. "Christine, you are the luckiest woman on the planet."

"Why is Christine lucky?"

Jenna whirled around and Molly straightened as Gavin approached the desk. Christine lifted a hand to her cheek, knowing she must be blushing tomato-red. How much had he heard of her coworkers' ridiculous conversation?

"No reason," she told him, rising from the chair and straightening the hem of her silk blouse. "What are you doing here?"

"Come on, now." Molly grabbed Christine's arms and pushed her around the side of the desk. "Is that any way to greet your future bride? We were just talking about your April wedding. How many groomsmen are you planning to have? I'm just curious, you know?"

Christine squeezed shut her eyes for a quick moment and prayed for the floor to open up and swallow her whole. When everything remained the same, she glanced at Gavin with a shake of her head, mouthing "sorry."

To her utter shock, he seemed to take the whole situation in stride. He flashed his charming grin at first Molly and then Jenna. "Christine will make a beautiful spring bride."

The two women practically melted to the carpet even

as Christine felt her normally nonexistent temper rise to the surface.

"Molly," she said with a calm she didn't feel, "could you watch the phones for a minute? I'd like to talk to Gavin in private."

"Private," Molly repeated in a singsong voice. "I know what that's code for."

Christine gave her a withering stare. "No. You. Don't."

The woman's smile faded, and she slid into the receptionist's chair as if a teacher had just reprimanded her. "Take all the time you need," she said.

Jenna nodded. "I can help, too."

"Thank you. We'll be in my office." She raised an eyebrow in Gavin's direction, and when he winked, she thought she might feel steam coming out of her ears. She turned and stalked down the hall to her office.

"I like the sound of *private*," he said as he closed the door behind them.

"Are you out of your mind?" she demanded through clenched teeth. She wanted to scream the words, but the last thing she needed was Maddie or Valene, who was still in town from the weekend, running in to check on them.

"I don't think so." He took a step toward her, but she held up a hand, palm out.

"You let them believe we were getting married in three months."

Gavin was staring at her left hand, and she quickly pulled it to her side when she realized she was shaking.

"They seemed to be under that impression before I arrived on the scene."

"It was a mistake," she whispered, her cheeks growing hot again. "I was trying to correct it. We're supposed to be having a long engagement. Long enough that it will seem natural when it ends."

He shrugged. "What does the timing matter? It doesn't hurt anyone."

Me, she wanted to shout. *This whole thing is hurting me. Killing me.*

She drew in a deep breath. She would not break down in front of him. "What's going on between us?" she asked quietly.

He blinked then said, "We're friends."

Oh, gah. The friend zone. Was there anything worse?

"You're scheduled to return to Denver next week. What happens then?"

She held up her hand, the diamond flashing under the office's fluorescent lights. "What about this?"

"I've been thinking about that." He shoved his hands into his pockets and stared at a spot beyond her shoulder. "I know this thing started as a favor. You helping me out to distract my family."

She nodded and wished she'd never agreed to any of it.

"But we've had a ton of fun these past few weeks. It's been a blast."

A blast. A blast right through her heart.

"What are you saying, Gavin?"

He met her gaze then, but she couldn't read the expression in his eyes. He smiled, all easy charm, and it was like looking at a stranger.

"Austin's a quick flight to Denver. We can still hang out. Long weekends. Holidays. I come down to Texas often enough."

"So we'd keep dating?" Christine pressed a hand to

her chest. Somehow she thought she'd be overjoyed at his words. He didn't want their time together to end. But the ache in her heart grew deeper with every passing second.

"That's the plan. Of course we'd have to deal with the pretend engagement but—"

"You'd be my boyfriend?"

He lifted one hand and massaged the back of his neck. "If you want to put a label on it."

Her eyes narrowed, and he must have realized that was the wrong answer, because he flashed a sheepish smile. A "getting out of the dog house" smile.

"We spent the night together," she told him.

"It was wonderful," he agreed. "When I think about you in my arms, it makes me want—"

"Then you left," she interrupted, needing to keep this conversation on track. Even if she felt like the two of them were stuck on a runaway train heading for certain disaster. "You rushed out of there like I'd done something wrong."

"Not you, Christine. Never you." He shook his head. "But this arrangement started with me asking you to live a lie. I feel like I've taken advantage of you, and the fact that we slept together only makes it worse."

Ouch. Just when she thought the pain couldn't cut any deeper, Gavin managed it.

"I've got my life in Denver," he continued, running a hand through his hair. "You're here."

"A quick flight away," she muttered, repeating his words.

"I never imagined things would go this way. I care about you, more than I ever thought possible."

It was difficult to focus on his words over the roaring in her own ears. Christine had spent most of her life feeling like she wasn't enough. That she shouldn't expect too much. That scraps of affection or love with conditions placed on them were her lot in life.

Being with Gavin had changed that. She'd changed, and even if it meant losing him, she wasn't willing to go back to being the doormat she'd been before.

"I love you," she said quietly and the words felt right on her tongue. Based on the stricken look that crossed Gavin's face before he schooled his features, he hadn't been expecting her to say them. She tried for a smile, but it felt as if her cheeks were made of ice. "I didn't mean for it to happen. I didn't even want it to happen." She managed a hoarse laugh. "You're kind of irresistible."

"I'm not," he immediately countered.

"I wish that were the case," she told him. "Do you know I've had a crush on you forever?"

He shook his head, his jaw going slack.

"Yeah," she breathed. "So when you asked me to pose as your girlfriend—and then fiancée—for a few weeks, it was a no-brainer." She made a fist and gently knocked on the side of her head. "Turns out I should have thought it through a little more. I thought it would be a fun lark, you know? My chance with a guy so far out of my league it's like we aren't even playing the same sport."

"That's not true," he whispered.

"Which is exactly my problem," she admitted, crossing her arms over her chest. "Because you made me believe we had a chance. I lost sight of the lark part of things and began to believe what was happening between us was real."

"Christine, you have to understand—"

"Let me finish, Gavin. I need to say this, and you need to understand it." She pressed a hand to her hammering heart. "I'm more than I ever believed, and you helped me see that. I wish I could have gotten there on my own, but I'll be forever grateful for the gift you've given me. I know now that I deserve all my hopes and dreams coming true when it comes to love."

"You do."

"You deserve to believe in yourself, too."

He took a step back as if she'd hit him, then gave a startled laugh. "I don't think my self-esteem was ever in question."

"There's more to you than your career and your penchant for hurtling yourself down treacherous mountains or climbing sheer rock faces or any of the other extreme activities you do."

"I don't think so," he said with another hollow laugh. "All that extreme business keeps me pretty busy."

"You're a good man." She ignored his attempt to add levity to their conversation. "You have a big heart and a protective streak a mile long. You're dedicated and kind—"

"Tell that to the companies that I've managed to put out of business for the firm's clients."

"You have so much to give if you'd allow yourself to see it. I can imagine you as a husband and a father—"

He held up his hands. "Whoa, there."

But she wasn't finished. "I can imagine growing old with you and being at your side for whatever life brings. I don't want a casual, long-distance…whatever with you, Gavin. I want it all." She swiped at her cheeks when tears clouded her vision. "I *deserve* it all."

"Yes," he whispered then closed his eyes. When he opened them again, the emotion she'd seen there moments earlier had vanished, and she had to wonder if she'd imagined it in the first place. "But what if I'm not the man to give it to you?"

She drew in a breath and said the words that she'd never expected to utter. The words that broke her heart. "Then I'll find it with someone else."

Gavin stared at her as if he couldn't believe she'd be able to dismiss him so easily. But it wasn't easy. It felt as though she'd reached into her own chest to squeeze her heart until she could barely tolerate the pain. At the same time there was no doubt in her mind that she'd walk away if he couldn't give her what she wanted.

As hard as she'd fallen for him over these past few weeks, she'd also learned to value herself. She wanted to be with a man who could do the same, and while it might destroy her to have to accept Gavin wasn't that man, it was a chance she had to take.

"I don't know what to say," he admitted.

That simple statement made her shoulders sag. It seemed so obvious. She'd laid her heart out bare to him. He could cradle it in his arms or walk away and ignore her feelings or, worse, stomp all over her love for him. She hoped beyond hope that he'd choose her, that she hadn't misread or created in her own mind the deep emotion she saw in his green eyes.

"I think," she whispered, slipping the diamond ring from her finger and holding out to him, "that tells us both everything we need to know."

He stared at her for several long moments and then took the ring from her, shoving it into his pocket. She hated to see the pain in his gaze. Even though her own heart was breaking, it didn't give her any relief to know that Gavin was just as unhappy with this turn of events.

Still, she wouldn't compromise on what she knew she deserved. Not for him or anyone.

"You should probably go," she whispered, gesturing to her desk crowded with files. "I have a lot to get through this afternoon."

He gave a jerky nod but didn't leave. It was as if he was rooted in place, unable to move forward or back.

"Gavin, please. Don't make this harder on either of us."

"So it's the end?" he asked as if he couldn't quite believe it.

And she wasn't willing to cut him off entirely. It would be like chopping off her own arm. "For now. We'll still be friends...of a sort. Unless..."

He swayed toward her, pulled by an invisible thread. "Unless what?"

Her mouth felt like it was filled with sawdust. How was she supposed to answer? She'd told him she loved him, and he'd given her nothing in return. "I'm not sure," she admitted. "Maybe one of us will figure it out."

"Okay, then," he said, his tone hollow. "Goodbye, Christine. For now."

Then he turned and walked away.

Chapter Sixteen

Gavin drove around for hours after leaving Christine's office and eventually ended up on the highway, heading east toward Houston. He'd turned off his phone after five calls in a row from Maddie, four from Schuyler and one last call from Valene.

Obviously, word had gotten out that he and Christine were over. He still couldn't quite believe she'd…what? Broken up with him? Yes, they'd spent the past several weeks together but could it really be considered dating given how their relationship started?

His heart stuttered at the thought of losing her, offering a clear answer that his brain was trying to ignore.

She said she believed in him, told him she loved him, and somehow that honest admission had made every doubt and fear he'd ever had buzz through his veins like a swarm of angry bees.

It was one thing to be a part of her life within the

confines of their arrangement. Quite another to truly open himself up to her. He might be a success at plenty in his life, but he'd never been able to handle personal relationships for more than a short time.

His belief that he wasn't built for lasting love now felt like a cop-out. He could be fearless on the slopes or in his job but he was a coward when it counted.

The pain in her beautiful blue eyes had been like a knife to the chest. He wanted to be angry with her. They'd had a deal, and she'd gone and changed everything with her sweet honesty.

He turned up the radio, trying to drown out the voices in his head telling him he was an idiot. Two hours later he pulled into the long, winding driveway that led to his childhood home.

Once again he thought about the charred shell of the Robinson house. He couldn't imagine that kind of tragedy befalling his parents' home.

He parked and started up the walk to the front door, which opened before he'd made it to the top step.

"What a wonderful surprise," his mother said, opening her arms.

He enfolded her in a tight hug, probably taking more comfort from his mom's embrace than a grown man should. He was too emotionally spent to care.

"I wanted to see you before I head back to Denver."

She pulled away, patting his arms. "I thought you were in Austin until the end of next week?"

"I… Yeah…looks like I'm going to be leaving earlier than planned."

He followed her into the house as she glanced over her shoulder. "Any special reason?" she asked and something in her tone made him stop in his tracks.

"They got to you," he muttered.

"Who?"

"The trifecta of terror." When she didn't stop walking toward the kitchen, he trailed after her. "Otherwise known as my three sisters."

"Would you like a glass of tea?"

"Sure. Thanks."

"I made banana muffins this morning."

"Okay." He took a seat at the island, drumming his fingers against the cool marble countertop. "Which one of them called?"

"I spoke with Maddie about an hour ago," his mother admitted. "She was worried about you and wanted to know if you'd contacted your father or me."

"Does she know I'm here?"

Barbara pulled a glass from the cabinet then took a pitcher of iced tea out of the refrigerator. "I texted her when I saw you coming up the drive. All three of them were worried."

He snorted. "Doubtful. More likely they all wanted to lecture me on how badly I messed things up with Christine."

She set the glass of tea in front of him then took a glass container of muffins from the pantry and opened the lid. "From the look on your face, I don't think you need that lecture."

"Which wouldn't have stopped Maddie."

His mother inclined her head as if considering that. "You're right."

He plucked a muffin from the container and popped the whole thing into his mouth.

"Those are made for biting," his mother gently admonished.

He finished chewing and then swallowed. His mom was an excellent baker. "Gets to the same place either way."

She smiled. "Just like there are many paths to love."

"Wow," he murmured.

"Not the smoothest transition, I'll admit. But I assume you've driven all this way because you want to talk about your troubles."

He shook his head. "I want to eat muffins, drink iced tea and find a stupid action movie to watch on TV. I don't want to talk."

When Barbara said nothing in response, Gavin sighed. "Can I have another muffin first?"

"Bring it into the family room. We'll be more comfortable there."

He grabbed a muffin and his tea and then followed her into the wood-paneled family room. Dropping down on the overstuffed couch, he placed the glass on the coffee table and ate the muffin, again in one bite.

"It was all fake," he blurted, rubbing a hand across his eyes.

His mother's gentle gaze didn't waver. "Your relationship with Christine?"

"The engagement, the ring…everything." He nodded. "Schuyler was pushing me about my love life at Maddie's wedding, trying to set me up with every single woman she knew. It's been like that for a while. I'm not sure why everyone cares so much about me settling down, but I got sick of having people in my personal business. Who cares if I don't date seriously or stay single forever?"

"Your sisters want you to be happy," Barbara said.

Gavin leveled a look at her. "It's not just them. You

and Dad are the same way. No one believes I can manage my own happiness. I know you mean well, but it makes me crazy. Did you ever think that I'm just not cut out for a committed relationship?"

"Not once."

His chest constricted at her quiet confidence.

"You're wrong," he whispered. "Clearly. Just ask Christine."

"It doesn't sound as if your feelings for her are fake."

"Not now," he admitted. "I guess not even at the beginning. I always liked her…" He closed his eyes for a moment. "I'm embarrassed to admit I never really noticed her before Maddie's wedding. She was the nice girl who worked for Dad."

"She was more than that."

"Yes…well…" Condensation pooled around the lip of the iced tea glass, and he ran a finger across it before taking a long drink.

"Tell me how this fake yet not-so-fake relationship started."

"I lied to Schuyler at Maddie's reception. Told her I had a girlfriend so she'd stop with the matchmaking business."

"Did she stop?"

"She didn't believe me," he said, shaking his head.

"Your sister knows you well."

"Lucky me."

"True."

He felt the wisp of a smile curve his mouth. Neither his sisters nor his mother would let him get away with much, and he loved them for it. Mostly.

"She was pushing me on the identity of my mystery woman and why I hadn't brought her as my plus one.

I'd been dancing with Christine earlier in the night and told her how annoyed I was with the pressure to settle down. I'm not sure why, although I was grateful at the time, but she stepped in with Schuyler and claimed that *she* was my girlfriend."

"Schuyler believed that?"

His smile grew as he thought about Christine coming to his rescue that night. It had been refreshing, spontaneous and sexy as hell. "Christine is a great office manager, but she might have missed her calling with acting. She convinced Schuyler. She convinced *me*."

"Do you know she's always had a bit of a crush on you?"

"Not at the time." He frowned. "How did you?"

"Oh, sweetie. It's a mother's job to understand those kinds of things. That's part of the reason it made me happy to hear you two were together. She's got such a good heart, and you deserve someone like that."

"I don't," he whispered. "I hurt her, Mom."

"Because your feelings weren't the same as hers? I saw the two of you together. It didn't look fake." She leaned forward on her elbows. "No offense, son, but you aren't an actor."

"I cared…" He paused then said, "I *care* about her. I didn't expect it and things would have been so much easier if we'd stuck to the plan of having fun while I was in Austin. The engagement raised the stakes even more. Then it became more. I even suggested that we keep seeing each other after I go back to Denver."

"Where's the problem?"

"She told me she loved me." His body went tight as he waited for his mom's response.

"How dare she," Barbara murmured.

"Exactly."

His mother reached over and gave him a soft swat to the side of the head.

"What was that for?"

"Maybe I'm hoping to knock some sense into you. An amazing woman said she loves you and that's bad?"

"It means she has expectations," he said, then cringed.

"And?"

"I've never been great with that. I don't date seriously. I'm not built for it. Why can't anyone understand that?"

She held up her hand and ticked off responses on her fingers. "One, because it's not true. Two, because it's a weak excuse. Three, because you love her, too."

He automatically shook his head. "I don't. I can't."

"Gavin."

"Mom, every woman I've ever dated has told me I'm not husband material. I'm perfect for a good time, a few laughs and fun weekends away. I don't stick."

"They were wrong."

"I've dated a *lot* of women," he said quietly, embarrassed at having this conversation with the woman who raised him but needing someone to understand just the same.

"I'm aware," she answered.

"I've messed up with plenty of them. Not on purpose but in the same way I ruined things with Christine."

"You only have to get it right once."

He shook his head. "I don't…" He closed his eyes and let the truth wash over him. "I love her," he whispered.

"Yes," his mother answered simply.

"But what if I hurt her and—" His lungs burned as he drew air in. "What if I'm not enough? What if I can't be the man she deserves? What if I end up with my heart broken?"

"My sweet boy," his mother whispered as if she was comforting a toddler with a skinned knee. "You are so brave and adventurous."

"No. I'm a spineless coward. When things got serious, I turned tail. She has no reason to give me another chance."

"She loves you."

As if that was reason enough.

"But—"

"Are you going to try to make it work? No one can force you. Not your sisters or me. The choice is yours, Gavin. How much do you love her?"

"With more of my heart than I even realized existed."

"What's the worst thing that could happen?"

He blinked as understanding dawned. "Giving up on this chance at happiness. I have to fight for her to take me back. If she doesn't, I'll respect her decision. But if I don't try, then I'm going to live the rest of my life regretting it."

"Can I give you a piece of advice?"

He laughed softly. "Isn't that what you've been doing this whole time in your subtle way?"

Barbara patted his hand. "Make it count. You're all about taking risks, and the stakes don't get any higher than when you're putting your heart on the line. Go big or go home."

"Really?"

"Would you ski down a bunny hill when the double black is there for the taking?"

He laughed. "You're comparing Christine to a ski slope?"

"I'm telling you not to hold back."

Okay. He could do that. His mother was right. He'd hurt Christine and now he had to convince her to try again. She deserved to have him risk everything.

He stood abruptly. "I've got to go."

"Back to Austin?"

"To Denver," he clarified, then held up a hand when his mother frowned. "Trust me. I'm going to make this count."

"I do trust you."

"Thanks, Mom. For everything." He gave her a quick hug, then headed for his car. His dad walked into the house just as Gavin was exiting.

"Gavin." His father's expression was stony. "We need to talk about—"

"I'm fixing it," he answered without breaking stride.

"Good luck, then," his dad called.

Gavin would definitely need it.

Christine checked her makeup in the compact mirror she kept in her desk drawer Thursday morning. Not bad, she thought, given that she'd spent most of the previous night in tears.

She hadn't heard from Gavin after he'd left her office on Monday, not that she'd expected to. Hoped, but not expected. The news of their breakup—if she could call it that—had spread like wildfire through the office. If she had to guess, she would have said that several curious ears had been pressed to the door of Christine's office to overhear the heartbreaking conversation.

She'd tried to play it off and had managed to hold herself together when Maddie came in and threatened revenge on her brother for being an idiot.

Christine had claimed ending the engagement was a mutual decision, and in a way it had been. She simply hadn't been willing to take the scraps of affection Gavin offered. Not when she loved him so deeply. It was his own fault. He'd been the one to help her see that she deserved more than she normally expected. Unfortunately, that newfound understanding made it impossible for her to accept anything less from him.

It was only when she'd gotten home and curled up on her couch in private that the heartbreak had truly washed over her. Princess Di had joined her on the sofa, shoving her snout into Christine and then climbing onto her lap. She'd wrapped her arms around the sweet dog and cried for far too long.

So for the past two days, her routine had been the same. Game face at the office then allowing her mask to crumble once she returned home.

Today she'd woken up with the equivalent of a broken heart hangover. It would have been nice to call in sick and curl in a ball on the couch with a carton of Häagen-Dazs and the TV tuned to some reality-television marathon. But she had to pull herself together. So she'd applied makeup, slipped into her favorite dress and then headed for the office. She'd stopped to buy a dozen donuts on the way in, hoping the offering of dough and sugar would somehow prove to her coworkers that she was moving on.

As if.

She shoved the mirror into a desk drawer and headed for the conference room. Maddie had called an all-staff meeting in order to go over the latest sales figures and strategies for salvaging their declining business.

All eyes turned to Christine as she entered the room.

"Am I late?" she asked, tucking her hair behind one ear.

"Right on time," Zach answered from his place near the projection screen at the front of the room.

When Christine went to slip into a chair near the door, Maddie, who stood next to Zach, gestured to her. "We've got a place for you up here."

"Okay," Christine agreed, hoping no one expected her to speak at the meeting. When she was seated, Maddie clasped her hands in front of her chest.

"Now that we're all here," she announced, "we've got a special presentation today. Could someone dim the lights?"

Christine frowned as she glanced around. No one else seemed surprised at how oddly the meeting was starting.

Maddie took the seat across from Christine and hit a button on the laptop that sat in front of her on the conference table.

A background of a tropical scene with the words, "Love is the Adventure" superimposed on top of it displayed on the wide screen.

"It doesn't matter to me where I am…"

Christine froze as Gavin spoke into the silence of the room.

"As long as I'm with you."

She darted a quick glance at Maddie, who grinned broadly as she hit the computer's keyboard. A digitally edited photo of Gavin and Christine appeared on the screen. She recognized the original photo—it had been taken at the Fortune family reunion. Gavin had an arm slung over Christine's shoulder, pulling her tight to his side. She was leaning in, her head resting on his shoulder, and they both were smiling broadly.

The happiness radiating from her in the photo was undeniable, and a fresh wave of pain stabbed at her heart. But what surprised her was that Gavin looked just as happy, at peace and content in a way she thought she'd imagined during their time together.

Instead of the background of the Mendoza Winery, it looked like they were standing in front of the Eiffel Tower.

"Whether we're traveling to the great cities of the world," he said, his tone both tender and deliberate, "or to a tropical beach…"

Maddie winked at Christine as she clicked a button on the keyboard. Christine couldn't help but smile as her face, along with Gavin's, appeared superimposed onto the bodies of people lounging on the beach. The next photo showed them skiing, and in the following one they were traversing the Great Wall of China. She laughed, as did many of her coworkers, as the photos became an unofficial "where in the world are Gavin and Christine" montage.

Gavin continued to narrate all the adventures they could have together, and hope bloomed in her chest like the first crocuses of spring pushing through hard ground. That was the life she wanted, filled with fun and adventure, and most of all with Gavin at her side for every moment of it.

When the original photo popped up on the screen once again, someone in the back of the room flipped on the lights. Christine's breath caught as Gavin came forward.

"But in the end," he said, pinning her with his gaze, "I don't care where we are or what we do as long as we're together. I thought I had things all figured out but you changed everything for me. You changed me."

She shook her head automatically. She was the one who'd changed over these past few weeks. How could he—

"I love you, Christine," he said softly as he came to stand in front of her chair. "I can't imagine my life without you. I don't want to be half in or to put any limits on us. I want it all. I want to be the man you deserve." He reached out a hand, and she placed her fingers in his, the warmth of his touch sending sparks shooting along her skin. It had only been a couple of days since she'd seen him, but she'd missed this like he'd been gone for months. When she'd heard through the office grapevine that he'd returned to Denver, she figured it was the end.

But now he was offering her a new beginning.

He pulled her to her feet and lifted her hand to his mouth, brushing a soft kiss across her knuckles. "You deserve to be loved for exactly who you are. You're beautiful inside and out, kind and generous, and you make everything in my life better." He squeezed her fingers. "You are my life."

"Oh," she breathed. She wasn't sure she could put together any actual words without bursting into tears.

"If you give me another chance," he continued, and she felt her eyes widen as he dropped to one knee, "I'll spend the rest of my life showing you how much you mean to me."

There was a collective gasp in the room as he took out a small black box, opening it to reveal the sparkling diamond solitaire she'd already come to think of as hers.

"I don't want to wait," he told her with a hopeful smile. "I can't imagine losing you and I promise I'll never give you a reason to doubt me again. I love you so damn much, Christine. Will you marry me?"

Words. She needed words. Around the galloping beat of her heart and the blood hammering through her brain, she managed to nod.

"Yes," she finally whispered, and Gavin let out a pent-up breath that told her he hadn't been confident in her answer. But she had no doubt she'd love this man forever.

"I love you," she said as he slipped the ring onto her finger. "I'll love you for all of my life, Gavin."

As he stood and kissed her, a cheer went up throughout the room. Christine only had eyes for Gavin. She knew her life would never be the same and she wouldn't have it any other way.

In the past month she'd discovered a strength in herself she hadn't known she possessed and a love with a man who made her happy in ways she could never have imagined. She planned to hold on tight for whatever adventure life brought her way.

Epilogue

"I touched a fish," Christine said with a wide smile. "You must be sick of hearing me say that, but I still can't quite believe it." She giggled. "I swam with fish in the ocean and I didn't drown. It was like I was the Little Mermaid. Everything was beautiful. I can't believe I missed out on that for so long."

Gavin leaned in for a quick kiss, tucking a loose strand of hair behind her ear. They sat on two lounge chairs at an exclusive resort outside Cancún, watching shades of pink and gold streak across the evening sky.

"I'm glad you enjoyed snorkeling," he said. "Are you ready for parasailing tomorrow?"

"I'm ready for anything with you," she confirmed, then placed a hand on her stomach. "But let's not talk about it or I might lose my nerve."

"You can do it," he told her, taking her hand as he leaned back in his chair. "I believe you can do anything."

She bit down on her lower lip as tears pricked the backs of her eyes. Would she ever get used to his unwavering support?

She watched the waves curling against the shoreline for several minutes, letting the sound of the surf relax her. "I still feel a little guilty leaving Austin when things are so tumultuous with the agency and the Fortunes."

Gavin squeezed her fingers. "We're here for the weekend, sweetheart. Maddie and Zach totally support you taking a couple of days off."

Christine nodded. Gavin had suggested the spontaneous trip to the beach over dinner with his family the evening after he'd proposed to her. Her first instinct had been to say no, but both Maddie and Kenneth, who'd driven over from Houston with Barbara for the impromptu celebration, had agreed it was a fantastic idea.

Schuyler had taken her on a quick tropical-vacation shopping spree since Christine's only bathing suit was one she'd owned since college.

Her new life would take some getting used to, but she wouldn't change a thing. Every day with Gavin would be an adventure, whether he was at her side as she conquered her fears or they were settling into a normal routine in Austin. Gavin seemed to enjoy being back in Texas, opening his law firm's Austin branch.

They'd already talked about finding a house together, and Christine had agreed to sublet her condo to her sister when they did. Her parents had been supportive and surprisingly excited for her when she'd shared the news of her engagement with them. Aimee hadn't said much but she'd shoved a wedding magazine toward Christine and mumbled that she'd marked the pages with "not hideous" bridesmaid dresses.

She hadn't bothered to reveal the details of how her relationship with Gavin had actually started. No one seemed to doubt his feelings for her. After years of feeling like she didn't fit, Christine had discovered that believing she was worthy of being treated with love and respect made all the difference. They had a long way to go to become the close-knit family her mother hoped for, but Christine actually believed they had a chance of getting there.

So much of that had to do with how she'd changed and grown in the past few weeks. She was becoming exactly who she was meant to be and felt more confident than ever. She credited Gavin for helping her to see herself in a different way.

"I don't think I've ever enjoyed the ocean like this," Gavin said, his thumb tracing small circles on the center of her palm.

"Come on," she chided. "You don't have to pretend like this is something new for you. I know you've been to beaches all over the world."

"Yes," he agreed slowly, "but I was always moving, looking for the next thrill. Now I'm content. You're the best adventure I can imagine, and I don't need anything else."

He tugged on her hand and scooted to one side of the cushioned chair. She moved next to him, resting her head on his chest as he wrapped his arms around her.

"Thank you," he said against the top of her head, "for seeing something in me that I couldn't see in myself. I love you, Christine."

"I love you, too," she whispered. The connection they shared meant everything to her, and she was excited for a lifetime of both big adventures and tiny moments with

Gavin. Her heart overflowed with happiness as they watched the sun dip below the horizon. Each day would be a new beginning and she'd cherish every single one.

* * * * *

MILLS & BOON

Coming next month

SURPRISE BABY FOR THE HEIR
Ellie Darkins

'I'm pregnant.'

The words hit Fraser like a bus, rendering him mute
and paralysed. He sat in silence for long, still moments,
letting the words reverberate through his ears, his brain.
The full meaning of them fell upon him slowly, gradu-
ally. Like being crushed to death under a pile of small
rocks. Each one so insignificant that you didn't feel the
difference, but collectively, they stole his breath, and
could break his body.

'Are you going to say anything?' Elspeth asked,
breaking into his thoughts at last. He met her gaze and
saw that it had hardened even further – he hadn't thought
that that would be possible. And he could understand
why. He'd barely said a word since she'd dropped her
bombshell. But he needed time to take this in. Surely
she could understand that. 'I'm sorry. I'm in shock,' he
said. Following it up with the first thing that popped
into his head. 'We were careful.'

'Not careful enough, it seems.' Her voice was like
ice, cutting into him, and he knew that it was the wrong
thing to say. He wasn't telling her anything she didn't
know.

Fraser shook his head.

'What do you want to do?' he asked, his voice tentative,

aware that they had options. Equally aware that discussing them could be a minefield if they weren't on the same page.

'I want to have the baby,' Elspeth said with the same firmness and lack of equivocation that she had told him that she was pregnant. How someone so slight could sound so immovably solid was beyond him, and a huge part of her appeal, he realised. Something that he should be wary of…

Continue reading
SURPRISE BABY FOR THE HEIR
Ellie Darkins

Available next month
www.millsandboon.co.uk

COMING SOON!

We really hope you enjoyed reading this book. If you're looking for more romance, be sure to head to the shops when new books are available on

Thursday 10th January

To see which titles are coming soon, please visit

millsandboon.co.uk/nextmonth